Ever After Between the Lines
A ROMANCE COLLECTION

CARRIE ANN RYAN

Ever After Between the Lines
By: Carrie Ann Ryan
© 2020-2025 Carrie Ann Ryan

This book is a work of fiction. Names, characters, places, and incidents either are products of the author's imagination or are used fictitiously. Any resemblance to actual events, locales or persons, living or dead, is entirely coincidental.

No part of this book can be reproduced in any form or by electronic or mechanical means including information storage and retrieval systems, without the express written permission of the author. The only exception is by a reviewer who may quote short excerpts in a review.

All content warnings are listed on the book page for this book on my website.

NO AI TRAINING: Without in any way limiting the author's [and publisher's] exclusive rights under copyright, any use of this publication to "train" generative artificial intelligence (AI) technologies to generate text is expressly prohibited. The author reserves all rights to license uses of this work for generative AI training and development of machine learning language models.

Praise for Carrie Ann Ryan

"Count on Carrie Ann Ryan for emotional, sexy, character driven stories that capture your heart!" – Carly Phillips, NY Times bestselling author

"Carrie Ann Ryan's romances are my newest addiction! The emotion in her books captures me from the very beginning. The hope and healing hold me close until the end. These love stories will simply sweep you away." ~ NYT Bestselling Author Deveny Perry

"Carrie Ann Ryan writes the perfect balance of sweet and heat ensuring every story feeds the soul." - Audrey Carlan, #1 New York Times Bestselling Author

"Carrie Ann Ryan never fails to draw readers in with passion, raw sensuality, and characters that pop off the page. Any book by Carrie Ann is an absolute treat." – New York Times Bestselling Author J. Kenner

"Carrie Ann Ryan knows how to pull your heartstrings and make your pulse pound! Her wonderful Redwood Pack series will draw you in and keep you reading long into the night. I can't wait to see what comes next with the new generation, the Talons. Keep them coming, Carrie Ann!" –Lara Adrian, New York Times bestselling author of CRAVE THE NIGHT

"With snarky humor, sizzling love scenes, and brilliant, imaginative worldbuilding, The Dante's Circle series reads as if Carrie Ann Ryan peeked at my personal wish list!" – NYT Bestselling Author, Larissa Ione

"Carrie Ann Ryan writes sexy shifters in a world full of passionate happily-ever-afters." – *New York Times* Bestselling Author Vivian Arend

"Carrie Ann's books are sexy with characters you can't help but love from page one. They are heat and heart blended to perfection." *New York Times* Bestselling Author Jayne Rylon

Carrie Ann Ryan's books are wickedly funny and deliciously hot, with plenty of twists to keep you guessing. They'll keep you up all night!" USA Today Bestselling Author Cari Quinn

"Once again, Carrie Ann Ryan knocks the Dante's Circle series out of the park. The queen of hot, sexy, enthralling paranormal romance, Carrie Ann is an author not to miss!" *New York Times* bestselling Author Marie Harte

Inked Kingdom

A MONTGOMERY INK BONUS ROMANCE

Inked Kingdom

I fell for Sarina the moment I saw her.
When the Kingdom tore her from me, I promised revenge.
My claim was forfeit the moment she ran, but now I will follow.
I will find her.
I will earn her.
And I will burn the world if they dare touch her.
Again.

Chapter One
STONE

THE FIST SLAMMED INTO MY JAW, THE CRUNCH of flesh to bone echoing in my head. I stumbled back and tried to fight, but the person holding me back tightened their grip, my arms pinned behind me.

"Fucking take it, Stone," the man in front of me grumbled as he hooked his fist out again, this time connecting with my ribs.

I let out a shocked gasp, annoyed with myself for doing it. Eddie's eyes narrowed into slits, the glee in them familiar. Eddie loved doling out pain and seeing others fall.

The fucking bastard. The fact I'd broken just the bit that I had would egg him on, and I had been doing so well not saying a damn word. As long as I didn't make a sound, Eddie would get tired and stop.

Now he wasn't going to stop anytime soon.

Fuck.

"The King already told you what you could fucking do with your retirement, Stone. You think you're too good for us? The King *made* you. He took you from nothing. Kept a roof over your head when your own father didn't even want you. When your dear old mother left you to rot in the alley with your brother. The King kept you alive when that rat bastard of a brother finally kicked the bucket as he should have long before. Who the fuck do you think you are?"

Rage ravaged my body, threatening to overpower me and make me lose control. If I lost control, I'd die. I wouldn't be able to face Eddie and keep up with the man behind me long enough to draw in my next breath.

"I'm not a pretty boy like you, it seems," I finally answered, with a smirk of my own, and the man holding me kneed me behind my legs. I let out a curse, and Eddie grinned.

"That's a pretty boy. Look at you, pretending you're some tough shit when all you're going to do is go cry to your mother." Eddie grinned again. "Oh, you can't do that because your mom is dead. I guess that's what happens when you go against the King. You know she screamed when she died. Bent to save you, and yet it's not going to be enough. She's dead. Now you're going to join her soon. I can't wait to tell the King to send you to meet your mom. She was hot, though. Kind of miss the fact that I never got to tap that."

Fury boiled through me, and I pulled at the other man, at Rook.

His name wasn't Rook. That was his title. Eddie was the Knight. We were part of the Kingdom, its organization outside of Desolation, New York. We ran guns, booze, drugs—anything to make the King richer.

I had been born into the life, I hadn't had a choice.

I might say that I could get out, but there was no leaving it. The only person that had left had been the one person that I'd loved.

Only Sarina was gone. She had been the Princess, daughter of the former Knight, sister of the older Rook, before everything had changed.

Now her family was dead, and Sarina was gone, and I was alone here.

Alone in a city of crime, of terrible choices, no getting out.

Somehow I was going to leave.

I had no other choice. If I wanted to live to see my next birthday, or fuck, see the next sunrise, I needed to leave before the rest of the Kingdom put me in front of the King.

"Fuck you." I growled out the word, knowing I needed to leave. I needed to be who I needed to be and fuck everyone else.

There was no way that I could stay here. No way that I could survive if I stayed with the Kingdom, in New York, or with any attachments to the Ruin.

The Ruin was made up of the major powers of crime and unorder congregated in Desolation, New York. It connected all the bosses, the cartels, the mobs, the games, and the outsiders. Anyone who was anyone in our part of the country was connected to the Ruin.

And I needed to sever that connection if I wanted to survive.

If I wanted to have her.

I had claimed her once, and she had left. Not to leave me, but to save herself, the one thing I hadn't been able to do on my own.

She ran from me once, from my world, from *our* world, and now I needed to find her. But the first thing I needed to do was get out of their hold.

"You really thought you could do it," Eddie said as he shook his head. He gestured behind me, and I frowned because the man holding me didn't move. No, instead, there was a sound of boots on cement and someone being dragged.

I froze, ice sliding up my veins. I looked at Jeremy.

Jeremy was the single friend I had left in the Ruin. He was a runner like me, but he tended to make poor decisions. Even worse than I did when it came to this life. I didn't do drugs. I didn't beat women. I didn't use anybody other than myself. Jeremy tried his best to emulate that but sometimes made the wrong choices.

Still, Jeremy was my only friend.

Eddie looked at me then and pulled the Glock out of his holster.

"You both thought you could leave?" He shook his head. "Guess you were wrong, weren't you?"

"I swear, I wasn't going to leave. I love the Kingdom. I love the King. I bow before him." Jeremy began to ramble, tears slid from his eyes, and I just blinked, wondering what the fuck Jeremy had done.

Because while I was going to leave, because I had to, Jeremy was supposed to wait. He had wanted to stay. He would never betray me or his King. What the fuck had he done to warrant this reaction from the Knight?

"The King sends his regards, Jeremy. Next time, don't fuck his daughter."

Jeremy let out a scream, and then there was nothing, just the sound of a gunshot echoing between my ears and my stomach falling out.

This couldn't be happening. Jeremy couldn't be dead. The Knight hadn't just killed a man in cold blood in front of me. But of course he had. They'd done it before. And if I wasn't careful, they'd do it again and again until there was no hope.

No salvation.

Jeremy fell, the single perfect precision hit right in the middle of his forehead. Eddie sighed and put the gun back in his holster.

"We're going to have to get the cleaner in here to clean

this up," he growled. "Do you want to use ours or someone else's?"

"Call Arlo." Rook chuffed behind me. "That way, our guy doesn't have to get his hands dirty. Arlo will be good at it."

Ice crawled all over me. Arlo was the cleaner for higher-ups in the Ruin. Nobody knew exactly what he did, but as Arlo worked for the Petrov Bratva. He was a big mean son of a bitch.

Nobody messed with him, and if Arlo was coming here to clean up the mess Jeremy made, he was here to clean me up too.

I swallowed hard, looked at my dead friend, and I wondered how the fuck I got here.

I was such an idiot.

I needed to get out of here. I needed to get out of the life that I had no choice in until now.

I couldn't even feel remorse for the friend that was dead. I didn't have time or the luxury to *feel*. Everything was numb. Hollow. Unending.

Jeremy was dead. And he had cried.

And I was next.

"I think the King wants to do this personally for you, boy," Eddie said as he shook his head. "I'm not going to waste a bullet on you."

Then Eddie moved forward and snapped out his wrist. The taser hit me right in the chest, sending electric shocks down my body. I hadn't even realized that the Rook had let me go, was laughing behind me. I fell to my knees, and then the taser was gone, and they were kicking. Steel-toed boots hitting my side, my ribs. Something cracked and I coughed up blood. And then there was a fist to my temple, and there was nothing.

"Wake up, dumb ass. Open those eyes."

I looked up into the dark eyes of the man above me and figured maybe this was how I was going to die. Maybe the King didn't want anything to do with me after all.

"Come on, before they take you to the hub, the Ruin doesn't need to see your dead body. And neither do I."

"Arlo?" I asked as I coughed.

Arlo looked down at the blood that I had sprayed on his chest and rolled his eyes. "Thanks for that. Come on, let's get you out of here."

"What the fuck?"

"You want out? I got you a car. No questions."

"But how? Why?"

"See, those are questions. And I don't want fucking questions."

"I don't understand."

"You don't need to understand. Just get the fuck out of here, Stone. You want to survive? Leave."

"But what about you?"

"There are different ways to survive, Stone. You know that better than anyone else." He tossed the keys at me, and I caught them with my left hand, my right one still aching from when Eddie had stomped on it.

"What are you going to tell them?"

"Again with the questions. It's like you want to be killed."

He shook his head and walked off without saying another word, as if speaking to me had been too much for him in the first place.

I looked over at the small nondescript sedan in front of me and wondered what the fuck was going on. My head ached, and I had a feeling I might have a concussion, but I ignored it.

I got in the car, started the engine, and wondered if I was trusting the wrong person. After all, I had been trusting the wrong people my entire life. What was one more wrong choice?

I needed to go, needed to find my home. The only home that I could think of was the one who had left me, the one who had needed to run, the one I hadn't gone after.

But there was no time like the present.

My only friend was dead, taken away when I was out cold, and I hadn't even had time to mourn or wonder what I could have done.

My family was long gone, taken from me before I'd had the strength to fight back to try to save them.

All that would be left for me at the Ruin were the death and destruction of whatever the King declared.

So I started the engine and I pulled away, wondering what the fuck Arlo was thinking and how the fuck I was going to repay him.

In the end, it didn't matter because I was looking for her.

For Sarina.

My life was forfeit.

The claim I once had on her long gone.

My past lay in ruins, but she was the one for me.

She would be my salvation.

Or my ending.

Chapter Two
SARINA

I tossed the recycling in the dumpster and shook my head. Well, standing in an alley surrounded by dumpsters and trash was at least better than my former life. It wasn't glamorous, but it was mine.

My back ached, my feet hurt, but to me, that just meant an excellent job for the day. I still had another shift at the bar later, but for now, being a barista at Café Taboo paid some of my bills.

That's why I worked as a bartender at Ink on Tap, the gay bar down the street that my best friend owned, in the evenings.

I didn't have a life, but that was fine. Who needed a life when you were working two full-time jobs and sleeping when you could? I didn't need a life outside of that.

At least, that's what I told myself.

After all, I had lived dangerously and a little more high-octane when I had been in high school. I didn't need anything more than this.

I rolled my shoulders and turned towards the other side of the alley to get back into the café and finish my shift. I tripped over a rock, my whole body turning to ice as I looked at the person in front of me.

It was a ghost. It had to be a ghost because he couldn't be there.

After all this time, that couldn't be Stone Anderson standing in front of me. The one person I had left, the one person that had taken everything from me.

Or rather, perhaps I had taken everything from him.

I had given him myself, my innocence, my heart, my future, and he had thrown it away because he chose his family over me.

He had chosen everything over me.

"Stone," I whispered, my voice cracking.

"You remembered me."

I blinked at him, my hands shaking. "What happened to your face?" I asked, wondering why that was the first thing that came out of my mouth. Of course, it couldn't be helped. He looked horrible.

Perhaps beneath the split lip, black eye, and swollen cheekbone, there was still that gorgeous ruggedness that was Stone, but I could barely see it. No, instead, all I could notice were the imperfections, the signs that perhaps he hadn't left the life like he had promised me he would.

He had stayed behind when I left, and whatever had wrapped its hands around his neck had taken more from him that I could comprehend.

"Sarina," he whispered, his voice a growl. It did things to me, just like it always had. That was the problem with Stone.

No matter what I did, I couldn't think when he was around. He made me lose all sense, lose all reality.

Because he was supposed to be my everything. My salvation. My one true everything.

And then he had chosen the Kingdom.

Chosen the place that had killed my father. Killed my brother. Killed everything.

Chosen the place that had wanted me. Not for who I was, but what I could do for them.

They had wanted my body, my soul. They had wanted everything other than who I was and what choices I could make.

Stone had chosen them.

How was I supposed to look at the man in front of me and want anything other than to run?

So I did. I left the alley. I turned on my heel, and I ran.

My feet dug into the gravel, and I ignored the blisters on my heels. I ignored Stone's shout.

I ignored him.

I'd have to call Hailey later and let her know why I had

left in a hurry, but she would understand. She had to. She and all of her family always understood what was going on. It was as if they had a sixth sense. They would understand why I had to leave. They might not know every detail, they knew enough to understand my running. At least for the day, and if Stone wouldn't walk away, perhaps forever.

I had been hiding in Denver for four years, but maybe this would be my last moment. Maybe I would have to fully leave and never come back. Never return to the place that I had called home for so long.

I ran down the block, and nobody paid me any mind.

They were all focusing on their own lives, their own problems. Nobody cared about the woman in the apron running for her life.

I had left my purse behind, everything. The only thing I had was my phone, and whatever wits I had left.

Because if Stone was here, the Kingdom couldn't be far behind.

And I needed to be safe.

I couldn't be near them.

Because if the Kingdom found me, I would be dead. My life would be forfeit, as would everything else I had ever thought I could possibly have.

Because once the Kingdom had you, there was no leaving. The King had wanted me for his Queen, even at a barely legal age.

He had seen what Stone had, and had wanted me. His

own Queen had died only six months prior, and everyone said it had just been an accident. We all knew that was a lie. The old Queen, Gwen, had been the Guinevere to her Arthur and had found her own Lancelot. She had cheated on the King, fallen in love with the wrong man. With the one man, she couldn't have and he hadn't been ruthless enough to save them.

She died at the hands of her own King, of her husband.

And the King wanted me.

And when I said no, he killed my brother, his Rook.

And when my father, his Knight, had fought for me, he killed him too.

Their blood still stained my palms; I could see them in my dreams, hear their screams. In the end, there was nothing I could do.

I had run. I hadn't run far enough, it seemed.

It was never going to be far enough.

Stone had found me. And soon, the new Rook and the new Knight would as well.

Stone was their runner, their tracker.

And the others would follow, and I would die. Because I would die before I fell before the King as a supplicant.

Before I became his bride.

Before I filled his bed.

I would die.

I pounded on the backdoor to Ink on Tap, praying that Rebel could hear me.

"What the fuck, Sarina?" Rebel asked as he pulled open the door. He was shirtless and in sweats and looked like I had just woken him up. Maybe I had. It was still early enough in the day that he was probably sleeping upstairs in the apartment that he owned rather than working on opening up the bar. Of course, nobody would be here other than him for the next hour or so, but it didn't matter. I needed to find a place to be safe. I needed to be safe.

"Can I come in?" I asked, my whole body shaking.

Rebel gave one look at me, tugged me in by my apron, and slammed the door behind me, locking it. "What's wrong? Are they after you?"

Rebel had left the Kingdom long before I had. He had dropped out of high school and ran before they could destroy his soul and his heart. That was over fifteen years ago, and now he owned Ink on Tap, the prominent gay bar for the area, the one that was inclusive, a safe house, and a safe place.

It was my salvation, the one place I could be myself.

The one place Rebel could be his self.

And I was going to have to leave it.

"Stone's here," I blurted.

Rebel cursed under his breath. "Is he alone? How did he find you?"

"I think he's always known where I was. Of course, he would."

"Fuck. Okay, we can get you some new identification, get you out of here."

"I left my purse and everything behind. I'm such an idiot. All I have is my phone."

"Okay, we'll get you out of here. I know somebody up in Wyoming. They can keep you safe."

"Really? Is that going to be the best I can do? Running for the rest of my life?"

"I don't know what else we're supposed to do, babe. I'll go with you. So you're not alone."

"You can't give up everything."

"I would. You know I would. My family's long dead and the King won't even remember who I am. After all, he didn't know me as Rebel."

I nodded and sighed. "Okay. I guess I'll leave? I don't know. I don't know what I'm supposed to do."

Rebel opened his mouth to speak and then frowned, pulling out his phone. "Well. It seems that Stone found you. Fuck. Okay, we'll get you out another way. Unless they have us surrounded." He let out a breath. "It's been so long since I've done this. I'm rusty."

Stone's voice came through the doorbell camera alert. "Sarina? I'm alone. I left. I promise you. I left."

Rebel and I both froze, my palms damp, bile filling my throat. "Did he say he *left*?"

"That's what he says. Fuck, it looks like somebody did

a number on him." Rebel met my gaze. "Sarina, babe. Stone would never have hurt you. You know that. He might have stayed to protect his brother, but he always promised that he would never hurt you."

"Why are you throwing that back in my face?" I asked, my laugh hollow. "He did hurt me. Just not in the way that he might think."

"Of course he did. He's a man. He's a dumbass. He stayed in the Kingdom to protect his brother, but he's out there, looking pretty hurt, and I don't know, something doesn't feel right about this."

Tension slid up my shoulders again. "What do you mean?"

"There's nobody on my surveillance, Sarina." He showed me his phone, at the eight cameras and their feeds. "Not a single thing. And none of my contacts have warned me that any of the Kingdom's coming here. I'll reach out if you want to see what's going on with Stone, but this doesn't feel like a setup."

"Isn't that going to be the last thing that anybody says before they find out it was a setup?"

"Maybe. But come on, let's go see what Stone wants. I'll protect you."

"I'm not going to have you hurt because of me."

"It would never be because of you. You know that."

"Rebel, we left."

"And maybe Stone did too."

I swallowed hard and rolled my shoulders back. "Fine,

he's never going to go away. It always seems like he can find me. I'll see what he wants, tell him to go, but you stay safe. I don't want him to see you."

"Sarina."

"What? Let me protect you for once. Maybe it's my turn. I shouldn't have come here. I put you right in the thick of things all over again."

"I'm here to protect you. Remember that."

"No, we protect each other." I kissed him hard on the mouth, and he rolled his eyes before he followed me towards the backdoor.

"Stay out of sight."

"Fine, but let me put on shoes. I'm not going to fight off a team while I'm barefoot and shirtless."

"If anyone could do it, it would be you," I teased, trying to lighten the tension.

"Sarina," Stone said again, through the doorbell camera. Rebel had the camera set up to hear what Stone was saying outside, and that was the only reason I felt somewhat like I could have control here. It took me forever to find my control, my own life.

I opened the door partway, the glass partitioning it off. It was bulletproof glass, and there was no way Stone could make it through. At least, that's what I told myself.

"Sarina. You ran."

"Of course I ran. What are you doing here, Stone? I'm not going back."

"I'm not going back either. I'm free." He shrugged, then winced, pressing his hand to his side.

"Stone." I reached up, almost getting to the door to help him, then realized what I was doing.

He wasn't going to get me this way. Nobody was going to make me feel like an idiot. "I'm fine. Just need to heal. It was a goodbye present from Eddie and the others on my way out."

"You're gone then. You just left."

"There was no just about it, but I'm out. I'm not going back." He let out a shaky breath. "I should've left long ago. I was a fucking idiot. But I needed to stay for Phoenix."

"I'm sorry about your brother." I swallowed hard. "I heard about what happened."

"Sorry about a lot of things."

Phoenix had been Stone's older brother and had died in a shootout with a rival gang. I didn't know the details, only that Phoenix was dead, and the sole reason that Stone had stayed was gone. And yet, Stone hadn't come. I had waited foolishly, as if expecting him to show up and for us to pretend that nothing had changed between us and that he had finally had a reason to stay.

In the two years since Phoenix's death Stone hadn't contacted me, hadn't shown, and that had been the final nail in the coffin of whatever dreams I had once had.

I left the Kingdom because there was only death of my

soul and my body back for me with the King. I had left, with a promise from Stone that he would come for me.

And then a single note saying he couldn't because Phoenix needed him had shattered everything. Had torn away the fragile bonds of whatever promises we had made to one another.

With the death of Phoenix shocking around our underworld, I had thought maybe I had a chance. Maybe he would come back.

He hadn't. Stone hadn't come.

And so, these past two years, I had found a way to be myself, the person that I was.

Stone hadn't come for me. I had come for myself.

"I came for you; you don't have to do anything. I'm going to stay for a while. Figure out who I need to be. But Sarina? I'm back. I'm here."

I looked at him then, looked at the man I had once loved, and I could see the parts that I had loved before, the parts that I had been connected to, but he wasn't him. I loved Stone Anderson. I had given everything to him, and he had stayed to protect his family, and while I understood that, I needed to defend myself. For once, I needed to do something for myself.

"I'm glad that you're out. But I'm not the same person. I'm not the girl that needed your help to get away from the King. I'm not the girl who watched her father and her brother die. You're free, but I've been free longer. Be safe, Stone. But I'm not yours anymore. And maybe I never was." I raised my chin, then closed the door in his face, locked it, and ignored Rebel's look. Instead, I fell to my knees, my hands ice against the cold metal steel of the door, and let the tears fall.

I had loved Stone before.

And perhaps part of me always would.

He was my past, not my present.

And if I wanted to survive, I couldn't let him be my future.

Chapter Three
STONE

THANKS TO ARLO'S INTERVENTION, I HAD BEEN in Colorado and away from the Ruin and the Kingdom for four weeks now. Four weeks of me trying to figure out what the fuck I was going to do.

Sarina hadn't wanted anything to do with me, and frankly, I didn't blame her. I had shown up out of the blue, not knowing what the hell I wanted, and she hadn't wanted me. Had practically shoved me out of the way. And I get it. She walked away, and I probably would've done the same in her case.

I missed her, damn it. Of course, I had missed her when she left before, when she had gotten out and taken the step before I had. She was far stronger than I was, far stronger than I would ever be.

Not that she would let me tell her that. No, she wanted nothing to do with me, and while I was a bastard, an asshole, I wasn't about to force her into spending time with me. So that meant I had to stay away. At least until I found some form of steadiness.

I didn't go into Taboo or Ink on Tap. Those were the two places that I knew for sure that she worked.

In the past four years, she seemed to have found her place, a set of friends, maybe even a family here.

And I wasn't part of that.

Maybe I didn't need to be part of that. Hell, I wanted to be part of that. She was my goddamn forever, and I just wished somehow she would let that happen. She would fall for me again and not want to let go.

Only, if I pushed, if I crowded in, she'd hate me more than she already did. And considering I knew she despised seeing me, that was saying something.

"You ready to go, Stone?" I shook myself out of my funk and looked up at Luc, my boss.

I had been out of a job, in need of funds, and a new way to start my life.

In a past life, I had once considered becoming an electrician. I was good at it and can usually rig up anything around me that was needed.

That was what the King had used me for when I wasn't a runner.

So I used the skills I had honed in the business to find a job here.

Now I worked at Montgomery Inc. and was working my ass off.

When I wasn't helping Luc with setting up the electric, I was lifting and hammering and sawing, doing whatever else I needed to do for the company.

An entire family owned and operated this place. It was nice seeing how one member of the family was the architect, the other the lead contractor, and one even a plumber. Luc was the electrician. He had married into the family; his wife Meghan was the lead landscape architect. They built homes and some commercial buildings, but whatever contract they got, they seemed to put their all in, always to code and worked with high-end materials.

They were the real deal, completely the opposite of what I used to do.

I felt like maybe I could find a home here, not that I thought I'd ever actually be able to stay. No, eventually, I'd have to go. Because I knew the King wouldn't let me stay for long. Maybe it was a good thing that Sarina was gone then. That she wanted nothing to do with me, because when the King found me, when he sent his men after the runner they had lost, if he even cared that much, they would find her too, and I would never let anything happen to her.

I was down on the ground, my hands covered in dirt as I lifted a box for Luc, when I heard a familiar voice. A voice that broke me.

I stiffened, even as Luc grinned widely on the other side of me.

"Hey man, we're going to take a break."

I cleared my throat and looked up at the dark-skinned man. "Excuse me?"

"My wife's here."

"Oh."

I stood up next to Luc and wiped my hands on my jeans. "I've met Meghan."

"Yeah, she's pretty great, isn't she?"

Only it wasn't Meghan I was looking at. Yes, Meghan, with her dark hair and bright blue eyes was gorgeous, but she only had eyes for Luc, just like I only had eyes for the girl next to her.

Sarina stood there, her hair piled on the top of her head, her hazel eyes wide as she looked at me.

Whatever color had been in her face from her laughter earlier was gone. Instead, it leeched from her skin as she stared at me as if she had seen a ghost.

Maybe she had.

I wasn't supposed to be here. I had done my best to stay away. Why the hell was she here?

Luc cleared his throat and looked at me. "I know you're running. We all do. I guess you know Sarina?"

"From a lifetime ago."

When we had been young, foolish, and thought we could take on the world. But in the end, we hadn't been able to do anything. We hadn't been able to save ourselves.

"You know, I almost made a mistake before by leaving and not fighting. You might be trying to figure out who you are, but if you think she's worth it, apologize. Make sure she knows she's the center of your universe. And don't fuck it up."

I looked up at the other man and frowned. "You can tell all that from a look?"

"You can tell a lot of things when you've been there before."

Luc shrugged, set down his equipment, then walked over to his wife. "Hey there, baby."

"Hey there, baby, right back."

They kissed each other like they weren't on their worksite, as if they hadn't been married for years.

"What'd you bring me?"

"Hailey was busy today, a conference downtown had heard about Taboo, and now she's stressed out. She sent Sarina here with our lunches, and I said I would help."

"It's nice to meet you, Sarina," Luc said as he held up his hand. Sarina smiled, but it didn't reach her eyes. After all, she was looking at me, then she shook her head, smiled for real, and took Luc's hand.

"It's nice to meet you. Hailey always talks so well about the family. I'm glad I could finally come out here."

"I'm glad you could too." Luc swung his arm around Meghan's shoulders. "Are you going to join us for lunch?"

"Oh, I should go back. Hailey needs me."

"Okay then, just let me know what you need. I'm going to go take my wife to neck around the side."

"Luc!" Meghan laughed, but she didn't counter that. Instead, she followed him, leaving Sarina and me alone.

"You're here," she whispered.

"Yeah. I've been working here for a bit." I cleared my throat. "I didn't know you'd be here. I know you said you wanted space, and I figured I'd do the one thing I should've done a long time ago and fucking listen to you."

She shook her head and looked down at the baskets around her. "I just brought lunch for the crew. Hailey does that every once in a while. Her bakery is right next to Montgomery Ink. The two families own the business, and they're all close."

"That's cool. Luc was telling me a little bit about it."

"So, you're an electrician now?" she asked as she stared at me.

"I always have been. I didn't do it for the right things."

"No, I guess you didn't."

I shuddered, pushing away thoughts of what I'd been forced to do in the past, because I wasn't that person anymore, at least, that's what I told myself.

"Anyway, I'll leave you be. If that's what you want."

"I don't know what I want, Stone. How are you here?"

"I don't know. I didn't expect you."

"Well, to say that I didn't expect you would be an understatement."

"I'm sorry. For taking up your space. For being here. But I missed you, Sarina."

"It's been years, Stone. I already told you we're not the same people."

"You're right. We aren't. I'd still like to get to know you."

"Really?" she asked, and I could tell she didn't believe me.

"I do. I want to get to know you. I'm here for the long haul, Sarina." As long as they didn't find me. But neither one of us needed to say that.

"I left all that behind me. I don't know if I'm ready to see it again."

"I'm not that person. I left. I should've left a long time ago, but I never crossed *that* line. I was never that guy."

We both knew what I was talking about; there was no need to say the words aloud.

"I was so afraid that you'd be pushed into it. I never thought you'd willingly take that step."

"Sarina," I whispered.

"I'm just so afraid. What if you wake up and realize that you miss that life?"

"No," I said vehemently. "I'm not that guy. I left because I needed to, because I wanted to. Because I missed you."

"Don't put that all on me. Don't say that you left only for me."

"I didn't. I left because I wanted to, because I needed my life back. I stayed because of my brother, and that was wrong, but he's gone. They all are. I don't want to be part of that life anymore."

"That life is long behind me, Stone."

"Good. Then let's start over."

I held up my hand. "Hi, I'm Stone."

She looked up at me, then down at my hand, her body shaking slightly as she sucked in a breath.

"Stone," she whispered. Then she let out a breath, met my gaze, and slid her hand into mine. "I'm Sarina."

"Sarina," I whispered, relief hitting me like a two-by-four.

"I'm scared," she said, with a hollow laugh. "What if you leave again? What if I have to leave?"

"I'm not going to let anything happen to you, Sarina."

"We both know you can't promise that."

"I'll try my damned best. But we're going to start over, remember? I'm just Stone. You're just Sarina."

She looked at me then and shook her head. "I don't think there's anything *just* about that. But we can start over. Because walking away from you hurt, it killed me, and I don't think I'm strong enough to do it again." And so we stood there, as others milled about, and I stared at the woman that I loved, the girl that had walked away, and the woman she had become.

I had to hope this wasn't a dream, that this wasn't going to fall around me.

I knew better.

I had always known better.

I just hoped it wasn't too late.

Chapter Four
SARINA

My feet hurt again, but this time I still had a slight bounce to my step.

I couldn't help it. It had been a week since I had seen Stone at the job site, since I had told myself that I wasn't making a mistake.

And I wasn't making a mistake. Because I had already made one before, by pushing him away. He had been hurting, had been in pain, and I had pushed him away to protect myself.

I shouldn't have done that. Yes, I was scared. Yes, seeing Stone had brought back memories of pain, agony, and shame.

He had always treated me well. He had always treated me like I was cherished.

He hadn't forced me to stay behind for him. He had watched me go, had stood back to make sure I was safe.

That's what I had to remind myself.

Yes, he had stayed, no, he hadn't come after me until I felt like it was too late, but he hadn't blocked me in.

"You feeling okay?" Rebel asked me from the other side of the bar, and I smiled at him, this time knowing it reached my eyes.

"I am, ready for the night to be over though, no offense."

He just grinned at me. "Oh, no, because your honey bun is coming to stay with you for the evening. I wouldn't want to stay either."

"Rebel," I said as I blushed.

"Honeybun?" Jeremiah, one of my regulars, asked as I handed him his beer.

"It's nothing," I grumbled, glaring at Rebel. "Stop it."

"Stop what?"

Rebel beamed and leaned forward towards Jeremiah. The two had been having a serious flirt for the past couple of months, and I wish they would just ask each other out already. However, fate was a tricky mistress, and they were taking more time.

"Her old boyfriend is back in town."

"Well, if you broke up with him, it must have been for a reason," Jeremiah said. "We don't want you hurt."

My heart swelled, and I could see it did for Rebel too from the look in his eyes. "He didn't hurt me. I had to leave a situation, and he couldn't come with me."

It wasn't exactly true because he *had* hurt me because he stayed away for so long. Only that hurt was also on me.

It wasn't all his fault, nor was it all mine. Sometimes I had to remember that it was the King's fault, the Kingdom, and the Ruin.

Those who had sent us to a life that we couldn't escape. They were who had hurt us both.

I wasn't afraid of Stone. I never had been. I was afraid of what he had represented, what had almost swallowed us both.

That wasn't the case anymore. I wasn't that person anymore. I had to hope that Stone wasn't that person either.

"Anyway, her ex is back in town, and he makes her smile like that, so I'm calling it a good thing."

I blinked and looked over at Rebel. "Really?"

"Of course. I'd say he's your lobster, but we know that lobsters don't mate for life," Rebel joked.

I rolled my eyes. "Please stop telling me random crustacean facts."

"I'd like to know random crustacean facts," Jeremiah said, his gaze only for Rebel. I looked between the two of them and held back a smile. If crustacean facts and trivia were what was going to bring these two together, I wasn't going to stand in their way.

I cleared my throat. "I'm going to go clean up on the other end, and then I'm heading out. Are you two okay?"

"I think we're just fine," Jeremiah answered, and Rebel rolled his eyes.

"You think that line is going to work?"

"I think I have a few more," Jeremiah drawled when I rolled my eyes. I grabbed my bag from underneath the bar, and headed towards the other end.

I'd have to wear my cross-body bag for the rest of the evening, but that was fine. I didn't want to interrupt them again accidentally. Not when things might be working out.

"Hey," Stone whispered from my side, and I let out a breath, my stomach tightening. I had known he was there, of course. The hairs on the back of my neck had stood on end, and I always knew he was there.

There was something about him. Something that hurt and ached and made me want to give in.

That was Stone. That was always Stone.

"Hi," I said as I looked up at him, at his deep green eyes, the way his dark hair fell over his face.

He needed to shave, and I liked it. That slight stubble that I knew would scrape rough against the inside of my thighs.

I blushed, wondering where the hell that thought had come from, and from the way that Stone's eyes darkened, he must've guessed where my thoughts had gone.

"When are you through tonight?" he asked, his voice a low growl.

"She's done now," Rebel said, not tearing his gaze from Jeremiah's.

I swallowed hard. "Apparently, I'm done now."

"Good, I'll walk you home?"

"Oh. Sure." Disappointment slid through me. In the week since we had reintroduced ourselves to one another, pretending the past hadn't existed even while it wrapped its claws around our throats, we had gone for coffee, for food, but we hadn't kissed. Hadn't done anything.

Had he wanted to start over completely by just being friends? Or was it something more? Was he just taking it slow?

I wasn't sure, but I couldn't read him, and it killed me.

Because I wanted to know, I needed to know.

I was just afraid if I asked, the answer would hurt.

Just like always, everything hurt when it came to Stone and the Kingdom.

"I have my bag, so I'm ready to go."

"Good. Come on, let's take you home."

I walked out from the side of the bar, waved at Rebel and Jeremiah, who weren't even looking at me, and found myself holding Stone's hand. His palms were rough, calloused, as if he worked hard with his hands, and I couldn't help but imagine his hands on me.

Why the hell did I feel so freaking horny? I had had sex before, mostly with myself, but it counted.

Why was it that every time I was around Stone I

swooned and couldn't focus? Why was I always wet when he was around?

There was something wrong with me.

"Where are your thoughts going?" he asked as we walked down the street towards the small set of apartments where I lived. It was ridiculously priced in downtown Denver. However, I was subletting from a woman who wasn't charging too much. I wasn't sure why, and I wasn't going to ask questions, but everything was legal according to Rebel, so I would focus on that.

"What?" I asked.

Stone met my gaze, shook his head. "You're in your head, and I don't know why."

"I think you can guess why," I muttered as we walked up the stairs towards my fourth-floor apartment.

"Okay, so you're working two jobs then?" he asked as I let him inside, feeling as if the space was far too small with him around. He was wide, all muscle, and he filled any room he was in. But right then, it felt like it was more as if I couldn't breathe when he was around. Or maybe I could never breathe when he was around.

"Yes, between both jobs, seven days a week and far too many hours, but they're good to me, and I'm saving up."

"This apartment can't be cheap," he said as he looked around the fully furnished sublet apartment. There were light colors, a modern kitchen, and a small sofa. My bed was in the corner, as it was a studio and not much square footage, but it was enough for me—more than I ever had growing up. Oh, my father had had a decent home before the Kingdom had enveloped us, but then we had moved into the compound, and I had only been given what they allowed me to have, what the King had bestowed upon us.

Because I wouldn't give him what he wanted, it wasn't enough.

"The price isn't that much. It's a sublet. And I think just good luck."

"It's great. I'm renting a hole in the wall in Aurora, and I'm pretty sure that the rats are bigger than I am, but it works."

I frowned. "I'm sorry. Did you sign a lease? We can find you something better."

"It's week-to-week, which is why it's such a shitty place. I was just afraid at first that I'd have to leave quickly, and I didn't want to sign anything. You know?"

"I do, because you're under the radar, just like I am."

"I hate that we are. I hate that he probably knows exactly where I am."

"I know he knows where I am," I said as I shrugged, setting my bag down. "He always knows. We can pretend and change our names, get a fake Social Security card, and go about all the normal ways to hide, but he'd always find us."

"That's why you never changed your name."

"I changed my last name, but there wasn't a point. He always knows where we are because if he can't find us, he has connections with the Ruin, and they can find anybody."

"There's no hiding unless you're dead."

I hadn't meant to say that, and with the storms in Stone's eyes, he didn't like to hear it. "I'm so fucking sorry."

"There's nothing to be sorry about," I said, shaking my head. "You didn't do anything wrong.

"Then why do I feel like I did something wrong?"

"Now that I think about it, you stayed to protect your brother. You survived because that was the situation we were in. I only got out because you found a way for me. And I think I hated myself more than you for you not being able to come with me."

"Sarina," he whispered as he moved forward, his hands cupped my face, and I let out a breath, the warmth of his skin on mine almost too much.

"I hated myself for leaving you behind. For not being strong enough to stay to fight for us. I know you had to stay. I know there wasn't another choice. I think, though, I hated you more than I wanted to when you couldn't come with me later. When your brother was gone, and there was nothing else."

"He chained me in the basement," he muttered, and I froze.

"What?"

He let me go then and began to pace, and I felt the coolness of lack of his touch.

"He chained me in the basement when my brother died. Beat me, did...well, things. I don't want to go into detail because I don't want to think about it. They were training the new Rook, the new Knight, and I was just the runner. They wanted me to kill this kid, this fucking kid, so that I could take over the Rook position, and I wouldn't." Stone met my gaze. "I wouldn't. And when they killed my brother, there was nothing else for me. I tried to leave, and they wouldn't let it happen. I stayed for as long as I was forced to, and then there was nothing else for me."

"Stone," I whispered.

"A friend helped me out, though I don't think he is actually a friend. An ally that I hadn't realized was an ally until it was almost too late to. He got me a car, helped me get out while I was thinking about just taking the bus to get here to you."

"Because you knew where I was," I whispered, my hands shaking.

"Of course I did. I always knew where you were, because I needed to make sure you were safe. That's why I stayed. Well, part of it. Because I needed to make sure you were safe."

Tears slid down my cheeks, and he cursed under his breath. "Stop it. I wasn't blaming you."

"I know. But damn it, Stone, why did we lose so much time?"

"We don't have to lose any more."

And then his mouth was on me, and I was lost. He tasted of coffee and Stone. I moaned into him, craving him. He was the drug, and I was the addict, and it had been too long since my last hit.

An eternity since my last hit.

I slid my hands up his back, digging my nails into his shirt, and he groaned into me, pinning me against the wall. I hadn't even realized that he had backed me up next to the front door until I was there and I groaned, arching against him. My nipples were hard, pressing against his chest, and he smiled against me. "You taste so fucking good. Like a memory, sin, and a promise all rolled up into one."

"I could say the same of you. I missed this, Stone. I missed you."

"It's only been you," he whispered, and my eyes went wide.

"What?"

"Since you left, it's only been you."

I swallowed hard. "I waited too. I didn't realize I was doing it, but I waited."

He groaned, his thick cock pressed against my belly. "Fuck. I'm not going to last long."

"Then this first time, we don't have to last. I just need you."

"Deal."

And then he was kissing me again, pulling up my shirt. I tugged at him, ripping at the bottom of his shirt until he pulled back, shrugged off his jacket, and remove the shirt over the top of his head. He was all ink and long lines of muscle. My hands ran over the scar on his chest, the other on his hip, another on his bicep, and he cursed under his breath.

"The only scars I have are the ones of my own making. Ignore the rest."

"Only if you ignore them too."

And I tugged off my shirt, leaving me in my bra, and his fingers went to the scar between my breasts.

"I'll kill him for you."

"No. He's nothing right now. Don't let him in here."

The King didn't matter right now. He couldn't. I couldn't let him be part of this.

I may wear the King's scar on my flesh, but I wasn't his Queen. Wasn't his anything.

Stone growled, and then he kissed me again, and I was lost.

I tugged on his pants, and we each toed out of our shoes, stripping each other gently. We were still standing, my back pressed against the cool wall.

"I need to be inside you," he grumbled as I reached between us, gripping his cock. He was wide, long, and I couldn't touch my fingers as I wrapped around him.

"Were you always this big?" I asked, looking down.

He grinned. "It looks like I'm going to have to refresh your memory." And then he reached down, lifting me by my thighs, and speared into me.

I was wet, soaking for him, and he slid right in with ease.

I looked at him, my breath coming in pants as I looked down between us, at the way that we connected, his cock deep inside my pussy.

"Stone."

"Fuck, I didn't mean to go so fast, but I slid right in."

"Because I'm always wet around you," I said as I clenched my inner walls. His eyes crossed, and he groaned, kissing me again. And then I wrapped my legs around his waist and urged him.

"Please. Fuck me. We'll make love later, but now I just need you to fuck me."

"Deal." Then he moved, sliding deep inside of me. He slammed me into the wall over and over again, and I arched for him, meeting him thrust for thrust. I'd be bruised later, but then again, as my fingers clawed down his back, he'd carry my mark as well.

And that's all I wanted, for him to carry my mark on his flesh, his soul, just like he had branded me long ago.

He flipped his thumb between us, over my clit, and I met his gaze. My mouth parted, and I came. It was a rush, passion and promise and heat all at once as my cunt clamped around his dick, my entire body breaking out into goosebumps as I came, my head thrown back, my body in need.

Stone bit down on my shoulder, grunting as he

followed, filling me as if the both of us hadn't been able to hold back. It was hard, rough, and it was perfect.

It was only then that I looked down and realized he hadn't used a condom.

Stone was the only person I had ever had sex with, and if he was telling the truth, and I had to hope he was, I was the only person for him.

"Fuck, I didn't protect you."

"It's okay. I'm on birth control. I'm clean."

Stone let out a shaking breath, his dick still twitching deep inside me. "I'm clean too. But hell. I need to do better about taking care of you."

"It's okay. It's okay."

And then I kissed him, falling in love with him all over again.

The boy that I'd loved, the man that I yearned for, and the promise I knew needed to be kept.

He was Stone, he was mine, and I had to hope that in these moments we had for one another—that this couldn't be the end.

Chapter Five
STONE

The sun warmed my face as I looked up into it and let out a deep breath. It had been a long day on-site, and I was exhausted but still revved. I needed to head home, shower, and then I was going to meet with Sarina. Somehow she had taken me back. It wasn't as if we had forgotten what had happened, but maybe we were just figuring out who we could be now.

I liked working for the Montgomerys. They were good people, took care of their crew, and didn't mind that I couldn't tell them everything.

Maybe it was because I figured a few of them had secrets of their own, or had been through shit the same as I had. But they didn't ask questions. Everything was above board and legal, because hiding from the Kingdom didn't happen. I knew they knew where I was, but they hadn't come for me yet. So that was something I would eventually have to deal with.

The Montgomerys didn't mind that I didn't answer their questions. They appreciated the fact that I did good work and was doing my best to learn.

They did care that I didn't have a truck or vehicle, but between walking, and the city's mass transit, I was making do.

I had never not had a bike or a vehicle. I had always had something. It had been a point of pride for me.

I had left my bike back at the Kingdom, and when I had come here, I had sold the car Arlo had given me, not exactly legal since the car hadn't been in his name either, but it had worked.

The place hadn't asked questions, and I hadn't volunteered anything. I'd gotten the money I needed to get my life started, as well as any money I had on hand, and that was it.

That meant I didn't have a vehicle, I had a shitty apartment, but I was saving.

And, if I was honest, I felt like I was also taking advantage of the fact that Sarina let me stay over.

Her sublet was small but fucking nice.

She had made a life for herself, and I was grateful for that.

If anyone had needed a new way to live, a new focus, it was her.

And she was making it happen.

I was so fucking proud of her.

I knew she was working too hard, and while I was too, I didn't want her to have to.

Maybe I could figure out a way to help her. To make it so she didn't have to work as hard. Not that I figured she'd let me help her. She was so goddamn stubborn, but then again, I wasn't that far off.

That's why I hadn't taken the ride offered when Storm and Wes Montgomery, two of the family members that owned the company, had offered to drive me home. They didn't need to see where I lived, even though they had the address. I didn't need to see the pity on their faces. And frankly, I didn't need the charity. I liked them, but I didn't know them. I needed to do this on my own, even if I might be making a mistake. I had made enough mistakes in the past, didn't want to make any new ones.

I turned the corner, my thoughts on what my next step would be when I heard it.

A single booted foot on gravel, one that shouldn't be there. Because nobody had been following me, I had been alone, and yet the hairs on the back of my neck were rising.

I turned and ducked the fist in the nick of time, but missed the man behind me.

"The King sends his regards," a muffled voice whispered into my ear, and then the fight was on.

Someone grabbed me by the back of my neck and pulled me backward. I stumbled a bit, catching my balance, and stuck my elbow out, hitting the other man in the chest. He moved back, and I punched out, slamming my fist into the mouth of the other man.

It was the Rook and the Knight. They had come for me. They wanted me.

Fuck. I'd been too complacent. No, I hadn't been able to hide entirely, as you couldn't hide from the Kingdom, but they'd still found me. I didn't even have a fucking weapon on me because I didn't want to carry.

But I knew they wouldn't care. I only had my small knife, not even a true weapon, and it wasn't going to be enough. And I couldn't reach it with my hands pinned behind my back, eerily reminiscent of the last time this had happened and I had watched Jeremy die.

Rage filled me at the thought of Sarina being in that position this time instead of Jeremy. I would never forgive myself if she got hurt. I couldn't let them find her. I couldn't lead them to her or have them know that I was close to her again.

I tried to get away but froze as the feel of a blade nicked at my neck.

"I wouldn't move, boy. You never know how clumsy I can be."

"Fuck you," I grumbled, knowing if they were going to do it, they'd have already killed me. They were just waiting. For what, I didn't know, but it had to be something. They wanted me, and now they were going to get me.

I just couldn't let them have Sarina.

"You shouldn't have left. The King wants your head, and he gets what he wants."

"I'm not your fucking pawn. I never have been."

"Really? Because you never moved up in the ranks. Never had enough dick to make it happen."

I snorted. "You don't want to hear about my dick, boy."

"That what you're going to go with? Well, too bad you're going to die out here all alone. Kind of sad, really. Then again, you always were. Couldn't keep your woman, couldn't keep your friends or family. You already have one foot in the grave, Stone. You shouldn't have run out on the King."

"Fuck. You."

I spat out the words, blood seeping from my cut lip, as the Knight hit me again and again, the Rook holding me back.

I couldn't do much, not with a knife at my throat, but I knew they couldn't kill me, not here out in the open.

At least, that's what I'd hoped.

"What the fuck is going on?" a familiar voice called out from a passing truck. The tires squealed as the brakes slammed, and then the Knight cursed under his breath.

"You're lucky this time, boy," he spat, literally spitting in my face.

I growled, and then the Rook let me go, the knife easily tucked away in his pocket.

They ran, Wes and Storm coming at me. "What the

fuck? Stone? Dear God. Come on, let's get you to the hospital."

I shook my head, wiped my mouth with the back of my hand. "I'm fine. They didn't break anything." I winced, rubbed my side.

"At least they didn't rebreak my ribs."

"Jesus Christ, Stone." Storm shook his head. "You need to see someone."

"I can't. You know why."

They might not know the details, but they knew why. I had kept my secrets on purpose. So I wouldn't go anywhere, but I was damn grateful to see Wes and Storm right now.

"Are they going to come after you again?" Wes asked, his hands on his hips as he glared in the distance.

"I don't know. They should give me space, but hell, I just don't know." I let out a breath, defeat lying heavy on my shoulders. "I won't come back to work. I won't put your family in jeopardy."

Storm frowned. "That's not what we said. We're worried about you."

"What about your family?"

"They didn't jump you on-site. They jumped you around the corner because you're walking home alone. We just won't let that happen again."

"What do you mean? You're going to fight back whoever tries to jump me?"

"No, we'll just make sure you're not alone."

"And for how long?"

"Till they give up? We don't know," Storm growled. "It's not like this is something we're used to, Stone."

"I figured that. You guys shouldn't have to deal with me."

"You shouldn't have to deal with this either. It looks like you're trying to start a new life with your girl out here."

"I'm not a good man, you guys." I swallowed a lump in my throat. "I never have been. Maybe I'm just getting what I deserve."

"Well, that's just a crock of shit," Wes added. "You got out. You do good work here. And while I don't want to hurt anyone, I don't want you to get fucking hurt."

"Well, they found me anyway."

"Did you use your real name on your paperwork?"

I nodded. "They'd have found me no matter what. Might as well not get you guys in trouble."

Wes and Storm met gazes and nodded tightly.

"I know someone that can help," Storm added, and my brows raised.

"Excuse me?"

"He's a friend of the family, at the other part of Montgomery Ink."

"What the hell do you mean?"

"Best not to ask questions. We'll see what we can do to make sure that they know you're off-limits."

"What kind of shit do the Montgomerys get into?" I asked, blinking.

"As I said, don't ask questions." Storm shrugged, and I looked between the twins, wondering what the hell I had gotten into and why I felt oddly safe.

"Now get in the fucking truck, and we'll take you home."

"Can you take me to Sarina's instead?" I asked, my voice low.

"Need to check on her?"

"Yeah. And just, well, you know."

"We do," Wes whispered under his breath, and I got in the back of the truck, wondering how the hell I had met these people and how my life had turned into this.

They dropped me off in front of Sarina's building, and I said my thanks, wondering if I would see them again. They said they had people to help? Maybe. Or maybe I had gotten a concussion, and I was dreaming all of this.

Nobody gave me a second look as I walked up the stairs, and I didn't know what to think about that, but I ignored it. My lip was bloody, I knew I would end up with a black eye, but I didn't look too bad, I figured. I had tried to clean myself up in the truck, but in the end, Sarina would know exactly what had happened.

I should have just gone home. I shouldn't show her this again. What the hell had I been thinking? Maybe I had gotten a concussion.

I turned on my heel to walk out and the door opened and Sarina's voice soothed my soul.

"Stone? What happened?"

I turned, swallowed hard. "I should go home."

"They found you," she whispered, before she tugged on my wrist and pulled me inside. She closed the door behind her, locked the three deadbolts, and put her hands on the door, shaking as she rested her forehead on the metal.

"I shouldn't be here."

"Did they follow you?"

I shook my head, winced. "I don't think so. Wes and Storm scared them off."

Her eyes widened as she looked at me.

"Sarina," I whispered, and swallowed hard.

She moved forward and cupped my cheek, her gaze filling with tears.

"You're hurt. They found you."

"I'm fine. They jumped me, but I'll be more careful next time. Or, I don't know, Sarina. They're always going to be there. There's no hiding."

"I know, I've always been on the lookout, same as Rebel. There's no living your own life if they don't want you to."

She tugged me to the barstool and then pulled out an extensive first aid kit.

"This brings back memories," I said softly.

Her lips quirked into a sad smile. "I know. We've done

this before. I did this for my father. My brother. I watched them die, Stone. I watched it all. I don't know if I can do it again."

She reached out, wiped the blood from my lip, and then cursed.

"We can fix it."

"How?"

"I don't know. But I'm not that man anymore. You're not that girl. We'll find a way out. We're already halfway there."

"Halfway there, and yet it seems like we have so much further to go. I can't watch you die, Stone. I can't have our past come back."

I tugged on her arm and pulled her close to me, holding her as tightly as I could without hurting either one of us. "I don't know what I'm going to do, what we can do. I'm never going to let them hurt you."

"What if we don't have a choice, Stone?"

I swallowed hard, but I didn't answer. Because I would die before I let them hurt her, or I would kill anybody who got too close.

What was another mark on my soul, after all?

Chapter Six
SARINA

My hands kept shaking as I made coffee. That wasn't the best thing for someone who worked at a café as a barista. But I needed to focus. I needed to work, make money, and maybe find a way for Stone and me to leave again.

It was so odd to think how quickly the two of us had become a pair again. As if no time at all had passed between us, and yet all the time had passed.

I let out a deep breath, opened and closed my hands, and did my best to focus.

Hailey was next door with her husband, delivering drinks to the tattoo artists while I was left operating the espresso maker, working on a latte for an order. The rest of the staff was friendly, welcoming and didn't ask too many prying questions. I had always found that slightly odd since they tended to ask and pry with everyone else.

But maybe it was because they knew I couldn't answer. Or at least give the answers that they wanted.

The Kingdom was watching. In the back of my mind, I had always known that. It was why I took the precautions that I could and why I always felt as if I needed to be two steps ahead. The fact that the Rook and the Knight had been here, had come all the way from Desolation, New York, worried me. I didn't know if they had truly gone back. What if they hadn't? What if they were waiting for us to make a mistake again?

I didn't know what I would do if I lost Stone. Or if I lost myself.

I had been honest with Stone before. Falling into a relationship might have been the worst mistake of my life, but walking away from him hurt just as much. Because I loved him. I loved who he was and how he made me feel.

So somehow, not being able to find a future, or at least look into seeing who we could be, pained me.

This wasn't what I had signed up for. This wasn't what I thought I could be, but now here we were, there was no going back. I had taken Stone into my bed and had brought him into my heart long before he had come to Denver to find me.

"Are you okay?" Hailey asked as she moved forward, her hand on my wrist.

I looked up at her and blinked, and gave her a watery smile. "I think I didn't get enough sleep."

She met my gaze, and I wasn't sure she believed me. It was the truth, but not why I felt like this.

"Okay, well, if you need anything, you let me know. I'm here."

I swallowed hard. "Thanks for everything."

"Why does that sound like a goodbye?" Hailey asked, her voice soft.

"It's not."

I swallowed hard. At least, I don't think so.

"Your shift was over twenty minutes ago, Sarina. Why don't you head home? Take the afternoon off from the bar."

I shook my head. "That would be nice, but I don't have the option of doing that."

"No, I don't think you do. You work so hard, Sarina. But I hope you know we think of you like family here. You and Stone."

I frowned. "Really?"

"Of course. Stone works for the other Montgomerys, just like we're family with these Montgomerys. I know this is probably invasive even to mention, but I heard about what happened."

I froze. "What did you hear?"

Hailey winced, and it was such an odd expression on a beautiful face. "I heard that Stone was hurt. That Wes and Storm found him. I'm glad that they found him. And while I don't know all the details, my husband said that things are being taken care of."

I shook my head. "I can't talk about it, Hailey."

"I know. I just want you to know that we love you, and we're here for you. Don't run, okay? We'll help keep you safe."

I met her gaze. "I don't think you know who you'd be fighting to try to keep me safe."

"No, I don't. It's completely out of my wheelhouse. I'm here if you need me. And if you do need to go, know that you can always come back. This will always be your home."

She squeezed my hands and then she walked away. I sighed, knowing I needed to leave. Maybe I needed to leave town. It might be safer for those that I had come to care for. But where would Stone and I go? And would I even go with him?

He had been back for two months, we had been together for only a month of that time, and he had already been hurt.

The Kingdom had already come to Denver after so long of leaving me alone.

Was it because Stone was the last straw? Or had they just been waiting until I had been lulled into complacency?

I wasn't sure, but I needed to make a decision.

I grabbed my bag and walked out of the back alley, heading towards Ink on Tap. My senses were on alert since I was afraid that *he* would find me any moment. The King hadn't wanted me in ages. Maybe this wasn't about me.

Maybe it was because Stone had left without permission. Hopefully, the King would forget Stone eventually, and someone else would make a mistake. Or another club or group would anger him, and he'd focus all of his attentions on them. That was what had happened with me, and it had given me over four years of relative peace. I might have been constantly on edge, but that was the path I had been set on from birth. The path I couldn't walk away from.

"Sarina?"

I turned, my hands outstretched, my taser in my right hand, and I looked up at Stone.

He held both hands up and cursed under his breath. "Fuck. Sorry, the bus was late, and I came here to walk you to the bar."

Relief speared through me, and I threw my arms around him, careful not to accidentally tackle him. "You scared the crap out of me."

"I can see that. I'm glad you have your taser."

"Who knows if it'll ever be enough," I whispered, and I kissed him softly.

"I hate that you're so on edge, that you're so afraid."

I shook my head. "You're in the same boat."

"Maybe. You were safe before I came here."

"Was I? Or was I just led to believe that?"

"I don't know, baby. Let's get you to work. Maybe Rebel will hire me too." He winked at me, and I grinned.

"He's always looking for a bouncer. It is a gay bar."

"Hey, I'll have you know I will protect anybody in that bar. As long as you're safe."

"I missed you," I whispered as I leaned into him.

"I missed you, too."

And I knew we both weren't talking about the afternoon and morning that we hadn't seen each other. No, it had been a long four years, four years in which we'd had to stay apart to keep each other safe, and it had taken me a while to realize exactly why.

We turned the corner, and Stone let out a shout. I hit the ground as he pushed me down, covering my body. Gunshots rained above us, and I screamed, trying to cover Stone as well, but there was no use, nowhere to hide.

We were slightly behind a dumpster, but it wasn't enough.

"As I said, the King wants you back. You don't get to decide to leave."

Stone growled, pulled me back from the ground, and I ignored the sting in my palms from where I had hit the gravel and now bled.

"Stay here."

"No," I shouted, my throat tight. I gripped his wrist. "Don't go."

Stay safe.

"They're going to kill you."

"No, they're going to kill you," I spat.

And then we were surrounded. They had guns, knives, and they came at us.

"You really shouldn't have left. And to think, you had had everything. A home, food in your belly, protection. And then you left." The Knight looked over Stone's shoulder. "Left to find her. The little bitch the King doesn't even want anymore."

I should have felt relief at that, but I couldn't, not when this could be the end.

The Knight came forward, glaring at Stone.

"You always were a little bitch, just like her."

I moved without thinking, aware that only the Knight had a gun in his hand. Everyone else seemed to just have knives. Not that there was anything *just* about that.

I moved forward, my taser out, and I got him in the belly. The Knight let out a shocked scream and hit the ground.

Stone cursed under his breath, pulled me back, and kicked the gun underneath the dumpster.

"Run," he yelled at me as the others moved forward, shock in their gazes that I would be the one to do that.

The Rook came at us, knife out, and Stone moved quickly, faster than I had ever seen him move before. He gripped the Rook's wrist, twisted. The other man let out a shout. The knife fell to the ground with a clang, and then Stone punched him hard in the face.

Another man came at us, and I kicked out, using the training that I had had from self-defense, and kicked the other man in the balls.

I tugged at Stone, knowing we needed to get away, but there were too many of them.

They couldn't get the gun, but they had knives, and I wasn't sure a taser was going to be able to get all of them.

I looked at Stone, so afraid I had made the wrong choice, that he would die and it was going to be my fault.

The Rook came at us again, the Knight still twitching on the ground, and then the most sacred sound in the world came.

Sirens hit my ears, and Stone and I froze, hands up in the air as the police came, then their words shouting at us to freeze, to not move. The alley filled with the authorities, and Stone and I went to our knees, trying to explain what happened.

Considering the way that it looked and the fact that Rebel and Hailey came out, her husband and the other tattoo artists with her to give their explanations as well, I knew that we would be okay.

The King was going to lose some of his inner circle, at least for the moment, but we weren't going to die right then.

Somehow.

I looked at Stone, my eyes wide, and prayed that this could be the end. Or at least an end.

It would be too much trouble. That anyone the King sent from the Ruin towards us would be sent right back, worse off. That Stone was out.

That I was out.

My father had lied. And then he had died. My brother had done much the same.

Stone was here. And he had protected me, and he had let me protect him.

I had to hope that this would be it. That this could be the start of our future.

The sounds of bullets, of shouts, of screams would echo in my mind until the end of my days, but maybe this could be the end. Or an end.

And finally, a beginning.

Chapter Seven
STONE

I'd gotten my first tattoo when I was fifteen years old. My father had sat me down, and the Kingdom's artist had branded me. I wore their ink on my flesh and their scars on my memories. But not my soul anymore.

I wasn't that man anymore.

It had been a year since the cops had come. Since everything had changed.

The Kingdom hadn't sent another man. We hadn't even heard from them. The Knight was still in jail, the Rook having gotten out on a technicality, but he hadn't come by either. Last I had heard, the King had sent him off, exiled him for failing to get me. For failing to get Sarina.

In the end, it didn't matter because they wouldn't be coming for us anymore.

I had gotten a few more tattoos since, mostly all of them thanks to the Kingdom itself. You wore your ink on your body to prove who you were to those in charge, and I wasn't with them anymore.

The only tattoo I'd ever gotten for myself was a small S hidden among my sleeve.

An S for Sarina, though some had thought it was for me.

I hadn't begrudged them on that or made them think anything different.

Now this ink was for me.

I let out a deep breath, letting the Montgomery behind me have as much space to work with as possible. We were covering up the brands that were from the Kingdom that had nothing to do with my present or my future.

Doing coverups were a lot more fucking painful than the tattoos to begin with, but I didn't mind. If this were my penance to pay for the mistakes I had made in the past, I would freely pay them.

Sarina sat in the next booth over, a woman with dark hair with pink streaks bent over and working on her back. Sarina was getting ink for herself, not a coverup, like me. She could focus on her future ink and paths, while I still had a long way to go working my way through my sins.

We were making this work for the two of us. Though I wasn't sure what would happen next, we would find a way to make all of this work. We were already well on our way to doing so.

We weren't the people we had been years ago. And for that, I was grateful.

I had been young, rash, and stupid the first time I had been with Sarina.

Now I was making choices for myself, and we were finding our path together.

She wore my ring on her finger and would soon carry my name as well.

She grinned up at me, and I smiled back, ignoring the pain as Austin went over the mark, again and again, doing his best to cover up the sins of my past.

I had fallen in love with Sarina long before I realized what love was.

She had been my salvation, my path, my future.

And now she was the promise I had never meant to make, the promise I had thought a dream.

The Kingdom was long gone. We were never going back.

In the end, however, she was my empress, my queen, my everything.

And I was one lucky son of a bitch.

****

Want more of Carrie Ann's romances?
Try Inked Persuasion

Montgomery Midnight Kisses

A MONTGOMERY INK BONUS ROMANCE

Montgomery Midnight Kisses

Alex Montgomery wants to do the unthinkable—surprise his planner-loving wife with a weekend away from the twins and his boisterous family for New Year's Eve. Tabby has a surprise of her own, one that the Montgomerys might just throw a cheese-filled party for even after the holidays. It's been four years since Alex and Tabby fell in love. Now it's time to see what happens after the happy ever after.

Chapter 1
ALEX

THE CHRISTMAS TREE SPARKLED BRIGHTLY IN the corner, and Sebastian and Aria were near it, playing with their toys. I rubbed my temples, trying to remember what I was supposed to be doing next, but I couldn't focus.

My twins were sitting underneath the Christmas tree, only a couple of days before New Year's Eve, and I was *happy*.

If I'd thought of this moment when I'd been younger, I couldn't have ever imagined this form of happiness. I had spent my most recent years, before getting married, thinking I didn't deserve joy. That I was never going to have it again.

And now it seemed as though maybe I had it. I still wasn't sure I deserved it, but I was never going to let it go.

"Daddy!" Aria said, waving her block in the air. I

smiled, my heart growing in size once again, and went to sit cross-legged beside them. Sebastian immediately tumbled into my lap, bringing his stackables with him. Aria sat in front of me, showing off her toys.

"Look at you both! I don't think I could ever do this good a job. This looks outstanding. You're doing a good job."

Aria smiled up at me. "Daddy, help. Please."

They spoke in more than just one or two words at a time, but sometimes they were in such twin-speak that getting out of it to talk to me wasn't high on their priorities. Tabby was usually better at getting them to speak in anything other than that twin-speak. But that was my wife for you, ordered and talented.

"Okay, let me help you with this. Although, pretty sure your Uncle Wes would be better at it."

"Your daddy is just as good as I am at this," my brother Wes said as he walked into the living room. He turned to me, a grimace on his face. "And, my wife should be here soon to help with the bathtub."

I groaned and moved another block to the top of the tower to help Sebastian. "You can't work on it?"

Wes walked forward, shaking his head. "Oh, I could do it, but you want me to work on plumbing and not my wife, who's a master plumber? No, that's not going to happen. I'm a builder, an organizer. I don't do plumbing. Not when my wife will beat me with that pipe wrench just for stepping on her toes."

I snorted. "Well, hell."

"Hell," Aria said, and I groaned as Wes laughed.

"You are not helping," I said, and kissed the top of my daughter's head as she moved closer. "Don't say that word. That's daddy's word."

"Daddy says hell?" Sebastian asked, and Wes started cracking up.

Maya walked into the living room and shook her head. "Okay, why are all of my brothers idiots?" Maya asked, laughing.

Aria clapped her hands. "Idiot."

"Hey, stop teaching the twins new words," I chided. Tabby was going to kill me when she got home.

Maya just laughed. "I'm pretty sure my husbands have taught my kids all the bad words. I am innocent here."

"Whatever you say, sis," Wes said, laughing, clearly not believing Maya just like I wasn't.

My sister moved forward, a smile on her face. "Okay, I have Tabby's bag packed, and the kids' bags packed."

I frowned. "I already packed the kids' things," I said.

"You did, and I added extra things because I'm going to be the one with your kiddos, so I wanted to make sure I had everything."

I sighed. "I'm not going to be gone for that long."

"We're not going to see you until next year," she teased. "You never know."

"You make my head hurt," I said, before I set Sebastian down next to his sister and stood up again. "Thank you both."

"We have a key, and Jillian and I will take care of the plumbing and the stove," Wes said.

I winced. "You guys know how to fix stoves?"

"We do, although we may just end up getting you a new one."

I shook my head. "You don't need to buy us a new stove. That one works perfectly fine."

"That one is the piece of crap that came with this house."

My siblings gave me more headaches than anyone else I knew. "Yes, and it has memories."

"No, you're just cheap," Maya said.

"Hello, I'm going to have twins to put through college. I *am* cheap."

"You make good money in your job," Maya whispered, while Wes was playing with the kids. "You can spend some of it on a new stove."

I sighed, conceding. "I know, and I will. But let's let Tabby pick it out. I'm sure she already has a planner with everything listed."

Maya snorted. "Well, she does keep me organized."

"You don't even work with her. How is she keeping the tattoo shop organized?"

"She taught me how to use planners correctly. I love your wife."

I grinned. I couldn't help it. "I love my wife too."

My sister gave me a soft smile, studying my face. "You sound all proud and happy just saying that."

"I really am." I paused. "Are you sure I'm not making a mistake with this whole weekend thing?"

Maya just rolled her eyes. "You are surprising your wife with a trip for New Year's Eve. A vacation when you guys haven't taken one since before the twins were born. With all that you've been through? You need this."

I blinked. "I can't believe we have been together for nearly four years."

Maya shook her head. "I can't believe all of us are married, and we're on our way to creating four dozen kids."

I laughed. "At least Griffin and Autumn are responsible with just a puppy."

"Yes, and that means they're always available to babysit." Her eyes twinkled, and I laughed.

"Are you sure they know that?"

"Between all of us, we have near a thousand babysitters. And Leif is old enough to babysit and one day, Lake will be able to help out too."

Lake was our new niece in Boulder and came down to Denver often to hang out with Leif, and vice versa. I loved that little girl, and it was nice that all of our cousins were starting to get married and have kids and start this new life.

It wasn't something for everyone. Griffin and Autumn weren't ever planning on having kids, but had a future that was all their own. I didn't know if Tabby and I would have any more children, but we had the twins, parts of my life I never thought I would have after losing everything before.

Maya tapped my temple. "Stop. You're getting in your head again."

I shrugged. "It's what I do. I'm the brooding one."

"And I'm the loud and sarcastic one," she said, raising a brow. The ring in it caught the light, and I smiled.

"I bet you're going to be the most kick ass mom at the PTA meetings."

Maya rolled her eyes. "Like they'd let me in."

"I don't know," Wes corrected. "Our generation is all inked and pierced. The people that show up in loafers and khakis are probably going to be outnumbered."

I laughed. "That's the hope. Plus, I think we're all in the same school district somehow."

"At least middle school and high school would be. Elementary school might be a little difficult since there's so many of us, we might be cut up into different districts," Wes said.

I met Maya's gaze and rolled my eyes. "You say that as if you don't already have it all planned out and color-coded for us."

Wes shrugged, handed a block to Aria. "Your wife and I are very organized. We have a plan. Don't worry. Everyone's going to be getting into good schools."

I snorted. "Good to know." I looked down at my phone. "You guys should head out so I can surprise her."

"You guys don't leave until morning, though, right?" My ass.

"Of course. And we'll drop the kids off in the morning and head out."

"I'm so happy for you guys," she whispered as she kissed my cheek. "You deserve this."

"Or I'm insane planning something in secret from a planner."

"She'll enjoy it because you did it. Now, if you did this every year without her being able to color code everything, you'd have to worry," Wes added.

"Thank you for that," I said dryly.

Wes and Maya left, and I made a note to look at new stoves and to remind Tabby that Jillian would be over to fix the tub later.

We were somehow homeowners, full-time workers, sometimes working a little too much, and parents. At one point, I had thought my life would be completely different, I had been married to someone else, had fallen into the bottle when things had gotten too hard, and somehow I had dragged myself out. And when I had dried up, sobered up, I looked into the future and found Tabby. Or more accurately, she had found me.

Most days, I still didn't think I deserved her, but she was there, smiling and ready to hold me every day I came home.

I was just lucky enough I got to hold her too.

"Honey, I'm home," Tabby said. "Your mother is amazing," she teased.

"Oh yeah?" I asked. My mother was in on the plan too and had taken Tabby for some post-Christmas holiday shopping. Apparently, Tabby wanted to send more gifts out to her brothers and new nieces and nephews. We had spent Thanksgiving out in Pennsylvania with her family, but Christmas and New Year's were going to be here in Colorado.

We were so enriched here in Colorado, and her family was very much so in Pennsylvania, so I didn't think we'd all ever live together, or even near each other. But we did our best to see each other as much as possible. I was grateful that Tabby let that happen. I would move to Pennsylvania in a heartbeat if I thought it would work out, but things worked here now. Maybe one day we'd find a cabin up in Pennsylvania and make that work, but for now, Tabby's family was out there, living with their whiskey bar, and us Montgomerys were here with our tattoos and construction.

"How was your day?" she asked, and kissed me softly.

"I worked some. The kids and I played with blocks."

I picked up Aria as she held up her hands, and Sebastian was already in Tabby's arms.

"Did you guys have a good day?" She nuzzled Sebastian's neck. He let out a little toddler squeal and kissed her hard on the cheek.

My chest swelled as I looked at the two of them and at the little girl in my arms. We were a family, the four of us. I still didn't know how I had gotten so lucky.

"So, Wes was here," I said casually.

Tabby winched. "How much?"

"Okay, first, don't ask things like that. You know, since you work there, and you're family, they're not going to charge you, but Jillian won't be here until tomorrow to fix it."

"I told Jillian to just come over, but no, Wes wanted to see it first so he could make plans or something. I don't understand your brother."

"He wanted to see if he could do it. I don't know, and then he needed to look at the stove." Wes had come over to help with planning the surprise, but I couldn't tell Tabby that.

"I figure we're going to have to get a new stove. I've made lists."

That made my mouth twitch.

"And from the look on your face, you probably joked that I had listed, but I do. It's time. We can afford it."

"Yes, and we'll make the decision together. We just won't let Wes show up with one."

"Knowing your brother, he'll pick the perfect one, but let's be sure. Let's make it ours."

"That sounds good." I rocked back on my heels as Aria started to fall asleep in my arms.

"So, what else happened?" she asked, staring at me.

I blinked. "What do you mean?"

"It's almost New Year's Eve, we are happy, it's the holidays, and you look like you're stressed out over something, and I have no idea what it could possibly be."

I sighed, held Aria closer. "I did something."

Her eyes sobered. "What's wrong, Alexander?"

I could have cursed. I swallowed hard. "Something good. I think."

"Please talk fast because you're worrying me."

She bounced Sebastian in her arms, but my son just stared at me, and I knew he was worried too. My kids were far too perceptive for their own good.

"I set us up a surprise trip. We are going to Vail tomorrow. For two days. We'll be celebrating the new year in a cabin that my friend owns, in the mountains, fireworks above us, if they get to do it this year, snow all around us, each of us holding hot cocoa, and just the two of us."

I looked down at the kids in my arms, and I didn't think they understood what I was saying.

Tabby blinked, her eyes filling with tears, and I cursed. "Or I can cancel. It's super easy to cancel."

She shook her head, went to her toes, and kissed me softly on the mouth. Aria and Sebastian were between us, clapping their hands together.

"I love you, Alexander Montgomery."

I frowned. "I love you too, Tabitha Montgomery."

"You planned a whole trip? Without me."

"You've been stressed recently, and I wanted to do

something to surprise you, and as the plans kept rolling on, I realized that I was probably doing something wrong."

She just smiled at me and shook her head. "A trip. The two of us. For New Year's. Alexander, wow."

"Not too much? I mean, we can still take the kids," I whispered, over their heads.

She shook her head. "Okay, let's go. I assume you have childcare arranged and everything packed and everything ready?"

"Yes," I said. "Maya will take care of the kids, she also packed, but I'm sure you can go double-check. That's why we're not leaving until morning."

Tabby's eyes widened. "Alexander," she whispered.

And I kissed her again, this time the kids wiggling between us as they started pulling at us for attention. I looked down at my daughter in my arms and my son in my wife's, and I knew maybe I made the right decision.

New Year's Eve, alone with my wife.

Just the two of us, a comfy bed, and hopefully, a good evening.

Because we had never spent the night without our kids before.

And here I was, surprising her with it.

Probably not the most intelligent decision I've ever made.

Chapter 2
TABBY

After nearly four years of marriage, I was more in love with Alexander Montgomery than I had been the first time I had seen him. Oh, that love at first sight, hadn't been reciprocated, not even close. He had been married after all. I had promptly slapped myself in the forehead for even allowing those thoughts to enter that realm. I had loved him in my own way from afar. And I had done my best to bury that feeling deep down so it wouldn't matter when nothing came from it.

Somehow, through the grace of fate, and whoever else was watching out for us, Alexander Montgomery was now my husband. And some days I felt like drawing hearts around his name in my planner and making plans. Only now I was living those plans.

Alexander wrapped his arm around my waist and squeezed.

"Why do you look like you just saw your favorite boy band member?" he teased, and I nearly tripped over my feet. He held me steady on the slightly icy sidewalk.

I smiled up at him. "You know what's funny? I was just thinking about you. I guess you could be in a boy band. There's enough of you in your family."

"Dear God, never mention that to Maya, or we're going to end up having to dress up for Halloween one year as her favorite boy band from the early two thousands."

My eyes brightened. "I need to take out my phone to make notes. It has nothing to do with what you just said."

He held my hand, brought it to his lips. When he placed a kiss there, I nearly swooned.

Alexander Montgomery was my husband. And I was going to sing it for all the world, and eventually, I was going to stop acting like the ninny that I was and live in a moment. But I couldn't help but squee internally.

"Did you just make a tiny little scream sound?" he asked, a brow raised.

I blushed. "I thought I was doing the squeeing internally. Apparently, I was doing it out loud too."

Alexander shook his head and leaned down to kiss me.

"Oops, sorry," a man said as he walked around us, coffee in hand. Had his cell phone to his ear and kept going, looking like he had business, *very important business.*

"It's the day before New Year's, and we're in Vail, Colorado. Why does he seem like he's on a mission?"

"Not everybody's on vacation like we are."

I threw out my other arm, careful not to hit anybody. "*Vacation*. What a wonderful word to use." I cringed and looked up at Alexander. "Is it weird that I'm saying this even though we don't have our babies here? They should be here and there as we're walking around, and they could see the mountains like this."

"They see the mountains every time we take them outside or if they look through a window. And they've been to Vail with us."

"You're right, but you were working. That wasn't a vacation."

"I was working on a photoshoot, and you were working with having to deal with two infants, in the cutest little snowsuits ever."

"Aren't they adorable? I can't believe they're already nearing three. Doesn't it seem like just yesterday we were finding out we were having them?"

"It does. I'm so glad you don't have to deal with that morning sickness anymore."

I smiled, but my stomach turned a bit. Hopefully, it was just at the memory finding its way to the present.

"What's wrong?" Alexander asked, and I shook my head. "Just remembering morning sickness."

"I'm just glad being sick all the time didn't last the full forty weeks like Maya's did the second time." He gave a full-body shudder. "I love my sister, and though she can be demanding in her amazing way, I hate seeing her be sick."

"I love your sister too. And yeah, you're right. Her being sick was horrible. But she's okay now."

"You think she and Jake and Border are thinking about having another?" he asked as we walked past a family with a bassinet.

My heart warmed, seeing the little family, and I looked up at Alexander. "I'm not sure. Maya was talking about it, and I'm pretty sure most everybody is open to more children, as Sierra and Austin are already working on the next adoption."

"Griffin and Autumn keep joking that they're going to have to end up with more playtime funds for each kid to the point that they're going to go bankrupt."

I laughed. "Griffin is a New York Times bestselling author who has two movies out at this point. He'll be fine. The fact that they even have a fund for each kid that they jokingly made so they can spoil our children is amazing."

"I do have the best brothers."

I elbowed him in the gut, and he laughed. "Excuse me. My three brothers are pretty amazing too."

"Dare, Lock, and Fox are pretty decent, but they're no Montgomerys."

I rolled my eyes at the age-old competition. Not that they were fighting over who was best, but they wouldn't be guys if they weren't finding a way to playfully growl at one another. Not that I would put it that way to them.

"I'm sorry that we're not with them this weekend."

"We weren't going to see them anyway. You surprising me like this didn't hurt those plans. We were going to stay home or maybe go to one of your countless siblings."

"I love how you say countless as if I don't just have seven."

"*Seven*, Alexander."

"Eight kids aren't that bad. And there's a set of twins. Like ours."

My eyes widened. "Do you think that we're going to have eight children?"

"Of course not. I was thinking about a rounded out ten."

I choked, and he pulled me out of the way of another family. "I hope you're joking."

"I am. I wouldn't mind ten, or just the two that we have, not that there's anything *just* about them."

I smiled again. "I like our family, Alexander. How it is or how it may be. We did good."

His eyes warmed as we stood in front of a little coffee shop. "We did pretty well. And it's all because of you, my Tabitha."

"Aw, you're so sweet. This whole trip, us without the kids, and you laying it on kind of thick. I know what you want tonight," I laughed.

His eyes darkened and leaned down and brushed his lips on mine. "Oh, I have a feeling I'm going to get exactly what I want."

"You are lucky there are children around, or I would tell you exactly what I think about that."

"Okay, I concede. However, I do believe I smell hot chocolate."

I whirled and clapped my hands together. "And chocolate shavings. And caramel sauce. Oh my word, I'm excited." I bounced, and Alexander laughed behind me.

"You already sound like you've had the sugar."

"Perhaps. But you cannot deny me this."

He tugged on my arm slightly, and I turned to him. "I can't deny you anything, wife of mine."

And I melted right there. Sometimes Alexander was quiet, a little gruff, in his own world. He had been through his own personal hell and had fought his way back. It only made sense he was like that.

However, other times he was so open and caring and puddle-inducing, that I couldn't help but fall in love all over again.

We waited in line, and I got a caramel drizzle hot cocoa, and Alexander ended up with a peppermint white chocolate hot chocolate. Or was that a peppermint hot white chocolate? I wasn't quite sure what they named it, but it tasted amazing.

As we walked back towards the home we were staying in, Alexander stopped me at the edge of the road and rubbed his thumb along my nose. "What?" I asked, a smile on my face.

"I love you."

He looked down at me. "I love you too. Even with the cream on your nose." He kissed me soundly, and someone cheered. I waved at the stranger. "Thank you!" I called out.

Alexander chuckled beside me, tangled his fingers in mine, and we crossed the street towards the house. He let me in, and I sighed as the warmth seeped into me. I hadn't realized how cold I had been getting until we were inside.

"You know someone that owns this place?" I asked as we took off our coats and got comfortable.

"A buddy of mine. He won a Pulitzer and wants to work with me. Offered me the place when we were talking about me wanting to surprise you with something."

My eyes widened. "Oh my. Look at you staying with the fancy people."

My husband blushed adorably. "I try. Are you almost done with your hot cocoa?"

I chugged the rest of it and handed him the recyclable cup. "Perhaps."

He shook his head, took care of her cups, and went to turn on the fire.

"Now cuddle with me, woman," he growled, and I sank into him.

I pulled out my phone, and he smiled. "Calling the kids?" he asked.

"I'm calling Maya, who can show me our babies. It's been three hours since we spoke to them."

"I'm shocked you didn't call them out there."

I blush. "I tried on one corner, but there wasn't great service, and I wanted to see their little faces on FaceTime."

Alexander took the phone from me, kissed the top of my head, and dialed. He had longer arms so I could lean into him as we waited to see our babies' faces.

Instead, Jake, one of my Maya's husbands answered. His nose ring was in, and he was smiling wide.

"Well, hello there, you two. Thank you for not calling naked."

"Jake," Alexander growled behind me, and I laughed. "We want to see our babies. Of course, we're not going to call your naked."

"Shame," Jake said, and then ducked his husband's fist jokingly.

"We've got them right here," Border said, and Jake turned the camera so we could see them.

Maya had her youngest, Skylar, on her lap. Sky was near the same age as Sebastian and Aria. Sebastian and Aria were both on Border's lap, while the trio's four-year-old, Noah, sat between them, reading a book to them.

"Noah, are you reading?" I asked.

"I'm trying," he said, smiling big.

Jake chuckled into the phone. "I'm pretty sure he has the thing memorized, but he's reading full sentences now. He's the smartest baby out there."

"Jake," Maya snapped, and I just grinned at the family.

"Babies," I said, as Aria held out her little chubby fist.

Sebastian waved, and we kissed into the camera, and I fell in love with my babies all over again.

"Did you have a good day?" I asked, and both of my babies told me all about their day with blocks and reading and all the sugar they were currently ingesting.

I raised a brow to Maya, who just shrugged.

"We're their aunt and uncles. We're allowed to do that."

"Okay, but next time we watch Skylar and Noah, be prepared."

"As always," Border grumbled as he held both of my babies.

The man was gruff, a little rough, but the sweetest when it came to our children.

I had a wonderful family. Had grown up with the best sort of people. Oh, I had been blessed by adding even more impossible, caring, and loving people to my brood.

I hung up with the babies, and I wiped tears.

"What's wrong?" Alexander asked as he set the phone down and turned me in his arms.

"Nothing's wrong. I'm just really happy."

He gave me a dubious stare. "I am," I whispered.

"You say that, and then you're crying."

"You've known me for how long? You know I cry when I'm happy and overwhelmed."

He held my face and kissed me softly. "Thank you for letting me take you out like this. For surprising you. I know we're not the usual people that go off schedule, but when this opportunity came up, I wanted to see if I can give you another holiday present."

I reached out and brushed my fingertips along his lips. He kissed them gently, and I nearly swooned again.

"I'm so blessed that I have you," I whispered.

"I thought that was my line," he whispered.

"You say that, and yet sometimes I can barely breathe even just thinking of you. I'm so glad that you picked me."

He frowned.

"I didn't pick you, Tabitha. You were mine, always. Just took me a while to figure that out."

And I fell in love with my husband, Alexander Montgomery, all over again.

We had been nearly beaten, robbed of our own fates, and yet we had come together.

And tomorrow, we have one more day in this year before we headed into the new year and our new plans.

And before we did that, though, I needed to tell him one more thing.

But I would wait till tomorrow.

For now, I just wanted to hold my husband and remember the present.

Something I usually forgot to do in the heat of family and plans.

So tonight, I would remember.

Chapter 3
ALEX

My hand slid over Tabby's hip, and she moaned into me, rocking that pert little ass of hers into my cock. I nibbled on her neck, slowly slid my hand up her waist to cup her breast. I plucked her nipple with my thumb and forefinger, and she moaned again.

"Alexander," she whispered.

I grinned. "Good morning, wife."

"Alexander," she moaned again. I loved the sound of my name on her lips. I slowly rocked against her, kneading her. She lifted her legs slightly, and I grinned before I gently probed her entrance and thrust ever so slowly into her wet heat. She moaned, her pussy clutching my dick.

"You're so hot, wet," I mumbled.

"How am I already so wet, and my eyes aren't even open?" she asked, her voice lazy. I slowly worked my way in and out of her, no rush, *need*, the desire to be with the one woman that I loved beyond all measure. She kept her leg up while slowly rocking back towards me. When I lowered her legs slightly, pressed her thighs together even as I worked in and out of her, the sensation sent moans out of each of us.

"Whoa," she whispered, and I grinned, moving slightly so I could kiss her on the lips as she looked back at me.

"You're so fucking beautiful," I whispered.

"I need you," she moaned back. I pulled out of her inch by inch, trying to catch my breath. Her mouth parted in dismay, and I smiled before I rolled onto my back, pulling her with me. She let out a little shocked gasp, and I grinned as she hovered over me, her breasts in front of my face. And because I couldn't help myself, I sucked at them, biting her nipples slightly. She shivered, both of us swallowing hard as she slowly sat on my cock.

We both sat still for a moment, each of us looking at one another as we breathed, and then she began to move. I let my hands roll over her hips, her breasts, up to cup her face to bring her down to my lips. She rocked on me as we each brought each other to pleasure slowly, her with a shocked gasp that had a pretty little blush spread over her body all the way down to her nipples. Me with a guttural moan as I filled her, both of us shaking in the end.

Tabby fell onto my chest, breathing heavily as I wrapped my arms around her and slowly slid my hands up and down her back.

"Good morning," I whispered, nibbling at her earlobe.

She grinned against my neck. "Good morning, husband. We don't get to wake up like that every morning these days."

She sat up slightly, and I looked up at her. "I do miss it, though Sebastian and Aria tend to wake us up a little bit earlier than we like most days."

She smiled and sank into me again. Yes, but we still have our nights, you and I."

"And our afternoons sometimes."

Tabby chuckled and held on to me, "True."

She snuggled into me more, and I pulled the sheet over her.

"What are our plans today?" she asked.

"Whatever you'd like. It's the last day of the year after all."

"Let's get cleaned up, showered, and go see more of the town. And maybe some more hot cocoa."

I laughed, kissed her soundly. "That sounds like a plan. And then we can come back here and see what happens in the afternoon. And in the evening. And late at night. And then tomorrow morning."

She giggled and kissed me again. "I love you, Alexander Montgomery."

I looked up at her then and sobered. "I love you too. With everything that I have. I'm so damned lucky that you're mine."

"I was just thinking that," she whispered.

"Yeah?" he whispered.

"We did get serious all of a sudden," Tabby said softly.

"True, but it's the end of the year, we're supposed to think of futures."

She smiled softly, kissed me on the lips. "We are. Now, come on, we can try shower sex."

I laughed, realized I was still inside her. "You know, I'm not as young as I once was," I growled.

"True, but you can still do other things while you're waiting to recover." She winked, and I laughed outright. The girl I had fallen in love with had been a little quieter and had stood up for herself, sure, but hadn't always asked for what she wanted.

And now she demanded it with love and humor, and I loved her even more.

I had made mistakes. So many damned mistakes when it came to my life and how I treated my family. And somehow, I had been forgiven. Nothing had been forgotten, and it couldn't be. But we had all worked together to find a future that we could work through. And Tabby had been instrumental in that.

I wouldn't be the man that I was today without her.

I wouldn't have the two other lights in my life without her.

"Why are you looking at me like that?" she asked as we walked into the largest shower I had ever seen. There were six heads there, and we didn't need to use all of them, though I wanted to try at some point, just to see.

"I was just thinking about how much I owe you."

She frowned. "You don't owe me anything, Alexander."

"I don't know if owe is the right word. But you helped me with so much, to find out who I am. And I'm always going to be grateful for that."

Her smile warmed. "Again, you don't need to be grateful or owe me for anything. You just found yourself, it took you a while to figure that out. I got to find myself along the way, too."

"True, and now we're all sappy and romantic together. Even when some days we don't get sleep and we're covered in vomit, even when the kids are almost three."

Tabby gave a small smile. "Well, that tends to happen when they get excited, and they egg each other on."

"I'm so glad we're able to start sleeping again," I said, as I put shampoo in my hand and began to wash Tabby's hair. She stiffened a bit, and I looked down at her.

"What is it?"

"Oh, I'm just thinking that one day the twins are going to be teenagers and keeping us up late at night when we're waiting for them to come home, or when they're just hitting puberty and we're going to have the sex talk, or when we're nervous about having to walk them down the aisle because they're getting married and then they're having babies, and all of that is going to end up with no sleep."

I shook my head as I moved so she could rinse her hair. I started washing my hair and frowned at her. "I'm sure parents get to sleep when the kids are older. Austin and Sierra get some sleep, even though not all of their kids are as old as Leif."

"Leif is different," Tabby said with a laugh. "He is the most well-adjusted and well-behaved kid I know."

I winced. "And now that you've said that, when he hits college, he's going to be partying all the time."

Tabby lowered her brows as her teeth worried her lip. "Do you think he's going to go to school?"

"What do you mean?" I asked with a frown. "They were talking about college, weren't they?"

"Or art school," she whispered.

My eyes widened. "Really. Why didn't I know this?"

"Because Leif loves his Aunt Tabby, and talks to me about certain things."

I thought about her words for a moment. "Leif at art school. That'd be kind of cool. Is he afraid to talk to Austin and Sierra about it?"

"No, he's talked to both of them about it, and they know that he took a gap year before he started school because of the adoption and everything. He wanted to be there for the family, even though they said that he could leave, but I also think he wanted to find out who he wanted to be. He didn't get as much time with Austin and

Sierra as he might have." Leif's entrance into the family had been unexpected, to say the least.

"We all understood when he decided to take a year between high school and college. He's working at the shop and the construction company. He's not just sitting at home playing video games, even though that sounds kind of fun."

"I agree. Leif wants to find out who he wants to be before he starts spending all that money on classes when he may be making the wrong decision."

"Art school. Do you think he's going to end up like Maya and Austin? Maybe open up another tattoo shop in Colorado? We could take over the world."

Tabby smiled. "I think that might be a good bet. But don't tell anyone else yet. Let's see what happens."

I grinned, then leaned forward and kissed her again. "That sounds like a plan. I wonder who Sebastian and Aria will end up being."

"They'll probably come together to take over the world or destroy it. That's what twins do," she said dryly.

"I'll be sure to tell Storm and Wes that," I added with a laugh. We finished our shower, and since apparently just being by my wife made everything go a little quicker, we used the bench in the shower exactly how I had imagined it. Sated, clean, and starving, we put on our clothing for the day, and headed out to get hot cocoa. And breakfast. But mostly hot cocoa for Tabby.

"I know that Hailey makes the best hot cocoa at

Taboo," she said, speaking of the cafe next to the tattoo shop in downtown Denver that was part of the family. "However, this is amazing."

"Tabby does make it better, but this is fantastic. A great way to end the year."

She smiled up at me, blinked before she sat down her cup as she looked at me.

"What is it?"

"Just a little dizzy," she said.

My eyes widened, and I leaned forward. "What's wrong? Do we need to go to the hospital?"

"Alexander, just because every time a Montgomery falls in love, they end up in the hospital doesn't mean I need to go right now."

"We have our own wing," I teased, looking down at her face, a little worried. "You're pale, where you should be all rosy because it's cold outside."

She let out a breath and blinked up at me. "Alexander, I think it's time I tell you something. I wanted to tell you a couple of days ago, but then we had this trip planned that you planned out of the blue, and yesterday was just so nice, I think I need to sit down."

There was a bench near us, and nobody really around us, so I sat down next to her and cupped her face. "We can go back. What's wrong?"

She smiled softly, leaned into my hand. "Nothing's wrong. I think everything is right."

Her eyes filled with tears, and alarm shot through me.

"Talk to me, Tabby. What's wrong?"

And then she pulled away slightly, took my hand, and gently placed it on her lower abdomen. It took me a second. I was an idiot after all, and then my eyes widened.

"Are you serious?" I breathed, my voice scratchy.

She smiled softly. "I'm very serious," she whispered. "It seems like Aria and Sebastian are going to get a sibling after all."

A wide smile broke out onto my face, and I stood up and threw my hands in the air, cheering.

Tabby laughed, her whole body shaking. "Well, I can see you're excited," she said, laughing.

"Are you kidding me? Holy hell. A baby." I paused. "We're never going to sleep again," I added, speaking of our shower conversation.

Tabby just rolled her eyes. "No, but we'll make do. We have already. And you never know, this could just be one baby instead of twins, and we could handle one. After all, we handled two."

I shook my head. "You just dared the gods. We're going to end up with triplets."

Her eyes widened, and she paled again. "Oh, no," she said with a laugh. And I plucked her off the bench and picked her up. "I love you so damned much."

"A baby," I whispered.

"A baby," she whispered back.

And then I leaned down and kissed her again, hard.

Another Montgomery to add to the world.
I couldn't wait.

Chapter 4
TABBY

"I'm freezing."

At least, that's why I tried to say. It was more of a chattering moan as I tried to keep my body wrapped tight into a ball.

Alexander winced. "Maya said she'd packed for you. We're in Colorado in *winter*. I didn't realize she'd pack you a dress that showed so much of your legs."

I narrowed my eyes. "You say that, and yet you can't get your eyes off said legs."

Alexander looked up, a wicked grin spreading over his face. "I can't help it. I just had those legs wrapped around my neck. I *love* those legs."

I blushed and was grateful for it as it warmed me marginally. Or maybe I was going numb and was on the way to the warmth before freezing to death.

"And you're not the only woman in a short dress. It seems to be the thing at a Vail New Year's Eve party."

I looked around the small gathering at the local ski resort and community center and smiled at the other women in short dresses. They smiled back, but I had a feeling that they had chosen their own clothing.

"I know I went through most things that Maya had packed, but I got distracted with the twins and something that needed to be done for work, and I didn't finish going through a list. I didn't even get a chance to make a full list."

Alexander winced, and I reached up and placed my hand on his cheek. "It's not your fault," I whispered. "And, we're inside, I'm just still cold from the walk over here."

"There's no parking here at *all*, or I would have driven you here, dropped you off, and then walked over myself."

"And I told you I was fine. And I am. I'm all nice and warm now."

"Come on, let's go get you some hot apple cider."

I beamed and slid my hand into his. "You going to be okay here tonight?" I asked, my words slow.

Alexander gave me a soft smile. "Of course. I'm an alcoholic, Tabby. I'm always going to be an alcoholic. But I don't want to drink now. And I won't tomorrow." It was a common refrain that he said, and it soothed to him as much as it did me. My husband was one of the strongest people I knew. He had followed his demons and had come out the victor. Bruised, bloody, a little broken, and a whole lot lost, but he had found his way.

And I loved him so damn much.

I wiped away tears, and Alexander's eyes widened.

"What's wrong?"

"I'm just a little weepy. I guess I can blame it on hormones."

His smile was bright and wide. "Hormones," he whispered. "We're having a baby," he said.

"We are", I said on a laugh.

"When do you think we're going to tell the rest of the family?"

"I'm pretty sure we're going to have to tell them soon, mostly because I keep having to go to the restroom at work with nausea, and your sister Meghan has already guessed. I didn't say anything," I added quickly.

"Because you needed to be first, but she was the reason that I went and got the test anyway."

"So how long have you known?" he asked as he handed me a hot cider. I took a sip, and it warmed me from the inside out. I did a little dance on my feet, pleased with the taste and warmth. "Only for five days." Alexander's eyes widened.

"I was waiting to tell you as a surprise and wanted it to be a cute little thing. I wasn't nervous that you were going to be upset or anything. Far from it."

"Good. Because I'm fucking excited, babe."

"I'm excited too. I still can't believe we're doing this again."

"I can't wait for Aria and Sebastian to find out. They're going to be excited."

I smirked. "You think so."

"I know so. They love their nieces and nephews. And now they won't be the babies anymore."

"They aren't the babies anymore anyway. Your family keeps breeding. Hell, so does mine."

He shook his head. "That is true," he said softly. "You know, we're probably going to need a bigger house," he said casually, as if he hadn't thrown me for a loop.

My eyes widened. "What? But I love our house."

"I love our house too, but we are the only ones not living in a house built by my family."

I rolled my eyes. "As I've helped with every single house that's been built, I know that. But we found the perfect little home for us."

"Emphasis on *little*, babe. Aria and Sebastian are sharing a room now because they're young enough. But they're not going to want to when they get older. They may love each other and enjoy spending time with one another. But, eventually, they're going to have their own interests, and it would be good to let them have their own space. And then, as I've seen with my siblings, the twin bond means that they're always going to be connected, but we don't want our next child not to feel like they're not part of it. So we need to give them all their own rooms."

I shook my head. "You've thought about this in detail."

"When we were dealing with the plumbing a couple of days ago, and then the stove, I realized that I think we're ready to move on. We both do well, and it's time for us to maybe buy a Montgomery home."

I laughed. "Your family will be happy."

"Yeah, they will. We're a little proprietary."

"I am shocked you could ever say that. Considering I *literally* have a tattoo inked into my flesh with your family brand."

His eyes darkened as he gently placed his fingertips over my hip with the Montgomery iris lay.

"Apparently, I'm a little proprietary as well."

I shook my head. "I love you. And yes, I love our house, but it's time we find a new one."

"We can rent that one out, use it for another source of income, or sell it. It's a great time for sellers right now."

"Okay, you're right. I'm just kind of sad that we're going to be saying goodbye to an era."

"We're going to be a possible family of five. That's an era too."

My eyes filled with tears, and I looked around at the group of people that were all strangers, dressed in their finest, who were enjoying themselves. I didn't want to be there, not with them. I wanted Alexander alone. "Let's go back to the house. You and me. We celebrate New Year's as the ball drops, and as it hits midnight, just the two of us. And then tomorrow we'll go home and start the next phase of our journey."

His eyes warmed, and he leaned down, pressed against my lips. "You know what? You're right. I'm glad we had some time to ourselves, but hell, I miss that big family of ours."

"And we're just getting bigger, I said, tapping my belly.

He placed his hand over mine, squeezing slightly. "I'm so damn lucky that you're in my life."

"I was just thinking the same," I said and smiled. "We've changed so much, and yet, I feel like it was just yesterday I saw you walk into the office and see me for the first time."

He frowned. "What do you mean?"

"I don't know, it's just one day. I felt like you saw *me* rather than the little friend that was always around."

"I think I needed to figure out who I was first. Before I was able to open myself up to you."

"I get it. I'm glad I got to find out who I was by myself and to build my own wants and needs in life without pining for you all the time."

"Well, you can pine for me any day of the week. I'll come running."

"Somehow, that was sweet and romantic," I said, and laughed.

Alexander bundled me in my coat as we said our goodbyes and thanks to those running this small party of strangers, and I shiver. "I know my coat goes past my knees, but I'm going to freeze."

"I'll take care of you. I promise." He gripped my hand, and we made our way back towards the house. It was only two blocks away, and it wasn't below freezing yet, thankfully. There had been a slight warm front that morning, so while it was cold, it wasn't bitterly cold. There was snow on the ground, but nothing new. So while I was chilled, I wasn't in danger of getting hypothermia. That meant the dress wasn't that bad, and Maya had chosen my favorite one. I loved my legs in it. And from the way that Alexander growled every time he looked down at them, I knew if he did too.

We had to cross a small park towards the house, and I looked down at Alexander's watch and frowned. "It's later than I thought," I said with a gasp.

He blinked, looked down, and smiled at me. "Well, do you think you can handle the cold a little bit longer?"

And with the snow around us, the mountains not that far in the distance shielding us, and the moon bright above us, I looked up at him, placed my hands on his chest, and grinned.

"Ten," I whispered.

"Nine," he said.

"Eight." A kiss.

"Seven." A caress.

"Six." A touch.

"Five." A brush of lips.

"Four." A rasp of breath.

"Three." Another kiss.

"Two." Then another.

"One." And one more.

"Happy New Year, wife of mine," Alexander said.

I smiled up at him and kissed him softly. There were cheers, people shouting, and happiness and celebration surrounded us.

But I only had eyes for my husband.

"Happy New Year, Alexander Montgomery."

"Now, let's get my wife inside where she can warm up, because I'm about to wrap you up like a burrito. You're not going to start the new year off with a cold. And our baby needs warmth."

I nodded, just starting to feel the cold. After all, Alexander warmed me up nicely most days. We practically ran to the house, and I stood in front of the fire as he started it.

And then he held me close, and we kissed, and kept kissing.

He slowly stripped my dress off of me, and I toed out of my shoes, my hands on him. And when we were both naked, lying on a soft rug in front of the fire, he slid into me, my body warm, sated, just from his touch.

We made love in front of the fire, both of us breathing into one another as we shook and tried to catch up.

And when I came, I whispered his name, and he filled me, both of us holding onto one another for dear life as the fire made us sweat-slick, and our passions burned even brighter.

"I think we need to start all new years like this," he whispered. "Naked and having sex in front of a fire? I like it."

"You know, I'm okay with that," I said, and I leaned into him.

We cleaned up, fell asleep naked on the floor, covered in a blanket. When my phone buzzed around three in the morning, I frowned and reached for it, groaning.

"It better not be a drunk dial," Alex grumbled, covering his eyes with his hand.

Maya's name flashed on a screen, and I froze, gripping his hand. "It's your sister."

"Maya? What's wrong?"

Maya's voice was raspy when she answered. "Hey there, I know it's late, happy New Year."

"Maya," I said, as Alexander sat next to me, his body's stiff.

"Everything's fine, but Sebastian has a fever. It's pretty high, so we're going to go into the emergency room just to check. Your doctor's meeting us there, and since we're all on each other's paperwork, it should be fine. But I wanted to let you know. Border is going to stay home with the other kids, so Aria's safe. But Jake and I are going in with Sebastian. My parents are coming over to help Border."

"We're on our way," I said, having put her on speaker.

"Thank you, Maya," Alexander said. "Just... thank you. And keep us updated."

"He'll be okay. You don't have to drive down the mountain in the dark."

"We're packing now," Alexander said as I stood up, my knees shaking.

"He's going to be okay. I promise you. He just has a little cold."

"And he needs his mom and dad," Alexander said sharply.

"I know, baby brother. We'll see you soon. I love you."

She hung up after promising that she would keep us updated, and I ran to the bedroom. We hadn't unpacked fully, something that I usually did, but we wouldn't have been here long enough for me to get situated fully.

We threw things into the suitcase, not bothering to worry about what was in its proper place or not.

"We have everything important if we forgot something silly, whatever," Alexander said, and I nodded tightly. "It sounds like a plan. Are you okay to drive?" I asked.

He kissed me hard on the mouth, pinching my chin. "Yes. I think you're the one that's shaking more. Keep the baby safe, I'll keep you safe, and we're going to go see our son."

The normally hour and forty-minute drive took nearly

two hours thanks to the cold, the darkness, and us being careful, but we practically ran into the emergency room. Jake was there, a smile on his face. "He's fine. His fever spiked already, and they gave him some meds, and he's sleeping. It's just a cold that his body fought a little too hard."

I hugged Jake tightly and followed him to Sebastian's room, where Maya was, holding Sebastian's hand while our son slept.

Tears fell down my face, and I clung to my sister-in-law hard before I sat down and pushed Sebastian's hair from his tiny little face. Alex was behind me, mumbling things to the others.

"Thank you," Alexander said. "Just thank you."

"Always, little brother. We'll stay for a little bit. That way, the doctors can catch us all up, and then we'll go home and update the family. We'll keep Aria safe. You stay here. I'm sorry to cut your weekend short."

I looked up at Maya and shook my head. "Our weekend is exactly what we needed, but we're here now. And we're never going away again," I said, as tears fell freely.

Maya narrowed her eyes at me. "You're crying more than I thought you would." Then her eyes widened. "You're pregnant."

"Maya, you should've let her announce that," Jake mumbled.

"Probably," I said with a watery laugh as I wipe my

face. Alexander handed me a tissue. "Thanks, babe. We're going to tell everybody soon. But yes, we're pregnant. And we're pretty much going to sell our house and buy a Montgomery one, so it's a little exhausting. But thank you for taking care of Sebastian."

Maya, the most verbose woman I had ever met, was at a loss for words as she just blinked at me. "Well, baby brother, when you go all out, you go all out."

Alexander shook his head, a smile playing on his face. He leaned forward, kissed Maya on the cheek, then did the same to Jake just because it made Jake laugh. "Go home, we'll take care of this. Thank you for being here. We'll update everyone soon."

After everybody congratulated each other and hugged, they left and I smiled. I leaned into my husband and watched my son sleep.

"Happy New Year," I whispered.

Alexander kissed the top of my head. "Happy New Year. I love you."

And as Sebastian slept, I knew we would be okay. Just one little bump, but we had been through worse. But we were together. And that's a blessed new year.

Chapter 5

ALEX

"I seriously cannot stand this. I'm so happy," my mother said as she bounced a bright-eyed and healthy Sebastian on her hip. Sebastian just grinned and leaned into his grandmother. My son had felt better the next morning and had been discharged from the hospital soon after. We had all been surprised that he had bounced back as quickly as he had, but then again, he was a kid. That's what they tended to do. They scared you to death, then showed you how amazing they were.

I was just glad that Sebastian was okay, and Aria seemed to have skipped being sick at all. Maya's kids had also ended up being okay, and the bug had only hit Sebastian.

"I'm excited too, Mom," I said, as Sebastian reached for me. My mom pouted ever so slightly, even though I knew it was in jest, and I took my son from her arms.

"So many babies," she whispered. I shook my head and looked around at my large and ever-growing family. I had seven siblings, countless cousins, and even more friends of the family that were constantly in and out of my parents' home and ours to celebrate different occasions. Tonight, however, was just the main eight, our spouses, and our children. That was still well over twenty people, with lots of babies crawling around, some in slings, other children just old enough to start creating their own little baby gangs of their own.

Leif, an adult now, even though he still felt like my little baby nephew in my head, was holding Aria as my daughter gazed adoringly up at him. Leif could do that. He just made everybody happy.

Austin and Sierra were beside him, their other children either in their arms or walking around them.

Everybody just looked happy, as if everything we had gone through together made it worth it. And that was right. Over time, we had lost part of ourselves, had been hurt, but had ended up stronger for it. But I would have rather not gone through any of that. I would have rather found peace and happiness without the pain, but we couldn't go back and change that. We could only look towards the future. That was something that had taken me far too long and even more mistakes for me to realize.

"What has you all melancholy?" my mother asked, and I looked down at her. "Nothing. I was just thinking about how far we've all come."

She shook her head. "We've done okay for ourselves. We keep growing, to the point that I don't know if we're going to fit in this home much longer."

I smiled at that. "We'll find a way. I'm sure Dad and Storm will start building on, just a wing for the grandkids."

My mom rolled her eyes. "Don't suggest that to him, or he'll start doing that."

"First, they have to work on my home, so that should give you a reprieve."

My mother's eyes brightened. "You guys are moving into a bigger home, one built by our family. It's about time," she chided, though jokingly.

"I'm so sorry it took us forever to find a home to find the time to move, what with the twins, and the jobs, and life."

"You're not going to be doing it alone. You always have the Montgomerys."

"Yeah, I do."

I kissed the top of her head, and Sebastian wiggled down from my arms. He ran over to his sister, who Leif had put down, and the two hugged before going with their cousins.

I couldn't help but smile, knowing that soon there would be more Montgomerys and more children added to the mix. We were loud, probably a little annoying to anyone outside our family, but happy.

Tabby walked over, a platter of cheese in her hands,

and I laughed. "You're officially one of us," I said, as I stole a piece of brie and popped it into my mouth.

"Miranda sent me over with this for this side of the room. Apparently, we're running out of cheese."

The entire room quieted, and all stared at her.

"It's okay. Luc and Decker are out getting more. It's fine. This is not an emergency. I know we joke that this family is addicted to cheese, but please do not start a riot because you only have a single extra-large cheese platter left."

"Did they bring the big car?" Border asked, his voice low, sardonic. "Maybe they should've brought a couple of trucks just to bring over the wheels of cheese."

Everyone laughed at that, considering Border wasn't one to joke often.

"I have no idea where this fascination came from. You were not this addicted to Irish Cheddar and Gouda when I first met your family."

"We were, just in a quieter sense. And then one of our cousins made a joke about how cheese is life, and we sort of rolled with it. Like the proverbial wheel of cheese."

My wife rolled her eyes as I took the cheese platter from her. The hoard descended on it, and I laughed, keeping my mother and pregnant wife away from any flying elbows.

"All this cheese probably isn't good for the digestion. Do you eat fruits and vegetables?" Tabby asked, and my mother gestured towards the half-eaten vegetable tray.

"We eat those too. And meats, and fresh chicken, and even carbs. We like to joke about cheese."

"One day, I'm going to add a little block of cheese to the Montgomery iris and see who notices," Maya said, and Austin shuddered beside her. "Please don't. For the love of God, please don't."

"It's just a farce at this point," Tabby said. "But I love it. I just miss soft cheeses."

"Tell me about it," Jillian said, her hand on her slightly larger belly. "For a family that loves dairy as much as we do, we sure do tend to procreate enough that half of us aren't allowed to eat the cheese that we so love for long periods of time."

"It is true. Maybe we could start a family tradition of loving something that isn't on the no-no list for pregnancy?" she asked sweetly.

I leaned down, brushed a kiss on Tabby's lips. "We'll find you something. Maybe something that's just for our little part of the family."

"Well, then we're going to need to know what it is," Maya added. "So we can claim it as the whole family's."

"She's right, you know," Tabby said. "Once you go Montgomery, you're one of them. Forever."

She said it as if she were talking about a cult, and people laughed, but I just held her close, and Sebastian and Aria came towards us. I leaned down, lifted them both into my arms, and handed Aria over to Tabby. She laughed, and the four of us held one another and watched as my family devoured cheese and vegetables and spoke of what they were planning for the new year and what they thought would happen next.

I didn't know what was coming next for the Montgomerys or where we would end up, but I knew where we had been and where we were now.

And that was just fine with me.

It was time for someone else to find their happy ever afters, to fight and crawl, and maybe not find pain at all when it came to a future.

We were settled here, finally, and after a long few years of memories that some of us would rather forget, I was happy with that.

I had kissed my wife at midnight under the moonlight on New Year's, and that's how I wanted to spend the rest of the year, with my family, my friends, and with a future I knew that'd be ours to hold, forever.

I hope you loved this holiday special from the Montgomerys!
The next set of Montgomerys begin in Fort Collins in Inked Persuasion!

Inked Fantasy

A MONTGOMERY INK BOULDER ROMANCE

Inked Fantasy

A single night changes everything.

It was only supposed to be a single date... but a few surprises make for an interesting night.

Chapter One
"JACK"

I CAREFULLY LIFTED THE LOWBALL GLASS TO MY lips, letting the smoky aroma of the whiskey settle onto my tongue as I finished my sip. As I set the glass down, I looked around at the high-end bar, noting the people surrounding me. Nobody should recognize me here, not when they were all focused on their own lives. Their own desires. Tonight wasn't about who they were or what they wanted from me.

No, tonight was about pleasure and an evening that I hoped the person I was set to meet would never forget.

I took another sip and nodded at the bartender. The man nodded back and handed over my check.

"Just one for you, sir?"

I gave him a small smile, shaking my head and put down cash. No names, not for now.

"I'll be meeting someone soon, and I wanted to make sure I settled the bill."

The bartender frowned, tilting his head as he studied my face. "We could have added it to your bill at your table. You didn't need to worry yourself."

I just shook my head. "No, I don't mind. Now, by any chance, have you seen a woman with a white rose in her hair?"

The bartender's gaze widened for a second, and then he smiled as if he were in the middle of the game with me. *With us.* "No, but I'll keep on the lookout. A blind date?"

My lips twitched into a small smile again, and I took another sip of my whiskey. "You could say that."

"Okay," he said, looking as if he were more intrigued than ever. "That sounds like a story. And I do believe your date has arrived," he said, his eyes widening marginally as he looked over my shoulder.

I turned, my glass in my hands, and stared at the woman with dark hair and light eyes. She had on a black wrap dress that clung to her curves and made me want to pull delicately on the strings at the side. I wanted to see what would happen when the dress fell off her shoulders and pooled down at her feet.

There were many things I wanted to see happened tonight, and if I were lucky, I would be trying every single one of them. In vivid and intricate detail.

I downed the rest of my drink, not taking my eyes off

of the white rose in her hair, and set the glass next to me on the polished wood of the bar.

"Thank you, Trevor."

Trevor, the bartender, cleared his throat. "You're welcome. Do you know where your table is, sir?"

"No, but I can ask the hostess. She said my table would be ready whenever my date arrived."

"If you're sure. Enjoy your evening, sir."

"I'm counting on it," I said, not bothering to look back at Trevor. No, my eyes were for the woman in front of me.

Jane.

At least that was the name that she had signed her texts with.

I could use Jane as her name for the evening. A perfectly normal name, for a perfectly pleasant woman, at least according to her texts.

But there was nothing normal or nearly pleasant about the goddess in front of me.

And I couldn't wait to get to know this Jane.

I prowled toward Jane, and her gaze went to the rose in the pocket of my jacket. Her eyes darkened for a minute, and then she met my eyes, a smile playing on her face. I stood in front of her, then inhaled the hint of her floral scent. Nothing overpowering, just a tease as to who this woman could be.

"Jack?" she asked, her eyes dancing.

"Of course, I love the rose," I said, and I reached out

and slid my fingers delicately through the end of her hair, careful not to jostle the rose, but needing to touch her.

This Jane, this stranger.

She cleared her throat, danced from foot to foot on her tall heels. "Well, should we see the hostess about our table?" Jane asked, her voice a little breathy.

I licked at my lips and nodded. "They told me it would be ready as soon as you arrived. We won't have to wait."

"Oh, that's good. I mean, not that I mind waiting, but it would be nice to sit down. I'm not that great in heels," she said, laughing a bit before looking down at her feet. She wore sky high fuck-me heels and seeing that made my cock ache. I swallowed hard, willing myself to slow down.

I needed to slow down.

"They do wonders for your legs. But don't worry, I do not want you in pain."

I turned as the hostess came to us, a smile on her face. "Mr. Smith?" she asked, and I nodded, a smile playing on my lips.

"My date is here, as you can see, we're ready when you are."

"And we're ready here, your table is near the waterfall as you asked. Follow me, and I'll lead you to your table. Your waitress will be Corinne, and she will go over the specials with you as well as the wine list. We do have two new wines tonight that our chef and sommelier are really excited about." Our hostess continued to talk as she led us to the table, and I looked down at Jane, unable to keep my eyes from her. She was beautiful and looked like she smiled often, and yet had a side to her that maybe others didn't see.

I couldn't wait to get to know this woman tonight and see where we ended up.

"Here you are, have a lovely evening," she said, as I moved to one side of the table and held out Jane's chair. "Here you go," I said, and she gave me a small look, shook her head as a smile played on her face, and sat down.

"What was that for?" I asked, keeping a smile down for myself.

"You're acting like such a gentleman."

"And you don't think I can be a gentleman?" I asked, raising a single brow.

"I'm sure sometimes you could play at one, but I'm already enjoying tonight. Thank you for making me feel like a princess."

"I was thinking goddess earlier. And my acting the gentleman is what tonight is supposed to be about. Having fun, no names, just us, an evening for whatever we want."

Jane smiled and leaned back ever so slightly. The action caused her breasts to rise as she took a deep breath, and I did my best not to focus on that.

"I'm glad that my friends were able to help me get out tonight. It's been far too long since I've been out to dinner with a handsome man."

"I do believe that was my line, although I was going to say something about your beauty."

"You don't need to butter me up," she said, laughing, and I shook my head, laughing right along with her.

"You are beautiful, but sometimes I'm not great with words."

She tilted her head at me, stared. "Do you think that?"

"Sometimes. It depends on if the words are important or not."

"That's a good answer," she whispered, and the waitress came to speak about specials and wines.

"The sea bass sounds wonderful, honestly," Jane said as the waitress finished, waiting for our drink order. "I know this is just for drinks, but my mouth is practically watering at the sound of the Chilean sea bass."

"It does sound delicious, although the filet that she spoke of, the one that is smoke rubbed? That also sounds divine."

Corinne nodded between us, a small smile on her face. "You can't go wrong with either, and I have a lovely wine pairing for each."

I met Jane's gaze and smiled softly. "What do you say we each order one, and I'll let you have a bite. Just a taste."

I could see the waitress blush near me out of the corner of my eye, but it was the delicate pink of Jane's porcelain skin that enraptured my gaze.

"I think I can do that," Jane said, clearing her throat. "I guess I'll take the sea bass."

"And I'll take the filet, medium rare?" I asked, and Jane nodded.

The waitress left after taking our order, and I leaned back in my chair, looking at Jane and wondered where we would go tonight.

"So, Jane, what is it you do?"

Jane shook her head. "I thought we weren't supposed to ask questions like that? That way, we would never have to lie," she said, and I sighed.

"Maybe. Or maybe the story is just the beginning."

She laughed softly at that and took a sip of her water. "Or maybe you don't want to tell me anything about you so that I can make a big story about me. How about this?" she asked as she settled into her chair. "My name is Jane, at least for the evening. I'm here because I haven't been out of my home in so long, I think I've forgotten what the outside world looks like. I was told I would have a lovely evening with a wonderful man, one who I have texted often this week, and I would have as much fun as I desired." A pause. "Anything I desired."

I cleared my throat as the waitress set our glasses of wine down, as well as the breadbasket. She left in a hurry, seemingly aware that she had interrupted something. However, Jane and I were in public, and if I wasn't careful, I was going to toss her on top of this table and have my way with her.

With the look in Jane's eyes, she had the same thoughts.

"I was told," I began, "that tonight would be any fantasy you desired."

"And now you sound like a gigolo," she laughed, and took a sip of her wine. "Oh, that's amazing. Crisp."

I took a sip of mine and nodded. "A little oaky, I like it."

"So, you're not a gigolo?" she asked, her eyes dancing with laughter.

I smiled, set my glass down. "Not even close. But I can pretend for the evening if you'd like?"

She shook her head, her cheeks bright red. "No, I would just like you to be you, Jack."

I swallowed hard, and looked into those eyes, and knew if I weren't careful, this evening would unravel, and my secrets would come to light.

Instead, I lifted my glass to hers, and she did the same. "To tonight. A night of fantasy. Of the only promise worth making."

She smiled, her eyes going dark. "To tonight."

And we each took a sip of our wines, and I knew the evening had just begun.

Chapter Two
"JANE"

I sipped the last of my chocolate martini and let the sugar and sweetness settle over my tongue. I loved all things sweet. It was an addiction, and I didn't mind. It was *my* addiction.

An addiction I knew that could rival the man in front of me if I weren't careful.

"Are you ready to go upstairs, Jane?" Jack asked, and I swallowed hard, then licked my lips.

"Forward, aren't you?"

Jack's eyes crinkled at the corners, the fine lines there deepening. "I thought we both had an understanding of exactly where this was going. Was I wrong?"

I set my glass down and dabbed at my mouth with my linen napkin before setting it on the table. "I think we both know where this is going, and I didn't say I disliked the forwardness."

Jack smiled, and it lit up his face and seeing that tugged at something me. I ignored that tug. That wasn't for tonight. No, tonight was about mystery and finding out exactly who I could be with this man, in this moment, and under these circumstances.

Tonight was about fantasy and fun.

I reached out for my small jeweled clutch and looked up at the man who couldn't stop staring at me.

"I'm ready when you are," I said, purring. I wasn't great at flirting, wasn't great at the role of the seductress, but it was fun to play. And after all, tonight was only about play. Tomorrow the carriage turned back into a pumpkin, my shoes would turn to slippers, and my form-fitting black wrap dress would turn into yoga pants and a tank top. My hair would fall from its curls, and I would pile it on the top of my head. I'd take out my itchy contacts, slide on my glasses—after I scrubbed my face free of makeup and put on an anti-swelling mask and under-eye ointment.

That was the true me.

But Jane...Jane could be whoever she wanted to be.

Jack stood up, held out his hand, and I slid my fingers along his. "Come on then, the night's only beginning."

I clenched my thighs together for just a moment, aware that anyone looking at us would know exactly what we were about to do. But it's what I wanted, same as Jack, for us to be in our own world, while the rest might look on, but not matter in the end.

I wrapped my arm around his as I stood, and the two of us made our way through the lobby of the five-star hotel and to the elevators into the back. Jack used a special key on the private elevator, one that not every patron would have.

"The penthouse?" I asked, surprised, even though I shouldn't have been.

"You said in your texts you wanted tonight to be special, and I am loath to not provide."

"You sure do sound like a male escort," I said with a laugh, ignoring the look from the woman in pearls as she walked past us.

Jack winked over my head, and I held back a grin. "You keep saying that so loudly, and people are going to think you paid for the night."

"How do they know you're not the one who paid for me?" I teased, surprising myself. Jack threw his head back and laughed, looking like the most interesting and attractive man I had ever met in my life.

And I couldn't wait for what happened next.

We walked into the elevator as the doors opened, and I swallowed hard, my palms going damp. The elevator doors closed, and I bit my lip, not knowing what would come next, the anticipation heady. Jack slid his hand over my hip and squeezed, and I turned into his hold.

"Jack?" I asked, and in answer, he pressed his lips to mine. My mouth parted, and I groaned into him. He slid his other hand around me, gripping my ass, pushing me into his hard erection. I moaned, practically climbing up him like he was a tree, and he deepened the kiss, tangling his tongue with mine. He moved, my back pressing against the walls of the elevator, my arms above my head as he ran his hands up my side and cupped my breasts.

"I can't wait to strip you out of this, but there won't be enough time." He kissed me again and then pulled away, righting my dress before he did the same to his clothes.

The doors to the penthouse opened as soon as he straightened, and I nearly fell, my knees weak. Jack seemed to realize that, and he gave me a worrying look before gripping my elbow.

"I'm fine," I whispered.

Jack met my gaze and held his hand on the door to the elevator so it wouldn't close again. "Are you sure? We can stop this right now."

"That's exactly what I don't want. Come on, let's continue. You said the night was only beginning. We can't end it now."

Jack searched my face before nodding tightly. And then he led me into the penthouse suite.

My jaw dropped, and I looked around, stunned. "I didn't even know this was here."

Jack shrugged and looked for all the world like he did this every evening. I knew for a fact he didn't, but him playing the role made me smile. The floors were made of marble, the walls textured with antique wallpaper and faux that made it look as if it were a palace, rather than a hotel room in downtown Denver.

"Is that a piano?" I asked, and blinked.

Jack grinned. "A baby grand. I think they were sad they couldn't fit a full grand in here."

"Oh, how horrible, *only* a baby grand." I smiled.

"Too bad I can't play," Jack said, laughing.

"We could always pretend. But I feel like we would both end up hurting our ears in the process."

"Too true. Now, there's a full bath here in the guest area, but there's also the master bath in the back, one with a waterfall, and a full five-headed shower."

I blinked. "Five heads as in to get all angles, or for five different people enjoying it?" I asked, laughing.

Jack grinned. "I'm not sharing you, so we're just going to have to deal with the two of us."

My brows raised. "So, we'll be taking a shower together?"

"Maybe. There's a bench in there. I'd like to try."

I blushed and cleared my throat. "Sure of yourself, are you?"

"You knew precisely what tonight was for when you showed up," he growled, and yet his voice was soft at the same time. I couldn't help but breathe hard and try to catch up.

"So, there are the showers," I said, clearing my throat after a moment. "And you said a guest area?"

Jack smiled. "There are two guestrooms, along with

their own foyer and sitting area. This is the main sitting area, but let me take you to the master bedroom."

I shook my head, looking at all the opulence and wondering why it was needed. "I would have been fine with a single bed, and maybe a desk." I blushed as I said it.

Jack looked at me and chuckled deeply. "That's good to know. But I wanted to show you, as my sister would say, the sparkly."

"So, you have a sister?" I asked eagerly, leaning forward with a smile on my face. This was the game, and I was having too much fun with it.

Jack frowned. "I shouldn't have said that. No details tonight. Right?"

I shrugged. "At least for now. We'll see what happens later."

I knew I wasn't good at this, and I would probably spill everything, break the fantasy. But, for now, I wanted to have fun. And here we were.

Jack led me past a dining room that had an actual chandelier and a small kitchenette area until he reached two double doors.

"Are you ready?" He asked.

"I'm exhausted from walking through this room already."

He grinned and then opened the double doors.

My mouth dropped open, and I swallowed hard. There was a bed in the center, raised slightly, and it looked larger than a king. There were sitting areas to my left and to my right, along with a balcony on the opposite end. I knew the one door was probably a closet area, or maybe another sitting area, or perhaps even an office. The other looked to be the bathroom, all marble and chrome, and I didn't know where to look.

"This is ridiculous," I said with a laugh.

"Pretty much," Jack said grinning. "But it's ours for the evening."

"I have no words," I whispered, and Jack turned to me and leaned forward.

"I don't think there needs to be any. Other than are you ready for the evening?"

"Always."

"Good," he said, and then his mouth was on mine again. I moaned into him, and he wrapped his arms around me, sliding his hands down my sides. He moved again, cupping my ass as he spread my cheeks apart while pressing himself into me. I writhed against him, needing more. When he trailed his lips down my neck, I shivered in his arms. His fingers went to the tie at my side, and I licked my lips. He met my gaze and then undid the bow. My dress fell to the side slowly, the fabric gently caressing my skin as it parted.

I gasped, the sensation too much, even just from that bare moment in his look. He licked his lips and then trailed his gaze over me, as if needing to sate himself in the view. I felt as if I could feel every single caress of his vision, and I couldn't stop my moan. He smiled, and then reached out, his thumb gently sliding along my nipple.

"Black lace, it suits you."

I blushed. "Not usually."

"I'm pretty sure everything suits you…Jane," he whispered.

He slid his hands down my sides, his knuckles along my belly, and then traced the lace of my thong around my hips.

"Beautiful," he whispered, and then he leaned forward and licked along my collarbone. I shivered, my knees going weak, and he pulled away again before moving me toward the bed.

"I can't have you fainting on me."

"You sure feel high and mighty of yourself," I teased.

"I can't help it. You seem to do that to me," he whispered, and then he kissed me again.

I shivered in his hold, and then let him stand me next to the bed. It's so high that my ass barely touched the top of it.

"Will this work for you?" he asked.

I nodded. "Yes," I whispered.

"Good." And then he tugged the rest of my dress off, the silk pooling at my feet. I stood on my tiptoes in my heels, and he knelt in front of me, sliding his hands down my calves. It sent shivers up my body, and I did my best not to groan again.

"Let me take these off you. I don't want you to be in pain," he whispered.

"I can handle the heels."

"But I need you to have all of your energy for what I'm about to put you through," he whispered, and so I let him untie the straps at my ankles and slowly slid my feet out of my heels. My ankles quit their protesting, as I gradually set my feet to the ground, and then he was there, nibbling up my thighs, and sending quick kisses that nearly had me coming right there.

He smiled and then pressed a sweet kiss over my center.

"Jack," I whispered, doing my best to remember his name.

"Yes, Jane?" he asked, his voice soft, a throaty purr against my pussy.

"Keep going," I whispered.

"As my lady commands." He unhurriedly tugged the lace off my hips and tossed it aside after I stepped out of my thong.

"Beautiful," he whispered, I was falling into temptation, past nearly falling, and going full straight down the rabbit hole.

He kissed me again and stood up, reaching around me to undo the clasp of my bra. I let the lace fall and sucked in a breath as he lapped at my breasts, using his free hand to squeeze my breasts, gently, and then firmer. He plucked at my nipples and then slowly trailed his hand down my belly to my core. He speared me with two fingers, at the same time sucking on my breast. I came, so quick to the trigger that I nearly fell, and I felt like I had never come so hard, so quick before. Maybe I had, but I couldn't remember. The only thing that mattered was the man holding me, making me feel like he would never let me go.

Jack lifted me up into his arms, cradling me to his chest, where he kissed me again, and I leaned into him, smiling sleepily.

"Enjoying yourself?" He whispered.

"That was amazing," I gasped, and then he slowly slid me into bed, and I nuzzled into the comforter.

"But what about you?" I asked, looking up at him.

He trailed a finger down my cheek. "Rest, you'll need your energy."

And at this throaty growl of his voice, I closed my eyes and drifted off, knowing as soon as I woke up, the night would be far from over.

Chapter Three
"JACK"

I PULLED JANE INTO MY ARMS A LITTLE BIT tighter, grinning as she nuzzled into me. She was all smooth curves and soft skin against me. After she had fallen asleep, nearly passing out from her orgasm, I'd made sure she was comfortable, stripped out of my clothes, and curled around her naked. I couldn't help it. I needed to be skin-to-skin.

And after all, this was Jane. This is what we wanted.

I studied her face, the strong lines of her cheekbones, the little tilted uptick of her nose at the end. She had long lashes, and her makeup was still pristine. I knew who had done her makeup for tonight and they would have made sure it would stay on, though I knew it might not once we took our shower.

If we got there. Right now, though, I was completely

satisfied laying here with Jane in my arms and pretending the rest of the world didn't exist.

In the morning, we would go about our responsibilities, and we would leave Jack and Jane behind. It was what was needed. Jack and Jane may never meet again, but they would have this evening.

Jane's eyes opened, and I smiled down at her. "Hello, sleepyhead," I whispered.

"L—Jack."

I shook my head and tapped her on the lips in warning. "Are you ready?" I asked, my voice a growl.

Her eyes widened, and she swallowed hard. "Always." I kissed her hard, delving my tongue against hers. She groaned, raking her nails down my back. I shifted above her and cradled myself between her legs and reached for the condom.

Her eyes widened, and I smiled. "I need to protect you, Jane," I whispered.

"Oh," she said, and I kissed her again, before kneeling between her thighs. I rubbed along her clit, along her swollenness, and smiled. "You seem ready for me already. So greedy after two orgasms."

"I can't help it when it comes to you, apparently."

"You can't help to come when it comes to me," I teased.

She rolled her eyes. "That was a ridiculous joke."

"Well, I am ridiculous. Sue me." She snorted, and I

leaned down to kiss her again, before slowly rolling the condom down my length.

"Are you ready?" I asked.

"You need to stop asking me that or I'm going to have to take care of the problem myself," she said before reaching out, not to touch herself, but instead gripped the base of my cock over the condom. I nearly passed out but told myself I was stronger than that.

Clearly.

I grinned, then positioned myself at her entrance. "I thought I would be a little more suave."

She squeezed me again. "Let's see exactly how you can work it, Jack," she teased, and I winked before I slid inside, deep with one thrust.

She let out a shocked gasp, and I froze.

"Jane?" I asked.

"I'm fine, I just, wow…I was ready, and yet still wow."

I chuckled, my cock twitching deep inside her. "I'll take that as a compliment," I said.

"If you begin to move, we can call it a compliment," she said, squeezing her inner walls. My eyes crossed, and I swallowed hard, before I lowered my head, kissed her again, and began to move. She wrapped her legs around my hips, and I slowly worked my way in and out of her, nearly shaking and already sweat-slick at just the beginning of our evening.

She moaned, meeting me thrust for thrust, both of us moving like we had done this a thousand times before.

But this is Jack and Jane's first, something that just helped the moment.

I rolled over to my back, needing to see her, and she hovered over me, a smile on the face.

"Jack," she whispered.

"Jane," I reached out, cupped her breasts, flicked my thumbs over her nipples. "Dear God, you're beautiful."

She trailed her fingers over the ink on my chest and arms, and then through my beard.

"Jack," she whispered, and that was all she needed to say. She put both hands on either side of my head and rode me, rocking her hips like a seductress, a siren that called my name.

I thrust up into her again, and her eyes went dark, her mouth parted, and she let out a little oh, and then she came. Her body flushed. Her nipples going even darker, harder. I followed her, my balls growing tight, and I came, my body shaking. Both of us were sweat-slick, holding one another, and she collapsed on top of me. I held her close, sliding my hands down her back.

"Wow," she whispered.

"Just the beginning," I muttered.

"I think we're getting a little too old to call that just the beginning."

I laughed and slapped her ass. She looked up at me, shocked. "Jack!"

"I think you liked that," I muttered. "Shut up," she said, not denying.

"It may take me a little longer than when I was younger, but I still want to try that shower. And maybe that chair."

"It's a hotel, who knows who's had sex in that chair."

I was still deep inside her, and both of us shuddered, laughing. This is what I had wanted, sex, fantasy, and comfort. Perfection.

"In the shower. After a minute. Let me hold you."

She smiled softly, her body going liquid, and she lowered herself on to me. And I held her.

My Jane.

At least for the night.

Chapter Four
"JANE"

My phone buzzed and I groaned, rolling from the man's arm that was wound tightly around me.

He grumbled something under his breath, and I smiled softly before reaching for my phone.

AARON

I figured you should get a text for checkout time. You have two hours. Enjoy your morning.

I looked at the clock, and my eyes widened. Not only had I slept in my contacts and my makeup, even though it was probably running down my face after the shower sex that we had had, I still could not quite believe it was already nearly eleven.

My fingers quickly went to my phone.

> ME
> Thank you! We're still in bed.

I flushed and could not believe I was texting my brother-in-law about being in bed.

I can practically hear Aaron's laugh from here.

> AARON
> Have fun. Glad you guys had a good night. But I don't need any details. Madison says she does. I don't want to know.

I laughed, said my goodbyes and thank yous, after checking on his charges, and set my phone down.

"Was that my annoying brother?" the man in my bed asked, his voice low and a little grumpy.

I smile. "Yes, just making sure we didn't overstay our welcome."

"Well, what time is it?"

"Nearly eleven."

Liam Montgomery sat up, his eyes wide. "What?"

I laughed at my husband and leaned forward and kissed him hard on the mouth. "I think midnight has struck, or maybe it was three in the morning when we finally went to sleep. Jack and Jane are gone, but I'm here."

Liam tucked my hair behind my ear and kissed me again. "I love you, Arden. Arden Montgomery."

I sighed at the name, loving the fact that my husband was so sweet, and all mine. All hardness and inked flesh that I could get my hands on. Mine, mine, mine, mine.

"You sound like a seagull from that movie with the fish," Liam said, laughing.

My eyes widened. "Did I say that out loud?" I asked, laughing.

"Pretty much. But, I kind of like it."

I leaned forward and kissed him again, and he groaned. He reached out and cupped my breasts, and I pulled away. "Hey, I wasn't done," he grumbled.

I shook my head. "We should get ready for the day. I can't show up to your brother's house looking like this." I pointed to my bedhead and whatever makeup I still had on my face, and Liam just shrugged. "They know what we were doing last night."

I blushed and shook my head vigorously. "They better not know everything, Liam Montgomery."

"You know, as much as I enjoyed being Jack last night, there's nothing better than hearing you call me by my given name, first and last."

I licked my lips. "I was thinking that I love being called Arden Montgomery. Look at us, no longer in fantasy."

"It was fun while it lasted, but I still got to say, this penthouse? You and that fucking hot dress and those fuck-me heels? Amazing night. But I also love cuddling with you on the couch while we watch movies and read books."

"Sometimes you just make my heartache," I whispered, tears falling down my cheeks.

Liam frowned and wiped the wetness from my skin. "No crying. Tonight's a good night. Last night was a good night. And this morning is even better."

"I know. I love you so much."

"And I love you, too. And, I want to go home," I whispered.

Liam's gaze met mine, and he nodded. "I'll go use the guest bathroom to get ready, because I know if I go in with you, we're going to take a little time."

I blushed. "Probably. There were three benches in there, and we only got to use two."

He growled, kissed me hard on the mouth, and hopped out of bed. I couldn't help but watch his ass as he moved away. After all, my husband had a great ass.

And I couldn't help it. He was naked. What could I say?

I rolled out of bed, stretching. I knew I'd be sore, but that was fine.

It was a great night off, but we had responsibilities at home, and I just needed to be there.

I showered, ignored the fact that I looked like Beetlejuice. I quickly blew dry my hair. Mostly because if I didn't, it would be a complete rat's nest, and I didn't have all of my curly hair products with me. I had wanted to travel light, although I wasn't completely Jane. Jane would have a single toothbrush and call it an evening. Arden had an entire suitcase.

I couldn't help it. I needed to be prepared.

I met Liam in the living room of the penthouse and looked around. "This is ridiculous," I said.

He shrugged, his cheeks going red slightly.

"I made a shit-ton of money as a model, and I make decent money in my current job. I'm allowed to every once in a while spoil you."

"Maybe," I said with a laugh. "But this is a little ridiculous."

He shrugged. "Very much so."

I looked around again. "Though we could maybe fit the entirety of the Montgomerys in here," I said, teasing.

"There's far too many of us for that, and I'm not footing the bill for that," he said and laughed. He kissed me hard again and then took my suitcase. "Come on, my wife, let's head home." He put both suitcases in one hand, squeezed my hand, and led me out of the penthouse.

Once in the sunlight that peeked through the car window, we were no longer any remnants of Jane and Jack. Just Liam and Arden.

A married couple—the first of Liam's siblings, and mine—and happy.

I had met Liam when I had been at one of my lowest points. Where I had thought that death would be welcome because the pain of living had been almost too much. I was still sick. I still had flare-ups. I still was in the hospital more than I'd like to admit. But I wasn't alone. Not that I had ever really been alone, because my brothers had always been there. But now they could focus on their wives and their children because Liam would always be there. Along with his family.

We had all grown leaps and bounds over the past few years, and I still couldn't quite believe that I had landed Liam Montgomery. The love of my life.

He looked over at me then, his aviators showing my reflection, and I knew he could see my heart in my eyes.

I couldn't help it. I didn't hide it from him.

He brought our clasped hands to his lips and kissed the back of my hand.

We pulled into Aaron Montgomery's driveway as the front door opened.

Jasper, my white Siberian Husky, practically leaped out of the doorway, barked happily, and sat patiently, even though he was shaking, on the grass waiting for us. Liam parked, and I jumped out of the car, all thoughts of pain from my lupus gone from my memory.

I knelt, hugged Jasper tight, and kissed the top of his head. "There's my baby boy."

I looked up as Lake came toward us, her hair piled on the top of her head, and her chin lowered just a bit.

"Mom?" Lake asked, and my heartbeat sped and felt like it grew five sizes.

"Hey there, baby. Did you have a good night with

your Uncle Aaron and Aunt Madison?" I asked and opened up my arms.

My daughter, of only a few months, ran into my arms. I hugged her tight, inhaled that sweet scent that was all Lake, and held back tears.

"Hey, Dad," she said as she pulled away and held Liam close.

I heard Liam's breath catch, and I knew he was ready to sob right along with me. She had only started calling us Mom and Dad two weeks ago. We had been Liam and Arden during the foster process. And as the adoption had become final, we were still getting our bearings.

But our ten-year-old daughter, Lake, was the light of our lives.

I knew that while the rest of the Montgomerys were slowly breeding an entire generation that would rival the originals, Lake might be our only child. And that would mean the world to me.

I had fallen in love with this little girl from the moment I had seen her, and I had nearly cried myself to sleep in tension and stress every night until the adoption papers had finally been signed. But now we were a family, the four of us with Jasper, and I couldn't believe that this was my life.

Aaron and Madison stood in the doorway, giving us a piece of privacy, even if we were in the middle of their yard. Madison was crying, leaning against Aaron. My brother-in-law was also crying.

We were a bunch of softies, and I loved it.

I looked up at Liam, my Jack for the evening, but my husband forever, and I smiled.

Last night had been a night to be wrapped up in fantasy and bliss. But fiction could tangle with real life.

And as I held my daughter close, my best boy puppy leaning hard into my side, and Liam holding us all, I knew that my reality was far richer than any fiction I could ever imagine.

A Very Montgomery Christmas

A Very Montgomery Christmas

It's holiday time with the Boulder Montgomerys and there are more than a few changes coming. Between family dinners, various cheese boards, late nights, and dramatic announcements, the family that has stayed together no matter the cost proves just what makes them special this holiday season.

Chapter 1
LIAM

"Jasper, buddy. What are you doing?" I asked, shaking my head. I knelt down in front of our white Siberian Husky and ran my hands over his face and flank. He licked at my chin, and I rolled my eyes before kissing him on the top of the head. I stood up next to him and grinned down at the dog Arden and I considered our son. "You're acting antsier than usual. What's going on?"

Considering Jasper was getting a little bit older in years and way more behaved than this usually, I was worried. He had been Arden's before we got together. In fact, he was the reason we had found each other after seeing each other in the hospital the first time we had met.

I shook my head, thinking about it. I had been hurt at a wedding after scaffolding had fallen and had changed my life. Arden had been in there for a reaction to the sun, just another one of her many problems that came with having lupus.

She had been in such pain, had had red splotches all over her face, and had felt like crap. I had needed stitches and had a probable concussion.

She had looked so freaking beautiful.

I'd walked away thinking I'd never see her again, despite the fact I'd wanted to. Jasper later had been the one to run away from Arden while taking a walk, something he had never done before and, God willing, hadn't done since. He had run right to me as if bringing us together again.

I'd like to think of him as our good luck charm, but right now, he kept barking and running around and chasing his tail. I had to wonder what the hell he was doing.

"Hey Dad, sorry, we were playing hide and go seek, and I think he's winning."

I swallowed hard as I looked up at Lake, my heart doing that little pitter-patter twist whenever my daughter called me Dad.

It had been less than a year, really only a few months, since Lake had come into our lives and been formally adopted. It had been an odd and stressful time through the system for Lake to be ours. We were still getting used to this whole family thing, but we had a daughter. Ten years old, sweet, kind, a little quiet, and totally in love with Jasper.

Jasper went from paw to paw, shook his tail, gave that doggy grin, and went right over to Lake. She let out a little giggle and ran her hands down him before hugging him tightly. Jasper, the little suck-up, wrapped one paw around her, rested his little head on her shoulder, and let out a contented doggy sigh.

Jasper was just as pleased at having the new addition to our family as we were. We had known that Jasper would be great with kids and babies, but we hadn't known the connection the two would share.

We were in the process of finding another dog as well, because Arden needed a medical alert animal around her in case she had another spell or reaction to her meds. Jasper was great at what he did, but as he was getting older, we all wanted to make sure that Arden had someone else trained and would let Jasper relax a bit. Jasper had many more years with us, but he didn't need to be working full time.

And now that meant that Lake would get a new puppy brother or sister. And maybe one day a human one too. But as we were only a few months into this big family thing, I didn't want to put the cart in front of the horse. After all, the rest of my brothers and sisters were having all the babies these days, and Arden and I felt like we were catching up.

"Sorry if I worried you," Lake said and winced. She ducked her head, and I swallowed hard. I knew all that was in Lake's file, everything that she had gone through before we had found her. Or, in essence, she had found us. But we didn't talk about it outside of therapy. That was fine. We had time to do so. And I hoped to hell she would. If not with me, then with Arden or one of her many aunts and uncles. I didn't like the fact that she had gone through what she had, but she was ours now. Our perfect daughter, and now that she was in her double digits, one day, she would be a teenager, and I'd have to deal with the next phase of being a parent.

"Why are you growling?" Arden asked as she walked in, her eyes bright. She was wearing a sexy red top that showcased her curves, but not too much, just enough for me. She wore black leather leggings with lace cutouts, knee boots and looked gorgeous.

"Just thinking about the future."

"You're doing that whole Papa Bear Montgomery thing, aren't you?"

"I can't help it. Just thinking about the guys or girls she's going to want to date later, and it's going to freak me out."

My wife laughed. "It's only been a few months. Breathe first. We have time."

"I'm going to have to talk with Austin. He'll know what to do." I'd make lists and read books in order to figure out how to be a father of a teenager. Giving her boundaries while not acting like an overprotective idiot was going to be a balance I wasn't sure I'd be able to find.

Arden rolled her eyes. "I guess Lake and Leif are

decently close in age when it comes to the cousins," she said, speaking of my cousin Austin's oldest son.

"Yeah, everyone else seems to be a bit younger. But Leif has already taken her under his wing and drives up here to hang out with her and show her the Montgomery ropes. I kind of like it."

"He's a terrific kid. And, your cousin Meghan has a son and daughter close to Lake's age, and everyone else isn't too far down the line in the grand scheme of things."

Hearing Arden's voice relaxed me, and I tried not to let the unknown of the future bother me as much as I was letting it. It was odd since it was usually the opposite when it came to Arden and me. "That's true. And who knows, maybe our next kid will be the same age or even older."

We were whispering now, aware that talking about it too much might stress out Lake. But she knew that we weren't done creating our family yet, and I wanted to make sure Lake had all the family she could handle. Lake wanted siblings just as we wanted a larger family.

"One step at a time. We're still getting used to this whole thing," Arden said, before she kissed my jaw. "Plus, my brothers are all working on starting families, and Macon's son wants to hang with Lake more. So, it's not just Montgomerys. You have to deal with the Bradys too."

"You're right, you're right," I said, before I kissed her softly on the lips.

She scrunched her nose. "Watch the lipstick. I don't want it to come off."

"That's why you're not wearing gloss."

Her eyes narrowed. "It's starting to scare me how well we know each other, especially since you know why I'm wearing matte lipstick instead of lip gloss."

"Because I want to kiss you. I learn what I need to in order to have those lips on me."

"Are we ready to go?" Lake asked, before she stood up and twirled around in her dress.

"We are, but first you need to find your shoes," Arden said.

Lake blushed. "Oops. I forgot." She padded off to her room, Jasper, on her heels.

"Christmas dinner with the Montgomerys. It's going to be interesting."

"Mom's been stressing out," I said softly.

Arden looked at me. "Why? Is everything okay? I thought things were good between everybody."

Finding out that the secrets of my family had been a little deeper than we had all ever guessed hadn't been easy for us, but we were better because of it. However, that wasn't what was wrong for the evening.

"This is her first real Christmas as Grandma. I think she's stressing Grandpa out to the point that he's ready to come sleep on our couch," I said dryly.

"Just joking, right? They are doing okay?" Arden bit her lip. I wanted to lean forward and lick at the sting, but

I knew Lake would be back into the room at any moment.

I nodded. "Just joking. We know that Grandpa Montgomery is ready to play Santa to the hilt. He actually has a suit, you know."

Arden laughed. "That I can picture. He has to compete with his brothers."

"We all know that each Grandpa Montgomery likes to make Christmas the biggest that they can. At least we're not having a huge conglomerate dinner. Tonight is just the Boulder Montgomerys."

Arden smiled. "And at least my brothers aren't coming to this since that adds an entire football team."

"No, but they'll be here for New Year's. Along with Marcus's family and a few others. As it is, we have my family, Zia, and Meredith, and Ronin, Kincaid, and Julia. I don't think my mom even owns enough chairs, come to think of it."

My wife laughed. "I'm sure they'll make do. It does get a little confusing around you guys, though."

"I'm ready." Lake walked in and twirled again.

"Almost," Arden said, and held out her hand. "This morning, we opened nearly all the gifts, and last night we opened your Christmas Eve gift."

Lake smiled. "And it was awesome. I've never had a Christmas like this. I mean, you always saw it in the movies, and I thought it was just something that they did for Hallmark and all that. But like wow. I just...thank you guys. I didn't really need anything for Christmas. Because I had you guys, and I know that's cheesy to say. But we're Montgomerys now. Cheese is what we do."

That made me laugh, I couldn't help it. "Have you been talking to my sister?"

"Aunt Bristol says that cheese is life. And I tend to agree."

My ten-year-old sounded so prim and proper just then that I knew she was mimicking a family member, but she was right. We had a fascination with cheeses in our family, and now it just became a snowball of jokes, hilarity, and damn good cheese.

"I'm glad you had a good morning with us for Christmas, and you have all your gifts, except you have one more that I'd like you to open."

Arden met my gaze, and her eyes twinkled.

I nodded, and I went to go sit next to the tree.

"There's one more here. Did you see it?"

Lake's eyes widened, and she and Jasper came to the tree, and she looked around.

"I thought we did everything. You didn't need to get me anything. I promise. I love you guys so much."

I swallowed hard and nearly started crying just then. But I knew that if I did, we wouldn't stop, and we'd be late for dinner.

"You are the best Christmas gift, birthday gift, 4th of July gift, any gift a dad could ask for," I said as I tucked a curl behind her ear.

"Okay, great, now I'm crying," Arden said, and she wrapped her arms around Jasper as her favorite dog licked her chin. "Seriously you guys are so cute."

"We try," I said dryly.

"Now, Lake, your surprise is right at eye level. Do you see it?"

Lake looked around, her eyes wide, and she shook her head. "Is that a new ornament? Is it for Jasper? I don't get it."

I met Arden's gaze, and she rolled her eyes. "I knew you would make it complicated," she said. "We should have just wrapped the thing."

"But I liked the ornament," I said dryly, and I pulled it off the tree before handing it to Lake.

It was a little snow globe with a tiny dog bone inside.

"What's this?" She asked, holding the ornament with care. "It's so pretty. I love it. Is the ornament for me and the tree?"

I met Arden's gaze, and I couldn't help but give her a wobbly smile. "It's part of it," I whispered.

"Is it for Jasper too? Because of the dog bone."

She let him sniff it, and I winced, afraid that he was going to break it. Not that Jasper wasn't the most careful dog I had ever met, but things happened. But both were so careful and reverent with each other that I shouldn't have been worried.

"It's for the family, but it means that there will be one

more family member in our tiny little Montgomery family."

She froze, her eyes wide before she looked between the three of us. "You mean I'm getting a brother or sister?"

"Liam, you need to stop being the writer and just put it all out there," Arden said softly, and she moved to hold our daughter close.

"Yes, one day we're going to do our best to get you a baby brother or sister. We've already talked about that, remember?"

"I remember. And I've always wanted a brother or sister. I'm okay with that. Even if she comes from your belly."

Arden kissed our daughter again, and I swallowed hard. "You are the greatest treasure we could ever imagine having. And I love you very much, and one day if we are blessed, you will have a brother or sister. However, for now, remember what we talked about with Jasper?"

Lake froze, and her eyes widened. "We're getting Jasper a brother or sister?"

"Yes," Arden said, laughing.

Lake looked at me and started bouncing on Arden's lap. My wife winced, but she didn't say anything. It didn't matter what happened just then, not with the joy radiating off of Lake's face.

"What does that mean? Is this ornament for them?"

I nodded. "We are getting another puppy, just like Jasper, but you are going to help us pick them out."

Lake moved her gaze between us. "But I thought he was supposed to help Mom. Isn't he supposed to be trained to be able to get along with Mom first? I'll love whatever puppy you bring. I promise."

That did it. I wiped my face as Arden openly wept. "I love you so much," Arden whispered.

Lake looked confused between us. "Why are you crying? Did I say something wrong?"

"You did nothing wrong," Arden said softly. "And yes, because he or she will be for me, we're going to do our best to make sure that we make the right connection, but all of these puppies are trained to help with medical alerts, like what I need. But you will help me make the final decision because they're going to be part of our family. Not just mine."

"I'll help. I promise. Jasper, you're going to have a brother or sister!" She carefully handed me the ornament before flinging her arms around Jasper. Jasper barked in glee once, lifted his chin, and the two of them began dancing around the living room. Jasper looked like a puppy himself, and I couldn't help but laugh.

"Things are about to get a bit louder here," Arden said dryly.

"Things were too quiet before the two of us met, don't you think?"

Arden met my gaze and smiled. "You're right. I was locked in my home, and I didn't have a way out. Jasper was my only real connection to the outside world except for my brothers, who were constantly trying to bug me."

"Because they love you."

"That may be true. But I had closed everyone else out of my life. Then you came along and bulldozed your way into my world. You and your massive family."

"It's what we do," I said with a laugh.

"Thank you for being my first favorite Montgomery," she whispered.

"You know, you're my first favorite, too."

"I love you, Liam."

"And I love you. Now, let's go bring the family to my mom and dad, and tell them the good news. Because I don't think my mom's going to be able to handle us if we're late."

"We would never be late. Not when it comes to your mom. She's already a fantastic grandma."

"And with the way that my siblings are producing, she's going to get a lot of practice."

"I honestly don't think she's going to complain."

I kissed Arden again and helped her stand up before we straightened up Lake's dress, made sure Jasper was all brushed and ready to go, and then the four of us were out of the door, heading towards my mother's house, and the start of our family dinner. And I had a feeling even with a dog, a babbling Lake, and Arden and I laughing along, we might be the quietest of the bunch.

And that was saying something.

Chapter 2
ETHAN

I stumbled into the living room searching for my shoes. Why my shoes would be in there and not in the closet where they should be, I didn't know. Well, I did. It was the new addition to the house that was approximately three months old, the love of my life, and currently screaming his little lungs off.

"It's okay, little Kingston," Holland cooed, holding the baby up to her chest. She does a little swinging motion around the living room, bouncing him to try to calm him down. Colic was no fun, and he had decided that he didn't want to breastfeed anymore, but also missed breastfeeding at the same time. So we were dealing with bottle feeding, pumping, lack of sleep, and a crying baby.

And I've never been happier in my life.

"It's okay, we're going to go see Grandma," Holland whispered. "And Grandpa, of course."

That made me snort. I went down to my knees and spotted my shoes under the couch. I rolled my eyes and pulled them out. "Grandpa knows that Grandma is the one that we're going to see. She's in baby fever at the moment."

"You know your father is in just as big a baby fever as his wife is."

"True, but he lets us believe that it's only Mom."

"They're just so good at being grandparents." She cuddled Kingston to her chest.

I leaned down, brushed a soft kiss over his downy head, and then kissed my wife on the lips. "Hi," I whispered.

"Hi. I don't remember what sleep is, Ethan. I mean, I vaguely remember lying down and waking up after a few hours feeling refreshed, but I don't think that exists anymore."

I felt the same, but I wasn't about to tell her that. She needed me to be the strong one, even if it was a lie. "It's fine. People can work on thirty minutes of sleep. There have been papers on it."

"Papers written by liars," she whispered fiercely, still swinging Kingston in her arms. He quieted down some but kept chirping little chirps of dismay.

And we all knew what he wanted and why he wasn't getting it.

"Is Lincoln on his way?" Holland asked, her eyes wide, pleading.

"Yes, he texted he was leaving the store. And then he texted at the stoplight, saying he was almost there. He checks in more than I do."

Holland rolled her eyes. "Well, that's a lie. You both check on me so much during the day. It's like having you here, except for you're not here to help me lift things."

"I can work from home more," I said. "Julia said she'd work with me on it."

Holland shook her head. "No. Because I want to still love you, and if you were working from home twenty-four hours a day, I am going to get testy."

"You know, I don't know how I should take that," I said dryly.

"You should take that in the grace that has been given. That I love you, I like you, and I'm stressed."

"I can't believe my mother did this four times."

"Maybe babies were easier back then," Holland said, and met my gaze. We both snorted, keeping our laughter at bay as to not jostle Kingston.

"Please don't tell your mother that I said that."

"Of course, I wouldn't say that. Because if I did, my dad would come up with a story of having to walk uphill both ways in the snow barefoot to get formula."

"That sounds about right," Holland said, continuing to swing. She wasn't wearing any makeup, her hair was piled on the top of her head, and she was wearing her same pajamas. And a bit of spit-up we had missed in the last cleanup.

"We need to leave in an hour," I said softly.

She narrowed her eyes at me. "Are you saying that I don't look ready for tonight? That I am not the most gorgeous specimen, you had ever seen?"

She might have been glaring at me, but I saw the laughter in her eyes.

"You are gorgeous. And if you show up like that for Christmas dinner, Mom will love you even more, and never let us hold Kingston for the rest of the evening, possibly not the week."

"She does love holding our baby. Just wait till Bristol pops, then your dad will finally be able to hold one of his grandkids."

"They'll just trade them off, with Lake dancing around them, telling them about her day."

Holland's smile was wide, filled with love. "I'm just so happy. I can't believe that this is our life."

"It does seem a bit shocking," I said dryly.

"Do you think Aaron and Madison are going to start trying?" Holland asked. "I know they were talking about it casually, and they want their kids to grow up with ours."

"As I don't think any of us are done having kids, despite the lack of sleep right now, they still have time. I don't know their plans because I don't want to be that guy who asks and steps into a painful moment. You know?"

Holland's smile softened, and she raised her chin. I leaned down, took her lips as was offered, and sighed.

"You're such a good man. I love you."

"And I love you too. So, who's going to be at this thing tonight?" I asked.

Holland just rolled her eyes. "These are your family members, shouldn't you know?"

"I'm exhausted. I don't remember anything."

"Yes, because I've had so much sleep, as we've discussed." She laughed. "Zia and Meredith should be there, as is Julia and her husbands. They've sort of all been added to the Montgomery family, even if they have families of their own."

"We do tend to do that."

What was unsaid was the fact that we were not spending time with her family. We were trying to mend those bridges, get better at it, but it wasn't easy. And I wasn't even sure that we wanted to accomplish that.

Lincoln's parents were on a winter cruise, something they had bought two years prior, thanks to a sale, and had done their best to get out of. But we would hear none of it, and they would be back for New Year's, and we would have Kingston's second Christmas a couple of days after his first. They had been so apologetic that my mother-in-law had burst into tears, but everything was okay. This way they would have their own special moment with Kingston and us, rather than being part of the large Montgomery one. We tended to be overwhelming on the best of days, annoying as hell on the worst.

"Is he here yet?" Holland asked, looking at the front door.

I shook my head. "He needed to pick up the groceries so we can make our side dish. We'll be cutting it close, but we'll make it work."

"Can you work on the diaper bag? Make sure we have diapers this time?"

"We had diapers last time," I said, groaning.

"We had diapers for a six-month-old, not a three-month-old. They somehow got added in, and then we had to double-tape him up so that it wouldn't fall off, leaving a huge accident everywhere. As it was, he already exploded out of the back of it, so I was covered." She groaned. "Since when did our romantic conversations include baby poop?"

"About the time that we found out you were pregnant," I said, and then kissed her on the cheek. "I'll work on it. And I hear the garage door now. Lincoln's on his way."

"Oh, thank God," she whispered, and then we turned to see our husband walk through the door. His hands were full of cloth and linen bags, stuffed to the brim with groceries.

"I went crazy. I know I had a list, and then I remembered everything that we hadn't put on the list, at least some of the things, so now we will have food for the week, maybe. Hell. I'm sorry, I'm late." He smacked a kiss on my lips and handed over the bags. "I need a drink," Lincoln said, shaking his head.

I took the bags easily and put them on the kitchen counter. "You're welcome to have a drink, and I'll do the driving tonight."

"If I have a drink, I'm going to fall asleep, and that probably won't be the best idea for me to be snoozing at the family dinner." He kissed Holland softly, and Kingston began screaming. My shoulders dropped, sighing, but then Lincoln plucked Kingston out of Holland's arms and put him to his chest. "There you are. Daddy's here."

Holland and I rolled our eyes, and I set to taking everything out of the bags. Kingston immediately quieted down, his big eyes staring up at his daddy.

I was Dad, and Lincoln was Daddy. We were going to try for that nomenclature for now. It may get confusing, but we would make it work. We weren't the only ones in our family in a poly relationship, so we were taking cues from my cousins who were raising kids with more than two parents. They were making it work, and we were following their path, doing our best to make it work for us as well.

Kingston was going to be always held, always loved, and know that no matter what, at least three people loved him with all of their hearts.

And that had to count for something.

"You know, last week, he would only stop crying for

Holland, the week before, only for you," Lincoln said, staring at me. "This kid is taking turns on his affections. And I don't mind it."

"I do," Holland said, covering her face with her hands. "I need a shower, to do my hair, do everything. And I think my right boob is leaking." She looked down at her shirt, at the wet spot currently increasing with every breath. "Yep. I'll need a pump at some point. Damn it. We're going to be late."

I shook my head. "No, it's fine, we'll get there." Late, but this was our lives now.

Kingston took that moment to spit up all over Lincoln, and we all sighed.

"I'm on it," I said, stuffed everything in the fridge, and tried to do mental math as to how we were going to make that side dish.

I took the screaming Kingston from Lincoln's arms, and Lincoln pulled his shirt over his head. I did my best to ignore the way that his muscles moved, the beautiful lines of his torso, but it was difficult. Even Holland was staring, and Lincoln just grinned. "You know, this is how we got in this mess in the first place."

"Maybe, but I don't mind." Holland laughed, and I shook my head.

"I'll clean up this little guy. You guys clean up each other. But separate showers, or we're going to be late." I narrowed my eyes at the two, and they just shook their heads. "Later."

"You say that as if I have any energy to please our woman." My husband looked over at our wife. "Sorry, babe."

"Oh no, I get it. At this point, I would just have to lie back and think of England, and I don't think that'd be fun for any of us."

"You better be lying back and thinking of one of us," I growled playfully, and brought Kingston into his nursery. We had gone with yellow flowers and giraffes, with splotches of green, and bumblebees. It was a happy, fun nursery and only clean at this point because we had hired a maid. Between the three of us having full-time jobs and working more than forty hours a week usually, we didn't have time, and we made decent enough money that we could help someone else feed their children by paying them to clean our house. They also helped us with prepared meals for the fridge, but they wouldn't be here for the holidays because we wanted to make sure they had time with their family after we paid them holiday bonuses. That meant, somehow, we needed to feed ourselves, and it was like we had forgotten how to as soon as Kingston was born.

I missed sleep.

Kingston started burbling, lifting his little feet in the air, and I undid his little onesie and changed his diaper. He was such a happy baby when he wasn't screaming. I knew he was in pain, and hopefully we would find a way through colic and get to the point of being parents where we could sleep again. My mother said it happened in about eighteen years, so I was counting down.

"I love you so much," I said, before kissing Kingston's little belly. Kingston just grinned a little gummy smile, and I quickly pulled another onesie on him. We were contemplating putting him in something cuter, but he was just going to mess it up anyway, so we had a dozen onesies ready all over the house.

We had a lot of family members, and that meant a lot of baby gifts. Thank God.

"Okay, this is as clean as I'm going to get," Lincoln said as he walked in. He wore partially unbuttoned linen pants, no shoes, no shirt, and his hair was wet and slicked back from his face. "You need to go shower too. There's spit-up down your back."

I sighed. "Damn it. I already showered. But thank you." I kissed Lincoln hard on the mouth as I handed over Kingston, and Lincoln put a blanket over his shoulder and lulled Kingston to sleep. I somehow showered quickly, found my shoes again as I dressed, and walked into the living room. Holland was there, her hair braided up in a complicated updo, but it was still wet.

"I know it's cold, and I'll put a hat over it, but this is as good as it's going to get."

"You look beautiful," I said, and kissed her softly.

She was wearing a dark red dress and black tights with black boots and truly looked gorgeous.

"Thanks for saying that. I think the dark circles under my eyes despite makeup really make the outfit."

"They match ours," Lincoln said dryly.

I went to pick up my keys and looked around and cursed.

"Stop cursing in front of the baby," Holland said. "His first word is going to be the F-word if we're not careful," she scolded.

I winced. "You know what we forgot?"

And Lincoln sighed. "Well, it looks like someone's going to be missing green bean casserole."

"It was the easiest thing to do. It's just cans mixed together in yummy goodness," I sighed. "I need to call my mom," I said, and Lincoln nodded, searching through the kitchen.

"Maybe there's something we can bring. Crackers?" he asked.

"Oh, this is good. We totally have this under control," Holland said, and I groaned.

Mom picked up at the first ring. "Are you guys on your way yet? Or having a little bit of trouble getting out the door?"

She always knew us better than we knew ourselves. "The latter. But I don't want to jinx anything by saying we're clean and ready to come over."

"Just bring extra clothes for all of you. We know how babies are. And don't worry about bringing the green bean casserole. I already made one, knowing that if you got busy taking care of that beautiful baby and yourselves, it might get forgotten. Either we'd have double, which is fine because I know that's your favorite side, or we would have a backup."

I had her on speakerphone, and Lincoln and Holland looked at each other and then smiled at me, looking a little sheepish.

"We're sorry. We're trying to help out, but we just messed up."

"You did not mess up," my mother said sharply, if not unkindly. "You guys are raising a baby with colic, still running Holland's shop, you're still working full time, Lincoln is under an immense amount of pressure, thanks to his upcoming show, and it's the holidays. You're allowed to be stressed out. Now come over here so I can hold that baby, and my baby," she added. "Well, I guess it should be all of my babies because I love all three of you. But quickly. You do not need to bring food. Just yourselves. And don't forget diapers. Although I do have some just in case."

I laughed, Holland and Lincoln joining me. "I love you, Mom."

"I love you too. Now be quick." She hung up, and I slid my phone into my pocket, looking around the house. "I hope to hell we have everything."

"Language," Lincoln laughed.

"I'll get better at it. Maybe. Maybe once you do," I added.

Lincoln shrugged. "You're right. His first word's going to be a curse word."

Holland shrugged. "It's going to end up being Dad. I'm outnumbered, two to one."

"But we love you anyway," I said, kissed her on the mouth, then Lincoln grabbed the diaper bag and headed out, Kingston in Holland's arms, being quiet for once, and I grabbed the extra go bag for us.

I had always wanted a family. I just hadn't known how it would come about. I had done my best never to think about what my future would be because I hadn't known how Lincoln would fit in. And now he was my touchstone, just as Holland was my everything. Somehow, I got so damn lucky I could barely breathe. But now we were here for Kingston's first Christmas, and I knew that no matter what happened next, I always had my family.

Spit-ups, crying jags, lack of sleep, no green beans and all.

Chapter 3
AARON

I knocked on my parents' door, Madison leaning into me, a smile on both of our faces.

"You know, you could just go in," Madison said, and I shook my head. "No, because it's the holidays, and my mom's going to want to open the door and greet us."

"That makes sense," my wife said, and I just held back a grin. *My wife.* I still couldn't quite believe that I could say that.

I had always known I'd wanted to get married and start a family. But actually having a wife? Finding someone that I genuinely loved beyond all measure and knew I would spend the rest of my life with? I still couldn't grasp that that was my life sometimes.

The door opened, and my mother stood there, clapping her hands. She had on her Christmas best, the pearls around her neck shining under the light, and a wide smile on her face. The pearls had been a gift from Dad for their twenty-fifth anniversary, and she only broke them out for special occasions. "You're here. You're here."

"Oh yeah?" I asked. "I'm not late, am I?" I leaned in, kissed my mother on the cheek, and moved back so Madison could hug her. I was still holding two casserole dishes, as well as presents on one arm, and Madison had two sets of gifts in her arms, but we were good at juggling.

"Come in, and you're not late. You're always on time. Bristol and Marcus are here, as are Zia and Meredith, and Julia, Ronin, and Kincaid are here as well."

I blinked, trying to put names to faces even though Bristol was my sister, and the rest were practically family, even if they weren't Montgomerys.

"Wait, so there are only two sets of siblings here?"

My mother waved off my words as she took the casserole from my hands. She immediately handed them over to my dad, who rolled his eyes and smiled.

Dad leaned forward. "Arden, Liam, Lake, and Jasper will be here any minute. They had a slow start because they had a couple more presents to open. And the new parents will be here soon. They had an even later start. But things tend to get that way when you have a new bundle of joy demanding all of your time."

I looked at Madison, who blushed and shook her head.

Okay, soon then.

"But you know you would think with three of them

that they'd be able to handle the timing better," I joked, and my mom narrowed her eyes at me.

"Be nice, or I'm going to have to slap you upside the head. And don't think I won't. Because I will, young man."

My dad just laughed. "You know she will."

"Yes, but I didn't think she'd be so blatant about it," I laughed.

"Of course I will, Aaron. Be kind. You never know when it will be your turn to be the new parents that are never sleeping."

"You never know," I agreed causally. I handed Mom one set of presents and then took the rest from Madison to empty her hands. "Okay, I think we got everything that we needed for everyone."

Mom looked at us, her eyes wide. "I thought we said we were only doing presents for the family. As in, Secret Santa."

I rolled my eyes. "You know that this is the first year that we have grandkids and nieces and nephews in the family. Of course we're going to splurge."

Madison laughed. "And, we got something for everyone, but it's the same thing, so I hope that's okay."

My mom's eyes filled with tears, and I knew today was going to be a long day of happiness and crying. But I didn't mind. It was what we wanted.

"Oh, that's so sweet. So this is all for us?"

"Yes, at least for each household, and we do not expect

presents from everyone. We just saw something and knew it would fit perfectly even though it was going against the rules."

"My little rule-breaker."

I rolled my eyes. "I'm not that bad, Mom."

"You are, but it's why I love you—at least one of the many reasons."

We set the presents in front of the tree, and Madison knelt to start putting things in the correct order. I helped her down, making sure she was okay, and she just rolled her eyes at me.

"Go say hi to your sister and brother, and the rest of them, stop worrying over me."

I shook my head. "I'm always going to worry over you," I whispered, before I kissed her again and made my way into the dining room. Bristol was sitting in a large armchair in the corner, her feet up, and looking absolutely miserable.

"So, how are you doing, late sister?" I asked before kissing her on the forehead.

"I am two days overdue, exhausted, and I think my ankles are the size of grapefruits."

"Oranges, darling, just oranges," Marcus said, leaning into his wife. The man smiled, his dark brown eyes bright even if I saw the worry in them.

"You guys doing okay?" I asked, being serious this time.

"We're doing fine," Bristol said on a sigh. "I guess."

I looked at Marcus to confirm.

"We are doing okay. We're just tired."

"I don't get to sleep anymore. Heartburn sucks, life sucks, and I just want the baby to come out. Get out, get out, get out, get out!" she said, pointing at her stomach.

"I'm sure that's how it works," Zia said as she walked in, her purple hair in ringlets all around her face. She usually never wore it in that style, and I liked the look on her for the holiday season. She wore a plum-colored dress with leather and lace swatches and lace tights and looked kick-ass. And since she could probably kick my ass, I didn't mind.

Meredith, her wife, and sort of my ex, came in behind her and kissed me on the cheek.

"Hello, Merry Christmas, happy holidays, blessed yule."

"And all of that back to you," I said, grinning. "You two look great." I looked down at Meredith with her equally leather and lace outfit, though her hair was bright blonde and had an undercut that I wanted to try one day. "Sorry. We're late," I said.

Meredith waved it off. "You already apologized to your mom, and technically you're not late. We're all early."

"My mom wanted us out of the house and here resting since Bristol had a shot of energy after our lunch," Marcus explained.

"So you already had Christmas with your parents and family, then?"

Marcus nodded. "Yes, and we're still all planning New Year's with the whole group. Between my sisters, their spouses, and their kids, it's going to be louder than usual."

"We're used to loud," Bristol said, patting her belly. "And you never know, by this time next week, we may have a baby. And no sleep. Much like Ethan and his crew."

"And there will be only two of you," I said.

"So I hear. Where's the other trio?" Bristol asked frowning.

"Oh yeah, where are Kincaid and crew? I have a gift for Kincaid after he helped me with something."

"Aww, look at you with your man crush," Bristol said, and Madison walked in and wrapped her arm around my waist. I did the same to her, and leaned my head on top of hers. She fit perfectly against me, like she was made for me. I said that often to her, and she just rolled her eyes and called me sentimental before blushing and leaning into me for a kiss. I was one lucky bastard.

"Hey, you're here," Julia said as she came up to me. I opened my other arm, and she snuggled into me, just like Madison was doing. She waved at Madison, and the two pulled away from me to hug each other.

"You look great," Madison said, looking at Julia. "Seriously great."

"It's that beach glow," Julia said, grinning.

"I still can't believe you guys went to the Caribbean the week before Christmas and still made everything work out."

"We had everything planned long before, and then the baby came with Ethan and crew, and I was terrified that it was going to be too much on the rest of the staff with both of us being out, but somehow we made it work."

"Because you guys are all good at what you guys do," I said, smiling down at Julia before looking up at Kincaid and Ronin.

"You guys are here," I said, and hugged the two guys.

"Of course we're here. It's Montgomery dinner. I'm here for the cheese," Kincaid said and nodded.

"Hey, long time no see," Ronin said, and I rolled my eyes. He worked with Marcus, and the two were busy as hell, despite the fact that they were closed for part of the holidays. However, that meant they had to do all the backup work they couldn't get to when the library's hours were open.

"Oh, I have something for you," I told Kincaid, as the other man tilted his head and studied me. "Really?"

"Yeah, just a thank you gift for help with my latest pieces."

"I don't mind."

"You didn't have to do anything for me."

I shook my head. "Yeah, I did. You're a world-renowned photographer, and you've worked your ass off. And you spent a whole day working with me taking photos of my pieces for my next show, so you did not have to do that."

"But as I said, I didn't mind. It was fun. Something different."

I shrugged. "Now look at us, all so talented, and working on what we love."

"I don't remember what it feels like to put a cello in front of me. I can't reach it," Bristol complained, patting her belly. "Come on, baby. I want to meet you. Get out, get out, get out, get out."

I snorted, but I didn't say anything. It felt like Bristol had been pregnant for a year, but soon there would be a new bundle of joy, promptly screaming and vomiting and keeping everyone up at night. Honestly, I couldn't wait.

"I can't wait to see you as a mom," I said, echoing my own thoughts.

"I don't know if you're making fun of me or being sweet? I can't tell sarcasm anymore. I think it's part of the whole pregnancy brain."

"I wasn't sarcastic. You're going to be a great mom. You're already great at pretty much everything that you do."

"Aww," Zia said, as she wrapped her arm around Bristol's shoulders. "Look at your brother being so cute. What does he want?" she asked.

"I don't know, but it can't be anything good," Bristol said, narrowing her eyes.

"It's like you guys don't trust me."

"We're here," Ethan called from the front door, and I heard the voices of a few others arriving. Everyone began the exodus toward the new arrivals. Marcus hefted up his wife, and I did my best not to smirk, knowing that I would get beaten if I used the word hefted out loud. And probably deserve it.

"So are we," Liam said. We all met up in the living room, the noise getting louder as Jasper and Lake started dancing in the middle of the room.

"Kingston is so cute! I love my cousin so much." Lake leaned down to see the baby and started talking about what she had for Christmas and saying hello to everybody. She ran into my side, wrapping her arms around my waist. "Hi, Uncle Aaron. I love you."

I swallowed hard, the emotion getting to me. "I love you too, Lake."

It felt like we had had her in our lives for years rather than only the single year.

She had been a Montgomery for even less than that, and she had taken to us far quicker than I had thought possible. But that's what happened when you had the Montgomerys, Arden's family, and so many of us around making sure she knew she was loved and would always be with us.

Madison leaned into me and sighed. "I think I'm going to be sick," she mumbled, and my mother's eyes narrowed.

"Madison?"

"I'm sorry I've got to go." She turned on her heel and ran, and I followed her.

"Be right back," I said, and closed the bathroom door behind us.

"Stop it. I don't need you to be here. You don't need to witness this."

"I love you, I'm here to hold your hair back." She went down to her knees and promptly threw up everything that she'd eaten that day, though it hadn't been much. She had already thrown up a few times that day.

"Damn it, I don't want to go back to the hospital," she whispered, as I ran a cool cloth over her face.

"I have ginger ale and crackers," Mother said the other side of the door. "Let me in, son. I want to make sure that my little daughter is okay."

"Might as well," Madison rumbled as she leaned against the bathtub. "They're all going to guess what's wrong sooner or later."

"There's nothing wrong," I sighed. "Everything's just right. We're just having a wicked fashion about it."

"Whatever you say. I think I'm going to be sick again." And she promptly did so, and I opened the door for my mother as soon as Madison was done.

"So, morning sickness?" Mom asked as she knelt beside my wife.

"How could you tell?" Madison still had her eyes closed, looking far too pale for my liking.

"I had four babies, and now my babies are having babies."

"It's bad, Mom," I mumbled. "She has hyperemesis gravidarum."

Mom's eyes widened. "Oh, no. Is that why it's so bad? You look like you've lost weight, Madison. How far along are you?"

"Heading into the second trimester, thank God. I had to stay in overnight with IV fluids before Thanksgiving," she mumbled.

Mom glared at me. "And you didn't tell us?"

"Because we had a lot of family things to deal with, that was difficult, and we could handle it."

"Does Lincoln know?

"I knew," Lincoln said, leaning against the doorway. "And I was going to tell all of you if it got any worse. And hey, it looks like it's getting worse." As Lincoln and Madison were cousins, we felt it only right for us to tell him because Madison needed a family member to lean on. Telling the entirety of the Montgomerys would have been too much.

"We didn't want to tell everyone until we knew I could get at least into the second trimester. I'm sick, but I'm going to be okay. The baby's fine. I just have severe morning sickness. And it sucks."

"I would say so," Mom said. "Okay, let's clean you up, and we'll bring you out, and you can sit down next to Bristol. Holland is going to sit down right next to you because that girl has not gotten any sleep, and we'll probably stick

Arden with all of you because I know she's in the middle of a flare."

My eyes narrow. "Is she okay?" I ask.

"I'm fine," Arden said, and I realized that nearly everybody that I knew and loved was standing in the bathroom doorway and watching the proceedings.

"Oh no," Madison said, and groaned into her hands.

My mom clucked her tongue. "We'll bring her out in a second, and then we'll celebrate a new baby. But come on, give her some privacy."

"What's privacy?" Liam asked. "We're Montgomerys. We don't believe in privacy."

My mom narrowed her eyes, and then my dad groaned before pulling the rest of the siblings and family members and friends of family out of the doorway.

"Come on, my girls will sit down on that big couch of mine, and we'll bring everything to you. You won't have to lift a finger."

Madison gave me a wobbly smile. "I seriously love your family, Aaron."

I looked down at my wife, the soon to be mother of my child, and my own mother, and smiled.

"And I love my family too. More every day."

I was one fucking lucky Montgomery and an even luckier man.

Chapter 4
BRISTOL

I put my feet up and groaned. "Why am I one hundred and seven weeks pregnant. Why does someone think that this is okay to do to me?" I asked, and narrowed my eyes at my loving and handsome and evil husband.

Marcus just shook his head. "I realize that you didn't get pregnant all by yourself, and I had some help in that, but you look gorgeous, so don't growl at me."

"Ixnay on the growlingay," Ethan whispered as he held Kingston to him, trying to get the little tyke to calm down. He was screaming, the colic a little too much for my nephew. And then my brother-in-law Lincoln took Kingston from his husband's arms, and the baby quieted down. My brother narrowed his eyes at his husband, and Lincoln just grinned before leaving the living room.

"I'm pretty sure he did that on purpose," Holland said, staring at her husbands and baby. "This week is all about Lincoln, but I think if we're true to form, next week Kingston will stop screaming while he's in my arms."

I blinked and looked over at my sister-in-law. "That's a thing? They take their turns?"

"Kingston seems to. And we're going to pretend that that's normal," Holland said, before she yawned so wide I swore I could see her tonsils. "Sorry," she mumbled and leaned against the soft cushion. "I think I've had around eight minutes of sleep this week."

"That bad?" I asked, anxiety filling me. I put my hands on my stomach, felt a kick, and patted the little baby's foot. "I really like sleep."

"And you do a lot of it," Marcus teased, rubbing my ankles.

"You're lucky I love you, and you're lucky that you're rubbing my feet right now, or I would kick you. I just really want you to keep rubbing."

"Anything you say, wife of mine."

"That's the way," Aaron said, laughing as he handed his wife Madison a glass of water. "See? We need to follow Marcus's advice. He knows what he needs to do as a husband."

"Do whatever she says," I agreed, and Marcus just rolled his eyes at me. "Sure, honey, whatever you say."

"See," I said, raising a hand, and then I groaned, with the baby kicking at my bladder. "I'll have to get up soon to pee. This baby keeps kicking and rolling in certain places."

"Are you dilated at all?" Holland asked, and Ethan shuddered.

"Please stop talking about my sister and dilation. There were a lot of things I learned during the childbirth process, things that will never leave my mind again, but I don't need to associate them with my sister."

"Amen," Aaron said, and I flipped them both off, grateful that Lake, the only one of my nieces and nephews who were old enough to understand the gesture, wasn't in the room at the moment.

"Grace and elegance, that is Bristol," Liam muttered, and I growled.

"I am past due on this baby, the size of a beached whale, and still retaining so much water at this point, I feel like I could float. Or maybe I'll sink like a stone because I'm so heavy. Don't make fun of me."

"Ah, the joys of pregnancy," Holland said, laughing. "Just wait, Madison, this will be you."

My newly pregnant sister-in-law turned impossibly green. "I think I'm going to be sick." She scrambled off the couch and ran towards the bathroom, Aaron, on her tail.

"I'm trying not to take that as an insult, but it's pretty difficult not to," I said dryly, and everyone laughed.

"You know, the one good thing about adopting is that I don't have to deal with whatever pregnancy brain you have. However, a new baby brain, even if the child you adopt is ten years old, is something."

"Oh, I know," I said, shaking my head at Arden. "Plus,

I hear you're getting a new puppy. There's got to be puppy brain."

"Oh yes, I had a lot more energy when Jasper was a puppy, but thankfully I have Liam to push around. And Lake will be there to help with training and picking up poop. See, that's why you have kids. To help you with chores," Arden said.

And my mom came into the room, laughing. "This is why I had the four of you. It helped me keep the house clean." She paused, looked at all of us, and burst out laughing.

"I think she's making fun of us," I said, looking at my husband. "But, I'm too tired to piece together how."

"I'll explain it later."

"I know you guys are talking about the next baby coming," Holland began, looking at Arden. "Do you have a preference for an infant? Are you going with an older child again like Lake?" she asked, and I leaned forward as much as I could over the bump that was my stomach and looked at Arden.

"No preference," Arden said. "Older children are usually harder to place, so we made sure that they knew that we were happy with either. As much as I had always thought about having children and being pregnant when I was little, and losing that part of that plan when I got sick might've hurt, I'm okay. Honestly. You don't need to step on eggshells when it comes to being pregnant and everything, okay?"

I swallowed hard and met Arden's gaze. "Are you sure?" I asked.

"I'm sure. I get to experience the joys and not joys of pregnancy between the three of you and between all of our friends because you guys never hesitate to share everything," she said with a wink, and I laughed.

"Sorry, we do get into detail."

"It doesn't help that we're all at some stage of pregnancy and baby-making at the same time," Holland added.

"And so I get the joys of that with you guys, I get to feel little feet and elbows against my hands when I put my palms over your stomachs. But then, even though there is that sense of loss and wonder, I get something else out of Lake. I'm a mom. It's our first Christmas with our baby, and though I didn't carry her to term, she's everything. She's my child. And I know deep down in my heart that it's no different than it would've been if I would've been the one that carried her." Arden sniffed, wiped her face, and then Liam was there, handing her a tissue.

"I love you," he whispered, and kissed her softly. Tears were freely flowing down mine and Holland's faces.

I hiccupped, and the baby elbowed me in the ribs prudently. "I think the baby is excited and wants to meet you soon. At least I hope so," I mumbled.

Marcus wiped my face, kissed my cheek. "We'll meet our baby soon. Don't you worry."

I was filled of worry, but I didn't say that.

"You still don't know if it's a boy or girl?" my dad asked, leaning against the doorframe.

I looked up at him and shook my head. "We wanted to be surprised. We went with neutral colors anyway, and my favorite color was blue growing up, so it's not like I need to conform to gender stereotypes."

Dad just grinned. "You're right. I know that you usually have lists of lists and would want things monogrammed with your baby's name."

"I know, that would have been nice. We have ideas for boys and girls and gender-neutral names. We'll see what happens when they show up."

"Sounds like a plan to me," Marcus mumbled, before he sat with his back against the couch, his hand on my calf as he slowly massaged it.

"I could get used to this," I said.

"Once the baby comes, he'll be holding that infant and trying to get some sleep, and there goes the massage," Mom said, and my dad rolled his eyes.

"I was always very attentive, Francine." He nearly leered it, and I shuddered.

"I don't want to know any of this," Ethan said as he walked back into the room, Lincoln behind him with Kingston in his arms.

"Hey look, Aunt Madison said it was time to open the gifts," Lake said, bouncing with Jasper behind her. He was like a big brother, constantly watching her, and I love the way the two interacted.

"Are you sure you're up for it, dear?" Mom asked as Madison nodded.

"Yes, since I'm still standing, and feeling okay, let's do this quickly."

My brother Aaron had his gaze on her, watching her like a hawk, and I didn't blame him.

I hadn't known she had been hospitalized for a night because of a lack of fluids, in so much pain, and she could be hospitalized again, and it worried me. With all of us going through our own issues, they'd wanted to keep it personal in the family, but now we all knew, and we'd be watching her. Even when I reached week two hundred of pregnancy.

"Okay, it's all the same gift, so only one of you needs to open it, so that way we don't stress out everyone."

"Well, here's mine," my mom said before handing it to Lake. "What do you say? Will you open it for Grandma?"

"I'll help," Lake said, and my mom sat down on the chair, Lake on her lap, and the two of them went to open the gifts. Kincaid had his camera out and took pictures of everybody, and I knew I was going to hate the way I looked, how bloated I felt, and how horrible I felt later, but I wanted this memory. And I knew that no matter what I felt about myself, it wouldn't matter.

Because we had our family. And I was blessed.

I started crying again, even before they finished opening the gift, and Marcus looked at me.

"What's wrong?" he asked.

"Nothing. Everything's fine."

He gave me a look that said I was insane, but he still loved me. He'd been giving me that look often.

Zia and Meredith came into the room then. Their hands clasped as they stood in the corner. The room was packed to the gills with people that I loved, and I just grinned at my ex-girlfriend and best friend, and she gave me a little wave. I knew the two were discussing babies and what would come next, and I wasn't sure what direction they were going for. I had a feeling, though, that a certain brother of mine would become a sperm donor if they had their way. For some reason, the small group of us had already discussed it, mostly because I was nosy, and I wanted to make sure my family was happy.

Since Aaron was close friends with Meredith, and Zia was practically a Montgomery, it would only make sense that that was the way they would go. They had already talked about it with he and Madison as a possibility, and soon there'd be more to our family.

And I couldn't help but cry at the love, the aching aspects of it surrounding us.

My mom let out a gasp, and Lake started clapping. "Oh, it's so pretty, thank you," Lake said, and I tried to move to look at it.

"Keep sitting, Bristol, before you topple over."

I blushed under my mom's happy chiding, and she turned the picture frame at us.

It was all of us, the Montgomerys, by birth, by happenstance, and by family.

Somehow the photographer, and I had a feeling it was Kincaid, had taken a photo of us all smiling or laughing and looking at one another or at the camera itself, but it was completely candid. Everybody looked wonderful, happy, and we're standing in front of Liam's cabin, the one we went to as a family as often as we could, with the mountains and blue sky behind us, and love on all of our faces.

"Kincaid took this photo while he was there, and I asked him if I could find the perfect frames for everybody and give it to you. I realize that technically it should be a gift from Kincaid, so think about it as from all of us." Madison began, leaning against Aaron.

Kincaid blushed and ducked a little bit behind his husband and wife. "It was no worries. I just happened to find a good photo, and Madison knew what she wanted to do with it."

"Each of you guys will have one for your homes. You can hide it and only bring it out when we're over, but it seems that we're going to need lots of babysitters," she said, patting her still flat stomach. "Meaning I expect you guys to have it out all the time."

I laughed as Marcus took out our picture and unwrapped it so I could look at it closer. I couldn't help but cry, looking at everybody. At our family. The one we'd made, loved, and cherished.

"This is perfect. There's so many of us."

"And only a snapshot in time," Marcus began, squeezing my hand. "That's not even all of our family, but so many."

"I don't know how I got so blessed," I whispered. "But I'm so happy."

We had been through so much heartache, pain, attacks. And somehow we had found our family, and it kept growing.

My father brought in a cheese board, and Julia followed him, another cheese board in her hand.

People started making up their little plates, snacking on the eight different kinds of cheeses they had in front of them. My mouth watered, but since most of it was soft cheese, I couldn't partake.

A Montgomery without cheese for an entire pregnancy was not a happy, bubbly Montgomery.

I needed to have that crocheted somewhere. We could hand out the pillow to every pregnant family member.

I looked down at Marcus, and he rubbed my knee.

"What's wrong?"

"Nothing. I'm honestly happy. This is the best Christmas ever. I wish we'd be able to share it with our little one."

Marcus kissed my knee. "We will. Maybe next Christmas will be their first Christmas. They'll come out when they're in the mood."

"It's a Montgomery and Stearn. They're going to take their sweet time no matter what."

Marcus shrugged. "I took my time finding you. They should take as much as they want."

"Look at you being so romantic."

I nearly leaned down to kiss him, but I knew the angle wouldn't work. Although at that exact moment, the baby decided to twist, and I groaned, clutching my stomach.

Marcus's eyes widened and he scrambled to his feet. "What's wrong?"

"I'm pretty sure Mom's going to need a new couch," I said, and everybody shot up from where they were sitting, and I looked down to where my water had broken.

"Well, it looks like a Christmas baby it is."

And I promptly burst into tears.

Chapter 5
FRANCINE

I HAD MADE MANY MISTAKES IN MY LIFE, BUT somehow I had ended up the most blessed and happiest woman in the entire world, at least from where I was sitting.

Liam had just returned to the waiting room after dropping off Arden, Lake, and Jasper at home. Lake had wanted to be there, but it was nearly midnight now, and she had fallen asleep. Arden had needed to take her meds and get some rest as well, as her flare-up was starting to get worse. But she was doing okay. And I was grateful for that. I love my daughter-in-law. She was vivacious, with whatever energy she had. She was brilliant, caring, and one of the most generous souls I had ever met. She had brought Liam out of his shell and brought him back to us.

I held back a sigh that twisted my heart, familiar but gentler than it had been over the years. I had almost lost him, not due to circumstance or outside forces, but because of my own decisions. We had nearly lost him, I thought, looking over at my husband. He gave me a small smile and squeezed my hand. He gestured towards Liam, and I knew his thoughts were along the same as mine. After over three decades of marriage, our minds tended to do that.

He might not be Liam's biological father, but he was his dad in every way that mattered. We may have stumbled on our way to this peace of mind, but now we were one big happy family that was slowly watching our children raise their children.

And sometimes the emotion was too great for me even to bear.

"You doing okay, Mom?" Liam asked, as he squeezed my shoulder. I leaned into my son, wondering when he had gotten so tall. Bristol was the only one my height, but my boys had gotten their height from the other end of the gene pool. They were all over six feet, broad, muscular, and sometimes strained my neck to look at.

But even with all that width and strength, they were gentle.

"I'm doing just fine. I'm waiting to hear more news coming," I whispered.

"It should be soon. And hey, if things speed up in the next hour or so, we'll have a Christmas baby."

"Of course, Bristol would want to do that. She needs to make sure everything is sparkly and in celebration."

"That's my baby sister," he drawled, before moving out of the way for Ethan.

"We need to head home," Ethan began, "though I'll stay. As long as you don't mind giving me a ride home?" he asked Liam, and Liam nodded.

"No problem."

"Thanks," Ethan said before looking at me. "We don't want Kingston to be sleeping here for too long, and honestly, I think I heard Lincoln sleeping earlier."

"It was only a little snore. I'm fine." Lincoln leaned forward, kissed the top of my head. He was just as big as my sons, and I felt like he was my own. I liked his parents, though I wished they were here more often. However, I got another son and daughter and the cutest grandbaby in the world out of it. So I didn't mind.

"You guys lasted longer than I thought you would," I said, and then leaned into put a kiss on Lincoln's cheek, and then Holland's. "Are you two safe to drive?"

"I'm good. That little power nap there helped," Lincoln said dryly.

"Tell Bristol we love her, and we'll come to see the new baby when they arrive," Holland said, and I leaned forward to kiss the top of Kingston's head. "We were just here a couple of days ago for Kingston's first round of shots, and we'll be here soon for the second round."

"That was a couple of weeks ago, darling," Lincoln said, and Holland crossed her eyes.

"Days, weeks, they're all blurring together," she said

on a laugh. "Update us, even if it wakes us, we want to know when there's a new Montgomery in the world."

"I'm pretty sure the earth will rotate off its axis just a bit when that happens," my husband said wryly. "Every time a new Montgomery is born, the world shudders."

That made me laugh. "That is our family slogan."

"Good to know," Lincoln said. "See you soon."

"And Merry Christmas," Holland added. They walked out, and I just smiled after them, my eyes watery.

"We did okay," my husband said, and I looked up at Timothy.

"Oh?" I asked.

"Francine, darling, we did better than okay. Look at all of them, bringing new life into this world, and soon we're going to have enough chubby cheeks to pinch and babies to spoil. And as soon as they make a mess or start to stink or make a loud noise and cry, we hand them off to their parents."

"That is the best part of being a grandparent," Marcus's mother said as she walked forward. I hugged her tight, and her husband gave a small wave. "Seriously though, you guys are going to catch up with us in terms of numbers of grandkids soon if you're not careful."

"You guys had a head start with your three girls," I said with a laugh.

"It's true. But I know Marcus and Bristol are going to want more than one, probably to catch up with the rest of

Marcus's siblings because you know how competitive they are."

I snorted. "We're going to end up with like eighty grandkids each, and that might be almost too much for me," I said.

"Maybe," Marcus's mom said with a smile.

"His sisters and husbands wanted to be here, and I have a feeling they will be here soon, just taking turns of who's watching the kids."

"That's what we're doing here. Eventually, we're going to overfill this waiting room."

"That's because this one is smaller than the one we usually end up in," Aaron said, leaning against the wall behind Marcus's family.

I looked over at him and down at the sleeping Madison in the chair next to him. She had her head resting on her thigh, looking sweet, and finally with a little more glow to her. She had been looking so ill before, I had worried for her. I would be a little grumpy that they hadn't told me she was sick, but I understood. They wanted time with the pregnancy news for themselves, but now they were going to have many eagle eyes watching her, making sure that she took care of herself.

"I could do well with never seeing the emergency room waiting room or the surgical area waiting room ever again," I growled. "But it's too much for our family."

"I agree," Marcus's mother said, her voice stern. "I

know you always joke about the Montgomery wing of the hospital, but it was getting a little ridiculous."

I visibly shuddered and leaned into my husband as he held me close. "I'm just sorry that we had to deal with it at all, but it's ok now that they're all safe. I'm going to knock on wood as I say that."

I laughed, and I looked around at my family. Kincaid, Ronin, and Julia had gone home, and we had promised to update them. They had stayed at the house to clean up and put all of the Christmas dinner fixings in the fridge. I was forever grateful that I could trust them to do that and had left them a key saying that they could keep it because they were family.

They had all blushed, sputtered, but I had left, with the feeling I had gained new children. I knew that Ronin had parents that they spent time with, but the other two could use more parental figures in their life. And my heart was big enough for all of them.

Meredith was on the other side of Madison, looking down at her phone, and I knew she was stressed out as well. I knew from what I could gather, either she or Zia might be next after Madison if all things turn out well, and so we would be waiting again for the next family member, even if she wasn't my blood.

Zia herself was in the room with Marcus and Bristol.

I loved Zia, and while I would have loved her to be my daughter in truth, having married Bristol, that meant I wouldn't have Marcus as a son-in-law. But now Bristol and Zia were best friends, and Zia was in the room with them, helping as Bristol's coach.

Zia and Marcus had become best friends as well, both ganging up to make sure Bristol took care of herself. And I loved to see it.

We were a loud bunch and all a little hungry, though we had all snacked a bit. This wasn't the Christmas that I had planned, nor was it one anyone had imagined, but this was what we were used to. In all honesty. A big family, someone changing the curve, and us being together. We would be able to eat more than cheese and crackers later, though I knew my children would be fine with just that. Their love of cheese knew no bounds, and they would all be surprised when they opened up their identical Montgomery family charcuterie boards that I had had hand-carved and branded with the Montgomery logo.

They would open it later, once we welcomed the new Montgomery into the fold.

"How much longer?" Aaron asked, and Madison woke up and scowled at her husband. "I hope you don't do this when I'm in labor. Constantly asking, are we there yet?"

"He was like that as a child and hasn't stopped," I joked, and Aaron blushed while everyone began to laugh. On the end of that laughter, the doors opened, and Marcus walked in, a grin on his handsome face.

"We have a girl, seven pounds, eight ounces, and perfect," Marcus said.

"What's her name?" Meredith asked, leaning forward.

"Bristol wants to tell you each personally," he said, shaking his head. "I think she's excited, and hell, so am I. I have a daughter," he whispered, and I started crying, leaning into my husband.

"Are we allowed to see her?"

"Yes, they're just getting everybody cleaned up and ready, and even though it's late, because it's Christmas, they're going to make an exception for us. Only two of you at a time, and I'll be in there with her." He turned to Meredith. "Zia is on her way out, and she promised not to spoil anything," he growled. "So, don't try to get the name out of her."

"Why are you looking at me when you say that?" Ethan laughed.

"Because I know you."

"Why don't you two go first," I said, looking at Marcus's parents. "The Montgomerys will bring up the rear. There's a lot of us."

"Oh, we'll have to call the girls. They'll want to come in too."

"They can come in the morning," Marcus said. "It will be a long night, and I don't want to tire Bristol out. Is that okay?"

"Anything you want, darling."

I watched Marcus's parents follow him in and leaned into my husband.

"A Christmas baby," I said, looking up at the clock.

We are six minutes away from December twenty-sixth, and a new Montgomery had been born on Christmas day. A Christmas miracle, a present, and everything I could ever ask for.

"Baby is going to be spoiled beyond all measure," Ethan said.

I snorted. "You say that as if Kingston isn't already spoiled by his grandparents."

"That's true," he said on a laugh. "But I'm glad we're all going to be able to have our kids grow up together. You know?"

I moved towards him, squeezed his hands, and leaned forward, so my forehead rested on his. "I know. And between your babies and all of your cousins having these babies, the next generation is going to be even louder than you guys."

"I honestly didn't think that was possible," my husband said dryly from my side.

"I'm a little scared." I smiled and leaned into my husband.

My kids brought up their phones and started updating those that weren't with us, and I just held my husband close, wondering how I could be so lucky.

When Marcus's parents came back out, crying and holding each other close, I rolled forward on the balls of my feet and bounced. "Come on, come on, I want to go see."

"Okay, I won't make you wait any longer," Marcus

said, and I followed my son-in-law towards Bristol's private room. I had given birth in a room with three other women and barely remembered it the first time. I think with Bristol, I had been alone, but I couldn't remember. All that mattered at that time were my babies and my family.

We walked into the room, and Bristol was sitting there, her hair piled up on the top of her head, and though she looked a bit tired, she was all wide-eyed and bright smile.

"Hi, Mom," Bristol said, and I looked down at the perfect little bundle in her arms. She was so cute and had the Montgomery nose, that much I could tell, and her father's dark brown skin. She was gorgeous, and I couldn't wait to hold her. But I also knew how a new mother could be and didn't hold out my hands. Instead, I squeezed my husband's hand and fisted my other at my side. "Oh, she's gorgeous."

"Here, you can hold her," Bristol said on a laugh. "You'll have to give her back soon. I love her so much."

Marcus sat on the other side, running his hand over Bristol's hair.

"She's beautiful," I said, as the light weight slid into my arms. "Every time another one of you has a baby, including all of my nieces and nephews out there, I'm always shocked at how tiny you are. But look at you, my little baby granddaughter. I love you so much."

"Can you tell us her name?" my husband asked, and I looked over at Bristol.

"Well?" I asked, a little anxious.

Bristol just groaned.

"Mom, Dad, meet your granddaughter, December Montgomery Stern."

I blinked away tears. "December, I love it."

"She's a Christmas baby, so I figured that we're going to do our best with future birthdays and everything else so she knows that she's special, that we should throw out all the names we had planned, and go with something full of joy. Montgomery will be her middle name, and it's a big name to fill, but I think she can do it."

I looked down at my precious granddaughter and smiled.

"Merry Christmas, December. Welcome to the Montgomerys."

I hope you loved this holiday special from the Montgomerys! You can find out more about Julie, Kincaid, and Ronin in Captured in Ink!

And the next set of Montgomerys begin in Fort Collins in Inked Persuasion!

Want to read a FREE bonus romance? Read INKED FANTASY for FREE here!

Over the Bridge

A MONTGOMERY INK LEGACY SHORT STORY

Over the Bridge

A secret romance.
Two friends turned to lovers.
But what happens when Sawyer and Kate want more?

Chapter One
KATE

Snow crunched underneath my boots as I made my way down the path. Tiny flakes of snow fell from the sky, as well as from the tall trees above, and I paused for a moment, lifting my face up to the breeze.

It wasn't too cold, even with the snow. Perhaps it mostly had to do with the two jackets I wore. Not to mention my fleece lined leggings. Even with the slight chill, the world had sung to me in this moment like one of those Disney princesses. It was a good day.

The sun shone brightly through the trees, and I stuck out my tongue to catch a few flakes.

"You do realize how much pollution is in the snow that you're currently trying to eat, right?" a deep voice said from behind me, and I froze for an instant, my shoulders tightening, my hands fisting at my sides.

I knew that voice. I heard it daily at work. While we

didn't technically work together, we were in the same building. My bosses, the Montgomerys, owned the entire building.

I was the admin for Montgomery security, which wasn't nearly the work some people thought. No, it was my job to keep the dozen or so full-time employees of Montgomery security on their toes. And frankly, to help keep them safe while they did their job keeping their charges safe.

The voice behind me belong to the newest tattoo artist from Montgomery Ink Legacy.

And every time I heard that voice, my emotions scattered into a thousand different directions. And most of the time I had no idea why.

"I'm not sure I asked you about anything," I said after a moment, not bothering to turn around.

"Wow. I was just trying to be helpful."

I turned to look at the bearded man with dark hair that nearly went to his shoulders at this point. He'd let it grow the past year since I had known him and was turning into quite the mountain man.

He had broad shoulders, a thick chest made of pure muscle, and thighs that filled out those jeans perfectly.

I did my best not to notice those thighs. I pulled my gaze back up and looked into his gray eyes and swallowed hard.

"I'll deal with the pollution to have my happy winter moment, thank you."

A smile slid over his lips that did something to me and I refused to look at them...for too long. "Enjoy your time pretending you're in a winter movie with hot cocoa waiting on you and everything."

"There might actually be cocoa waiting for us, you know." I wrapped my arms around myself, suddenly chilled. "When our friends said the wedding was going to be in Cherry Creek, I expected the real Cherry Creek. You know, the one in the city. Not where I nearly had to get off the roads trying to get up into the mountains."

Concern covered his features as he stepped forward. "I told you we could have driven up together. Are you okay? Did something happen?"

And right then and there was why Sawyer always confused me. I worked with his brother Gus daily. Gus was just as growly, and fiercely protective over his wife, Jennifer. He also always made sure that I had candy, nuts, or some form of cheese product on my desk. I liked snacks and was constantly on the move, so I needed the extra energy the way my metabolism worked.

Gus made me laugh, and I felt like I had found a new big brother.

Sawyer did nothing of the kind. We constantly butted heads, and while I knew Sawyer was one of the most brilliant people I'd ever met in my life, sometimes it felt as if he was trying to lord his intelligence over me. I knew that was on me. I had a complex when it came to smart men. Even those who only thought they were smart.

The problem was Sawyer was brilliant. I was good at what I did and excelled at patterns and keeping a place like Montgomery Security on track.

But my dyslexia made some things a chore. And sometimes it felt like I wasn't good enough. Like I didn't deserve to be there. And here Sawyer was, effortlessly brilliant and always right. Even if he didn't mean to be.

Like the fact that he had offered to drive us both up to this wedding between our mutual friends. I had gone to college with the bride, and Sawyer knew the groom from his previous job in the academic world.

Going from an actual nuclear physicist to a tattoo artist was quite the journey, but as I had seen Sawyer's work, his arc deserved to be showcased.

And his brain couldn't help but fire at a thousand percent.

"I'm fine." I winced. "Okay, I'm fine now. It was a little harrowing at the corner of that pass, but the ice wasn't too bad."

Sawyer moved forward, gripping my arms. "Are you seriously okay? Damn it. I should have insisted we drive together."

I shook my head. "If you had insisted, I would've rather walked."

Sawyer rolled his eyes. "Well, at least we're both in agreement you're stubborn as hell."

I pushed at him so he would let me go and gestured

toward the main lodge. While this place was also called Cherry Creek, it wasn't the high end shopping area with condos. No, this place was all about luxury in a scenic setting. It was your typical mountain lodge with a large lobby to the fireplace and comfortable overstuffed seating. And apparently all the rooms on the first floor had private hot tubs.

My room had not been ready yet when I checked in, as I had wanted to get there early knowing that driving was going to be an issue for me, so the person manning the front desk, Cameron, was storing my luggage.

Since Sawyer was also out on a walk without his belongings, I assumed the same had happened for him.

"Why don't we just head inside and see if our rooms are ready?" I asked.

"I don't know why you're being so grumpy with me." He knew exactly why I was grumpy with him. But I didn't want to think about that right then.

"Sawyer. It's going to be a long wedding if you're going to be like this."

His eyes danced, as he gestured us toward the small bridge that hovered over the frozen creek.

"What is it?" I asked, holding back a laugh.

"It's our thing."

I looked down at the bridge, then up at him, my heart racing. "How is standing on a bridge our thing?"

He leaned forward and brushed my hair behind my ear, making me realize my hat was starting to fall off. "I kissed you for the first time on the bridge in Estes Park. Do remember that?" he asked.

I swallowed hard, my hands once again fisting at my sides.

Because I wasn't stressed that he was here. Wasn't tense that I would have to be near him all weekend. No, I stiffened and did my best not to reach out because it was all I could do *not* to reach out to him.

Because in the year since we had met, I was slowly falling in love with Sawyer. The dorky, yet brooding, annoying, yet selfless man who was so talented at everything he did it sometimes annoyed the hell out of me.

And it was our secret.

"Nobody knows the two of us in real life, you know. At least not here. We can be whoever we need to be."

I finally unclenched my fists and did the one thing I had wanted to do since I had heard that deep growl of a voice. I put my hands on his chest before lifting to my tiptoes.

"That's more like it." He pressed his lips to mine, and I was once again lost. He tasted of the hot chocolate I knew he had scored from the lodge before he had taken this walk. And I slid my tongue against his, relishing in everything about him.

Secretly dating the tattoo artist next door for months wasn't easy. Especially when your bosses were in security and secrets for a living. But for once, I wanted something to just be for myself. So when Sawyer had kissed me for the first time, and then teased that it should be just between us, I had agreed. I slid my arms up around his neck, pulling him closer to me. His hands moved to my backside, squeezing as he pulled me against him. Even through my multiple layers, I could feel the heat of him, the strength.

It was so hard not to want him in public, but I liked having this one piece of myself that was just for me.

Because while I love the Montgomerys and all of our friends, everybody was constantly in each other's business. I had grown up as the little rich girl in a small town where everybody followed each and every step I took. They knew what I wore and too often, they would comment if my favorite milkshake of choice would change. And every single busybody mother would want to know exactly who I had a crush on and who I was dating. If I rode too quickly on my bicycle, or went too fast over a speed bump when I had been able to drive, the entire town knew. And they judged. There were no secrets at all. No privacy.

Even though I didn't live there, they still put my happenings in the town newsletter. Because the town was too small for a whole paper, but it was still a gossip column, complete with new sightings, bear issues, sales at the general store, and Kate's Mistakes.

It didn't matter that I lived in one of the largest cities in the United States now, they still dug into my personal life. When I had broken up with my longtime boyfriend before working at Montgomery Security, it had been breaking news. My mother and sisters encouraged it. Because the more I was seen about, the more they were. They relished in the limelight, and I wanted to hide.

As it was, it was hard enough to make sure that so-called helpful former neighbors didn't accidentally hurt my business. Because the Montgomerys were in charge of secrets, and my past was the exact opposite. Sawyer been my secret surprise and was perfect on multiple levels. Even though a small part of me wanted to shout it to the world.

He pulled away after moments, both of our breaths coming in pants. "We should head inside." His voice was low, full of promise. I nearly pressed my thighs together at the vibrations alone.

"Yes, our rooms should be ready soon."

He gave me an odd look before tucking her hands and moving us toward the Lodge. As people began to mill about, everybody starting to arrive for the wedding, I pulled my hand away.

He tilted his head at me but didn't look disappointed. Instead he looked as if he had been expecting it. And perhaps even wanted to keep hiding.

After six months of secretly dating, late night dinners, overnights where we made sure that other cars were never spotted, part of me wanted to just let it out in the open. We had had enough of our time together just for the two of us that having all of our friends and family locally in the middle of it wouldn't be that much of a big deal. I would even ignore the update in the small town newsletter because after all this time, things were different.

But maybe he didn't want to be different.

Once again, maybe I was thinking too hard.

He opened the door for me, and I smiled at him, trying to look as if I knew him as a friend, but not anything more.

I hadn't realized I was so good at deception until I'd fallen in love with Sawyer. I was even good at lying to myself.

Cameron, the young, incredibly attractive man behind the desk, smiled up at me.

"Hello there, Kate. I was just looking up your reservation as all our rooms are ready."

I smiled then. "That sounds perfect. I could use the time to warm up and freshen up before the event tonight."

There was a small cocktail party for the attendees, and the wedding was the next day. The rehearsal dinner had been the day before, but only family had been invited to attend. Which honestly, was the perfect amount of time for me in the mountains like this.

Cameron clicked a few keys, and then smiled at me. "Okay then, I have your room, a king-size bed with the hot tub. Let me just get you those two keys." He met Sawyer's gaze and I felt as though I wasn't in on the secret.

I frowned but figured the two keys were just automatic.

"And Sawyer, here's your key. The room has exactly what you requested." Cameron winked, and an uneasy yet anticipatory feeling spread over me.

"Did you already check-in?" I asked, doing my best not to sound too curious.

Cameron looked between us and cleared his throat. "You two were on the same reservation. One room, one king bed. Right? Or did I mess up?" He bit his lip, frowning.

My chest tightened for an instant, wondering how that could happen. But then again, Sawyer had made the reservations. *Two rooms*, and we would find a way to move between each other's. That way no one was the wiser.

Sawyer pulled my hat off my head and grinned. "You've got it right, Cameron. I think our girl here just needs a little more hot cocoa and maybe even champagne to fully wake up."

"That would be fantastic. Champagne makes me sleepy, but don't worry, I have everything set for you. Enjoy your evening."

I heard the relief in Cameron's voice, even as I looked up at Sawyer, wondering exactly what he was thinking.

Then again, it's exactly what I had wanted. Even if I hadn't let myself voice it.

"What are you up to?" I whispered.

"Anything I want," he said softly, and he pulled me to our room on the first floor.

The large bed filled most of the space, and somebody

had thrown white rose petals all over the beautiful duvet. Our luggage was already inside, along with a charcuterie board, a cheese board, a hot chocolate set up, and a bottle of champagne on ice.

As the door closed behind him, I whirled around.

"One room? Really?"

Uncertainty crossed his features, and he tugged on the bottom of my braid. "Did I mess up? I figured it would be easier to be honest."

In answer, I smiled brightly and threw my arms around his neck. "You're ridiculous. But I like it."

And I love you.

He smiled at me then, his eyes darkening before he crushed his mouth to mine. I moaned into him, needing him more than anything.

"We don't have a lot of time," he whispered against my lips. "We're going to have to make fast work of it."

"Are you going to count orgasms before dinner?"

He raised a single brow, looking sexy as hell. "I can."

Then he slid his hand beneath my leggings and panties and over my pussy. I gasped at the coldness of his fingers against the heat of my core, and he just grinned at me before slowly rubbing his middle finger over my clit.

"Sawyer," I panted.

"You're going to be saying my name a lot more often tonight. Now, let's see exactly how wet you are." With his gaze on mine, he slid two fingers deep inside me, stretching me.

I gasped as he worked in and out of me quickly. His fingers rough, he spread them, a gasp escaping my throat. The sounds of my wetness filled the room as I gasped into him, and he flicked my clit with his thumb.

And just like that I came, my inner walls clamping down around his fingers as my knees nearly gave out. He smiled then, slowly letting me come down as he slid his fingers out from beneath my pants.

When he moved to brush his wet fingers against my lips, I opened my mouth and let him slowly slide them inside. I could taste myself on his skin, and I shivered.

"That's it, imagine this is my cock."

"Why can't I have your cock?" I teased.

"You can. After dinner. First however, I want to fuck that cunt of yours just the way I know you like it. And when you get back from dinner, I want you on your knees. Naked. Your breasts covered in champagne. And then I'm going to fuck that mouth of yours until you're gagging and then I will lick up every ounce of you. And then I'll eat that sweet pussy, taking my fill, before I pound into you again, making you beg."

If it was possible to come at just words, I would have. As it was, my clit pounded in rhythm to my heartbeat, and I tore off my jacket.

Our movements were urgent, and yet somehow familiar. This wasn't our first time, and in this moment, I knew it wouldn't be our last. He was familiar, and yet every time we touched it felt like something new.

Something hidden. Forbidden.

Sawyer moved us to the bed, rolling to his back as I straddled him. I rocked over his length, leaving a trail of wetness behind as he squeezed my hips.

"Tease."

I smiled down at him before bending to kiss him softly.

We had forgone condoms a few months ago after getting tested. I had an IUD, and having him bare inside me was one of the most pleasurable experiences I could have ever hoped for. It also made it harder for both of us to make it last longer. Because we could feel everything, and sometimes I was just a hair-trigger away from losing the battle to keep the sensations going.

He slid his hand between us, working me up again, and I leaned up slightly so he could press himself against my entrance.

Our gazes colliding, I slowly sank down on him, his cock stretching me impossibly full. Tears pricked my eyes as I looked down at him, at the intensity there.

I didn't know if he loved me. I wanted to hope that he did, but we had been so good about keeping everything secret, we kept what we felt to each other in the shadows along with who, or rather what, we were. I wanted to tell him that I loved him. I wanted to tell the world. I also wanted to keep this moment just for us before it slid through my fingertips.

He froze for an instant, reaching up to wipe the tears on my cheek. "What's wrong, Kate? Am I hurting you?"

The fear and tenderness in his voice nearly broke me, so I did my best not to think about what could happen. And only let myself think of this moment.

"Everything is wonderful. Just keep going."

He remained still for another moment before seeming to believe my words. Then he moved, and I rocked with him.

He held onto my hips, keeping me steady as I arched for him, plucking my own nipples with my fingers, and loving the way he stared at me.

And when I came again, he followed me, filling me with everything that he had.

Only I wasn't sure it was everything.

I wasn't sure I wanted to ask if I could have it all.

Chapter Two

SAWYER

"Hey, can you hand me that sketch pad?"

I looked up at Leif Montgomery and nodded. "No problem. Are you working on the piece for Warren?"

"Yes, but I'm having issues with the angle because elbows are always so tricky."

"Tell me about it. Sometimes I wish I didn't enjoy trying to piece puzzles together like that."

"Figuring out how it can look good at multiple positions is always difficult. But I enjoy the process, even as I'm pulling out my hair."

"And what luscious hair that is. It would truly be a loss."

He flipped me off, and I went back to my sketches. I had two appointments already and had another one in about an hour. I was damn lucky to have even gotten the space at this shop. The flagship shop in downtown Denver was now known worldwide thanks to a few news articles and shows. Celebrities tried to come from all over to get their ink by a Montgomery. While there were only four studios underneath the umbrella of the Montgomerys, people wanted more. Except for the fact that the family wanted to keep everything in-house. A Montgomery had to be working at the Montgomerys.

My place happened to be the next generation place. Leif's father was the original owner and still worked full-time downtown. And when there had been a spot open at this location, I had been lucky enough to get hired. People had clamored for it because you cannot only learn a lot, but people want your art because of the traffic alone.

I was just grateful that I'd had an in thanks to my brother who worked next door at the security company. I knew that I wouldn't have been able to get the job if I didn't have the talents, but I also had to mesh with the family and everyone involved for me to be hired. It was a working environment yes, but it was also a group that hung out together, worked together, and dealt with a lot of shit together. So if you didn't get along or mesh, it wouldn't be the right fit. So when the Montgomerys had been looking for another tattoo artist, and I had been coming up into my own, the timing just worked out.

Leaving my job at my old company had been difficult. I loved working in science and trying to find ways to combat the energy crisis that we were in. But I had been burned out. Between other companies trying to steal ideas and government contracts falling through because of politics, I was just done. I felt like I couldn't think my way through the fog of monotony. I still worked on a contract basis with my old crew if needed. Because sometimes they needed someone to look at proofs and get all of the maps out. And it was nice for me to make sure that my mind was still working a way I needed it to.

But I enjoyed being a tattoo artist more than anything, which had surprised the hell out of my parents.

Not so much Gus. I didn't know why, but he seemed to understand that this was exactly what I needed to be before too long.

I was just lucky that Gus happened to know a family of tattoo artists. I knew I would find a job somewhere, but this place was perfect.

"Hey, are you coming out tonight?" my boss asked, and I shrugged.

We had been back from the wedding for a week now, and something had shifted. I wasn't sure if it was on me or Kate. Going to the wedding together like we had had probably been stupid. Kate and I both enjoyed sneaking around and living in the moment just with each other, not with everybody looking in.

Now that we were back, it was hard for me not to look at Kate. Not to go next door and brush my lips against hers and just see how she's doing.

We had lasted months with a polite distance even

while together, but one weekend had shattered that, and I didn't know what to think.

"Earth to Sawyer. You okay?"

I flinched, pulling myself out of my thoughts. I needed to keep Kate out of my mind for the moment—and what she meant. A safe place, but nothing too serious. Because if I made it any more than it was, no good could come from it for either one of us. I'd break her just like I always did. Because there was nothing left.

"Yes, I'm fine. Just thinking. And yes, I'll be there tonight. Who else is going?" I asked.

"Mostly our family, but not everyone," he added at the raising of my brows. The Montgomerys had more than a few family members, and I wasn't sure we would all be able to sit in the bar we were heading to.

"Mostly the people that work in the building, and their spouses. Everybody got babysitters, and we are going to have fun. It's about time. Brooke and I really need a night off."

"Why are you using your night off to hang out with us?" I asked, honestly curious. The two of them had a full family, with kids ranging in ages from infancy to elementary school age. I didn't know how the two of them kept up with everything. I could barely keep up with myself.

And the moment I still awake with Kate.

"We haven't had a night out with the group in far too long. We have a dinner date with just the two of us planned for next week."

"Two nights away in one month? Look at you being gluttonous."

He rolled his eyes at me, and we went back to work. My appointment came in, and I did my best to focus on what I was doing and not on the fact that Kate would be there tonight.

The two of us had been in the position to hide who we were to each other in public often. Yes, we worked next door to each other, but our evenings out were usually just for us, or with separate groups.

This would be one of the few times we would be in a situation like this. And since coming back from the mountains, I wasn't sure how long it could last.

I ran my hand over my chest, ignoring the ache there. There was a reason Kate and I worked well like this. I couldn't offer her forever, and she wanted something just for herself. Only I wasn't sure that was the case for her any longer. I had seen the longing look on her face, the way she had lit up when she could kiss me in public.

I was doing her a disservice by staying on this track. I knew it. I didn't have anything to offer beyond this. But she deserved so much more. Only I didn't want to let her go. So tonight I wasn't sure how long I would be able to keep my hands to myself, no matter how selfish that was.

I finished up the bumblebee tattoo for the grandmother of four, and headed to the bakery next door to get a hit of caffeine. I had stayed up far too late the night before tossing and turning, thinking of Kate. So any caffeine would be good.

I liked the fact that the café was right next door, and I could have just asked for them to bring something over through the connecting door. However, I liked the feel of the place. The large coffee mugs, the scent of baked goods and fresh ground coffee filling the air. Before I had even worked in the building, I used to come here to sit at one of the small tables and work on a few math problems with copious amounts of coffee. It was truly fate's good graces that brought me here for good.

As I walked inside, I bumped into someone, not paying enough attention. I reached out and gripped her elbows, only to realize it was Kate. She held a bakery bag in her hands that was currently pressed to my chest. She looked up at me with those wide green eyes that always took me in when I couldn't think.

I swallowed hard. "Hey."

"Hi, Sawyer." She licked her lips, and it was all I could do not to bend down and capture them with mine. She always tasted so sweet. I loved the taste of her lip gloss, the way that she would nibble at my lips and moaned when I did the same to her. I loved the way she made little mewing sounds as she was close to orgasm. When I would know exactly how to slide my fingers over her clit to send her over the edge. Honestly, the feel of her pussy clamping down around my cock as she came was one of the true wonders of the world.

And with how close we were just then, I had a feeling she could feel exactly how happy I was to see her.

Her cheeks blushed to an adorable pink as she looked down between us. "Somebody's happy to see me," she whispered, and I winked before letting go.

"He's always happy to see you."

"Are you going tonight?" she asked.

I was aware that we were standing in the middle the doorway, though nobody else seemed to notice. I cleared my throat and moved slightly forward so that way she had to walk backward.

"I am. Are you?"

"Yes. Is that okay?" She paused. "I don't know if I'm going to continue to be good at this."

I was aware that a few of our friends were now staring at us from behind the counter. And yet, I couldn't quite let her go.

I was such a damn bastard. "So what if I did this?" I asked. Her eyes widened in answer as I lowered my head to brush my lips against hers.

She smiled against me, and I wanted to take the action back. Because part of me craved more. I wanted to show her off to the world, and make sure she had everything she ever needed for the rest of her life. But I wasn't that guy. And yet here I was, kissing her.

She pulled away first, and I took a step back, wondering if I had messed up.

"I guess that answers that question," she said softly, confusion in her gaze.

Shit.

"It's about time," Raven said from behind us.

We both turned to her as she grinned.

"I don't know what you're talking about," I lied.

"I thought there was something between the two of you, but I was never sure, and Sebastian said I was wrong. However, this is great."

"It's just..." Kate began but couldn't finish her sentence.

"We are just hanging out," I blurted.

Raven frowned as Kate stiffened at my side, but I couldn't put us through anymore lies. At least not lies to myself. Right?

"Exactly. But we will be there tonight. I can't wait for karaoke." Kate smiled brightly, but I could not turn to look at her. Why couldn't I see what was in that gaze of hers?

"Okay. I'm sorry for even blurting anything to you guys. I was just excited and surprised. But don't worry, I won't text the group chat." She winked. "I know all about being the center of attention. I won't do that to you." She reached forward and squeezed her forearms before heading back to the counter, and I let out a breath.

"I probably should have asked."

Kate shook her head. "No. Because if you would have asked, I would not have had an answer. So this is for the best. Keeping secrets started to feel like shame. I don't like doing that."

But wasn't I lying to her?

The fact I didn't have a true answer to that worried me. But I pushed it to the side so I could at least catch my breath.

"Do you want me to pick you up?" I asked.

Her lips twitched. "I suppose we could drive together. Since the cat is out of the bag."

"I suppose that works." I winked, feeling as if we'd crossed a line that we couldn't come back from. "How about I be there at seven?"

"Yes. Okay. That's good."

In answer, I leaned down and kissed her again, before she scurried away back to her office. I found myself no longer in need of coffee. After all, I had enough energy bouncing through my system, and I wasn't sure when I was going to be able to get a full night of sleep again.

"Seriously, this is my favorite bridge," Kate called out over the music.

I just grinned down at her, my arm over her shoulder. It hadn't taken long for everybody to realize we had come in as a couple. People had countless questions, but after a few of our one-word answers, they had stopped asking. I knew I was probably the asshole, but I did not care in that moment. I just wanted to enjoy my night out with Kate. Because I did not know how much longer this would last. How much longer it *could* last.

She looked so happy underneath the multicolored lights, dancing in her seat as Greer sang a popular pop song.

"I didn't know you could have a favorite bridge?"

"I have like seven of them. And this is the top one. It's one of the parts of the songs that you can stand up and sing and shout right along with the artist and feel like a part of it. Not everybody truly does it, but a few artists like her do it perfectly."

"So I guess you and I truly have a thing for bridges."

She blushed and elbowed me in the side.

"Maybe. I can't help it. It's fun. But I promise never to force you to sing a bridge with me while we're on our bridge."

Our bridge.

Because it was the first place we kissed, the first place we had made plans—the first place I knew I was in trouble.

Just like I knew I was in trouble now.

She must've seen something in my face, because her smile faltered. "What's wrong?"

"Just a headache," I lied. "We *are* at karaoke."

"True. It is my turn next. Just don't make fun of me when I go full pop princess up there."

I pushed her hair back from her face and smiled. "I promise. I won't."

"Good. Because I will kick your ass."

"That's my Kate."

Her face softened before she jumped up to go take the mic. She spoke with the organizer for a few moments, going over the song.

I let out a breath as someone sat next to me, and I knew exactly who it was. My brother studied my face, a frown on his, and I was afraid of what he would say. Because my brother knew me more than anyone. While Kate was starting to get to know me far more than I thought possible, Gus knew all of my secrets. Or at least he knew all of them now.

"What?" I nearly barked.

"Are you okay?"

No judgment, no anger over keeping secrets. Just my brother worrying about me. And what was the kick to the chest? I nearly got up and ran out of the building so I wouldn't have to face that question.

Because I did not have an answer for him.

"I'm fine," I lied. "Montgomerys just know all, and Kate and I wanted this to be for us."

Gus shook his head. "I know Kate, because *small town*, and I figured that might be her excuse. She has enough big brothers working with her, that her wanting a moment to herself makes sense. But you? Does she know, Sawyer?"

I shook my head, my jaw tightening. "No. But it's fine. This is just casual. We're friends."

"You're welcome to keep lying to me. I know that you need to. Especially with everything that happened. But don't lie to Kate anymore. Please, because I love you, don't lie to yourself."

Before I could say anything, he got up and went back to his wife, Jennifer, who was giving me a curious look. Because she didn't know either. My brother had kept my secrets even though I didn't have a true excuse other than my own cowardice.

But I pushed it to the back of my mind as I stared at Kate. She gave me a tentative smile, and I grinned back at her, holding up two thumbs.

"Play 'Wonderwall'!" I called, and as she laughed, the crowd joined in, and Kate began to sing. Her perfect alto voice was soothing and catching. It wrapped around my soul, the one thing I couldn't allow, but I ignored all of the warning signs.

And I watched the woman I was falling in love with sing a song about broken hearts and past lives.

I told myself that this would be enough for both of us. That she wouldn't fall along with me.

Because I vowed never to love again. Never to fall fully.

And Kate would just have to understand.

And hopefully so would I.

Chapter Three
KATE

"I'm going to be late to work."

Sawyer just grinned at me in that far too handsome way of his, and I had to press my thighs together. I knew we were playing with fire. We had to steal these moments together as it was. Between his long hours, thanks to his competitive artwork, and the Montgomerys, and my even longer hours, times where we could be with one another felt few and far between.

It was funny because when we had been hiding our relationship—for lack of a better word—it felt as if we had more time together.

But now, all our friends and family knew we were sleeping together, and everything seemed to ramp up.

Including my attraction to him.

I hadn't meant to even be with Sawyer, let alone want him like this.

But I couldn't hold back my desire for him. And the best part was that he was in the same boat.

Every time he looked at me, I felt as if I could melt in front of him.

Just like he was doing right now.

He stood in the doorway to my bedroom, jeans slung low on his hips with the button undone, and I swallowed hard. He hadn't bothered to put on a shirt after taking his morning shower, so I could stare at the long lines of his body as well as gaze upon the artwork covering his skin.

Like most tattoo artists, he had the ink to show for it. He had done some of his own ink on his nondominant side, but most of it was done by friends and fellow tattoo artists over time.

He told me he had a vision of what he wanted, and every single piece had his own flair to it, and I loved it. Every piece was him. And I had licked every single one of those pieces.

I blushed hard as Sawyer slid his hands out of his pockets and prowled toward me.

Honestly, I couldn't think of another word other than prowled. He looked as if he were a large jungle cat, and I was prey in his path.

Only I did not want to run.

"I can be quick for you," he murmured as he came forward, his lips brushing my jaw.

My lips quirked into a smile at that.

"You say that as if it's a good thing."

Sawyer slid his hands underneath my towel and covered my bare pussy. "I can last all night. You know that. But I can get you off with just a flick of my fingers. You are so wet for me that my hand is soaked. Do I do that to you? You just look at me and you are already wet for me? Wet for me all night? Even though I needed to come four times last night? Is my Kate in desperate need for more? Am I not getting my Kate off enough?"

I leaned into his hold as he put his other hand around the back of my neck and pulled me closer. "I'm pretty sure I still have beard burn on my thighs from your attention last night. And that doesn't change the fact that we will be late if we don't get to work."

He slid his fingers between my folds, as if he were gently taking his time, not a care in the world.

And I couldn't help the moan escaping my lips.

"Sawyer," I whispered.

"That's it. That's my Kate. I want to see you come before we leave. I need to see you come. I want you to ride my hand, Kate. Ride it and tell me who owns this pussy."

I rolled my eyes even as he slid one finger deep inside me. He felt so thick within me, even though his cock was wide and stretching every time, I was still swollen from the night before so even his finger felt invasive. But in the best ways.

"I own my own pussy, thank you very much."

He grinned at me before spearing me with two more fingers. The movement sent the shocked breath out of me, and I gasped, arching my back. The towel fell, and my bare nipples pressed against his chest, hard little points of pressure.

"Who owns this pussy?" he growled, sliding in and out of me so quickly that the sounds of wetness filled the room.

"I do," I teased, and he stopped moving, leaving me breathless.

"If that's the case, then you don't get to come. You get to be on edge all day, besides rubbing your legs together, your clit pulsating knowing that it misses me. Because this is *my* pussy, Kate. You know the rules. If you want my dick, you need to know who owns this cunt."

A whimper escaped my lips as I tried to rotate my hips. He tugged on my hair, the sharp pain sending delicious vibrations down my spine.

"Bad girl. You don't get to get yourself off. Not until you tell me what I want to hear."

I smiled up at him, loving that he was like this. Sometimes we were soft and sweet. Other times he owned me. In any other moment, it would bother me to the point of hatred in any other point of my life, but not now. I wanted Sawyer to own me. In body and soul and just in this bedroom.

"You own my pussy," I whispered, my cheeks heating.

He moved his hand from my hair and down to my ass, squeezing. Then he slid his finger around my puckered hole, teasing. "Say it like you mean it."

"It's yours," I rasped. "All of me is yours. Just let me come. Please."

"Because you begged so nicely." And then Sawyer leaned forward and brushed his lips so gently against mine, tears almost pricked my eyes.

But I blew them away quickly as he moved his hand, rubbing the heel of his palm against my clit as he speared me with three fingers.

I went off like a rocket, my knees going weak as my orgasm slammed into me.

I didn't have to fear for my safety as I fell because I knew Sawyer would catch me. That should have worried me. Because I couldn't rely on him like this. Not when we both knew that we needed to talk about what this was. But in that moment, I couldn't care.

Because Sawyer lifted me up into his arms, the strength of him breathtaking. And he slid me down over his cock. I stretched for him, his dick wide and long and everything that I craved.

With my back against the wall, he pushed into me inch by inch.

I've brushed his hair from his face as I moved my hands to grip his shoulders.

"Sawyer," I whispered, tears once again threatening.

"That's it, Kate. Take me."

I nodded, and then leaned forward to take his lips because I couldn't let him see my tears. Only, from the way that his eyes tightened, I knew he'd seen.

But I pushed that away as he moved, his cock sliding in and out of me with the slow progression as I rolled my hips on him.

We moved as one, as if we had been doing this for a lifetime rather than just these stolen moments. I didn't know what I was to him other than the fact that I loved him. He always took care of me, always made sure I came first, and yet in this moment I didn't know what the movement meant.

When he slid his hand between us, his thumb rubbing over my clit, I shattered once more, coming along his cock.

I wanted him to follow me, needed him to follow me. But instead he pulled out of me and moved me to my feet. My toes were still curled from my orgasm, so it took me a moment to realize what he wanted. Then I put my hands on my dresser, facing the mirror as he stood behind me, bracing myself.

"I want to see your face. Let me see your face."

I nodded and arched for him as he slammed into me from behind.

He had one hand on my hip, keeping me steady as he pounded into me. And the other moved up my body, grasping my breasts, plucking at my nipples. He moved up to my throat, squeezing. I moaned into him, needing every inch. When I met his gaze, I fell.

I was in love with Sawyer.

But his eyes had blinked. And I couldn't read him. He

finally moved once more, shouting my name as he came, and I followed him, even as my heart pulsed.

Because Sawyer was pulling away. Not physically, not when he was still deep inside me. But in every other way.

Finally, before I could say anything to put a spark in a moment that we weren't ready for, I bent over to get the towel that I had dropped before.

"We are going to be late, and I should shower. Thank you for the orgasms," I said, my voice so falsely cheerful, that it made my teeth hurt.

Sawyer frowned before cupping my cheek. "One more shower? I promise to keep my dick away from you so we can make it to work."

I nodded, that same too bright smile on my face. "Of course."

He studied my face, as I did the same to him. Only I wasn't sure what he saw, because I couldn't figure out a damn thing on his mind.

I had already washed my hair, so I put a shower cap on as we quickly washed off the evidence of our lovemaking. Only I wasn't sure I could call it that. Not when I didn't know what he felt.

Sawyer turned toward me, soap in hand, and I once again looked at the shattered mirror tattooed over his heart.

Without thinking I traced along the edges, along the names etched on his heart.

I had asked him before, just joking at first, and then he closed up.

So when I slid my fingers over the evidence of his past once more, and he froze, I quickly pulled away and turned so he wouldn't see my face.

I didn't say anything, just like I knew he wouldn't either.

When we finished showering, Sawyer kissed me on the cheek before leaving to change. I did my hair and makeup, telling myself I was making too big of a deal of the evening. Sawyer didn't owe me his heart. Nor his secrets.

I knew that deep down.

And yet part of me, the softest part, needed it. I needed everything. I deserved it. And I hated even thinking about that.

I was nearly finished getting ready as Sawyer came up from behind me and moved my hair away from my neck. He placed a soft kiss along my skin, and shivers wracked me even as I choked back tears.

"Ready for this afternoon?"

I nodded, my eyes closed. "Yes. I can't wait for my appointment." I finally met his gaze in the mirror, my throat tight.

"I'm still annoyed that Nick is the one who gets to do your tattoo."

"Because he's going to help me design it. And I've been putting it off for two years."

"Then I get you next."

I rolled my eyes, my heart swelling. I knew I was thinking too hard about everything. We just needed to take things slow.

"We can do that."

He pressed a kiss to my temple, and then headed out as we had planned. We might work in the same building, but we had different hours. And he needed to head home to pick up a few things anyway.

I knew I would be sitting in Nick's chair for a while, so I made sure I wore a comfortable outfit for work. I was the admin for Montgomery Security, but I was also on my feet often. While I helped with scheduling and being the face for customers when Noah wasn't, I also had to go to certain client sites with the team. Sometimes they needed an extra set of eyes, or somebody to work with the person who needed security. My job had turned into a jack-of-all-trades, and I loved it. I loved constantly being in motion, even when sometimes it was just my mind.

So I put on flowing linen pants and a cute top, and boots that somehow still worked with the outfit. I could wear jeans if I wanted, most of the team did, but I was in the mood to feel a little more flowy. And my arms would be free for whenever I was ready for my tattoo appointment.

The perks of working where I did was that I got discounts at the coffee shop, the art house, and the tattoo shop. Not a huge discount because we wanted to make sure people made their money, but enough that it didn't hurt my bank account if I wanted one of the best tattoo artists in the country.

Part of me knew I should have waited for Sawyer to do my piece, but he could do the next one. The fact that he was thinking about the future made me smile. Because he was thinking we would be near one another at that point.

Or perhaps I was the one *overthinking*.

I pushed all thoughts of that from my mind however and told myself that I just needed to focus on work.

Not on the fact that I had a feeling that Sawyer didn't love me.

It had been all fun and games when we had been hiding, and now we were out in the open, and things felt different.

I stopped by Latte on the Rocks to pick up the coffee order for the team and smiled at Raven. Raven was married to Sebastian who also worked at the tattoo shop next door. The fact that most of the people that worked in these buildings were either Montgomerys or dating or married to one should probably worry me. But in reality, it just meant that people cared for each other, and they actually got along. That wasn't the case with most businesses. We were all professional, and yet I knew that if I needed help, every single one of these people would drop what they were doing to help me.

Just like I would do the same for them. I might not be dating a Montgomery, but I was part of the family.

Warmth spread through me at that thought before I looked over at Sawyer's face.

"It sounds like a full house today," Raven said as she handed over the two containers of drink orders as well as a bakery order.

I rolled my eyes. "We have a group meeting before our big install. And I know there's a few other things going on that they're going to need caffeine for. Thank you so much for getting it out ahead of time."

"It's what we do. Do want some help?"

"No, I've got it. You have thick handles on your bakery bags, so they don't dig into the skin."

Raven grinned. "That was a huge issue we had with our first bags. We had needed to go cheaper at first, even though it was still good quality, but they dug into our palms too much."

"I appreciate it."

But before I could pick up the bags in question, a familiar voice stopped me. "I'm here anyway. So you are going to have to deal with my help."

I turned as Gus moved toward me, and a bright smile slid over my face. "I thought you were coming in late this morning?" I asked. I looked up at the clock and was grateful that I hadn't been too late despite my extracurricular activities with Sawyer that morning. I just wasn't as early as I usually liked.

"Things worked out with the sitter quite well. Thankfully Jennifer and I will both be there. I saw you coming in here and I know we have a full house so therefore you probably would have your hands full. So I'm here to help."

"You're the best, Gus," Raven said as she beamed up at him.

Sawyer's brother just shrugged. "I'm really excited about whatever's in that big bag, so it's a purely selfish thing."

I snorted and let him help me gather the immense order as we headed out the door and toward our offices.

It wasn't that long of walk, and I was grateful that the café shared the same building. Although with the delicious baked goods and the scent that always permeated the air, sometimes it wasn't the best thing in the world.

"So, how's Sawyer?" Gus asked.

I rolled my eyes. "You are not even going to try for subtle, are you?"

Noah opened the door for us as we walked inside, and Gus just chuckled.

"Of course not. But I haven't seen my brother recently because he's been a little busy with someone else."

"Jealous, are you?" Jennifer asked her husband as she took the bags from my hands. "You smell delicious. I'm so glad that Greer and Raven moved in."

"The best decision the Montgomerys ever made was allowing my place to pop up," Ford said as he moved forward as well.

Noah, Ford, Daisy, Kane, and Kingston were all of the

Montgomerys who owned the business. Aria had also been part of it, but had been bought out so she could pursue her photography business.

Hugh, Gus, Jennifer, as well as ten other contract workers, all worked full-time. And I was the admin that had to organize them somehow.

I loved it.

"We are very spoiled," Daisy said with a grin. She leaned forward and kissed his cheek, and her husband just rolled his eyes.

"You say that but then our daughter always expects the same baked goods that we have. She's going to end up with a cavity."

"That's when you have them brush their teeth. It's called parenting," Noah said, and I laughed as Hugh grumbled something, and everybody sat down with their baked goods and copies, and we began our first meeting of the day.

"Kate, can you come out to the Henderson property?" Ford asked.

I looked at my tablet and schedule and nodded. "In three days' time, right?"

"Yes. It's going to be a lot more complicated than what I really wanted but we're going to need someone there to placate him. And since Noah can't be there, I need you to do it."

I snorted. "So I get to be the one in harm's way of his attitude?"

"Hell no. If he's an asshole to you, we don't take the job," Ford said precisely.

I nodded. "That's good to know."

"We don't need to take a job that treats us like shit. We have a waiting list as it is," Daisy said with a shrug. "The client wants us to go over everything twice, so he touches every step. Which might be fine in some cases, but instead, it feels as if he doesn't trust us. And everything takes three times as long. It makes me feel like a jerk for getting annoyed, to be honest."

"I don't mind at all. Plus I get to learn more."

"Thinking of getting your license?" Jennifer asked.

I shook my head. "No thank you. I like the paperwork part much more."

"That's like music to my ears," Noah said with a laugh.

I joined in as the rest of the team made fun of him, and I sat back in my chair, taking as many notes as I could. I loved this job. I wasn't treated like a second level person just because I wasn't out in the field often. I wasn't in charge of high-risk situations, and I didn't do installs and I wasn't a bodyguard.

By the time we were done with our meeting, I was ready to start the day, so I answered a few phone calls and got down to work.

Lunch passed quickly. I ate my salad at my desk, the amount of chipotle ranch dressing on it was probably illegal, and was surprised when my alarm went off.

"Yeah, it's tattoo time," Daisy said, clapping her hands. "If you're still over there when we're working, come on over to see it. If not, I'll stop by on our way out. I can't wait to see the art. Nick is so good."

"And yet Nick has never done a tattoo for you," he said dryly.

Daisy rolled her eyes. "Do you know how many tattoo artists are in my family? I have to get to all of them for at least two rounds before I can get to a non-family member. It's a process."

"Is there a list I should know about?" I asked, honestly curious.

"Yes actually. We each have it written down, at least for our own ink. I'm pretty sure Leif has one for every single person in the family. I don't even want to think about it." She gave a mock shudder, and I laughed.

"I'm going to go drop off a few things in my car, and then head over. I can't wait."

"Actually I need to head out to pick up something I left in the car too. I'll walk with you," Gus said.

I frowned at him. "Is there a reason you're walking with me? I thought we had enough security cameras in the parking lot." There had been a few issues recently, issues that still gave me nightmares. And I hadn't even been the one shot at.

"Nothing like that. I just figured since you were going out, I would go with you. And maybe stop by to annoy my brother."

That made me smile. "That always sounds like a plan."

We walked to the parking lot and parted ways while I dropped off my things and picked up a bag. And then we made our way back to the shop.

I frowned for a moment as two people walked around back, both of them talking in low tones.

Gus cursed under his breath, but I couldn't pay attention to him. Not when I realized one of the people was Sawyer.

"Kate," Gus began, his voice low.

But I ignored him.

Instead I just watched as the woman in front of Sawyer reached up and cupped his face. And Sawyer didn't move back.

Instead he lowered his head, his hands at his sides, as the two of them stood there in that moment, my heart shattering into a million pieces.

But before I could do anything, before Gus could explain his brother's actions, I took a step back and must have made a sound.

Because Sawyer's head shot up, and his gaze met mine.

And I did the one thing that I could do in this moment, when I knew I had been far more wrong than I ever thought possible.

I ran.

Chapter Four
SAWYER

"Fuck."

Laura dropped her hands and cursed under her breath. "I'm sorry. Was that her?"

I glared at Laura, even though this wasn't her fault. No, of course this wasn't her fault. Everything that we had gone through over the past fifteen years had everything and nothing to do with any actions she had made.

Instead, Laura had been the person stuck in the center of complications and brutality and loss repeatedly until there was no escaping.

And I had been the one standing beside her, and yet a thousand miles away.

"Yes. That was her." Guilt rode up my throat, and I swallowed back any bile that had come with it. I had done my best to keep my past in the past. Because every time I was forced to look at it, it felt like I was right back in it.

Feeling every single moment of loss and pain. I thought I was over this. I thought I could look toward the future and see something. Instead, all I saw was the past. It gripped me with its talons and plunged me into its darkness.

There were many reasons why I had left my old life behind. Some of it had to do with my passions and my needs. But a lot of it had to do with the man I used to be. Because I wasn't him anymore.

"You should have told her, Sawyer," Laura whispered.

I froze, my chest tightening.

"Laura is right." I glared at my brother as he spoke, but he held up his hand before I could say anything. "I don't know why you and Kate were keeping a relationship on the down low for so long. But it's not my business."

"You're damn right it's not your business."

"Sawyer," Laura whispered.

I flinched. "I am going to tell her."

"Everything?" Gus asked.

"Don't. Just don't. I fucked up."

"You did," Gus snapped. "Kate is a good person. But the problem is so are you."

My heart raced. "Why are you yelling at me about this?"

"Because you don't think you are. Because every single time you find a little bit of happiness you think you need to push it away. You think it's your fault that anything bad happens in the world." Gus paled and looked over at Laura. "I'm sorry."

"No, that's why I'm here. I wanted to tell him I was doing okay. That he doesn't have to worry about me. Stop worrying about what happened. I know you are never going to be able forget, but I am not on your chest anymore."

"But you are," I whispered, barely resisting the urge to rub my hand over the ink on my flesh. The ink that Kate had traced that morning.

"I'm not a problem. Maybe I should stop coming here. Maybe I should stop visiting you. I only came to tell you I was happy. And that I want you to be as well."

I began to pace, bringing my hand through my hair. "She was already falling away, Gus. This isn't going to help anything."

"I can talk to her," Laura said, her voice soft.

I shook my head. "I don't think that would help anything."

"Well, if your groveling doesn't work, I'll talk to her. Because you deserve happiness, Sawyer. So I'm going to leave and I'm truly sorry if I messed up anything."

"It wasn't you, Laura. I should've said something to her before this."

"And I shouldn't have touched your face. I'm just so used to thinking of you as the boy you were. Just like I was the girl before. But I'm not. Be well, Sawyer. And I'll do the same."

And with that she walked away, leaving me alone with Gus and all of the mistakes I had made.

"How do I tell her?"

"First you need to figure out what you want. Do you love her?"

I looked at my brother, my shoulders tense. "I never thought I would be able to."

"Maybe you should think of an actual answer before you talk to her then. You don't have to love her right now, but you have to respect her enough to know that if you can't love her, you need to let her go."

"I never should have let it come this far."

"That is bullshit. You are my brother. I love you with everything that I have. You are a damn fine uncle and brother-in-law. You are a fantastic brother and son. And yet, you are horrible to yourself."

"This isn't helping anything," I groaned.

"Maybe it's time we have this conversation. Yes, in the middle of our work parking lot. But there hasn't been a better time, has there?"

"Gus." My pulse increased and I couldn't look at him. I didn't want to do this. I wanted to go back to the way things were. Where Kate didn't have to know what I didn't have in me.

"No. You're going to listen to me for a moment. Because you went through hell and I will never understand how life could be so cruel. I will hate what happened to you, and the fact that nothing we had within our grasp could prevent that. But you saw Laura. She is the healthiest I've ever seen her. And she wants you to be happy. Just like we do. Laura, even through the worst, was never selfish enough to want to pull you from your current life. From your future. You were the one that always did that. So let yourself have a future. If not, then what is the fucking point of you being here?"

"Gus," I rasped.

"I was losing you day by day. I thought maybe when you changed jobs and found your art again you were back. But I was wrong. And then you started to smile again. And you started to leave the house. You were happier. It took me forever to realize it was because of Kate. Because you are finally letting yourself *be*. Don't let the past scare you from what could be now. Don't hurt her."

"I'm already doing it."

"So stop."

"You say that as if it's easy."

"Life is never easy. The choices we make, even the ones that feel insurmountable or the easiest thing in the world, always come with conditions. Find her. Fix this. For her and yourself. I love you, Sawyer. But don't let this catapult into something worse."

And with that, Gus squeezed the back of my neck, glared at me for a moment, and then left.

I looked down at my hands, feeling far more hopelessly than I ever had in the past. Or at least for a good long while.

I had to repair this.

Kate deserved better. She always had.

And the problem was, I knew exactly where she had run off to. That should worry me more than anything.

I ran around the corner and down two blocks to where the small creek that surrounded the area lay. We were in off-season, so the creek wasn't full or bubbling, but there was still enough of it for one of those picturesque moments if you were on a certain bridge.

Our bridge.

The one that I had first kissed her on, the one that I had first allowed myself to just be.

Kate stood there on the bridge, her back to me. The slight breeze in the air winnowed through her hair, sending tendrils backward. She turned slightly so I could see her profile, but she hadn't caught sight of me. She looked like a damn goddess there. With her hair billowing around her face, those flowing pants moving slightly in the wind.

As dusk threatened, the streetlights hadn't turned on fully, so I couldn't see her face. I couldn't read her features. That had been the problem the past week or so. Because she had started to hide her feelings from me. But even in our lightest moments, those feelings had broken through. And I had seen the rawness of them so well it scared me.

I was such a bastard.

She stood on our bridge, the one we had first kissed,

the one where I had taken it too far, and there was no going back to what was.

I knew my footsteps were loud as I walked up behind her, but Kate didn't say anything. Didn't move. Instead she just stared off into the distance, her hands on the railing. The metal and wood of the bridge was more decorative than anything. If a strong gust hit it, it was sturdy enough not to be blown away, but bicyclists didn't even use it really. It was just a place that was fragile enough that others stayed away from it, yet sturdy enough for you to walk over, or perhaps take a moment.

Just like we had done before.

And perhaps what we were doing now.

"Who is she?"

Her voice broke me. Because there wasn't sadness there. There wasn't anger. No, it was resignation. I would've even preferred it being devoid of emotion. Instead it was as if she knew where this would lead. And I didn't even know.

"Her name is Laura."

"That's not really an answer. But perhaps it is. Is she why you kept us secret for so long?"

I frowned, resisting the urge to reach out and touch her shoulder. I wanted her to face me. I needed to see her eyes. Only I knew once I did I would lose all sense of what I needed to do. Not what I wanted to do.

"I thought the two of us were keeping our business private because *we* wanted to. Because of your small town, and because it was nice just to have something for the two of us."

She turned then, a wry smile on her face. But it didn't reach her eyes. "You know what, that is true. I'm the one who agreed to secrecy. To hiding what we were to each other. Though I don't really know what that is, so the hiding it had been a good thing. It had given us time to be with one another, without any complications or worries or expectations. Except I might."

"Kate."

She shook her head. "I lied. Because I did have expectations. I didn't mean to. But I kept wanting more. And that's my problem. We never promised each other more. We didn't promise each other anything. So who is Laura, Sawyer? How many other secrets did you keep? How many other trysts did you keep in your pocket? Did you take her up to a mountain lodge? Where you pretended there was one room and one bed?"

"No. It's not like that."

"Then what was it? Where did I go wrong?"

I needed to reach out but I knew she'd reject my touch. And I'd deserve it. "You didn't go wrong. This isn't your fault."

"What is this? And who is Laura?" She shook her head. "Maybe I don't have the right to know. Maybe I'm just overreacting. But this isn't just about that woman touching your face. This is about you pulling back. This is about you not telling me a damn thing when you are inside me and we are naked. So please, just tell me something. Anything at this point."

"She's my ex."

Kate studied my face for a moment, even though I did my best not to show a damn thing, but her eyes filled with sympathy. "And you loved her."

"I did." I shook my head, my throat growing tight. I didn't talk about this ever. Gus and my parents were the only ones that knew. Jennifer didn't even know. I had done my best to bury that so well that I wasn't even sure I could say the words aloud.

"I'm sorry." Kate shook her head and wiped away tears. I made her cry. I had done the unthinkable and made Kate, the woman who tried not to show too many emotions, cry. She met my gaze as she rolled her shoulders back. "I'm clearly touching on something that I shouldn't have. I'm sorry. You're right. We don't have any expectations, and I don't deserve to poke at something that clearly hurts. So I'm just going to go. Because I don't think whatever situation this is...it isn't working anymore."

"Laura and I were together in high school," I blurted. "We loved each other in the way that high schoolers love each other. And while sometimes that could be the deepest of things that grows into adulthood, we were fourteen when we got together. We were each other's firsts and only for years. And then we were seventeen when that little test turned positive."

Kate's eyes widened, but she didn't say anything. For

that I was grateful because I needed to get this out before I broke.

"Seventeen and pregnant. We were juniors." I let out a rough chuckle that held no humor. "We still had another year of school, and Laura was walking around the halls pregnant, with everybody judging. Guys would slap me on the back and call me virile or judge me behind their whispered hands. But they *always* judged her. People were worrying about their next class, AP courses, where to go for college. We were trying to figure out birth plans and what the hell we were going to do with the baby. My parents were supportive. They were pissed off, but supportive. Laura's parents? Not so great. They kicked her out during the first trimester."

"That's terrible."

I let out a hollow laugh. "Yeah. Terrible. So Laura moved in with us, and we got married."

Kate's eyes widened. "You were married?"

Just one more secret, after all. "We got married in the summer before our senior year, when Laura was seven months pregnant. It was ridiculous. You don't get married when you're seventeen. When you're still in high school and having a baby. There were so many other decisions we could've made, but we made those. My parents were pissed off. They had been supportive through everything because they knew we needed that backbone. But we went behind their backs to get married. They didn't kick us out, but the look of disappointment and worry on their faces still haunts me."

"They must be really good people to have been there for you though."

"They are the best." And she had never met my parents because it wasn't as if I introduced anyone to them anymore. I didn't do serious. And yet, Kate had slipped through the cracks, and I hadn't even known.

I was silent for a moment, trying to collect my thoughts. Because I knew what I needed to say next. And since Kate could do the math, she probably knew some of it too.

"On our way home from the first football game of the season, a drunk kid from a rival school veered off the road and slammed into us. I was driving with Laura in the passenger seat. Her due date was in four days."

Tears fell down Kate's cheeks. "Oh Sawyer." She might not know the details of the rest of the story, but she could guess.

"We didn't lose the baby then. She went through childbirth, while each of us had stitches and she had a broken arm, and I had broken my foot. And the baby never took a breath."

"I'm so sorry. There aren't any words for that. I'm so sorry you both went through that so young or even at all. Sawyer…"

"We stayed married until our junior year of college.

Though she had dropped out by then. Everybody who would say such crappy things to us when she was pregnant became the sweetest, most caring people. They brought food, flowers. The donation center where we took all of our baby's items we had accumulated over time was grateful for us. Even though they knew the story. Everyone in our town knew the story."

Kate pressed her lips together, still crying softly, and I reached out to push her hair from her face. I needed to touch her, needed an anchor. Because I was selfish.

"Laura started doing drugs our freshman year of college. First to stop the pain, then just because she needed that new pain. She tried to hide it but was never good at that part. She would take our money and buy more pills. In the end, I wasn't strong enough to help her." My voice cracked. "Her parents took her away. The divorce papers came quickly, and I filed them. It was the best thing they could've done for us."

"Sawyer. It's not your fault."

"I was the one who wanted to go to that football game. Laura wanted to stay at home with her feet up because her ankles were swelling. But I was the one who had to go." And the two of us had fought terribly over that. Because she was afraid I was going to flirt with one of the cheerleaders that constantly flirted with me. None of my reassurances had helped. But we had been teenagers. Those were the feelings that you had. That was the normal part.

Kate reached out and put her hand on my arm, that

touch cementing me in the present when the past screamed at me. "It's still not your fault. It was that drunk driver."

"That kid paid with jail time and memories that he can't get rid of. I don't even think about that kid anymore. He was sixteen. He ruined so many lives. But we all had to deal with the consequences of our choices. Laura is doing fine now. It's why she came here. Because for the past fifteen years we keep sliding into each other's orbits just to say we're okay. We lived a half life and we didn't realize where our lives could be. I had nothing left. Or so I thought." I met her gaze, my hand shaking. "She has a life now."

"And she's the person tattooed on your skin."

I nodded and undid the buttons on my flannel. I pushed it to the side to show Laura's name and Megan's. "My first tattoo. I did the one thing that you're never supposed to do and put a person's name on your skin. But it was after we had divorced. I was only going to put Megan's. Our daughter." I swallowed hard. "But I felt like Laura had died that day too. At least the Laura that I knew. I didn't do this because I loved her. I did this because I failed her. I failed our baby girl."

Tears fell down her cheeks. "Sawyer."

"I'm not good enough for you, Kate."

"Sawyer. You went through the worst thing possible. But that doesn't mean you're not good enough for me. That's not fair to either one of us. I was standing here because I thought you were never going to open up to me. Because you thought we were better in the shadows. And I love you." Her eyes widened as she said it, and I had a feeling she never meant to utter the words. "I didn't mean for it to happen. But it did. I love you. And even if it takes you a while to come to that point, I'm here. Don't give up on us, Sawyer. You are good enough. I promise. If you can try. I'll be here to try too."

Every ounce of me wanted to say yes. To reach out to cup her face and tell her I loved her. To let myself feel for the first time in far too long.

But when I closed my eyes it wasn't Laura in that car.

It was Kate.

It was Kate bleeding out.

It was Kate screaming my name.

And it was Kate lying lifeless in my arms.

"I can't," I whispered, and Kate's face blanched.

"Sawyer."

"I lost something of myself before. I'm not the man for you. You deserve someone that can love you with their whole heart. You deserve the world, Kate. And that's not me."

And with that, I turned on my heel, knowing I was doing this for the best. Kate would get over it. She would realize exactly who I was.

And she would find happiness.

Just not with me.

Chapter Five
KATE

It had taken three days for me to find the courage to smile. At least a smile that didn't feel as brittle as dried out bark.

The problem with working with those you loved, those who could read through those fake smiles, was that you had to continue to work with them even through the peeking gazes that they could not quite hide. Oh, they thought they were doing a good job of it, but I saw the shared looks. Heard the slight whispers after I walked by.

Poor Kate.
Kate will always wait.
Kate will always be left behind.

At least this hadn't reached the town's newsletter yet. I'm sure it would. They hadn't even figured out I had been dating Sawyer, but they would figure out we had broken up. Though, could you really even count it as dating or breaking up? No, it had been hiding, me falling in love, and Sawyer running away from his feelings.

Maybe he would get his head out of his ass and think about wanting to move forward, but it wouldn't be with me. Because he might say he's not enough, but I clearly had been enough for him to at least take a moment and breathe.

He had been through one of the worst things possible, and my heart ached for him. I had shed countless tears over what he had gone through. There weren't any words for that kind of pain. But perhaps it was for the best that he had walked away. Because I had made a fool of myself by telling him I loved him when he had nothing left to give. Perhaps I thought his excuses were a lie. He had so much to give someone, even if his heart ached. Even if his past was a hellscape of horror. But he didn't believe it.

And I wasn't his.

And yet the problem with going to work and putting on a brave face, was that nobody knew why Sawyer wasn't coming to work. And why I looked like I had been run over by a car.

But they all knew something had happened.

I didn't hate Sawyer. I didn't even dislike him.

I knew he was hurting. And all I wanted to do was hold him so he could breathe.

I didn't need him to love me. I just needed him to love himself.

That was why I needed to get on with work and breathe as well.

Nothing good could come from my wallowing. At least in my case.

I would break down later. First, I needed to help with the Henderson account and make sure that everyone on the team had exactly what they needed.

While I was terrible at relationships and being a human being sometimes, I was amazing at my job. If I kept propping myself up enough, I would one day believe I was good enough.

Go team!

"Are you okay?" Gus asked, brow raised. The man had been so caring for the past three days. So gentle. Yes, Gus was the gentle giant usually, but he was the only one who knew as many details as possible. No wonder he had always been so delicate with me. As if he knew one day Sawyer might walk away.

I did not blame Gus for that.

Frankly I didn't even blame Sawyer.

I blamed myself for falling in love.

"I'm great!"

He blinked at me, and I realized I might've screamed that.

"Okay, I'm okay. However I'm here for work. I am going to go meet with Mr. Henderson and we are going to do a fantastic job on this account."

"How much coffee have you had?" Ford asked from my other side, and I rolled my shoulders back.

"One does not discuss how much cold brew one has had."

"Maybe one should discuss it," Ford said, blinking rapidly.

"I got this. You can trust me. I promise."

The guys shared a look, and I wanted to scream even though I knew they were worried about me for a reason. I was acting out of character, and this was my job. They needed me to be sane so I could keep everyone safe. I was the one who needed to get my head out of my ass this time. Not Sawyer.

"Really guys. I'm fine. I'm in a good place to talk with Mr. Henderson over there, and go through all of the plans again on the tablet, while you guys get set up. This was the plan, and you can trust me. I promise."

"We do trust you. That's why we're a little worried about you," Ford whispered.

I winced, even though I told myself I would stop doing that. "You don't need to worry about me. I'll be fine."

"Kate..." Gus began.

"Okay. I'm not fine right now. But that's okay. I don't need to be fine right now. But I do need to be pleasant Kate. Reliable Kate. Hard worker Kate. So that is what I'm going to do."

I made my way over to where our client stood, hands over his chest.

"Hello, Mr. Henderson. I have my tablet here so let's go everything step-by-step."

The man glared at me, his eyes glancing down at my jumpsuit and boots. It was a fashionable jumpsuit, one I thought looked quite professional. I hadn't wanted to show up in stilettos and a pencil skirt. I loved that kind of outfit, but I had a feeling Mr. Henderson wanted to see a little more work in the field versus in the office.

"Kate, right?"

I nodded, my smile bright. "Yes. I'm so glad that you remembered. Now, I do have all the plans in front of me, and I know you wanted to go through them. While the team is working on their set up, you and I are going to have a lot of fun with this app."

"I don't know if fun and apps have ever been said in the same sentence before," he said dryly.

That made me laugh for the first time in three days. "Honestly, you're right. However, I love organization and plans. So maybe it's fun for me."

Mr. Henderson, the man who had glowered and growled for most of the past few weeks when we had been dealing with paperwork, laughed.

Ford, Gus, and the rest of the team froze behind me, their gazes wide as they stared over at the unheard-of sound that was Mr. Henderson laughing.

I beamed at them, because yes, I might be broken and dying inside, but at least I was good at my job.

"Okay now, let's use that enthusiasm for good." I pause. "And by good, I mean spreadsheets."

The older man snorted, and we did indeed get down to business with our spreadsheets.

This project had multiple steps, places where everything could go wrong at once. This wasn't just a home or business that needed to be connected to high-grade security, there were also working parts that had to deal with team members on both sides, high level security issues, and even biomechanics. Noah was great at that part, but for now we needed to go step-by-step.

Mr. Henderson also had to answer to his board, so that would be another meeting. However, I would at least be useful in that.

"You really have this down," the man said after two hours.

I smiled up at him, finally feeling that I was doing something right for once. "I do. But don't sound so surprised. It is my job."

"You guys are the fourth company I've tried working with. Even though they do come prepared, they can't deal with my need to know every single detail."

"Honestly, what they may need is someone like me who can let you go through it while they're going through their parts of the plans. Because you'll notice that you have not stopped anyone from working this entire time. You don't need to second guess what they're doing, you need someone to go through it as they're doing it."

"Exactly. Because I need to be able to explain this to all 500 people that answer to me."

"And it's a big job. So that's what we are here for."

"And if you ever want a job with us, just let us know."

Flattered, I shook my head. "I'm really happy where I am." Even though I felt like part of that was a lie. Because the man that I loved was next door to me, and I had to find a way to get over that.

"Are you trying to poach our favorite admin?" Ford asked, and Mr. Henderson just grinned.

"Damn straight."

"I think this means I need a raise," I said, completely joking.

Ford rolled his eyes. "Now look what you've done," he said, and before I could answer, and explained that I wasn't serious, a sharp crack hit the air.

Mr. Henderson cursed at my side as Ford flung himself on top of me.

My back hit the ground, and the air was knocked out of me as Ford covered my body with his. Three more cracks echoed throughout the air, as Gus was yelling into the radio, and other people were saying things all around me.

And it took those few moments of them doing what they did to keep us safe for me to realize that somebody was shooting at us.

My pulse raced, and my palms went sweaty. I was never out in the field where I could get shot at. That was not my job. This was not a high-security section.

But as my mouth went dry, Ford took me behind a wall, and Mr. Henderson knelt beside me, checking me over.

"Are you okay?" He paused. "I was a medic."

I nodded, squeezing my hands open and closed. "I'm fine. Just got the wind knocked out of me."

"Good. Sit there." He looked over at Ford. "I think they're done."

"Hugh got him," Ford said quietly, and I really hoped that it meant that the guy was down and handcuffed, and not something worse.

My heart raced, and I tried to keep up with the conversation as the authorities arrived, and we explained what happened. They had already set up video surveillance, so the authorities knew exactly what had gone on.

I wasn't privy to the classified information on why the shooting had occurred. And frankly I was fine not knowing. I didn't want that to be part of my job description. It turned out that Hugh had knocked the guy out from behind and had indeed used zip ties to keep him secure. That was the only thing that made it so I didn't throw up right there. I did not like high stress situations. And I felt as though I would pass out if I thought about it too hard.

By the time we made it back to the office, every other team member had shown up as well. There was food, nonalcoholic drinks, and everybody was debriefed. It was all I could do not to throw up.

This had been a merciless week. And all I wanted to do was go home, get in the bath, and have a very large glass of wine.

"Kate? You okay?" Daisy asked, her voice soft.

I nodded, knowing it was true. "I'm fine. Really."

"All of you are required to talk with our team leader before you come back to work though. You know that right?"

I nodded, relieved. "You guys always take care of everyone's health. Mental and physical."

"Damn straight. Do you want a ride home?"

"I got her."

I looked up sharply at the sound of Sawyer's voice, and everybody stopped talking, staring at the two of us.

"If that's okay with her," Sawyer said as his jaw tensed.

"Are you sure that's a good idea?" Gus asked.

And I knew at that moment, if I didn't get him out of there, everybody was going to have an opinion about this. And I barely had one of my own. I didn't know why Sawyer was there, and I didn't even know if I wanted him to be. However, I needed to get us both out of there.

"It's fine. Thank you." I grabbed my bag and headed out of the room before anybody could stop me. This was probably the worst decision I could make. However, I just needed to get out of there.

I pushed past Sawyer on my way to the parking lot,

stopping at the small bridge that connected the parking lot to the main buildings. Then Sawyer had his arms around me and crushed me to his chest.

"I got here as soon as I heard. Are you okay?" He pulled me away for a moment, cupping my face as he studied me. "Are you hurt anywhere? Do you need to go to the hospital?"

I swallowed hard, shaking my head. "I'm fine. Ford pushed me out of the way." I cursed with how that sounded. "It was nowhere near me. But everybody had a reflex, and they got me out of the way. I'm fine."

"I didn't even realize you went out in the field like that. What the hell?"

"It wasn't supposed to be like that. And I'm not usually out there. You know that. We talked about that. Why are you here, Sawyer?"

"I should have been here before. But I can't make up for that other than to say I'm sorry. So damn sorry. You could have been killed. It scared the fuck out of me."

"I thought I didn't matter to you like that. You walked away, Sawyer."

"Because I'm an idiot. Because I wasn't allowing myself to feel. I thought that if I pushed you away, if you were safe in another direction, nothing could happen to you. And then look what happened. You were shot at today. My brother was shot at today too."

The pain in his voice nearly broke me. "We are both fine, Sawyer."

"You keep saying *fine*, but I don't believe it. You could have gotten hurt today."

"You're the one who hurt me." I hadn't meant to scream the words, but here we were, once again on a different bridge, with everything that I'd tried to bury deep spilling out of me. "You pushed me away. I said I love you and you said I wasn't good enough."

"No, I said *I* wasn't good enough," Sawyer snapped. "And I'm not. How could I be when I don't tell you that I fucking love you. Because I do. It scared me so much. Do you know that every time I close my eyes and try to go to sleep, I see you in the car next to me? I see that drunk driver hitting your side as you scream my name, and I can't help you. I see you die in my sleep and I can't help you. I can't do anything to save you."

Blood drained from my face as I stared at him, trying to comprehend his words. I felt like I was two paces back, only trying to catch up. "No. I didn't know any of this. Because you don't tell me anything. I'm not Laura. And it's not your fault what happened. You know this."

"It doesn't help the nightmares."

"Then talk to me. Talk to someone. You can't control fate. You can do everything in your capacity to keep us safe, but sometimes the worst happens. And that's terrible. You can't live your life expecting the worst."

"I nearly lost you today."

"You already did though."

"Give me another chance. I love you, Kate. I knew the

moment I watched you lift your face up to the sky and try to catch snow. In that moment I knew that you could be mine forever if I let it happen. But I wasn't going to let it happen. Because I was so damn afraid. Then you were almost hurt anyway. Please, take me back. Let me figure out exactly how to do this boyfriend thing. I'm not good at it, but I want to try. Please. I'm so sorry. I can't promise I will never hurt you again, because casual hurt still counts. Even when we don't try. But I'm never going to be that stupid again. I was coming back. I was going to come to your house tonight and grovel. And I will crawl right now on this bridge. Please take a chance on me. Again. Please be kind to the asshole that I am. And love me."

Tears were freely flowing down my cheeks as I gripped his shirt. "I already love you. You jerk. But every time you get scared you can't hurt me and push me away. You have to trust me. And yourself."

"And I'm trying with every ounce that I am. Every single day. I'm trying to earn you."

"You already earned me. You just need to find a way to believe that."

"I love you, Kate."

And for a moment, it truly felt as if I were watching this take place from far away. He had said the words multiple times on this bridge, and yet in that moment, it felt as if I had been waiting all my life. And here it was. It wasn't perfect, but it was ours.

I reached out to cup his face. "I love you, Sawyer. Let's not mess this up."

"Damn straight." He cleared his throat. "And I am ready to kneel down on this bridge and grovel."

"You can grovel later." I paused. "Bridge people?" I asked, and Sawyer threw his head back and laughed. It was the most beautiful sight I had ever seen.

"Apparently. I guess this means every time I see a bridge I have to tell you I love you. I don't like that."

When he crushed his mouth to mine, I was lost.

I knew this was only our beginning. But it wasn't an ending.

The world was unfair, it wasn't easy, but it was ours.

And I loved the man who held me with such care it was as if he knew either one of us could break. However, we would be there to catch the other. Something we hadn't allowed ourselves to think about before.

And so I kissed the man I loved on our bridge.

And later when he knelt down on one knee to propose on another bridge, I said yes.

And on yet another bridge I vowed to love him until the end of our days.

In years later when we watched our children ride their bikes over the bridge near our house, I held on to Sawyer, knowing that we were indeed connected by bridges.

And I would go over them every day just to see him smile and mean it, until the end of our lives.

What if It's You

A MONTGOMERY INK LEGACY ROMANCE

What if It's You

A chance encounter.
A second chance.
What happens when Jess and Demi find themselves in each other's orbits and can't say no?

Dedication

*To Emma, Olivia, and Prosecco.
The best trio as inspiration ever.*

Chapter One
JESS

"You really need to get out more."

I rolled my eyes at my best friend's words but didn't voice my opinion on the matter. Alecia was on a tear, so I let her do her thing. Honestly, it was the only way to move on in the conversation when it came to the woman I'd known for years and who stood up for me no matter what.

I merely had to deal with her incessant need to make sure I was happy and healthy.

"There are an abundant amount of ways for you to get out there and just relish in life. To *thrive*. There's that dating circle coming up next weekend. You should totally sign up."

I paused in the action of stretching and looked up at her. "Dating circle? Why does that sound like a quilting circle but with dating?"

I went back to stretching, as the two of us were about to jog in the park. The sun beat down on us, but it wasn't too hot this early in the day. It had snowed overnight and was now melting, so the paths were a little wet and muddy, but still full of people. The fact that it would probably be in the seventies or eighties later just told me it was a normal spring day in Denver, Colorado. There was still snow on the Rocky Mountains and some in the foothills, so I knew we would most likely have another blizzard before we hit true spring and summer. But for now it was perfect jogging weather as long as I wore a light jacket. However, I wasn't sure we would actually get to the whole jogging part if Alecia kept going on about my love life. Or lack thereof.

Finally, my best friend answered me, a grin on her face. "It's not quite a quilting circle...though maybe that's an apt description. It's more like speed dating, but without the pressure of a bell in your ear."

I continued to stare at my best friend as she pulled her dark hair back from her face, before pulling down the sleeves of her jacket to cover her light brown skin as a chill settled into the air with the wind beginning to pick up.

"I don't need a speed date. I just got out of a serious relationship. I'm not quite sure that me going to speed dating, or dating circle as you call it, is the right thing. You told me to get out, and I have tickets to that softball game. That's going out."

She rolled her eyes at me again. "I mean going out

with someone you actually want to sleep with. And Clive does not count as a long-term relationship."

I shook my head at her as we began our slow jog. Alecia could run for miles and did so in marathons. I could probably do a 5K, but I preferred swimming or some form of sport rather than slapping my feet to the pavement over and over again. I got bored easily and needed distractions in order to actually run.

"I dated Clive for eight years. I'm pretty sure that counts as a serious relationship."

At least we had been *together* for eight years. I hadn't realized he had been seeing other people the final three years of our relationship. But what did I know is I'd had to tell myself that I was in love with the person I was living with, and yet it seemed that I had been wrong. Terribly wrong.

"First off, you dated a guy named *Clive* for eight years."

I held back a snort, ignoring the tiny twinge of pain at my stupidity. "There's nothing wrong with his name. There's *everything* wrong with what's inside him."

"At least you're finally agreeing to say that out loud. You never let me talk shit about him, even during the breakup."

I shrugged, as I tried not to let my breathing sound too loud when we made up our way up the hill. Alecia didn't even sound out of breath, when I felt like I should start wheezing any moment.

"I hate being that person that bad talks about the guy you used to date. Because that means you were either completely blind to all his faults the entire time you were together or made terribly bad choices and have the worst taste. How am I supposed to trust myself again if I believe that?"

Alecia just gave me a sad frown as we made our way around the corner, both of us still trying to keep pace with each other. "I love you, babe. With all of my heart, but you're allowed to talk shit about the guy who cheated on you."

"Maybe." A wheeze slipped out, and I ignored the pain in my thigh. I hated running. "Maybe I can pretend it didn't happen and move on with my life. It is much easier to do that."

"If you say so, but since you said moving on, you need to do this dating circle. It's fun."

I gave her a slow blink as we turned the corner, my breathing finally settling once I found the pace that worked for me. Though the fact I kept thinking about my breathing meant I wasn't in the zone like she was, and I'd be bored any moment now. "So says the woman who has been in a serious relationship for three years."

Alecia beamed, her entire face lightening. "Emma and I love each other. They are the best part of me. And I want you to have what the two of us have."

Alecia and Emma were perfect for each other and while I wasn't sure they'd ever want to get married, they fit like they were made for one another. Once I'd thought I'd had it too—now I wasn't sure if it even existed for me. "I don't need it right away. It's been six months. I'm allowed to take my time."

"You're taking your time to the point that any tan you had from your breakup vacation down in the Bahamas with us is gone. You are so pasty white, you're practically a ghost."

I scowled at her underneath the brim of my cap. "I'm a redhead. That tan I had was a burn and freckles because while I thought I'd been reapplying enough sunscreen, I was wrong."

"And you are a gorgeous redhead, but you need to get out more. You just said so."

"I'm out here on a jog with you, and I have my tattoo session scheduled later today. What more do I need?"

"You need a date. When is the last time you went on a date with somebody that made your heart sing and your fingertips tingle?"

We stopped jogging, both of us staring off into the distance. I shook my head at her, wondering why that was the description she went with of all things. And yet, a face came to mind.

I had been twenty right before I met Clive and had been swept off my feet. Yes, Clive and I had been happy for a while, but we had never given into marriage pressure, or the children talk that we had with most people in our lives. Neither one of us had felt the need to move forward in our relationship. And possibly that should have been a sign.

But that tingling feeling? No I hadn't had it with Clive. Clive had been a warm settling.

That tingling all had to do with a woman I hadn't seen since I was twenty. When the semester was over for me, and she had a new, shiny diploma in her hand. After one final party when we had stayed up all night laughing with each other, we had parted ways.

Because each of us had our own lives to follow, and I wasn't even sure where Demi lived now.

"Who are you thinking about?" Alecia asked as we paused at a picnic table. I knew she was letting me catch my breath, so I let it happen.

I shook my head. "No one."

"Don't lie to your best friend."

I rolled my eyes once again. "Just Demi."

"Demi?" Alecia frowned before her eyes widened. "That gorgeous blonde with the high cheekbones? I remember her. Whatever happened to her?"

"She went back to England where her family is. She was only in Denver for the end of her program. And even then, she completed two years here before heading off to Oxford. I mean, *Oxford*. She was brilliant."

"Look at you gushing over someone you haven't seen in eight years. I remember her now. That long flowing blonde hair." Alecia let out a sigh and I kicked her in the shin gently.

"Excuse me, you're the one in a long-term relationship."

"And Emma would have the hots for her too. That's why the two of us are perfect for each other."

"They really do love you," I said with a grin.

"They do. But yes, I remember Demi. And that British accent? Swoon."

"It's always that North London accent that gets to me."

"It is why you watch so many period dramas," Alecia said as she pulled at my arm and made me continue to jog.

"Is it sad that that's the last time I felt that kind of tingling?" I asked, honestly a little worried.

"Yes, but it's fine. You are going to go out there and meet people. And I will make sure that happens. So will Emma. Because we love you."

My lips twitched into a smile. "I feel like you've both adopted your little bisexual friend instead of having kids of your own."

"It is what we do. We watch out for each other. And we can't wait for our baby to grow up and flee the nest."

"I think the phrase is leave, not flee," I said dryly.

"Whatever. Now, when's your tattoo session?" she asked as we finally made our way back to the parking lot. My previously pasty white face was now most likely blotchy red since I always looked like I was overheated when I worked out. I was in shape, but I seriously hated running. The things you did for your best friends.

"It's at three, and Leif and I are really excited to get started."

It had taken me nine months to get into the Montgomery Ink Legacy schedule. It would've taken me even longer to get into the OG Montgomery schedule in downtown Denver. But I happened to live closer to this branch. Everyone at both establishments was so talented, and I really loved the vibe. However, thanks to an article that had hit *Rolling Stone* about them, their waitlist had exploded. They still made time for walk-ins and did their best to accommodate everyone they could, but with what we wanted on my sternum, I needed something more than a walk-in.

"Are you sure you don't want me to go with you?" Alecia asked.

I shook my head. "You have to prep for your road trip. It'll be fine. I trust these people, and I'll show you all the photos."

"I'll be checking in on you. We both will." Her phone buzzed and she took it out of her side pocket, a wide grin sliding over her face.

I knew it had to be Emma, so I pulled out my water bottle from the door of my car and watched as my best friend danced on her tiptoes, texting the love of her life back.

"Well, I could tell who that is," I teased as she slid her phone back into her pocket.

"Oh shush." Then her face changed a bit, a serious

expression sliding over. "I want you to have what we do. I love Emma with all of my heart. They are the reason I get up in the morning most days. And I hate the fact that Clive took so many years of your life."

I swallowed back that familiar emotion—the fact I truly felt like I had wasted time. I reached forward to grip my best friend's hand.

"I lived my life. I don't want to think about wasting time or stealing it. Maybe I will go to that dating circle. Or leave the house more."

"I promise to push you where I think you need to, but not so hard that you hate me in the end."

I gave her a quick peck on the cheek, and then pinched her hip. "You're always going to push. But that's why I love you."

"I love you too, you dork." She paused for a moment before getting a wicked gleam in her eyes. I did not trust that gleam. "You know, Emma always said that we'd be up for poly if you'd like."

"It would make things easier," I said before we both burst out into laughter. While I loved Emma and Alecia, there was seriously zero attraction between any of us. The whole poly thing would've just been easy so I wouldn't have to go out into the real world. And we all knew it.

We said our goodbyes, and I headed home to shower and get ready for my appointment. I was a graphic artist by trade and worked long hours for multiple companies and smaller businesses. That also meant I was lucky enough to be able to work from home, and I was particular when it came to the art about to be laid on my body.

I wasn't the one drawing it, as it would be Leif's art on my skin. Though we had gone back and forth for a while now trying to pick the exact piece I wanted. I was very grateful this Montgomery was patient with me. Because after all this time on the waitlist, I was truly worried that my proclivities in wanting perfection was going to push him away.

But not so far.

Anxious, I ate, showered, did a little bit of work, and then it was time for my session.

Clive had never liked my ink. My right arm was a full sleeve of complex work, and my right hip and thigh were covered as well. At some point I would work on my left, but I was having fun with this one-sided part of me. My sternum would be what connected the two for now, and it felt as if this was my independence piece. Although I wanted this to be about me, not what Clive hadn't allowed me to do.

Hence the intricate artwork and flowers and tiny skulls that were all about me.

And nothing about him.

I made my way to the shopping center that held the tattoo shop, a security company, an art house, and a cute little cafe I loved visiting. Latte On The Rocks made some of the best lattes out there, and so I knew I was going to have to get one on my way in. Apparently, each place was owned by a different Montgomery, and I wasn't quite sure how that worked. I loved my siblings, but I didn't know if I could work with them day in and day out.

I picked up my lavender and honey oat milk latte, the special of day, and practically skipped over to Montgomery Ink Legacy. Music blared out of the speakers, but not too loud, and people were laughing, and there were others with headphones on as they slept through their tattoos.

I wasn't quite sure I was going to be able to sleep through this one like I had with my thigh tattoo. The sternum was going to hurt like a bitch.

People from all walks of life were in the booths, some with big beards and full tattoos, some with prim and proper dresses on and a bright smile as they got a tiny ankle tattoo. Everybody just looked so pleased to be there, and it was no wonder they had made the news.

Leif Montgomery walked toward me, his dark hair falling over his bright blue eyes as he grinned. He had a strong jaw, a slight beard, and what looked to be fresh ink on his forearm.

I pointed at it and grinned. "A new tattoo?"

He tilted his chin over at a big, bearded man in the corner, and smiled.

"Nick finally got me."

Nick grunted, but the woman in a business suit perched on his lap just laughed. "Ignore him. He's grumpy because I have to go out of town for a week."

"He's always grumpy, and I don't think we need that much PDA in this family establishment," Leif teased, his eyes filled with laughter.

"So says the man who practically made out with Brooke when she came over to have lunch with you earlier," Nick said pointedly, and I laughed as the two of them continued to razz each other.

"Come on over, are you ready for this?" he asked, and I nodded.

"I'm really excited."

"Well let's get to it. We're going to be in the private room in the back, though Tasha, my apprentice, is going to be in the room with us. No matter what, you're going to be covered, and we're not one of those shops that say you have to be topless in order to do the sternum tattoo."

I held back a shudder at some of the stories I'd heard, but the Montgomerys weren't like that. "It's why I came to you guys instead of some other place."

"You wouldn't believe the shit some people pull. But don't worry, we're going to make this work."

Tasha, a woman with blue hair, all curves, and a bright smile waved at us. "I saw the artwork, and I'm really excited to see it on your skin."

"So am I."

While we would be in the private room, the door was going to be open since it wasn't like I was going to be showing everybody everything, and I didn't mind. I wanted to be part of the group and the enthusiasm of the tattoo shop.

So as I settled down on the chair, going through the stencil, I froze as a lilting voice hit my ears.

"Jess?" a familiar voice whispered, and I froze, and turned to see someone from my past.

"Demi?" I asked, my voice a breathy gasp.

She had cut her hair since I had last seen her. Now it was shaved on the sides, but long up top so it was almost bob length when she swooped it over. Her bright blue eyes shone underneath the lights, and those cheekbones could once again cut glass.

She wore skinny jeans and a white button-up top tucked in at the front, but the three top buttons were undone so you could see her lacy undershirt, which was more like a bra.

She also had a fresh tattoo on her forearm and looked to be like an angel sent from the gods to bring me back to a time where everything had been a little easier, a little lighter.

"It is you," Demi said, that British accent doing things to me I didn't want to think about.

"You two know each other?" Leif asked, and I was pretty sure he could feel the heat between us. The chemistry that I had always had with Demi pulsated, and I did a quick check on her left hand and realized there was no ring. I caught Demi doing the same thing, and we both looked at each other, that wide smile of hers making those dimples pop out.

"I'm about to get a sternum tattoo, do you want to watch?" I blurted, and Demi just laughed.

"I would love to. I am going to go get a coffee first though, do you need anything?"

I pointed to my fresh iced latte on the bench, and she grinned.

"Okay, I'll be right back. Don't leave, okay?"

I swallowed hard and nodded.

"I'll be here."

"Good."

And then she walked away, and I couldn't help but notice the way that her ass filled out those jeans. There was a pointed clearing of a throat beside me, and I looked over at Leif.

"What?" I asked, my voice high-pitched.

"Nothing. Sebastian just finished the work on her, she's been in here a few times. Single from what I know. And freshly moved from London."

I narrowed my gaze at him, even as anticipation slid through me. "You know all this, do you?"

"People talk when they're in the chair. And I am pretty sure the entire room felt the chemistry between you."

"Don't call up the U-Haul just yet," I said dryly. He threw his head back and laughed, Tasha and the others who had heard joining in.

And when Demi came back to sit next to me, I was already on my back, the sound of the needle whirring filling my ears. "It's going to be a beautiful tattoo," Demi said softly, and I swallowed hard, ignoring the pain because I couldn't keep my gaze off her.

"I didn't know you were back."

"I didn't know if you would want to know."

And then even though Leif was literally poking a needle in and out of my skin repeatedly, I felt nothing. I was just looking at the woman who had made me smile all those years ago and had to wonder exactly why I couldn't look away from her.

And why I would ever want to.

Chapter Two
DEMI

"So you met her years ago? And now you guys have been texting for two weeks. I don't know, it seems kind of fast for you to get all bubbly and happy like this."

I paused in the action of buttoning up my top as my sister droned on and on about the timeline of my...whatever this was with Jess.

Considering Jess and I hadn't had a true first date yet, I wasn't quite sure how this was moving too quickly.

"It is our first date. It's not moving at the speed of light, as you call it. We've been texting because I've been out of town. You know I've been working, so this is our first entrance into the dating world. It's going to be fine." I wasn't sure if that last part was for her or me.

Elena just raised a brow. "You always get so gaga over anyone you date."

"I don't know why that's a bad thing. And I do not go *gaga*. Not that I even know what that means."

"You put everything into it. You trust them with your whole heart. And then when they break you, all you do is mope around, and I hate seeing you in pain. Maybe just protect yourself a bit more with this one."

Frowning, I finished getting dressed before going to push back my hair and figure out what to do with it. It had been down to the middle of my back for as long as I could remember. I had learned how to braid it, work in countless ponytails, curl it, straighten it, and just have fun with it.

And then on a whim, I had decided to do the big chop. Shave the sides of my head, and let the front come down over my face. Meaning I was constantly pushing it back and trying to figure out if I wanted a pixie cut, a short haircut, or something in between.

While it didn't feel like me, it totally felt like me at the same time. Then again, moving back to Denver after spending so much time in England felt like coming home. Which was odd, considering I had been born in England. I had only come to Colorado for a two-year program to work with a certain professor, and now I was back, once again working with that professor but as a colleague, rather than a student. I wasn't in the university program, rather working in industry, but he was the person I went to for advice, and quite nicely, vice versa.

"I really like that haircut," Elena said after a moment, and I met her gaze in the mirror.

"Really? You kept trying to curl it and play with it when I first got it."

"Because I've never seen you in that kind of style. I'm used to you looking all girly."

I rolled my eyes. "I still look girly, just with a short haircut. Way to be rude."

Elena cringed. "Sorry. I do like the haircut. You look hot."

"And that's so something I want to hear from my baby sister."

She laughed before hugging me from behind and kissing cheek. "I adore you. Have fun tonight and be safe."

"I don't know quite how to take that," I said after a moment.

"I just want you to protect yourself. I mean, you guys just happened to meet in a tattoo shop the day you're both getting ink? It feels a little too like fate, and you know I don't trust that."

I pressed my lips together since this was the same woman who, not five minutes ago, was worried I was moving too quickly. Now she was bringing up fate. "No, you're even more analytical than me. Don't worry, it's just a date. The fact that I'm even getting out there should make you happy."

"That is true. I was starting to think you were a hermit once we moved back here."

"Well, make up your mind. Am I supposed to be the hermit, or go out and have fun and get my heart broken?"

"How about you do neither?"

With that, Elena left me alone to my own devices, and I grabbed my wallet and keys, knowing that I was going to be later than late if I didn't get out of there in time.

In the two weeks since I had seen Jess, we had texted every day. Probably a little more than I had ever texted in my life. It had been surreal seeing her again after all that time.

We had known each other in school of course, but not that well. And then one night at a party, we had sat up for hours, and I had bared my soul in a way I'd never done so. We hadn't even kissed, hadn't even made a move on each other in any way. But there had been a connection soul-deep that should have scared me but hadn't.

But I had moved the next week and had been scared to do anything that might lead to something more. Not that I'd been so into myself I'd thought it was a sure thing. But I knew deep down, I'd catch feelings. And worse—what if she hadn't? And she had known I was moving as well, so it wasn't as if I had ghosted her. Whatever could have been… just hadn't happened.

Now it felt as if maybe everything was happening for a reason. Maybe I was leaning way too much into this fate thing.

I got into my car and drove down to the ball field, holding back a laugh at the date we had decided to go on.

Parking was a breeze thanks to my valet pass from work, so I got out quickly, slid my sunglasses back on, and searched the crowds for the woman with auburn hair and deep-set brown eyes. I could gaze into those eyes for far too long, and while that should worry me, it didn't.

Things happen for a reason, and what if it was okay to just lean in.

I spotted Jess quickly, and my heart raced.

"Keep it cool," I whispered to myself, as Jess came forward, wearing cut-up jeans and a jersey for the local team. She had on tennis shoes that didn't tie up but looked untied at the same time, and sunglasses perched on the top of her head. When she put her hand over her eyes to block them from the sun, I just shook my head.

"Hey there. You made it."

I smiled and tapped her sunglasses down so they perched on her nose.

"Oh. I always forget."

"So says the woman with a fairer complexion than me."

"I'm not quite sure about that. You've been in England for a while and out of the sun. Though I *am* slathered in sunscreen."

"Same. Thankfully, we should be in the shade for most of the game. I know where to choose my seats thanks to my coworkers."

"That sounds like a plan." We stood there for a moment, just staring at each other, and yet awkwardness didn't settle in. It just felt normal. As if we had just been waiting for this moment.

I reached out and took her hand, twining my fingers with hers. "Ready to head in?"

She beamed, a single dimple on her right cheek peeking out. "Yes. But I do need a hotdog. It's tradition."

Moving across the arena, I pulled her in the direction of the food and merch areas. "You know, usually I hate hotdogs. I mean, what's in them?"

"You don't ask those things."

"Exactly. However, it is a sporting occasion. And we are watching our state's major league softball team kick some ass."

Warmed, we made our way to the line, the number of people surrounding us growing as we got closer to the first pitch. "That's what I like to hear."

"A hotdog it is. Because it is some form of sports ball."

"What do you get on your hotdog?" Jess asked, her gaze on the menu in front of us as we waited.

I paused as we stood in line. "I feel like this is an important question I don't have a good answer for."

"I'm a purist. Which I know is crazy. I either go plain or a full chili dog."

"That sounds disgusting," a tall man said from beside her, but we ignored him.

"Well, I don't feel so bad then," I said with a laugh.

"So what do you get?"

"I like mayonnaise and mustard," I mumbled, and Jess burst out laughing.

The same guy shook his head. "Not a single layer of ketchup between you. However, that just means more for me."

I fist-bumped him, and then Jess did as well, and we ordered our dogs and beers.

"There's nothing better than a hotdog and beer at a softball game."

"I can think of a few things better," I said, meeting her gaze.

"Look at you," she whispered, though her cheeks matched her hair in that moment.

We took our seats, and I did indeed try a taste of her chili dog, and it wasn't that bad. And she was hesitant at first to try the mayonnaise but liked it in the end.

"I cannot believe I just ate that," Jess said with a shudder, and I slid my arm behind her in the seat, and we watched the game, talking and laughing the entire time. By the end of it, we were still hungry, but it wasn't quite time for dinner yet.

Jess smiled over at me as the game ended. "There's this gelato place in easy walking distance. What do you think?"

"I freaking love gelato. However, now I'm afraid of what your favorite flavor is."

"I don't have a favorite flavor. I go for whatever sounds good in the moment. Usually the special. As long as it's not bubblegum."

I nearly gagged and glared at her. "There's such a thing as bubblegum gelato?"

"I didn't think it was an American thing," she said with a laugh.

My stomach revolted at the thought, but I let it go. Sort of. "The horror. The actual horror. However, I really only like pistachio."

"That's okay, but I guess that means you're not going to want to share?"

I took her hand, laughing. "Of course I'm going to share. That's the whole point of getting different flavors."

"Okay, so I will be the wild card, and you'll be the steady one."

"That doesn't sound too bad."

We walked hand in hand and ordered our gelato. She ended up with this rocky road peanut butter monstrosity that tasted amazing. The flavors burst on your tongue, and I couldn't help but smile as she fed me off that little spoon.

"See? You have to try new things."

My tongue darted out, licking gelato from my lips, and her gaze went straight there. "I really don't mind trying new things," I said softly, my voice going slightly deeper.

We stared at each other for a moment before Jess finally broke the silence. "I can't believe you're back in town."

I paused, trying to formulate my answer. "It felt like home. Which is weird to say, but I love it here."

"I don't think I could be anywhere else. Though I've never been to England."

I wanted to show her, but that felt a little too fast for a first date. Maybe. "I'm from North London, and my family's still there. Though my sister lives here too."

"Oh? I didn't know she had moved here."

"I hadn't mentioned it?" I asked, and then she shook her head. "Yes, she's going to the same school I did. I don't know if she'll stay here, but she found a guy that she really likes. So who knows."

"I'm just glad you're here. Which sounds super cheesy, and way too big this soon."

"I was thinking about how the fact that we saw each other after so much time felt right... Now *that* felt like too much."

We stood there, melting gelato in hand, as I watched the way her throat worked as she swallowed. "What do you say we go back to my place and watch a movie?" she asked, and I nearly had to press my thighs together.

"That sounds like the best plan."

Somehow, I followed her to her house, trying not to drive erratically. I pulled into her driveway, following her into the garage before she closed it behind us. And then my lips were on hers. She let out a shocked gasp, before she wrapped her arms around my shoulders, and kissed me back.

She tasted of gelato and Jess.

I sucked in a breath, trying to focus. "I wanted to do this all those years ago. But I knew I was leaving."

"I was really fucking sad you didn't do this all those years ago," she whispered against my mouth, and then I was tasting her again, needing her.

"You know, I was going to take this slow," I said after a moment, licking my way down her neck. She tugged at my shirt, untucking it from the sides.

"Same. I was going to act cool, slowly get to know you, and then by date like five, I'd talk you into bed."

I laughed, before leaning down slightly to kiss her forehead. I was a few inches taller than her, but when she wore heels, we were the same height.

I really wanted to see her in heels.

Just heels.

My brain scrambled to keep up with her words. "Well, if we count our time at that party as a first date, it's been how many years?"

Her eyes darkened. "Exactly. And getting the tattoo was a second date. And then all of our texting can count as one."

"Of course, and then softball and gelato? That's two dates right there."

"It's just plain math."

"Girl math is the best math."

She kissed me again, and I was lost. She led me into her bedroom, both of us needing to take breaks so we could touch each other, taste each other. And as we stood at the end of her bed, a giant king-size with a fluffy white duvet and olive pillows, I kissed her harder before pausing.

"Shit. What about your tattoo? You got it on your fucking breastbone."

"Sternum tattoos take a few weeks to heal, but I am all good. I'm not sore anymore. I just have to be a little careful with the rubbing."

I swallowed hard, and then tugged on the bottom of her shirt. "So no rubbing in between your breasts."

"That means I couldn't wear a bra." And as she pulled the top of her shirt over her head, I swallowed hard.

Her breasts were bigger than mine, overfilling my hands. I reached out, my thumbs gently brushing along her tight nipples. She sucked in a breath, her mouth parting.

I licked my lips, my stomach tightening. "So I'll just have to be gentle this time."

"Just a little bit."

"The ink though? It's fucking brilliant."

The intricacy of the tattoo itself was stunning. I could stare at it for hours, and not just because I held her breasts in my hands.

"I've wanted it for a while, and I'm glad I did it."

I plucked at her nipples, pinching, loving the way that she sucked in a sharp breath. "You look damn beautiful."

"You seem far too dressed."

I laughed before leaning down and sucking one nipple

into my mouth. She gasped, sliding her hands through my hair as she pressed me closer to her chest. I had to be so gentle, as I never wanted to hurt her, so I bit and sucked, before laving attention to her other breast.

"Demi," she whispered.

"I've been waiting for you to say my name like that all day."

And then I pulled back and undid the rest of my buttons. The shirt fell to the floor, and she reached forward and undid my bra in an instant.

My smile widened at the efficiency. "I so love sleeping with women. We are the best at taking off bras."

"I know, right? It's all the practice."

She kissed me hard on the mouth, as my bra fell to the ground, and my breasts pressed against hers. "Damn it, I knew I would love the color of your nipples."

"Thinking about them often?" I asked, laughing.

"Far too much."

And then we were tumbling on the bed, her head lowered to suck and taste my nipples. We both writhed together, taking our time. I needed to be gentle with her, and I knew that, but I couldn't help but tug on her hair just a bit. When her eyes darkened, I gave a wicked grin.

"Did you like that?"

She nodded, her mouth parted, as I leaned down and slid my hand underneath the button of her jeans.

"How much did you like it?" I asked as my fingers slid

between her folds. "You're so wet. Soaking me. Have you been wet all day?"

"Yes, damn it. Even when I text you, I'm wet. And I have work to do."

"Poor baby. All wet and no one to get you off." I narrowed my gaze. "Unless you've been getting yourself off?"

She rocked on my hands, and the tip of my finger slid inside her. She moaned, and I went a little deeper, though with her jeans in the way, it was harder.

"Of course I got myself off." She blushed. "Once when we were texting."

"You should have told me." I leaned over and bit her earlobe before whispering, "Because I did the same thing." My finger pressed against her clit, and she came, shaking against me as she moaned my name.

I shifted down on the bed, undid her jeans, and pulled them off. "That's it, that's what I've wanted to see." I shucked her shoes, jeans, and panties to the side, and then I was between her legs, spreading her out before me like a feast.

"Demi."

"This is what I've been thinking about all day." And I kissed up her legs, taking my time between her thighs, gently biting. She writhed, but I didn't touch her there, taking my time.

"I can't, I can't." She reached down, tangling her hand in my hair, bringing me closer to her pussy.

"Well then, let's see exactly what I've been missing." And then I licked between her folds, loving the way she bucked off the bed. I pinned her down at her hips, taking my time, using my tongue around her clit, and then diving between. When I shifted to slide one finger and then a second inside her, she moaned, both of us trembling. I spread my fingers, rubbing hard against her soft inner walls.

"I can't—I can't do this again."

"You can and you will." And then I moved quicker, sliding three fingers in and out of her with rapid succession as I rubbed my thumb along her clit. I slid my free hand up to hold her breasts, being careful of the tattoo, and then she came again, clamping my fingers in such a hold I could barely catch my breath.

I pulled out of her and slid my fingers in my mouth, loving her taste. Her eyes went impossibly dark, and then she leapt.

Laughing, we wrestled on the bed and she had me pinned, though I let her. When she shoved off my pants and slid between my legs, I tugged on her hair, loving the way that she gasped at the slight pain.

"So you're going to taste me? Eat me out like a good girl?"

"Damn straight," she said with a laugh, and then she was licking and sucking, and I couldn't think. I had one hand in her hair, guiding her, the other on my breast, pinching my nipple. And when I came, I whispered her name.

Soon we shifted again, this time with my head between her legs, her head between mine, and we sucked, and we ate, and we pleasured each other until I could hardly breathe.

Then we found ourselves facing each other, my leg between hers, her thigh between mine, as we rubbed against each other—arching to the point of pleasure. And when we came one more time, I held her close and knew that letting her go would be the hardest thing I'd ever done.

So maybe I wouldn't let her go at all.

Chapter Three
JESS

"I don't know if I'm really an antiquing person," I said with a laugh as I leaned into Demi's hold.

"I'm totally not one, but I'm learning. My sister comes down here often and said I might like looking at this one place that has reasonably priced furniture. Not quite antique, but unique enough. Especially if I want to sand it down and refinish it."

I looked over at Demi and raised a brow. "You know how to refinish things?"

Demi snorted. "I've done a few projects—not well, mind you—but I'm learning. I figured we could do it together if all else fails. You're better at crafty things like that than I am."

I slid my hand over hers, our fingers tangling as we walked down the downtown streets of Boulder. We had taken the drive up to enjoy brunch and antiquing. The brunch wait was at least two hours, even on a weekday with a reservation, but that was fine. They would text us to come back, and then we would eat, have some mimosas, and go back to shopping. Walking around the college town that had exploded over the past few years was always nice. And frankly, the cities of Denver, Boulder, Colorado Springs, and Fort Collins were slowly becoming one megacity with the urban sprawl. So being able to find something a little different over time was nice. Plus you couldn't beat the mountain views here.

"Have you ever been up to Estes Park?" I asked and Demi shook her head.

"I haven't. Isn't the Stanley Hotel up there?"

I nodded, thinking of the historic and famous hotel that had everything to do with *The Shining*. "Yes. You can stay the night there, though I don't. I'm not in the mood for horror and ghosts, even if it might not be real."

"I heard the drive up there is beautiful though."

"It's gorgeous. And honestly, I like going up there when people come to visit from out of town so that way I can go to the chocolate place."

"Of course you would want to go to the chocolate place," Demi said with a laugh, squeezing my hand.

Technically, if we were counting dates, this was number eight. Or perhaps eleven. I wasn't quite sure where we were counting from, and in the end, I knew I would quit counting soon.

Things just felt good.

And that was probably a little scary, but then again, I liked that feeling. It had taken a single meeting at the Montgomerys' for everything to change, and I still couldn't quite believe this was real.

"Okay, so I guess we're going to have to find a chocolate place *here*." Demi began to look around the shops, a smile playing on her face.

In the past two months, we had spent every free moment we had together. Which sadly wasn't that many. Between both of our jobs, and life in general, it wasn't like we spent twenty-four hours a day together. And while everything had clicked between us, it was still relatively fresh and new. Sometimes it felt as if I was waiting for the proverbial shoe to drop. And that wasn't fair to Demi or to me. But it wasn't as if I could hold back. And that should worry me.

"Okay, you have scrunchie face."

I blinked up at my girlfriend. "What is scrunchie face?"

"You're thinking so hard that your nose scrunches in that cute little way. And while it is adorable, it worries me because I don't know what's going on in that brain of yours. Are you doing okay? What's wrong?"

I shook my head and gestured towards one of the freestanding benches they had for people to sit down and enjoy the architecture. We each took a seat, and she turned sideways, one leg up, her other foot on the ground so she could face me.

"Talk to me, Jess."

Her lyrical voice washed over me, and it felt like I had known her for ages. Honestly, it scared me how much everything felt right after only two months. While I had been with Clive for eight years. Eight years where I had thought he had been the one, but I had never been able to move forward. And he had never even tried. We hadn't been each other's person, and instead he had been with other people.

"I'm just thinking. I'm enjoying the time we're spending together…"

Her face fell, concern filling those beautiful eyes of hers. "That worries me, you know. The way that you say that as if there's an ending."

I cringed and reached out to grip her hand. She looked down at our connection and let out a slow breath.

"That's not what I'm saying at all. I'm really enjoying this. I love being with you, I love going antiquing even though neither one of us knows what we're doing. And I love the fact that we are waiting for two hours for brunch and neither one of us cares. It was in our schedule for the day knowing that we would wait. It just makes sense, even though we could have easily eaten at home."

"They have cream cheese stuffed French toast and crepes. Of course, we're coming here," she teased, but I still saw the concern in her gaze. "It's okay if you're worried that things are going too well. That's what I do often. My lot in life is to always wonder if I'm doing things wrong or if things are going well. I mean, I was a walk-in for that tattoo."

My eyes widened as I stared over at the woman who haunted my dreams and my living memories. "What? How did you manage that?"

"Each of them takes at least one walk-in a week. It's not a true walk-in. I called to see if they had any space for the week, and they fit me in. So I wasn't even on the waiting list. Sort of like a lottery, I guess? And I got lucky. And well, it happened to be the same day as yours. Which should honestly worry me a bit at the whole idea of fate, but maybe it's just because I needed a tattoo, and so did you."

I slid my hands over my sternum, where my now fully healed ink lay. "I almost canceled."

Her eyes widened "What?"

"Clive never wanted me to get this tattoo. He never liked tattoos on women."

Demi's eyes narrowed. "Are you serious?"

"Very serious. He thought it was trashy. And yet, I'm covered in tattoos."

"And so every time you got a new tattoo it was like telling him to fuck off?" she asked.

"Maybe. I just wanted to be *me*. And I thought with

every additional tattoo, when he stayed, maybe I was changing his mind. But it turned out he was just finding other women *without* tattoos to sleep with."

"I really hope that I never meet this man. Because if I do, I might actually have to kick him."

"He's not worth the foot pain."

"You say that, but I'm still upset that he hurt you."

I shook my head, still annoyed at what could have been—though I'd told myself never to live within those regrets. "The sad part is, I was almost relieved that it was over. Even though yes, he hurt me. But I thought he loved me. And I don't know… I didn't know if I was ready for being serious with anyone afterward."

Demi's eyes tightened for just an instant, and I nearly cursed myself.

"I'm sorry, I probably shouldn't say that to the woman that I'm seeing."

"No, I understand. We haven't had that kind of talk." She paused. "And I don't know if I'm ready for that kind of talk in public like this."

And I had just killed the mood. "Did you know that my friend Alecia was going to make me go on a dating circle and then I didn't have to because I met you that night?"

"Alecia said what?" she asked, throwing her head back and laughing. The two had met soon after our softball date that had turned into something more and had clicked immediately. In fact, Demi had met most of my friends and everything just made sense. She had slid into the friend group so easily it was a bit disconcerting. In fact, everything about this relationship was disconcerting because it felt so stress-free.

"I'm glad you didn't have to. Though I still don't know what a dating circle is."

"Thank you," I said, throwing my hands in the air. "That's what I said."

"You don't have to deal with that. Although I kind of want to know who Alecia would've set you up with," she said, teasing.

"I don't know, she's not really great at setting people up."

"Ooh, tell me more."

We stood up then and made our way back to the restaurant because we were at that two-hour mark. My phone buzzed halfway there, and I figured that was great timing. We went straight to our table, a tiny two-top on the balcony so we could see the mountains, and everything settled into place just a little bit better. We ordered our mimosas and coffee, and indeed got the French toast and crepes. I added a savory omelet to share, and I figured we'd want leftovers.

"Okay, tell me about some of her bad dates," Demi said, and I grinned.

"Well one time she introduced Claude to Rose, and it turned out that they were second cousins."

Demi choked on her mimosa and set down the champagne glass. "Are you serious? Did they know before or after." She paused. "Actually, don't tell me."

"They knew as soon as they met each other. She hadn't given last names, trying to be mysterious, I guess. But they showed up at the restaurant and laughed because they went to numerous family reunions together because they had the same grandma."

Demi wiped her face, and I just laughed with her. "Okay, that is bad."

"Alecia always said that they all would've gotten along well. Probably because they had similar genes," I said dryly, and Demi cracked up again.

"Demi?" a soft voice asked, and I turned to see a woman with blonde hair past her shoulders and bright eyes move forward. From her cheekbones, I knew exactly who this was.

I grinned as Demi turned, a similar smile on her face. "Elena. What are you doing here?" She stood up quickly and hugged her little sister tightly. "Elena, this is Jess."

"Oh it's so nice to finally meet you. My work schedule has been so hectic lately that we haven't been able to meet."

I stood up and gave her a hug, since she seemed to be a hugger, and stood back to smile at her. "I am so glad to finally meet you. What are you doing here? I thought you lived down in Denver."

"Same. But we heard about this brunch place and got on the waitlist."

"Same," Demi said. "Where's your table?"

"Well we just finished eating, we were in the front. Clive is paying though."

I froze at the name, but knew it had to be someone else. Clive didn't live in Boulder, and there were plenty of men named that. But Demi stiffened as well, and turned to me, worry in her gaze.

"Clive?" she asked, her voice strained.

"Well Robert. But his name is Clive Roberts. I always call him by his last name, but I've been hanging around his friends so much who call him by his first name, it's just stuck. Oh he's on his way here. I'm so glad that you can finally meet him. It was totally serendipitous that we're all here."

But I could barely hear her as she continued to say words that probably meant something important. Because the roaring in my ears intensified, and I watched as my ex-boyfriend came forward. For some reason, everything felt like a slap in the face. As if no time had passed and I was stuck on this Ferris wheel of hell.

His blond hair was pushed back though he was looking down at his phone. He had that strong jaw that led me into temptation in the first place. And was currently rolling up his sleeves of his long sleeve shirt to show off his forearms.

I used to love those forearms.

Elena smiled up at him, clearly unaware of the

tension. "Clive, honey. This is my sister and her girlfriend. Isn't it funny that they're here too?"

Clive finally looked up and froze like a deer in headlights.

We stood there, the four of us, with Elena's face finally falling as she looked between us, confusion etched on her features. "Jess? What's wrong?"

Demi cleared her throat and finally spoke into the silence. "Clive, it's well... I'm Demi. Elena's sister."

Of course Demi had been on the verge of saying nice to meet you, but it wasn't. Was it?

My world couldn't be this small. Millions of people lived here, and yet, it had to be *him*.

"What's wrong?" Elena repeated, and I put on a bright smile because this wasn't Elena's fault. At least I didn't think so. From what Demi had told me, Elena and her boyfriend hadn't been dating that long. Meaning she wasn't one of the people that he had cheated on me with. And part of me wanted to warn her about him, but I wouldn't yet. I would just try to get through this tableau, and not let the punch to the chest worry me.

"Sorry, Clive. Fancy meeting you here." There, that sounded like an adult. A slightly snarky adult, but an adult, nonetheless.

He blinked at me. "Jess. I didn't realize you were Demi's girlfriend."

Elena looked between us, before her eyes widened, and she pressed her lips together.

"Small world, isn't it?" Demi asked, and as our food grew cold behind us, and people were starting to notice the awkward meeting, I realized there was no way for me to get out of this with any form of grace.

"Oh," Elena said after a moment, her mouth parting. "Well. We should be off. We're in everybody's way. I'll talk to you soon?" She looked at Demi and then gave me a pleading look.

I had no idea what was on her mind, but frankly I wasn't even sure what to think.

She gave me a hug, and then did the same to Demi, while Clive didn't even look at us. He walked away, his hand going to the small of Elena's back, and I had to think I was seeing things when she stiffened. Or maybe, that's just what I wanted to see.

"Jess," Demi whispered, and I rolled my shoulders back, tears threatening.

Why would I be crying? It wasn't that I loved him. But it was eight years of my life slammed into my face.

"Let's finish eating, everything's going to get cold. And I really don't like cold eggs."

"Baby," she whispered, and I gestured towards our food and took a seat.

"No, let's finish our mimosas. It's a really small world, right?"

She gave me an odd look, before thankfully the waiter came by. "Could we get boxes to go? And the check?"

"Demi," I whispered.

"No, it's okay. Let's head out. I want to get home a little early. That way we beat traffic."

Such a lie, but I would take it. Hell, I would cling to it as if it were the truth.

Somehow, we found ourselves back in the car, the food carefully on the back seat, to-go coffees in the cup holders.

I put the audiobook we'd been listening to back on so I wouldn't have to talk. And yet, all I could do was see the man that I thought I had loved for eight years and wonder what the hell I had been thinking. Because I had believed in that love. I had believed I knew what I was doing. And I had fallen headfirst into love with him so quickly I hadn't looked back.

Just like I was doing again.

Was I making the same mistake?

When we pulled into my driveway, I gave a bright smile and tried to pretend I was okay.

"Thank you for brunch. It really was great. That cream cheese? Perfect."

"Hey, let's just get inside, okay?" Demi asked, worry in those gray eyes of hers.

I swallowed hard and picked up my coffee as she reached back to get her things and the takeout containers. We walked inside, and I took the food from her, and set it in the fridge, my stomach way too tense to even think about finishing it. I wasn't even sure I wanted to look at it.

Because Clive would just hit my memories once again, tainting everything.

Just as he always did

"I didn't know. I thought his name was Roberts."

I heard the sadness in her voice and hated that I was the cause. "He likes to go by that sometimes. But he was always Clive to me."

"I'm sorry. If I'd have known, well, I don't know what I would've done. But hell, I can't believe my sister is dating that cheating asshole."

"He might have changed you know..." I said, my voice slightly strained.

"I'll talk with her."

"No, I don't want him to think I'm trying to ruin his life."

Demi let out a breath. "But if he's going to ruin my sister's life, I want to take care of her."

"True. Well, I have a headache. So I should just go take a nap or something. I'll see you later?"

At the abrupt change in my tone, her eyes widened. "Jess. I don't want to go. Let's talk about this."

"No, I don't really want to. In fact, seeing him just reminded me how quickly I fell in love with him. And how things are moving so fast right now. So maybe it's good that I go take a nap. And just think."

Demi reached out but I took a step back, doing my best to ignore the look on her face and the ice spreading in my chest. "You can't break up with me over this. We just need to talk it out. Don't run."

"I'm not running," I lied. "I just need to think."

And as I stood there, heart shattering, she stared at me, and I was so afraid I was making a mistake. Only I wasn't sure if the mistake was staying or pushing her away.

Yet I had a feeling I had just taken any choice in that matter away.

Chapter Four
DEMI

I tried not to let the panic settle in, and yet it was all I could do.

Crushing weight settled onto my chest as I took a deep breath and reminded myself that it was okay. That nothing was wrong, and I was going to be able to fix this.

And yet in no way did that sound as if it was going to happen.

"Jess, what is going on in your head?" I asked.

That probably wasn't the best way to go about it, but as she began to pace, pulling that gorgeous red hair away from her face and into a ponytail, I realized that maybe I wasn't the only one on the verge of having a panic attack.

"All I know is that we were doing just fine, having a wonderful morning, until you saw him." A horrible feeling sank in, and I blurted out the question before I thought better of it. "Do you still love him?"

She whirled, her eyes going wide. "Of course I don't. I haven't loved him in a long time. But I was in love with the relationship I *thought* we had. I gave him eight years of my life, and I thought we were endgame. And it turns out he was cheating on me for how long?"

I tried to do the math in my head, and I could feel the blood rush from my face. "You don't think—"

"The timing isn't right from what you said. No, I don't think he was cheating on me with your sister. And even then, it wouldn't be her fault because he'd have been the liar. But I cannot believe that he's dating her. Of all the people in the world, it's your sister. Who you love and is the sweetest person in the world from what I can tell from your stories, and yet she chose *him*."

I didn't know what Elena saw in him other than she'd seemed happy. And now I felt like a horrible sister for not knowing more about this man—something I'd be changing soon. "Just talk to me. Don't push me out because you're scared."

"But shouldn't I? I fell into this so quickly. One minute I'm getting a tattoo, the next minute we're joking about U-Hauls."

I press my lips together, trying to calm down. "It was just a joke."

We had woken up that morning, both of us naked and sated and realized that I was out of clean jeans. I borrowed a pair from her, and while we weren't exactly the same size, it had somehow worked. I just rolled up the cuffs, so it looked as if I was going for that look rather than them being too short. I had made the joke that I should just move in, and rent the U-Haul, a common joke with our friends, and she had smiled right back to me. Had given me a fucking drawer.

And maybe that was moving too quickly.

I rubbed my fist over my chest, between my breasts, and tried to steady myself. "It's not like we're strangers. And it's not like I met you yesterday. We've had months."

"Two."

"And we knew each other before then."

"We knew each other when we were younger," she corrected.

"Fine. But time doesn't make the connection. Time doesn't change who we are. If you want to know more about me, just ask. I won't say that I'm an open book because those who say it are usually the most closed off, but all you have to do is ask."

"That's the problem. I know you'll tell me anything. And I want to know every inch of you, every mistake and glory and praise. I want to know it all. Just like I want to tell you everything."

"Then what's wrong with that?"

"Because I thought I was doing it right the first time. I believed in it. And he lied to me." Tears splashed down her cheeks as her voice cracked, and I moved forward, cupping that beautiful face.

"I hate him for hurting you. And I *hate* that he's

dating my sister right now. Something that I'm going to talk to her about."

"I don't want to break her heart because mine was shattered."

"Then let me piece it together. It doesn't have to be perfect. *We* don't have to be perfect. But don't shut me out because you're afraid of him."

"I'm not afraid," she lied, pulling back.

I let my hands fall as she paced again. "Maybe not of him, but what you're feeling. And so this is probably the worst time for me to tell you that I love you."

She froze for an instant, as the volley was thrown, my heart in my hand, hoping she would take it from me. She faced me then, that pale face growing even paler so that her freckles stood stark in comparison.

"You love me? How?"

"How could you even ask that? I love the way you make me feel, the way you laugh. I love how you see the world. I love that you opened your arms to me and introduced me to your circles knowing that I was still finding my way here. I did not grow up here, but this is my home. And I want you to be my home too. I know it's too quick, but who cares? We're not kids. We're not Romeo and Juliet."

"First off, it's a tragedy, and those were, what, thirteen-year-olds who were going through puberty?"

"Yes. Exactly. We're not them. This doesn't have to be

a tragedy. We can slow down, I promise. But I can't lie. I love you."

She was silent for so long that I was afraid I was making the worst mistake of my life. Baring all when I had jumped without looking. "I love you too," she whispered, and it felt as if the world had frozen all around us, time standing still as I waited for the next ball to drop.

"Then why do you sound so scared saying that?"

"Because I loved him."

"And you don't love him anymore. And I'll take however long you give me to try to heal that heart of yours. But let me love you."

A tear slid down my cheek now, and she moved forward, wiping it from my face. "I'm just so scared."

"You are the most fearless person I know. You jump in headfirst to everything else. So jump with me now."

"I wasn't supposed to fall in love again. I was going to take time."

"Take time with me."

Her lips quirked into a smile as my heart raced. "I don't know if that's how it works."

"Then we'll make it work this way." I sucked in a deep breath. "You said you love me."

"You said it first."

And then my lips were on hers, and I couldn't hold back. She wrapped her arms around me, and I kissed the woman that I loved.

It didn't matter that it had only been a couple of months, I had fallen head over heels, and there was no going back.

"You know what's the funny thing?" I ask softly, as we held each other.

"What?"

"When I moved back to England, I kept wondering if it could be you. What if it was you?"

"You're going to have to hold me back when I have another panic attack about something."

I nodded, elation threatening to take everything over. "As long as it's not about him. He doesn't deserve our time."

"Okay. So I guess I should go rent the U-Haul?" she asked, and I burst out laughing, sprinkling kisses all over her face, before tugging her down to the couch and showing her exactly how much I loved her.

SIX MONTHS LATER.

"I'm so excited you're closing on the house soon," Elena exclaimed as she taped up the final box in our living room.

In the time since we had finally said we loved each other, I had indeed moved in. However, I still had a lease on my place, so Elena had taken over the apartment. And now Elena would be moving into Jess's home so we wouldn't have to sell it and it would be closer to Elena's classes and work.

Jess and I had bought a house.

Apparently, we were going full blazes and not looking back.

"Things moved quickly, but it's the perfect place," Jess said as she came forward, tape and Sharpies in her hands. "Where is the clipboard? I feel like I need my clipboard."

"I've got it," Justin said as he walked forward, clipboard in hand. He leaned down and pressed a kiss to Elena's lips, and my sister beamed up at her new boyfriend.

Clive had been out of the picture right after brunch. Apparently, he hadn't stopped his cheating, and he was lucky he had run with his tail between his legs, because he would have had to deal my wrath if I ever saw him again.

Now, Elena was dating a man that we all loved, and they were taking it slow. At least slower than Jess and I were.

Alecia and her wife were in the back room, boxing up the last of our offices, and we were getting things ready to go.

Time indeed moved quickly.

"Thank you," Jess said as she took the clipboard from Justin, and the bearded and inked man went to go lift another box.

I smiled over at Elena, feeling lighter than I had in years. "I'm really glad that you brought him, because while I am strong, I really do like his muscles."

"You're welcome," Justin said as he flexed, and the rest of us laughed.

"Are you hitting on your sister's boyfriend?" Jess asked, wrapping her arm around my waist.

"Of course. I can't help it. He's so swoon worthy."

"He really is," Elena said as she stared off at him, and we all watched the way his ass moved in his jeans.

"Seriously, thank you for bringing him along," Alecia said as Emma laughed beside us.

"I feel like a piece of meat here, ladies," Justin said, but then he bent over slowly to pick up another box.

Laughing, I kissed my sister's cheek, and then smacked another kiss on Jess's lips. "Okay, we have to finish this up, and then we have reservations at the new brunch place." We had found a closer place with cream cheese stuffed French toast, and honestly, I was excited.

"This is why I'm here, not just for the ogling, but the French toast," Justin called out, and we all laughed, settling in.

I had always known that this would be my home, maybe not this place, maybe not these people, but the mountains and this air.

And yet, that invisible string that tied me to the woman that I loved had tugged me back when I hadn't realized it.

Jess smiled at me, before laughing at something Elena said, and I knew that this was my family.

The woman that I had let walk away after one evening of pure happiness, and now I would never let go of again.

And all thanks to the ink that had started it all.

And surely it wasn't our last.

Was it Over Then

A WILDER BROTHERS SHORT STORY

Was it Over Then

The Celebrity and The Bodyguard

They loved each other once.
Then they parted ways.
It's been years and neither one has forgotten each other.
But they also cannot have one another.
Or can they...

Chapter One
EVERLAND

"Everland!"

"Over here! Smile for us!"

"Everland, is it true that you signed onto the latest thriller movie?"

"Everland, have you signed the deal for your myopic yet?"

"Everland, why did you and Dean break up?"

"Everland, did you hear that Dean is engaged? Rumor is that he was with Rosalie for your entire relationship. Do you have any thoughts on that?"

"Everland? Do you think your current relationship troubles are why your recent releases have flopped?"

"Everland! Is it true that you had a secret love child with Harry, and gave it up for adoption? And that is why Dean cheated on you with Rosalie?"

I nearly tripped over my feet at the last question, but

kept my chin up as my bodyguard got me into the back of the SUV. He slammed the door, speaking into his headset as my driver skated away from the curb.

I took off my oversized sunglasses and rubbed my temples.

"Well, that was a new one."

I looked to my left at my long-time publicist and friend and shook my head at her.

"Which part, Laura? The fact that they called my latest releases a flop, even though I grossed over $100 million more than the budget the first weekend? Would you call it a flop if you're number one for four straight weeks?"

"They only call it a flop because you didn't do as well as the latest over-budgeted movie that *didn't* earn out domestically. At least according to them. Although, that move was more about blowing things up and showing off their dicks."

"That is true. Though to be fair, if any of the men in my line of work actually showed their dicks, there would be a real uproar. But no, they want full frontal from me, but a penis is scary."

Laura snorted. "Darling, a penis isn't scary, it's just not nice to look at."

I took the offered Perrier and grinned.

"I'm pretty sure I've dated more often than you have. When was the last time you saw penis."

She flipped me off. "We are not going to talk about

that. Covering your career really is more than a full-time job. I don't need to see a penis to enjoy life."

Ben, our longtime driver, laughed at that, his rough chuckle rare.

"See? I got Big Ben to laugh. I truly believe I have hit a new level of sarcasm."

I caught Ben's gaze in the rearview mirror, the humor crinkling at his eyes, and smiled. One day Laura and Ben would realize they were perfect for each other and they would run away and get out of this life I had accidentally created. But then I wouldn't know what to do without them.

"Actually, the new thing I was talking about was the love child. I hadn't seen that many of the threads. I am going to have to do some research."

I rolled my eyes before finishing my drink. "Somebody probably mentioned it on social media, a random comment that shouldn't have been seen, and now a thousand others have used it as click bait." I tried not to grind my teeth.

The problem with everybody thinking Dean had cheated on me with Rosalie, was that they were once again, not even in the realm of truth. Dean and I had been in a business relationship for five years. Five years where neither one of us had to deal with people wondering who we were with, who we were fucking, or if our hearts were broken. Yes, they hounded us for intimate moments, and were constantly watching my waistline to see when I would become pregnant. But for some reason, that seemed easier than letting the world know each of us were single. Happy about it. And working our asses off.

Between his two years long world tour, four albums, and my six movies a year, I wasn't quite sure when people thought Dean and I could actually be together.

Dean and I had a perfect business relationship. We hadn't even slept together in all the times that we had been forced to sleep in the same hotel room thanks to annoying paparazzi.

He was the consummate gentleman.

Then he had fallen in love with my stunt double.

I *loved* Rosalie. We trained together, she kept me active, and she was a wonderful person. And no matter how many times we told the world that Dean and I had broken up, and he and Rosalie were perfectly happy together, people made up their own story.

Dean got off scot-free. He was the man's man, the talented rock star who everybody loved. So the fact he could pull two women that happened to look incredibly alike? The press was eating it up.

Rosalie was a homewrecker, and I was the woman who couldn't keep a man.

It didn't matter that I loved them both and was now on my way to their wedding.

They'd labeled us, and there was no going back.

I groaned just thinking about it.

"Why did I say yes to being in this wedding?" I asked.

"Because Rosalie is your best friend, and Dean is your other best friend. So when two people you love fall in love, you're there for them," she replied.

I glared at Laura. "I thought *you* were my best friend."

I fluttered my eyelashes and Ben laughed again.

"Oh Big Ben, I thought you were supposed to be all stony and silent," Laura said.

"Laura, my darling, I'll be whatever you want me to be."

That shut Laura up, and I preened. The two of them were totally in love, and I couldn't wait for it to come into fruition. I was great at setting people up. Everybody in my sphere fell in love and found their perfect person.

I did not.

No, I worked hard. I ran a production company to help make sure women were in every place of production. I wrote fiction books underneath a pen name that were doing well and had hidden who I was until I had hit the New York Times. And then I had been outed, and I had begun to sell even more. I had an Oscar under my belt, four Emmys, a Golden Globe, and a Teen's Choice award. Plus a few others. I was an A-list celebrity according to the world, and I was so damn lonely.

"You know the reason I'm doing this is so that when the press finds out about the wedding, they'll see that I'm fine with it."

I didn't mean for my voice to sound so sad, but apparently, I wasn't that great of an actress.

"That helps, but that's not all." Laura reached out and squeezed my hand, something she rarely did. Though we were friends, we also had to put our business relationship first. It was the only way to make sure that we kept each other safe. Because somebody needed to be the taskmaster when I couldn't.

"At least he'll be at Bethany's place."

"It does work well that she happened to marry into a family that hosts weddings and has a private enough venue with amazing security. So far, the wedding hadn't leaked, but with so many of us landing in San Antonio and the surrounding private airports, people are going to realize a big named wedding is happening at the Wilder Resort and Winery."

"But for now, maybe the two of them can have a little bit of solace. And I can watch two of my best friends get married, while hanging out with another friend and her amazing family. And you two can maybe have a night off." I fluttered my eyelashes at Ben again, who shook his head as he turned into the private airport.

Laura just clucked her tongue at me as we made our way, thankfully without issue, to the private plane and got ready for takeoff.

"Can I get you anything to eat?" our flight attendant asked, a pleasant smile on her face.

I bit my lip. "I really want a hamburger."

"I can do that for you. Do you like cheese?"

"Yes, please. Do you have Swiss by any chance?"

The other woman smiled. "How about a mushroom and Swiss burger, and I have a poppyseed honey mustard that is divine on it. I know it sounds weird, but I love it."

I clapped my hands, suddenly ravenous. "That sounds amazing. I'm in. And whatever French fries you have. And champagne. Because we're here to celebrate."

"You've got it."

She took Laura's salad order, as well as Ben's order to match mine, and we got ready for takeoff.

"You must be in a mood if you are about to eat a hamburger." Laura just smiled at me.

"It's not like they have too many choices back there. We don't want to waste food. But I had hoped they had hamburgers."

"Still, I'm glad you're going to enjoy your food."

I raised a brow, and she just shrugged before going back to work. Ben was on his tablet, most likely going over the security protocols for the next few weeks.

We had this wedding, and then two weeks of intense traveling and promotion before my next shoot. Eventually I would have a vacation, but I wasn't sure when that was going to happen. Because of the promotion and shoot, me indulging in a greasy hamburger probably wasn't good for me since I rarely let myself have something that rich. I didn't care. I was allowed to eat food. Contrary to the public's belief.

Of course, if somebody saw me eating a hamburger and took a photo of it to put on social media, they would probably say I was eating my feelings because of my breakup. Because a woman wasn't allowed to eat a hamburger. I was so tired of being shamed for eating food. Because food was sustenance. And it gave me energy. I was tired of defending myself over everything. And since my mini-rant was now out of control, I knew I was past being hangry.

As we made our way from New York to Texas, I finished my burger—the mustard *was* divine—and went over notes for the next week. Every once a while I would look up to see Laura and Ben pointedly not looking at each other, and then glancing at one another to see if the other had noticed. They were so damn cute, and I knew one day my situation would have to change.

Because they would need time for themselves once they figured out what they were feeling. Just like Dean and Rosalie.

And here I was, once again alone.

A little boy with dark hair and bright green eyes filled my mind, and I did my best not to think about that memory. It had been years since I had seen Finley. Years since we had parted, not on the best of terms.

He had been my best friend, my confidant. When my dad had thrown me out when I was only twelve, it had been his house I had run to. His parents held me close and made sure I was safe.

And when my mother had finally left my father and remarried the most loving man ever, Finley had been there by my side to make sure that my stepdad wasn't anything like my birth father.

Finley had been my first kiss. My third date.

And my first time. We had been fumbling teenagers, laughing and overheated as we had tried to figure out what we were doing. And it had been awkward yet loving. It had been even better the second time. And the years after that.

Then life happened, and we had to grow up.

I had gone to New York to attend Julliard, grateful for not only my stepfather's connections, but for somebody actually seeing my drive and talent.

Finley had ended up in the Air Force Academy with glowing recommendations and a bright future ahead of him.

He'd always been one to care for others, always the one to put others before himself. So it had surprised me that that was a life of service he had decided to go down. But it was in the opposite direction as me.

Colorado Springs versus New York City.

I lived in the spotlight, a life with an art.

He'd lived in a world I had no concept of.

Because when I had tearfully kissed him goodbye, and promised I would write him, I had.

Only it had taken me a year to realize that he had never promised to write me back. He had merely kissed away my tears and told me to soar. *His Ever.*

And I hadn't seen him since. Not even when I had

gone back to our small town to visit my parents. Not even when I had seen his parents. I had to think it was on purpose at that point. That our return trips had never coincided. So I had taken that hurt within myself and pushed it into the characters I played.

But it was little wonder that I had never fallen in love again.

How are you supposed to find that kind of love when it had soared beyond the crest of truth at such a young age.

He had been my sun, and I his Icarus. I had flown far too close, and I had never found my footing again.

"Everland? Are you okay?" Laura asked, her voice low, worried.

I shook myself out of my thoughts, memories I had tried to forget for far too long, and smiled over at Laura.

"I'm great. Just ready to get the show on the road."

She studied my face, and then glanced over at Ben as if he had answers.

The trip from the private airport to the retreat wasn't too long. The landing strip had been built within the past year, thanks to people in Austin who had needed a better place to land. And it turned out that it was actually closer to the side of the I-35 core than Austin itself. That meant it was a quick trip to the gates of the retreat and through security.

I was slightly surprised at the intense security at each

gate, but considering who lived there full-time and how many people visited, it was nice to see.

"We booked a cabin for you on the other side of the winery on the private section. You'll be free from prying eyes and can relax without other guests around."

I looked over at Laura, surprised. "I thought I would be staying at the inn with the rest of the wedding party."

Laura shook her head. "The land itself has over two dozen small cabins, and larger ones if you like homes. There's also enough acreage that a few of the Wilders actually live on property in homes spread out on the other side of the acreage. The main inn has twenty rooms, and the whole place is rented out for the wedding itself. I'm staying in one of the rooms, but I thought it would be nice if you had space to yourself." She paused, blinking slowly. "I hope that was okay. I just thought you needed a moment to yourself before this next transition."

For some reason tears almost pricked my eyes, but I blinked them away and reached forward to grip her hand.

"It's perfect. Thank you." I rolled my shoulders back, oddly excited for this reprieve. Yes it would be stressful, or perhaps it would be just what I needed. Time for myself, to figure out exactly what I wanted next. While I watched two of the closest people in my life about to love each other forever.

That wasn't too bad of weekend.

The place was absolutely stunning. Set in the hill country of South Texas, it wasn't completely brown and full of cattle like my brain had thought. Instead there were green trees and odd pops of colorful flowers everywhere. It felt homey. Different than the forests of Colorado or countless other places I'd seen. But still beautiful.

The large barn and inn were a stunning white, with beautiful architecture and stonework everywhere. I knew the winery with actual vines were on the other side of the property, and there was a distillery, a couple of restaurants, and even a spa. I had a massage booked for the next day and I was excited about relaxing.

I didn't know exactly when Bethany had met her husband, but the two of them were absolutely adorable, and I knew Everett worked really hard with his family on all of this. It was sad though, that this was my first time coming here. I hadn't been able to make it to their wedding because I had been on the other side of the world and wasn't able to get out of my contract. I had sent a gift, but it wasn't enough. And I had celebrated with them again at their home in LA.

But now I would be able to see most of my friends here. A small slice of a giant world in the most uncommon places.

"It's good we're out here when we are. We will get out of here and meet with Rosalie and Dean first," Laura explained. "And then one of the Wilders' other team members will show you your cabin. I promise I'm not going to bug you this entire weekend. This is almost your vacation."

I rolled my eyes at her again. "I don't think you know what that word means."

"Because you haven't taught it to me yet," she teased. Ben laughed again, and Laura's cheeks blushed.

Maybe this weekend wouldn't only end with the marriage, maybe something else could happen.

Or maybe I needed to stop matchmaking.

We got out of the SUV as the Wilder staff welcomed us. They went over a few things about the property that Bethany had already explained to me before, and I couldn't help but look across the beautiful landscape and inhale that fresh air. It wasn't like the city at all, and while it was humid as heck, it was still moderately comfortable.

Thankfully it wasn't the hellscape of summer in Texas. "Everland?"

I turned at Ben's voice and smiled up at him. "Hey, Ben. Are you staying in the inn with the others or bunking with me."

He shook his head. "I'll be around for sure, however, it won't just be me. Actually, the team that trained me owns a slice of this place."

I blinked. "You know Bethany's brother-in-law?" I asked on a laugh. One of Bethany's brothers-in-law was married to the owner of the security company that not only kept the Wilders' running and safe, but they also provided bodyguard services for certain individuals around the world in our sphere.

I wasn't quite sure exactly how it all worked, but it was a particular set of skills.

"I do. Trace is the one who trained me back in the day and actually introduced me to Laura and the rest of your team."

It didn't escape my knowledge that his voice softened when he said her name. "How did I not know this?"

"Because while I might be your main guard, you do have six of us," he said dryly.

"Now I feel bad. How did I not ask?"

"Everland. You know my birthday, my mother's name, my niece's name, and you send gifts on their birthdays. You also know what I'm allergic to, and you always make sure that I get my favorite funky socks at whatever country you're in. It's okay that you didn't know who my former boss was."

I blushed, feeling awkward. "Apparently I need to know everything."

"And I'm going to need to know a few more things. Because it's only me with you on this trip as the rest of the team gets their vacations or work on the next phases, Trace is going to blend in some of their team with mine."

"I had wondered why it was only you coming with me, but I assumed one of the other guys would meet us here."

"Todd was going to, but then his sister needed him."

I pressed my lips together. My heart hurt because

Todd's sister had recently lost her husband, and he had needed to take a leave of absence.

"I still feel like I need to send something. Or do something."

"You made sure that there are meal services for that family for the next year. You're doing good." His gaze caught on something behind me, and he smiled. "Now I'm going to introduce you to the person that's going to work with me. Trace promises he is great. And he owes me a beer."

"I'm pretty sure you owe *me* one," the deep voice said from behind me, and I froze.

I knew that voice. It didn't matter that it had been twelve years since I had heard it. I knew that voice. I swore I could feel the heat of him behind me, even though I knew he had to be farther away than that.

I turned, hoping I was wrong, and at the same time, hoping, desperately hoping, that I was right.

Finley stood there, and my breath caught in my throat. He looked so much the same, and yet so different.

He had filled out, muscle upon muscle, and yet still looked as if he could sprint down the hall with no worries. His hair was a bit shorter than it had been when we were younger, and the screen I still pierced my soul.

I knew I should say something, to be angry that nobody had warned me. Then again, nobody knew about Finley. The press, and those who called themselves caring fans, who tried to dive into every aspect of my life, had never been able to unearth our history together. He had always been mine. My personal memory. My personal heartache.

He studied my face just as intently as I knew I was doing, and I wasn't sure what I was supposed to say.

Ben cleared his throat between us, and yet neither one of us looked over at him.

And then Finley reached out and traced the outline of my jaw and up towards my eye with his finger, something he had done countless times before.

"Hey, Ever."

"You...you're here."

"And you did good, Ever. I always knew you would."

And like that, the memory of every unanswered letter, every forgotten text and call slammed into me, and I rolled my shoulders back and turned away from the only man I had ever loved.

The one person who'd shattered my heart before I had even realized our time could be cut short in an instant.

Chapter Two

FINLEY

"I take it that's not exactly how you wanted it to work out."

I looked over at the very large man who I had known for a few years and had done my best never to be jealous of. That was all a lie.

Because I had definitely been jealous of Ben for far too many years. However, it was my own damn fault for my jealousy after all. If I'd ever followed through with any of my chances at reaching out, maybe the only woman I had ever loved in my life wouldn't be standing in this cloud of hurt and anger.

"No. Not at all. From the look on her face, do you really think it did?"

"Since I don't know what the hell just happened, I'm not going to blame either one of you right now. And honestly, you're lucky that I know you. Because if I didn't, we would have a problem with the way she looked at you." Ben narrowed his gaze. "Are we going to have a problem, Finley?"

I didn't back down from the narrowing of Ben's eyes. It grated that he was the one who was allowed to be so protective of Everland after all these years. However, this was Ben's job. I was just the one to pick up the pieces for a few hours.

Because she wasn't the girl that I had fallen for. The person who was all my firsts just like I was hers.

She was the woman who had taken over the world. The woman of grace, elegance, and power.

And I had watched her rise from the ashes of her childhood like a phoenix aflame. Part of me had always wanted to rise with her. To stand alongside her as she shone brightly.

Only I had needed to find a grounding of my own or I would have ended up as burned embers in her wake. Never on purpose. She would never have done that to me.

But I would have pulled her down.

We both had needed to grow up. To find our paths. And by the time I had gotten back from making far too many mistakes, and after far too many deployments, she had been in the arms of another man.

And to the outside world she had looked so damn happy.

And that was why I could not understand why she was here for the man's wedding.

"We are not going to have a problem. Although I would love to know why she's here."

Ben's brows rose. "You are on her security detail for the weekend. You damn well should know why she's here."

"That part I know." I began to pace, running my hands through my hair that was far too long now. I had been forced to cut it short for so many years, so my hidden rebellion had become a fashion statement. Now the rest of the guys on the team poked fun at me, but it was all in good humor.

But I didn't look like the man that Everland had known. Just like she didn't look like she had when I had left her. Or rather when we had left each other.

"I take it you know her. You're the guy from when she was a kid, right? Her high school boyfriend?"

I raised a brow. "Maybe."

Ben sighed. "The press doesn't know much about her childhood. She's done damn well at hiding all of that. She wanted her privacy. And Laura spends most of her time making sure whatever parts of Everland's life she could keep to herself she can. However, I'm going to need to know if you can deal with this if you want to work with her."

"Do you really think you can stop me?" I asked the man who I had once called friend.

"That doesn't sound like a great introduction," my boss Trace said as he came forward, a curious expression on his face. However, I knew beneath that curiosity was downright anger. Because I was not acting like the man he had hired. The stone-cold remote guy who could do what was needed. Who could stand on the sidelines and help whoever was in my charge.

There was no way I could be stone cold or anything like that when it came to Ever.

"Finley is Everland's ex-boyfriend. And we didn't know that. And now I'm worried."

Trace's gaze shot to me at Ben's words. "Are you fucking kidding me?"

I bristled. "It's not really any of your concern."

Trace growled. "That's a lie. I should have your job for this."

I sighed, running my hands over my face. "It was a long time ago. We broke up because she went to New York to start school, and I went to the Academy. It wasn't a bad breakup. It just is what it is. We were childhood friends. And that means I'm not going to let anything happen to her."

"What if you are the one who puts her in danger just by being there?" Ben asked softly.

I shook my head, rage coursing through my veins. "No one is going to get her when I'm around. No press, no busybodies who want information they don't have the right to have. I didn't tell you that I knew her because it's been so damn long, I just wanted to see if she was the same. I'm not going to make a big deal about it."

"I really don't believe you," Ben said as he crossed his arms over his chest. I opened my mouth to say something, but he shook his head. "But I saw the way she looked at you. I saw the way she reacted. I've known her long enough that I have a feeling if I were to take you off this case, she wouldn't like it either."

I straightened. "Really?"

"I'm not going to interfere. But I am going to be watching you."

"We are going to have a long talk once this is over," Trace warned.

I nodded tightly, knowing I might lose my job because I'd kept her a secret. But she had always been mine to protect. Secrets and all.

And now I needed to see exactly who she was now, and if she wanted to see the man I had become in the end.

Ben led me towards her cabin, and I was grateful it seemed that she had a little bit of privacy.

"We set this up so she has full cameras everywhere. And no guest can walk past this area unless they have a key card. Bethany has land out here that we use for guests who need space," I explained to the other man.

"We went over everything as we set up, but I'm grateful. She needs space."

I gave Ben a look, furrowing my brows, worry coursing through my veins.

"You're going to have to ask her." He answered my unasked question but I decided to ask anyway.

"I don't understand why she is attending and participating in a wedding between her ex and her former friend."

Ben just raised his brows. "I thought you knew her."

I paused, confused, until I realized that maybe not all was as it seemed. "Well shit."

"I'm not going to say anything. You should talk to her."

"I will never understand celebrities and their culture."

"You think I do? I was here to make sure that she can have a semblance of a normal life. With the peer social relationship that fans have with her? She doesn't get that life. She gets to go from secluded home, to private dinners, to private planes, not because she's full of it. But because people constantly touch or interrupt her. They want a piece of her, even if she doesn't have anything left for herself. So if you hurt her, I'll bury you on this land and they're not going to say a damn word about it. You understand me?"

I wanted to lash out. The man was far too overprotective of Everland. But I knew he was doing it on purpose. Because I had seen the new stories about her. I knew she didn't get the privacy and life she needed. He was doing his job.

And I would never fit in. I never had.

"I'll talk to her."

Trace snorted. "Good. Don't screw this up. Because I'm tired, and I'm not in the mood to get a shovel."

I barked out a laugh. "I'm pretty sure the Wilders have a backhoe to help you with that."

"Good to know." Trace gestured toward the cabin, and I rolled my shoulders back, making my way in the direction of the only woman I ever loved.

I didn't even have to knock before Everland opened the door and stared at me with wide eyes.

"Ben just let you come here? Without a word to me?"

"I'm pretty sure I can feel his eyes on my back. So if you gestured toward him, he could probably kill me with his pinky."

"Maybe." She stared at me and shook her head. "Why didn't you write me? You never answered a single letter. After all of these years, not a sound from you. I never saw you at home. I never saw you in any part of the world that I was in. It was as if you didn't exist. It was as if you didn't want me to exist in your life at all. And I hate the fact that the first words I'm saying to you after all these years is that you didn't write me back."

I moved forward then, hating myself. But she didn't pull away. "If I would've written you back, I would've dropped everything to see you. Or you would have done the same. And we never would have been able to figure out who we needed to be as adults."

"That's a bunch of shit. You know it."

I raised brow. "I didn't know you knew how to curse, Ever."

She stormed away from me into the cabin, and I

followed her. Thankfully I didn't think Ben was on my tail.

"I'm not a child. It's been over a decade. I've seen the world. I've done so much. And I couldn't share any of it with you."

"I saw the world too, just not the same way you did."

Her eyes filled before she blinked her tears away. "I only heard tidbits about where you went. Whispers of your deployments. I waited for years for you to write me back. For a single note that you were okay. And I had to hear it from my mom who heard from your parents that you were even alive. And finally they stopped asking because it hurt for me to hear. All I knew was that you were alive and getting out of the military. And I did not want to know anything else. Because you cut me out of your life. And now you're here acting as if no time has passed."

"We were crazy for each other, Everland. We were so consumed in one another we didn't have other friends. We had our lives, in the future that we made up in our heads without any planning. How were you supposed to become who you are if you were tied down to me in my constant moving and deployments. I never got to stay in the same place for longer than two years until recently. And I'm still living with my company. Getting a job with Trace is the most stability I've had since I left you at the airport."

"So you didn't write me back for my own good? That's bullshit."

"I didn't write you back because I was dying inside. And I wanted to leave. To drop out of the Academy, which would have stained my record and my life for the rest of my days because I needed to see you. And I knew I would drag you down with me. And I was a coward. For not writing back. Because I loved you. Damn it, Everland. I still love you. Watching you soar has been the most achingly painfully beautiful thing I have ever done in my life. You are so talented and the world has seen it."

"And I'm lonely!" she yelled.

I took a step forward, knowing I was putting my life in her hands at this moment. "I'm sorry. But you know if we would've found a way to stay together, we would've stopped trying to grow. And I was selfish enough to want to see you do amazing things."

Tears fell down her cheeks then, and I wiped them away with my thumbs.

"I want to hate you. But every time I've tried to fall in love on-screen it was you. And every time I try to do the same in real life, it was never you."

"Ever. I'm so damn sorry. I didn't know how to make our futures work if I didn't go cold turkey. And it was the hardest and most moronic thing I've ever done in my life."

"How are you here, Finley?"

"I was already here. Trying to find a way to get the

courage to come to you. And then I saw your name on the guest list and everything clicked. This was the time."

"So you waited for me? But you never tried?"

I winced before letting her go, beginning to pace her small living room. "I came to your house."

"No you didn't," she snapped.

"I did. You were with Dean. And the two of you looked so damn happy. I knew I was too late. I watched the world fall in love with you, and you go from relationship to relationship. Or at least the media said you did. They made up things about you, and maybe some of it was real. And I never saw that light in your eyes until you looked at Dean. I knew it was too late."

"You weren't. He's my best friend. And he needed time away from the spotlight just like I did. We never even had sex," she spat.

My chest tightened. "I hate the fact that I'm so fucking excited to hear that."

"I should've let you squirm some more. You really came all the way to LA?"

"Of course I did. I tried to stay away for so long because I thought it was what was best. I was wrong. And now I'm here, not asking for forgiveness. Not asking for your heart. I'm just here, needing to see you. Because I missed you, Ever. I miss you every day that we were apart. Even when I knew I should've stopped long ago."

"You were always more romantic than me," she said, her arms crossed over her chest.

"I can go. There's someone else that can take my spot, and I'll walk away. But just know that not writing you killed me inside."

"I hate the fact that I know if you would've written me back I wouldn't have been able to move on. Even though I really haven't. But I would've been a shell of myself. And I hate that you were right. Because you're never wrong, Finley. You're always so certain you're right that it kills me inside."

I moved forward and cupped her face again. "Let me protect you. Just for the weekend. Relax. Breathe. Take some time for yourself. Maybe I'll let you see the letters I wrote to you all those years ago."

Her eyes widened. "No. You did?"

"Every single one. I kept them. Because I'm a sap. I loved the woman that you were when we left. I would love to get to know the woman that you are now."

"I don't have any answers for you. I'm still so mad."

"And you have every right to be."

"But can you do the one thing that I really need you to do, even though it's a terrible mistake?" She asked.

I froze, swallowing hard. "Anything."

"Kiss me."

And I was lost, the girl of my dreams in my arms and I leaned down to press my lips to hers.

Chapter Three
EVERLAND

This was a mistake. A terrible mistake. But then again, I hadn't made enough of them recently. After that first kiss in my cabin, I'd pulled away and I'd told myself that would be it.

Then he'd shown me the grounds.

We'd gone to the winery, the spa, the distillery. He made sure I was safe while showing me his new world.

And it was like we'd never been apart.

Laura hadn't said a word, and I knew it was because Ben had filled her in. I didn't know what would come of them or what they'd say about my current choices—but that would come later. For now I lived in this bubble of time that didn't make any sense.

I was so angry with him...but I knew he'd been right. Because if there had been another way, I'd have found him before this. Instead, we were now who we needed to be in this point of our lives.

And now I had my arms around him again, knowing I needed to back away.

Only we weren't moving from each other.

It felt as if no time had passed, and yet he was still a completely different person. His lips were firm on mine, and I took a deep breath as I pulled away, trying to get my bearings.

"We should stop," I whispered against him, trying to breathe.

Finley went back slightly, before pushing my hair from my face. "We can." His lips quirked into a grin that hadn't changed in all those years. The grin that meant either trouble or the thrill of a lifetime. I had followed that grin into new experiences, and not all of them had to do with the love I felt for this man.

"We only have an hour before the rehearsal dinner. And I still need to get dressed and look as if I'm somewhat presentable."

"Okay. Because the press found out about Dean and Rosalie?"

I shook my head as I took a step back, trying to compose myself. Everything about me ached, and it had to do with this man. I wanted to climb him like a tree and just soak in the essence of him. I wanted his hands on me, and to feel him inside me. Over me. Just feel.

But I needed to take a moment to breathe. I hadn't even realized he would be here a few hours ago, and now here I was, falling into him as if I didn't have a way to hold back. I knew if I let myself fall completely, I would hurt him. Not because I wanted to, but because my life came with obstacles that others couldn't see and didn't understand. Maybe he had a glimpse of it from the other side. By protecting Bethany and those in his care. But his life was in the shadows. And being with me would tug him into the spotlight.

"I don't think they do. No news choppers yet. But I would assume Trace and the others would message you, right?" I answered, trying to keep my voice cool.

"Trace has been giving me updates, yes. Same as Ben. What put that look into your eyes?"

"What look?" I asked, trying to pretend I had no idea what he was talking about.

"The one that says you're trying to think of a thousand worries before they even pop up. You always had that expression on your face when you were worried about Juilliard. Worried about your mother. Worried about me. It's as if you take the weight of the world on your shoulders and you can't take a step back and believe that we're here for you too."

"I don't like the fact that you can read me so well after all this time. We were separated for years, and yet in one afternoon you can walk back into my life and fit in. I don't know how I feel about it."

"Maybe I wanted to surprise you like this. While I

knew you were coming here, I thought you were here as an ex-girlfriend of the groom. I wasn't sure a letter or phone call would be welcome. Hell, I wasn't even sure how to approach that subject."

"I don't think there is a map or flowchart for this. I never meant to find you again. I never thought I would."

"And I found you. I should have found you long before this. I'm sorry for wasting so much time."

I shook my head, trying to reel in my emotions. "If the press hasn't found out about this wedding yet, that's good. It will give them some privacy. But I love them both as my best friends. Just as Laura is my friend. Same with Bethany. Our world is so different than what others think it is and what others live through. So having small private moments like this is practically unheard of."

"I know you're trying to warn me away, but I'm not going anywhere. Unless you truly want me to. You don't have to worry about me, Ever."

I shook my head. "Somebody should. I don't know if I can just fall into what we were."

"I'm not asking you to. We aren't those people. We are who we are now. And I would love to get to know the real you. Not the one the media presents."

I winced. "There's a reason nobody needs to know the real me beyond my circle. And it's a tight circle, Finley."

"I'm glad you have them." He pushed my hair behind my ear, but before I could say anything, the front door opened. Finley whirled, pushing his body in front of mine, but visibly relaxed as Laura and Ben walked in.

"I was just here to check on you," Laura said, her voice oddly high-pitched.

I peered around Finley and held back a smile as I realized that Laura's perfectly coiffed hair was no longer smoothed and styled. Instead it looked like hands had roughly slid through the strands, and she had distinct beard burn on her neck. Ben, in contrast, looked like the cat who caught the canary.

"I was just about to get ready. You should come with me, Laura. I have a feeling we should talk." I gave her a pointed look and then glanced over at Ben. Laura, the ever unflappable woman in my life, blushed.

I beamed and gave Finley one last look of longing that I couldn't hold back, before pulling Laura to the bedroom to get ready.

"I see you and Finley are catching up. Ben was filling me in, and let me say, Finley is quite handsome."

"Yes, yes. You are right about that. And I know Ben has already done his background check once again."

"We just want to protect you. But Finley is clean. He wouldn't be on this job if he wasn't. You already look lighter."

"I could say the same about you."

Laura shook her head. "We're not here to talk about me."

"Maybe we should. Maybe it shouldn't be about me."

"Let's get ready for the wedding, and we can toast to unexpected circumstances."

I held up my hand and squeezed Laura's, feeling as if something had changed for both of us.

I just hoped it wasn't for the worse.

I WORE A SKY-BLUE BALLGOWN THAT MATCHED the wedding colors but wasn't truly a bridesmaids dress as I made my way through the small crowd that was here for the rehearsal dinner. Everyone went full formal for the evening and I felt like a princess.

Finley was at my side, acting as my escort and guard. I wasn't sure how I was supposed to feel about that, the way he was playing double duty. But all that mattered was I felt completely safe. I just had to hope my heart would remain safe through the weekend.

Taking a leap into the unknown felt as if I were jumping off a cliff.

Before I could dive any deeper into my own emotions, Dean came forward with his arms outstretched.

"There's the other love of my life." I laughed as he held me close and kissed me hard on the mouth. "I was beginning to think you were going to hide in your cabin with this mysterious stranger for the whole day."

Dean pulled away as Rosalie came forward and picked me up, twirling me around in those strong arms of hers.

"Dean cannot stop asking questions about who this Finley is." Rosalie also kissed me hard on the mouth before grinning up at Finley.

"It's nice to meet you. Welcome to our wedding. Are you working or are you finally going to be Everland's date. She's so hard to set up."

Blushing, I shoved at the bride and groom.

"You guys are ridiculous. Stop embarrassing me."

"Never," they said at the same time, and Finley let out a rough chuckle.

"I can see my perception of whatever the hell is going on was completely wrong."

"It's Hollywood. Whatever you think you're seeing is usually a lie. Sometimes on purpose, most of the time not," Dean said with a shrug. "But I'm glad Everland is here. Although I'm a little annoyed that Rosalie got her as maid of honor, and I couldn't get her as best man."

"Your brother is your best man, so I'm sorry that I couldn't take up both spots."

"You just like Rosalie more than me."

"That is true," I teased.

Finley's gaze shot between all of us, clearly catching onto the play by play. It felt odd to be my true self around both of my friends while others were milling about. The only people at this rehearsal dinner were those who loved Dean and Rosalie. Meaning they knew the truth about our relationship. Tomorrow at the wedding there would be a few more people who weren't completely in the know, so we wouldn't be this comfortable. But maybe it was time for me to finally be myself. Whoever that was.

"We're going to steal Everland for a few moments to go over a few things, and then we have dinner. Really, tonight is just an excuse to eat and drink."

"I'll be around, checking in with the team. If you need anything, let me know." Finley's gaze met mine and I swallowed hard. The promise and intensity in those eyes should have scared me. Instead all I wanted to do was indeed take that leap I never knew I craved.

"I'll be here. Promise."

He looked as if he wanted to reach out and touch me, so I gave him that option. I moved forward to cup his cheek. Then I went to my tiptoes and brushed my lips along his.

He froze, clearly surprised I would do this in public, before he kissed me back, this time a little harder.

"I'll keep an eye on you. Promise."

"I trust you," I blurted, surprising myself.

And when Finley walked away, Ben taking his place, Dean whistled between his teeth.

"Okay, I love him. I can't believe you just kissed another man public." Dean grinned.

"Was that weird? I've no idea what I'm doing." I blushed.

"It wasn't calculated, it was new. So damn happy for you." Dean hugged me tightly as Rosalie wrapped her arms around the both of us. The three of us stood in an odd hug, and yet it felt like home. These two were part of my family, and the world would never understand. But I had a feeling Finley did.

"You deserve this," Rosalie whispered.

"It's only been a few hours."

"And yet you had a lifetime before this moment. And I see the way you look at each other. It's like no time has passed. Maybe I'm sappy because I'm about to marry the love of my life, but I want my best friend to be happy too."

I bit my lip before we were summoned by the Wilder wedding planner, and I was saved from having to answer.

By the time the rehearsal dinner was done, I was exhausted, exhilarated, and wondering if I was about to make one of the biggest mistakes of my life.

"We have security up for the area, and the press hasn't caught wind yet. The night team is on, and Finley will be with you."

I froze at Ben's words and looked up at him while we continued our way to my cabin.

"Is he working then?" I asked, trying to sound nonchalant and clearly failing.

His lips twitched. "No. He and I are both off for the night. You have the rest of Trace's team on patrol."

I raised a brow even as my stomach clenched. "So I take it you and Laura will be able to have the night off?" I asked, teasing.

Ben blushed. "I don't know if that's any of your concern."

"What if it is?" I asked, teasing. "Either way, I'm happy for you."

"I would say thank you, but then you would think you won this argument."

"Maybe I did," I said with a laugh. I let out a deep breath before I made my way inside. "I love Laura. She's one of the best people I know. And she deserves happiness. And so do you."

"You're saying all these things, and yet, I don't know if you believe them for yourself."

I froze, running my hand over my chest. "I'm just trying to figure things out."

"I know you are. And you deserve to be happy. Also, if he hurts you in any way, I will murder him. Don't worry."

"I'm oddly worried now."

Ben's lips quirked into a smile before he led me inside. My heart raced as anticipation washed over me. Finley wasn't there yet, apparently having to complete his outtake paperwork for the day. The wedding was the next day, and I had tons to do, and yet all I could think about was tonight. And what would happen.

Or maybe what wouldn't.

I didn't know why I was putting so much pressure on myself. It was just one evening. One meeting with a man I had thought had been out of my life for far too long.

A hand brushed against my shoulder and I flew around, a scream ready to rip from my throat.

"It's just me," Finley whispered as he ran his hands down my bare arm.

"Scared the crap out of me. I didn't even hear you come inside."

He raised a brow. "Lost in your thoughts then? I knocked. Said your name."

I blushed, shaking my head. "Apparently. I'm usually better about that."

"I'm not going to let anyone hurt you."

"As my bodyguard? Or somebody that wants to be in my life."

"Whatever you want me to be."

"I don't have answers yet. But I've missed you. I'm still angry."

"Be angry. I deserve it."

"If this happens, no matter what this is, the press will find out. Any skeletons you have they're going to dig out. It's going to be relentless. I've never wanted to force that on anybody. Nobody deserves that."

"What about you? What do you deserve?"

"Does it matter? This is the life that I chose."

"You chose to act. To live in a job that thrills you and fulfills you. You didn't ask for anything else. They don't deserve anything else."

"That's not how things work."

"I'm game for anything. I walked away before because

we needed time. And then I walked away because I thought you'd already found your place. I was wrong. So I'm here."

"For how long?"

"For however long you need me."

"What if this is too much for you?"

"Then it is something we should face. Together."

I knew it was stupid. I knew too much time had passed and our lives were completely different, but it felt as if my heart had finally found what had been missing all this time. It was ridiculous and made no sense. And yet all I wanted was the man in front of me.

In answer, I went to my tiptoes and wrapped my arms around his shoulders. He bent his head, pressing his lips to mine.

And I was lost.

He tasted of coffee and Finley. It was all I could do not to lean into him and let him take me. Or maybe that's exactly what I needed.

He lifted me by my thighs, and I wrapped my legs around his waist. His slight beard was rough against my face and I shivered. I moaned into him as he walked us to my bedroom, his arms so strong that I felt safe. He would never drop me.

It wasn't supposed to be like this. Wasn't supposed to be this quick.

Or maybe it was.

He gently laid me on the bed as both of us moaned

into one another. And then he was stripping me, taking his time as he kissed up my sides, between my breasts. When he stripped my bra from me, I moaned as he licked my breast. Then he took one nipple into his mouth and sucked, using his hand to roll my other nipple between his fingers. I felt too many emotions, and I couldn't think. All that mattered was him.

He continued to strip me, raining kisses down my stomach, between my thighs. I when I was bare before him, he studied me, taking his fill.

"I've wanted to taste this pussy for years. Every time I tasted something sweet, I thought of you."

I blushed, my hands on my breasts. "That must make dessert quite interesting."

"I'm about to have my dessert." And then he lowered himself, sucking on my clit. I nearly shot off the bed, but he pinned me down, taking his fill. He licked and sucked, exploring every single inch of my pussy as he brought me closer and closer to the edge. When he speared me with two fingers, I was done for, clamping around him.

"You're so beautiful when you come," he whispered.

I couldn't think, couldn't do anything but feel him against me as I continued sliding through my orgasm. My toes curled and I sucked in a breath as I nearly went over again. Then he removed his fingers and sucked them clean, making me squirm.

I sat up quickly and stripped off his shirt. He smiled down at me, those eyes darkening into pools of emotion that I couldn't read, and I knew exactly what he was thinking.

I was his, just like he was mine.

And when I pushed him down on the bed and stripped off his pants, he smiled. When he slid his hands underneath his head to watch me, I gripped the base of his cock.

"Now that's a picture."

"You rarely ever let me do this before."

"I'm not going to stop you now."

I licked up his shaft and he groaned, lifting up his hips.

I opened my mouth for him, letting him slide inside. And then one of his hands was in my hair, and he was fucking my mouth, my tongue lapping against him.

I could taste the salt of him, and I bobbed my head, moving through the motions as he was the one who set the pace.

I let him take control and let him take me. And when he tightened beneath me, he pulled out, and I whimpered.

The sound of a crinkle of a wrapper filled the room, and then he sheathed himself and lifted one of my legs. I arched into him, and then he moved. He entered me slowly, his cock stretching me in the best ways possible.

"Finley," I breathed.

"That's it. Take me, my Ever. You're so damn tight."

"I need you to move," I whispered.

"That I can do."

And then he was pounding into me, thrust after thrust as each of us breathed into one another. He had me on my stomach, coming in from behind with my legs pressed together so it was tighter than anything I'd ever felt before. And then I was on my back with my legs wrapped around his waist as he slowly arched into me, the motions sending me over the edge and into bliss. I kept my eyes open, and my mouth parted as I came. And as he captured my lips with his, he followed me, his hips stiffening just for an instant as we fell into one another.

We had been everything to each other before. When we hadn't even known who we were.

And now?

Now I knew it had never truly been over.

He was the man I had always wanted. The man I had thought I left behind.

Now he was the man I wanted to keep.

Chapter Four
FINLEY

THREE YEARS LATER

"*Everland! Are you excited about your next movie?*"

"*Everland! What do you have to say about Dean and Rosalie welcoming their second child? Will you be their godmother as well?*"

"*Everland! Is it true that you were secretly dating your husband all these years?*"

"*Finley! Tell us more about your wife!*"

"*Everland! Tell us the name of your recent child! The world wants to know about your baby girl!*"

As I pulled my wife into the back of the SUV, I shook my head. "How on earth did they figure out we had a baby girl?" I muttered.

From the seat in front of us, Laura snickered. "Darling. They always find these things out."

"At least they don't know we're having twins," Ben said from the front seat, and I could see the tips of Laura's ears blush.

"Don't say that too loudly because then suddenly *I'm* pregnant with twins," Everland said with a laugh.

I leaned over and kissed my wife's cheek. "I wouldn't mind that."

She raised a brow. "Scarlett is only four months old. Give me some time, husband of mine."

I shrugged. "I'm not in a hurry."

Considering it had taken nearly fifteen years for me to finally get the woman of my dreams, I was good at being patient.

At least sometimes.

It hadn't always been easy. I didn't do the exact job I thought I would, and I didn't mind it. I still worked for Trace and Ridge with the Wilders. I was just in charge of the staff outside of the compound. I also didn't get to be Everland's personal bodyguard at all times. Because sometimes I wanted my attention on her, and not those who wanted to hurt her or wanted a piece of her.

Finding a balance was something we did every day, but I wouldn't trade it for anything. The world had opinions on who I was, and who they thought Everland was. Those opinions didn't matter.

They thought they could be in a parasocial relationship with us, though they could have vitriol and opinions about who we needed to be.

But those spaces didn't matter. We existed as who we were, and all that mattered was our inner circle. With the Wilders and the close friends Everland had put around herself all these years.

I might still have a few opinions on what others thought, but in the end, all that mattered was my family.

Including the small town that we visited together. It was our secret time and place where we could hide from the world before the world found us.

But for now, we were heading back to the Wilders'. We had one more wedding to attend, and Scarlett would be waiting for us on the plane with her nanny and personal bodyguard. We hadn't wanted her to be seen in public, so we had spent three hours away from our baby girl. The longest three hours of my life.

I knew I should have come forward long before I had. I should've taken a stand with the woman I loved. Then again, I loved the Everland she was now. And I would take every moment that we had.

Because it hadn't been over then. Not by a long shot.

"What's get you all sentimental?" Everland asked as she cupped my cheek.

"Just thinking about you."

"That's way too cute. Please stop," Laura said, and I chuckled.

"We're almost ready for vacation," Everland said, her eyes dancing.

"Honestly, love of my life, I didn't realize you knew what that word meant," I said dryly.

"She doesn't. You know she'll be going over scripts and paperwork for the company." Laura shrugged, her attention on her tablet as always.

"You say that as if you're not at my side the entire time," Everland said with a laugh.

"Ben, were going to have to make sure that the women of our lives actually get an evening off."

"You may be a tough son of a bitch, but I'm pretty sure they could take you," the big man said from the front seat.

"I never said they couldn't." And then I leaned over to Everland and whispered in her ear, "You can take me later.

Her cheeks blushed, and I kissed her softly before leaning back and letting myself breathe.

Soon we would be with Scarlett, and then the rest of the Wilders.

And we could finally breathe for a moment.

Our lives weren't for the restful, and I didn't mind. Watching Everland grow and thrive was everything that I needed.

I had walked away before, and I would never do it again.

Because she was my first love, my first friend, my first, and my only.

And I was never letting her go again.

Delicate Nights

A MONTGOMERY INK BONUS SCENE

Delicate Nights

Austin and Sierra from Delicate Ink have weathered terror, angst, and uncertainties but now they're happily married and the parents of two amazing kids. Only problem? They need a night to themselves and a long-awaited Montgomery Ink wedding might just be the perfect way to make that happen.

Chapter One
WEDDINGS

AUSTIN COULDN'T WAIT UNTIL THE RECEPTION was over. With so many siblings, it felt as if he'd been in wedding after wedding. And while his family meant everything to him, he really just wanted one night with his wife. Was that so wrong?

Yeah, he loved Alex like crazy and adored the fact that Tabby was now a Montgomery in truth, but he desperately wanted out of his suit.

And if he were honest, he wanted Sierra out of that damn dress of hers even more.

Okay, so maybe not *out* of the dress since now all he could think about was rucking that soft cream and peach lace up her thighs and taking her from behind. He'd tug at her hair, making her arch her back so she pressed her ass back into him as he thrust into her. Her butt would jiggle just right, and he'd have to grip harder, increasing his pace until they both came so hard they fell into a heap of sweaty limbs.

He swallowed hard, thankful that he was sitting down and had the tablecloth to cover his raging erection. Suit pants would do nothing to hide the fact that he was now so damn hard, he was pretty sure he would blow if Sierra so much as brushed against him.

Thankfully, for both of them, she was on the dance floor with their son, Leif, and unaware of where his thoughts had turned. Leif looked over and winked at him, and Austin couldn't help but grin back. Yeah, that kid was a Montgomery through and through.

He still couldn't quite believe that he had a teenager who was almost as tall as Sierra. He'd only had the boy in his life for a few short years, but now that time seemed to be going by faster and faster. Their other son, Colin, was out like a light upstairs in the main house with the four babysitters the family had hired to help ride herd on the Montgomery kids. With so many babies and kids running and crawling around, was it any wonder they'd had to hire out for a Montgomery wedding while they usually tried to take care of their own?

And what a wedding it was. Tabby and Alex had fought hard for their time together, and Austin was damn happy for both of them.

He'd be even happier once things ran down and he could take his family home, get them to sleep, then take his wife to bed.

Yeah, that sounded like the perfect ending to a long day full of family and friends. Even Tabby's family had flown in from Whiskey, Pennsylvania to be with her. Austin always found it weird that she had another family so far away since she was so ingrained in the Montgomerys and had been for so long. But her brothers and parents loved her hard and were pretty kickass people.

But hell, he just wanted everyone to go home so he could. Or at least have things get to the point where no one would notice if he and Sierra walked out after leaving the kids with the grandparents. He was kind of a dick right then for even thinking that, but it had been far too long since he was able to have a night with his wife. He missed her riding his dick as she screamed his name.

They'd been forced to be quiet for far what seemed like ages.

Sierra met his gaze across the dance floor and raised her brow. Yeah, she knew what he wanted, and he knew that she was feeling the same strain he was.

As much as they loved their kids—fucking loved them to the ends of the Earth and back—they needed one night to themselves.

But he had a feeling tonight wouldn't be that night, not with how much fun everyone was having.

Damn weddings.

"Dick straining your zipper, big brother?" Griffin asked as he took the empty seat next to him.

"There a reason you're worrying so much about my dick?"

Griffin snorted and took a sip of his beer. "Not so much. But you keep eye-fucking your wife like you haven't had a taste of her in months." He looked over at Austin. "That about right?"

Austin rubbed his beard with his middle finger. Damn Griffin for being so good at reading people. Made his work as an author better, but damned if it didn't make it hard to keep secrets sometimes.

"Autumn and I can take the kids for you tonight if you want. It might be easier for us to just sleep in your guest room so you don't have to deal with packing up the kids' shit. You and the wife can go get a hotel room and fuck until the sun comes up."

Austin blinked slowly before turning to his brother. "You really think Sierra is going to want to show up with *no* luggage at a hotel? And what about you and Autumn? I'd have thought the two of you would want some time to yourselves. And do I really look that hard-up?" He was a little worried about the answer to the latter since he was in public. No need to appear like some cretin in front of family. He could do that behind closed doors with his wife, thank you very much.

Griffin shrugged. "We have time to ourselves almost every night. Perks of being the best aunt and uncle around, who don't have kids of our own. But I know you and Sierra have been working really hard recently, and with two kids in completely different stages of their lives at home, you probably don't have a lot of time for just the two of you. So let us do this."

Austin frowned, bending forward so his forearms rested on his thighs. "Sierra doesn't like unplanned things."

"She might like this. Autumn can even pack her a bag, and we'll drop it off at whatever hotel you choose later tonight. Go. Have fun, and just be with your wife. We can handle the kids."

Austin ran a hand over his beard and swallowed hard, the idea of having a whole night alone with Sierra far too tempting to pass up. "Let me ask if she had any other plans for us tonight." For all he knew, she just wanted to go home and sleep after a long day of wedding festivities.

Griffin clapped him on the back. "That's what I wanted to hear. Go get your woman."

Austin was already prowling toward the punch bowl where Sierra stood talking with his sister Miranda. His baby sister must have noticed the glint in his eyes because she quickly skittered away, leaving Sierra snorting over at him.

"Really, Austin? How scary are you trying to be right now?"

"Enough." He quickly went over the plans Griffin had mentioned, and worry briefly crossed her face before she grinned. "What do you say, babe? Wanna take a night with me?"

"You're sure they'll be okay?" She bit into that luscious lip of hers, and he could only imagine how they would look wrapped around his dick.

"The kids, or Autumn and Griffin?" At her look, he ran his knuckles over the bare skin of her shoulder. He loved the way she shivered at just that small touch and couldn't wait to see what else he could do.

"I'd say both but...damn, Austin. I can't get the idea of your dick in my mouth out of my thoughts." She whispered the last part so close to his ear, he could feel the heat of her breath. This, of course, sent his cock straight to the almost-blowing stage, and he had to count to ten backwards before he could even say anything.

"Play with me, Sierra. Just for the night."

"Always."

He was surprised that he refrained from tossing her over his shoulder and carrying her out of the wedding at her answer, but from the look on his family's faces as they said their goodbyes, he had a feeling it had been close.

Whatever.

Chapter Two
BEDSHEETS

"That woman knew I was about to do you right now," Sierra muttered as Austin closed the room door behind them with a loud snick. "I mean, we're wearing *wedding* clothes and just checked in late to a hotel for one night without luggage. That practically screams sexcation."

She turned and watched Austin undo his tie. She was pretty sure if her panties hadn't already been damp from the anticipation of what was to come, she'd have drenched them at the sight. Who knew she could fall in love with wrists and forearms? She'd thought the term *arm porn* was just a joke until she met Austin Montgomery.

"So?" her husband asked. "This is a classy place, and after I fuck you hard a few times, we'll take a bath in that fancy-ass tub, fuck some more, then fuck again in the bed. Or...some mix of that. Then, later, when Griffin shows up with our things, we'll have clothes for tomorrow so we don't have to do the walk of shame. But I don't really give a care that the woman at the front desk knows we're about to have sex. My plan is to make you scream you so loud that she can hear you from there as you come on my cock."

Red Alert.

Wet Panties Ahead.

"Jesus," Sierra muttered. She was one damn lucky woman. And because her thong was far too wet for her to even walk at this point, she did the only thing she could do.

She slid her hands up under her dress and tugged the sides of the lace down before stepping out of them. Austin watched her every movement, the lead pipe behind his zipper growing before her eyes.

She'd always loved that her husband was a grower *and* a shower.

Fucking fantastic.

"Take off the rest of your clothes," she ordered, loving the way he raised his brow at her tone. "I don't want to spend too long trying to get that zipper down, or ending up in half a dress or just one sock. I want us both naked. Now."

"I thought I was the one who gave the orders, babe." His tone was so low, so *demanding*, her knees went weak. It had been so long since they played. They'd grown through the dynamics of their relationship and weren't the same couple they were when they first met. And for that, she was glad.

But right then, she could only strip out of her clothes and go to her knees at his voice, wanting a taste of what they'd once had but knowing it wasn't what they both *needed* any longer.

Just a taste.

Not a forever.

She already had her forever with him. And she loved their present, the promise of their future, but for this moment, they could step into their past and *remember*.

"Damn," he growled low. He stalked to her and ran his thumb over her lips. She opened for him, sucking. "You want my cock in your mouth?"

"Yes, sir." The word felt foreign on her tongue after so long.

He shook his head. "I'm Austin, Sierra. You're mine as I'm yours."

"Then, yes, *Austin*, I want your cock in my mouth."

"Then unzip me and start sucking. I want to come down your throat while you play with my balls. Then I'm going to eat you out until you run wet down my face. Sound like a plan, babe?"

In answer, she undid his pants and slid him out of his boxer briefs. He was so hard that he was already wet at the tip. She spread the wetness over him, and he shuddered before wrapping her hair around his hand and pulling her head closer to him.

She opened for him, needing him in her mouth. He tasted of salt and man, and she wanted more, *craved* more. Her husband let out a groan, and that just egged her on. So she looked up at him before swallowing him whole.

They both groaned at that, and she closed her eyes, getting to work. She loved going down on him, adored knowing every sound and movement he made was because of *her*.

She'd married the man of her dreams and got to sleep with the man of her heart *and* her fantasies.

She was one lucky Montgomery.

Before she could get her fill, however, Austin was in front of her, his mouth on hers, and his hand between her legs. He moved his hands with the experience of a man who knew his woman as he played with her folds and rubbed her clit.

"I know I said I'd be slow and savor you," her husband growled, "but I can't wait any longer."

In answer, Sierra arched up into him, needing more. "If you don't get inside me right now, I'll scream."

He kissed her harder. "I'll make you scream anyway."

Then she was on her back on the bed as Austin stood at the end of the mattress, thrusting into her with one deep movement. She gasped, his length filling her so completely that she knew she'd be sore in the morning even after all they'd shared together.

And she couldn't freaking *wait*.

They moved together as one, their bodies sweat-slick

and aching. She was coming before she could catch her breath, and then she found herself on top of him, riding him until they both came together.

Her nails dug into his skin, and his fingers gripped her flesh to the point of bruising. An aching pain that would be a constant reminder that they'd taken each other to the edge, to the point of ecstasy.

She'd never loved her husband more.

At least, that was what she'd thought until he brought her, breathless, to the tub and leisurely washed her skin, his lips on her shoulder as he achingly cared for her.

No, *now* she'd never loved her husband more.

"Mine," she whispered, her body feeling heavy and sated.

"Always, babe, always."

And then she slept in the arms of the love of her life, knowing that no matter what they went back to the next day, they had this night. And no matter how many years passed, she knew they'd always be breathless for one another, always ache with need at the mere thought of each other.

Sierra Montgomery was one lucky bitch, and she knew it.

Damn straight.

Chapter Three
HOME

Austin grunted as Colin stepped on his junk, but since the kid was bouncing on the couch as he wore out some of his never-ending energy, he couldn't really say anything. He hadn't been paying close enough attention and probably deserved a small, sock-clad foot on his crotch.

Sierra met his gaze across the living room as she winked.

He just laughed and set Colin on the floor so he could play with Leif like he had been before he decided to crawl all over his dad.

Austin met his wife's gaze again and couldn't get the image of her naked and sated from the night before out of his mind. They'd made love two more times after their bath and had slept for only a couple of hours before the bellhop had brought up their bags, courtesy of Griffin and Autumn.

And since neither of them could be without their kids for long, they'd had breakfast in bed before coming home and relieving his brother and sister-in-law of their duties. He owed the two of them for sure.

He also knew that Leif was getting old enough to watch Colin on his own. Perhaps, even in a few years. Somehow, his family had grown from just him alone in his house, worrying that he'd never find a way to fill the empty rooms, to something so full, he could barely comprehend it.

It still boggled his mind that he'd once had nothing but his shop and his dreams and now had more than he could ever wish for.

He had two amazing sons—one from a past where he'd lost so much, and the other from his present where he'd almost lost even more.

He had his home and business, a testament to everything he'd gone through.

He had the Montgomerys—those in Denver, Colorado Springs, Boulder, and Fort Collins.

And he had his wife.

His Sierra.

His everything.

What more did a bearded, inked man need?

A Note from Carrie Ann Ryan

Thank you so much for reading Ever After Between the Lines! Each of these stories are set within my main series and are a taste of what you're missing! I hope you loved these as much as I loved writing them!

If you want to make sure you know what's coming next from me, you can sign up for my newsletter at www.CarrieAnnRyan.com; follow me on twitter at @CarrieAnnRyan, or like my Facebook page. I also have a Facebook Fan Club where we have trivia, chats, and other goodies. You guys are the reason I get to do what I do and I thank you.

Make sure you're signed up for my MAILING LIST so you can know when the next releases are available as well as find giveaways and FREE READS.

Happy Reading!

From The Forever Rule
ASTON

The Cages are the most prestigious family in Denver—at least according to the patriarch of the Cage Family.
And the Cages have rules.
Rules only they know.

I ALWAYS KNEW THAT ONE DAY MY FATHER would die. I hadn't realized that day would come so soon. Or that the last words I would say to him would've been in anger.

I had been having one of the best nights of my life, a beautiful woman in my arms, and a smile on my face when I received the phone call that had changed my family's life.

The fact that I had been smiling had been a shock,

because according to my brothers, I didn't smile much. I was far too busy being *The Cage* of Cage Enterprises.

We were a dominant force in the city of Denver when it came to certain real estate ventures, as well as being one of the only ethical and environmentally friendly ones who tried to keep up with that. We had our hands in countless different pots around the world, but mostly we gravitated in the state of Colorado—our home.

I had not created the company, no, that honor had gone to my grandfather, and then my father. The Cage Enterprises were and would always be a family endeavor. And when my father had stepped away a few years ago, stating he had wanted to see the world, and also see if his sons could actually take up the mantle, I had stepped in— not that the man believed we could.

My brothers were in various roles within the company, at least those who had wanted to be part of it. But I was the face of Cage Enterprises.

So no, I hadn't smiled often. There wasn't time. We weren't billionaires with mega yachts. We worked seventy-hour weeks to make sure *all* our employees had a livable wage while wining and dining with those who looked down at us for not being on their level. And others thought we were the high and mighty anyway since they didn't understand us. So, I didn't smile.

But I had smiled that night.

It had been a gala for some charity, one I couldn't even remember off the top of my head. We had donated between the company and my own finances—we always did. But I couldn't even remember anything about why we were there.

Yet I could remember her smile. The heat in her eyes when she had looked up at me, the feel of her body pressed against mine as we had danced along the dance floor, and then when we ended up in the hallway, bodies pressed against one another, needing each other, wanting each other.

And I had put aside all my usual concepts of business and life to have this woman in my arms.

And then my mother had called and had shattered that illusion.

"Your father is dead."

She hadn't even braced me for the blow. A heart attack on a vacation on a beach in Majorca, and he was dead. She hadn't cried, hadn't said anything, just told me that I had to be the one to tell my brothers.

And so, I had, all six of them. Because of course Loren Cage would have seven sons. He couldn't do things just once, he had to make sure he left his legacy, his destiny.

And that was why we were here today, in a high-rise in Centennial, waiting on my father's lawyer to show up with the reading of the will.

"Hey, when is Winstone going to get here?" Dorian asked, his typical high energy playing on his face, and how he tapped his fingers along the hand-carved wooden table.

I stared at my brother, at those piercing blue eyes that

matched my own, and frowned. He should be here soon. He did call us all here after all."

"I still don't know why we all had to be here for the reading of the will," Hudson whispered as he stared off into the distance. Neither Dorian nor Hudson worked for Cage Enterprises. They had stock with the company, and a few other connections because that's what family did, but they didn't work on the same floors as some of us and hadn't been elbow to elbow with our father before he had retired. Though dear old dad had worked in our small town more often than not in the end. In fact, Hudson didn't even live in Denver anymore. He had moved to the town we owned in the mountains.

Because of course we Cages owned a damned town. Part of me wasn't sure if the concept of having our name on everything within the town had been on purpose or had occurred organically. Though knowing my grandfather, perhaps it had been exactly what he'd wanted. He had bought up a few buildings, built a few more, and now we owned three-quarters of the town, including the major resort which brought in tourists and income.

And that was why we were here.

"You have to be here because you're evidently in the will," I said softly, trying not to get annoyed that we were waiting for our father's lawyer. Again.

"You would think he would be able to just send us a memo. I mean, it should be clear right? We all know what stakes we have in, we should just be able to do things evenly," Theo said, his gaze off into the distance. My younger brother also didn't work for the company, instead he had decided to go to culinary school, something my father had hated. But you couldn't control a Cage, that was sort of our deal.

"Why would you be cut out of the will?" I asked, honestly curious.

"Because I married a man and a woman," he drawled out. "You know he hasn't spoken to me since before the wedding," Ford said, and I saw the hurt in his gaze even though I knew he was probably trying to hide it.

"Well, he was an asshole, what do you expect?" James asked.

I looked behind Ford to see my brother and co-chair of Cage Enterprises standing with his hands in his pockets, staring out the window.

With Flynn, our vice president, standing beside him, they looked like the heads of businesses they were. While they wore suits and so did I, we were the only ones.

Dorian and Hudson were both in jeans, Hudson's having a hole at the knee. And probably not as a fashion statement, most likely because it had torn at some point, and he hadn't bothered to buy another pair. Theo was in slacks, but a Henley with his sleeves pushed up, tapping his finger just like Hudson, clearly wanting to get out of here as well. Ford had on cargo pants, and a tight black T-shirt, and looked like he had just gotten off his shift. He owned a security company with his husband and a few other friends, and did security for the Cages when he could, though I knew he didn't like to work with family often. And I knew it wasn't because of us. No, it was Father—even if he had officially *retired*. It was always Father.

And he was gone.

"Can't believe the asshole's gone," I whispered.

Ford's brows rose. "Look at that, you calling him an asshole. I'm proud."

"You should show him respect," Mother said as she came inside the room, her high heels tapping against the marble floors. I didn't bother standing up like I normally would have, because Melanie Cage looked to be in a *mood*.

She didn't look sad that Dad was gone, more like angry that he would dare go against their plans. What plans? I didn't know, but that was my mother.

She came right up to Dorian and leaned down to kiss his cheek. She didn't even bother to look at the rest of us. Dorian was Mother's favorite. Which I knew Dorian resented, but I didn't have to deal with mommy issues at this moment.

No, we had to deal with father issues at this point.

"I'm going to go get him," Flynn replied, turning toward the door. "I'm really not in the mood to wait any longer, especially since he's being so secretive about this meeting."

As I had been thinking just the same, I nodded at Flynn though he didn't need my permission. However, just then, the door opened, and I frowned when it wasn't just Mr. Winstone walking into the conference room.

I stared as an older woman walked through the door following Mr. Winstone, and four women and another man with messy hair and tattered cut-up jeans that matched Hudson's walked behind them.

The guy looked familiar, as if I'd seen him somewhere, or maybe it was just his eyes.

Where had I seen those eyes before?

"Phoebe? What are you doing here?" Ford asked as he moved forward and gripped the hands of one of the women.

"I was going to ask the same question," Phoebe asked as she looked at Ford, then around the room.

Those of us sitting stood up, confused about why this other family—because they were clearly a family—had decided to enter the room.

"We're here to meet the lawyer about my father's death, Ford. Why would you and the Cages be here?" she asked, and I wondered how the hell Mr. Winstone had fucked up so badly? Why the hell was he letting another family that clearly seemed to be in shock come into our room? This wasn't how he normally handled things.

Ford was the one who answered though—thankfully—because I had no idea what the hell was going on.

"Phoebe, we're here for my dad's will reading. What the hell is going on?" he asked. Phoebe looked around, as well as the others.

I stared at them, at the tall willowy one with wide eyes, at the smaller one with tears still in her eyes as if she was the only one truly mourning, and at the woman who seemed to be in charge, not the mother. Instead she had shrewd eyes and was glaring at all of us. The man stood back, hands in pockets, and looked just as shell-shocked as Ford.

But before Mr. Winstone or anyone else could say anything, my mother spoke in such a crisp, icy tone that I froze.

"I don't know why you're acting so dramatic. You knew your father was an asshole. He just liked creating drama," she snapped.

As I tried to catch up with her words, the older woman answered. "Melanie, stop."

This couldn't be happening. Because things started to click into place. The fact that the man at the other end of this table had our eyes, and that everybody looked so fucking shocked. I didn't know how Ford knew this Phoebe, and I would be getting answers.

"We had a deal," my mother continued, as it seemed that the rest of us were just now catching on. "You would keep your family away from mine. We would share Loren, but I got the name, I got the family. You got whatever else. But now it looks like Loren decided to be an asshole again."

"What are you talking about?" the shrewd sister asked as she came forward, her hands fisted at her side.

"Excuse me," I said, clearing my throat. I was going to be damned if I let anyone else handle this meeting. I was The Cage now. "Will someone please explain?"

"Well, I wasn't quite sure how this was going to work out," Mr. Winstone began, and we all quieted, while I wanted to strangle the man. What did he mean how *the hell this would work out*? What was this?

This seemed like a big fucking mistake.

"Loren Cage had certain provisions in his will for both of his families. And one of the many requirements that I will go over today is that this meeting must take place." He paused and I hoped it wasn't for effect, because I was going to throttle him if it was. "Loren Cage had two families. Seven sons with his wife Melanie, and four daughters and a son with his mistress, Constance."

"We went by partner," the other mother corrected.

I blinked, counting the adults in the room. "Twelve?" I asked, my voice slightly high-pitched.

"Busy fucking man," Dorian whispered.

Hudson snorted, while we just stood and stared at each other.

This could not be happening. A secret family? No, we were not that cliché.

"I can't do this," Phoebe blurted, her eyes wide.

"Oh, stop overreacting," my mother scorned.

"Do not talk to my daughter that way." The other mother glared.

"It was always going to be an issue," Mother continued. "All the secrets and the lies. And now the kids will have to deal with it. Because God forbid Loren ever deal with anything other than his own dick."

"That's enough," I snapped.

"Don't you dare talk to us like that," the shrewd sister snapped right back.

"I will talk however I damn well please. I am going to need to know exactly how this happened," I shouted over everyone else's words.

Out of the corner of my eye I saw Phoebe run through the door. Ford followed and then the tall willowy one joined.

"Shit," I snapped.

"Language," Mother bit out.

I laughed. "Really? You are going to talk to me about language."

I looked over at James, who shrugged, before he put two fingers in his mouth and whistled that high-pitched whistle that only he could do.

Everyone froze as Theo rubbed his ear and glared at me.

"Winstone," I said through gritted teeth. "I take it we all have to be here in order for this to happen?"

He cleared his throat. "At least a majority. But you all had to at least step into the room."

"Excuse me then," I said.

"You're just going to leave? Just like that?" my mother asked.

I whirled on her. "I'm going to go see if my apparent *family* is okay. Then I'm going to come back and we're going to get answers. Because there is no way that I'm going to leave here without them."

I stormed out the door, and thankfully nobody followed me.

Of course, though, I shouldn't have been too swift with that, as the woman who had to be the eldest sister practically ran to my side, her heels tapping against the marble.

"I'm coming with you."

"That's just fine." I paused, knowing that I wasn't angry at these people. No, my father and apparently our mothers were the ones that had to deal with this. I looked over at the woman who Mr. Winstone and the mothers had claimed was my sister and cleared my throat.

"I'm Aston."

"Is this really the time for introductions?" she asked.

"I'm about to go see your sister and my brother to make sure that they're fine, so sure. I would like to know the name of the woman that is running next to me right now."

"I'm running, you're walking quickly because you have such long legs."

I snorted, surprised I could even do that.

"I'm Isabella," she replied after a moment.

"I would say nice to meet you Isabella…" I let my voice trail off.

She let out a sharp laugh before shaking her head. "I'm going to need a moment to wrap my head around this, but not now."

"Same."

We stormed out of the building, and I lagged behind since Ford was standing in front of Phoebe who was in the arms of another man with dark hair and everybody seemed to be talking all at once.

"I just. I can't deal with this right now," Phoebe said, and I realized that something else must have been going on with her right then. She looked tired, and far more emotional than the rest of us.

I looked over at the man holding her and blinked. "Kane?" I asked.

Kane stared at me and let out a breath. "Wow," he said with a laugh.

"We'll handle it," Isabella put in, completely ignoring us. "And if we need to meet again later, we will." Then she looked over at Ford and I, with such menace in her gaze, I nearly took a step back. "Is that a problem?"

I raised my chin, glaring right back at her. "Not at all. However I want answers, so I'd rather not have the meeting canceled right now. But I'm also not going to force any of my," I paused, realization hitting far too hard, "*family* to stay if they don't want to."

And with that, I turned on my heel and went back into the building, with Isabella and Ford following me. Everyone was still yelling in the interim, and I cleared my throat. As Isabella had done it at the same time, everyone paused to look at me.

"Read the damn will. Because we need answers," I ordered Winstone, and he shook like a leaf before nodding.

"Okay. We can do that." He cleared his throat, then he began going over trusts and incomes and buildings and things that I would care about soon, but what I wanted to know was what the hell our father had been thinking about.

"Here's the tricky part," Winstone began, as we all leaned forward, eager to hear what the hell he had to say.

"The family money, not of the business, not of each of your inheritance from other family members, but the bulk of Loren Cage's assets will be split between all twelve kids."

"Are you kidding me?" Isabella asked. "What money? We weren't exactly poor, but we were solidly middle class."

"We did just fine," the other mother pleaded.

My mother snorted, clearly not believing the words.

I glared at the woman who raised me, willing her to say *anything*. She would probably be pushed out of the window at that point. Not by me, by someone else, but she probably would've earned it.

The lawyer continued. "However to retain the majority of current assets and to keep Cage Lake and all of its subsidiaries you will have to meet as a family once a month for three years. If this does not happen, Cage Enterprises will be broken into multiple parts and sold." He went on into the legalese that I ignored as I tried to hear over the blood pounding in my ears.

"You own a town?" the other man asked.

I looked over at the one man in the room I didn't know the name of. "Not exactly."

"Kyler," Isabella whispered.

In that moment, I realized that I had a brother named Kyler—if this was all to be believed.

"This can't be legal right?" the tall willowy person said.

"Yes Sophia, it can," their mother put in.

Oh good, another sister named Sophia.

Only one name to go. What the hell was wrong with me?

I forced my jaw to relax. "Are you telling us that we need to have all twelve of us at dinner once a month for three years in order to keep what is rightly inherited to us? To keep people in business and keep their jobs?"

"We don't need the money, but everyone else in our employ does," James snapped. "As do those we work with."

"Damn straight," Dorian growled.

"How are we supposed to believe this?" I asked, asking the obvious question.

"First, only five must attend, and two must be of a

different family." The lawyer continued as if I hadn't spoken. "Of course you are *all* family…"

"Again, how are we supposed to believe this?" I asked.

"Here are the DNA tests already done."

"Are you fucking kidding me?" Isabella asked.

I looked at her, as she had literally taken the words out of my mouth.

"Isn't that sort of like a violation?" Kyler asked, his face pale.

"We need to get our own lawyers on this," James whispered.

I nodded tightly, knowing we had much more to say on this.

"There's no way this is legal," the youngest said, and I looked over at her.

"What's your name?" I asked.

"Emily. Emily Cage Dixon," she said softly, and we all froze.

"Your middle name is Cage?" I asked, biting out the words.

"All of our middle names are Cage," Sophia said, shaking her head. "I hated it but Dad wanted to be cute because our father's name was Cage Dixon, or maybe it wasn't. Is he also a bigamist?" she asked.

Her mother lifted her chin. "We never married. And no, your father's name was not Dixon, that was my maiden name."

"What?" Sophia asked. "All this time…are our grandparents even dead?"

"Yes, my parents are dead. The same with Loren's." The other mother's eyes filled with tears. "I'm sorry we lied."

"We'll get to that later," Isabella put in, and I was grateful.

I let out a breath. "In order to keep our assets, in order to keep the family name intact, we need to have *dinner*. For three years."

The small lawyer nodded, his glasses falling down his nose. "At least five of you. And it can start three months after the funeral, which we can plan after this."

"This is ridiculous," Hudson murmured under his breath, before he got up and walked out.

I watched him go, knowing he had his own demons, and tried to understand what the hell was going on. "Why did he do this?" I asked, more to myself than anyone else.

"I never really knew the man, but apparently none of us did," Isabella said, staring off into the distance.

"Leave the paperwork and go," I ordered Winstone, and he didn't even mutter a peep. Instead, he practically ran out of the room. James and Flynn immediately went to the paperwork, and I knew they were scouring it. But from the way that their jaws tightened, I had a feeling that my father had found a way to make this legal. Because we would always have a choice to lose everything. That was the man.

"It's true," my mother put in. "You all share the same father. That was the deal when we got married, and when he decided to bring this other woman into our lives."

"I'm pretty sure you were the other woman," the other mom said.

I pinched the bridge of my nose.

"Stop. All of you." I stared at the group and realized that I was probably the eldest Cage here, other than the moms. I would deal with this. We didn't have a choice. "Whatever happens, we'll deal with it."

"You're in charge now?" Isabella asked, but Sophia shushed her.

I was grateful for that, because I had a feeling Isabella and I were going to butt heads more often than not.

I shrugged, trying to act as if my world hadn't been rocked. "I would say welcome to the Cages, because DNA evidence seems to point that way, however perhaps you were already one of us all along."

Kyler muttered something under his breath I couldn't hear before speaking up. "You have my eyes," he said.

I nodded. "Noticed that too."

The other man tilted his head. "So what, we do dinners and we make nice?"

I sighed. "We don't have to be adversaries."

"You say that as if you're the one in charge," Isabella said again.

"Because he is," Theo said, and they all stared at him.

I tried to tamp down the pride swelling at those words—along with the overwhelming pressure.

Theo continued. "He's the eldest. He's the one that takes care of us. And he's the CEO of Cage Enterprises. He's going to be the one that deals with the paperwork fallout."

"Because family is just paperwork?" Emily asked, her voice lost.

I shook my head. "No, family is insane, and apparently, it's been secret all along. And it looks like we have a few introductions to make, and a few tests to redo. But if it turns out it's true, we're Cages, and we don't back down."

"And what does that mean?" Isabella asked, her tone far too careful.

Theo was the one who finally answered. "It means we're going to have to figure shit out."

And for just an instant, the thought of that beautiful woman with that gorgeous smile came to mind, and I pushed those thoughts away. My family was breaking, or perhaps breaking open. And I didn't have time to worry about things like a woman who had made me smile.

The Cages needed me and after today's meeting there would be no going back to sanity.

Ever.

In the mood to read another family saga? Meet the Cage Family in The Forever Rule!

From One Way Back to Me

ELI

When my morning begins with me standing ankle-deep in a basement full of water, I know I probably should have stayed in bed. Only, I was the boss, and I didn't get that choice.

"Hold on. I'm looking for it." East cursed underneath his breath as my younger brother bent down around the pipe, trying his best to turn off the valve. I sighed, waded through the muck in my work boots, and moved to help him. "I said I've got it," East snapped, but I ignored him.

I narrowed my eyes at the evil pipe. "It's old and rusted, and even though it passed an inspection over a year ago, we knew this was going to be a problem."

"And I'm the fucking handyman of this company. I've got this."

"And as a handyman, you need a hand."

"You're hilarious. Seriously. I don't know how I could

ever manage without your wit and humor." The dryness in his tone made my lips twitch even as I did my best to ignore the smell of whatever water we stood in.

"Fuck you," I growled.

"No thanks. I'm a little too busy for that."

With a grunt, East shut off the water, and we both stood back, hands on our hips as we stared at the mess of this basement.

East let out a sigh. "I'm not going to have to turn the water off for the whole property, but I'm glad that we don't have tenants in this particular cabin."

I nodded tightly and held back a sigh. "This is probably why there aren't basements in Texas. Because everything seems to go wrong in these things."

"I'm pretty sure this is a storm shelter, or at least a tornado one. Not quite sure as it's one of the only basements in the area."

"It was probably the only one that they had the energy to make back in the day. Considering this whole place is built over clay and limestone."

East nodded, looked around. "I'll start the cleanup with this water, and we'll look to see what we can do with the pipes."

I pinched the bridge of my nose. "I don't want to have to replace the plumbing for this whole place."

"At least it's not the villa itself, or the farmhouse, or the winery. Just a single cabin."

I glared at my younger brother, then reached out and

knocked on a wooden pillar. "Shut your mouth. Don't say things like that to me. We are just now getting our feet under us."

East shrugged. "It's the truth, though. However much you weigh it, it could have been worse."

I pinched the bridge of my nose. "Jesus Christ. You were in the military for how long? A Wilder your entire life, and you say things like that? When the hell did you lose that superstition bone?"

"About the time that my Humvee was blown up, and when Evan's was, Everett's too. Hell, about the time that you almost fell out of the sky in your plane. Or when Elliot was nearly shot to death trying to help one of his men. So, yes, I pretty much lost all superstition when trying to toe the line ended up in near death and maiming."

I met my brother's gaze, that familiar pang thinking about all that we had lost and almost lost over the past few years.

East muttered under his breath, shaking his head. "And I sound more and more like Evan these days rather than myself."

I squeezed his shoulder and let out a breath, thinking of our brother who grunted more than spoke these days. "It's okay. We've been through a lot. But we're here."

Somehow, we were here. I wasn't quite sure if we had made the right decision about two years ago when we had formed this plan, or rather *I* had formed this plan, but there was no going back. We were in it, and we were going to have to find a way to make it work, flooded former tornado shelters and all.

East sighed. "I'll work on this now. Then I'll head on over to the main house. I have a few things to work on there."

"You know, we can hire you help. I know we had all the contractors and everything to work with us for some of the rebuilds and rehabs, but we can hire someone else for you on a day-to-day basis."

My brother shook his head. "We may be able to afford it, but I'd rather save that for a rainy day. Because when it rains, it pours here, and flash flooding is a major threat in this part of Texas." He winked as he said it, mixing his metaphors, and I just shook my head.

"You just let me know if you need it."

"You're the CEO, brother of mine, not the CFO. That's Everett."

"True, but we did talk about it so we can work on it." I paused, thinking about what other expenses might show up. "And what do you need to do with the villa?"

The villa was the main house where most things happened on the property. It contained the lobby, library, and atrium. My apartment was also on the top floor, so I could be there for emergencies. Our innkeeper lived on the other side of the house, but I was in the main loft because this was my project, my baby.

My other brothers, all five of them, lived in cabins on

the property. We lived together, worked together, ate together, and fought together. We were the Wilder brothers. It was what we did.

I had left to join the Air Force at seventeen, having graduated early, leaving behind my kid brothers and sister. After nearly twenty years of doing what we needed to in order to survive, we hadn't spent as much time with one another as I would have liked. We hadn't been stationed together, so we hadn't seen one another for longer than holidays or in passing.

But now we were together. At least most of us. So I was going to make this work, even if it killed me.

East finally answered my question. "I just have to fix a door that's a little too squeaky in one of the guestrooms. Not a big deal."

I raised a brow. "That's it?"

"It's one of the many things on my list. Thankfully, this place is big enough that I always have something to do. It's an unending list. And that the winery has its own team to work on all of that shit, because I'm not in the mood to learn to deal with any of the complicated machinery that comes with that world."

I snorted. "Honestly, same. I'm glad there are people that know what the fuck they're doing when it comes to wine making so that didn't have to be the two of us."

I left my brother to this job, knowing he liked time on his own, just like the rest of us did, and went to dry my boots. I was working by myself for most of the day, in interviews and other "boss business," as Elliot called it, so I had to focus and get clean.

I wasn't in the mood to deal with interviews, but it was part of my job. We had to fill positions that hadn't been working out over the past year, some more than others.

Wilder Retreat was a place that hadn't been even a spark in my mind my entire life. No, I had been too busy being a career military man—getting in my twenty, moving up the ranks, and ending up as a Lieutenant Colonel before I got out. I had been a commander of a squadron, and yet, it felt like I didn't know how to command where I was now.

When my sister Eliza had lost her husband when he was on deployment, it had been the last domino to fall in the Wilder brothers' military career. I had been ready to get out with twenty years in, knowing I needed a career outside of being a Lieutenant Colonel. I wasn't even forty yet, and the term retirement was a misnomer, but that's what happened when it came to my former job.

East had been getting out around that time for reasons of his own, and then Evan had been forced to. I rubbed my hand over my chest, that familiar pain, remembering the phone call from one of Evan's commanders when Evan had been hurt.

I thought I'd lost my baby brother then, and we nearly had. Everett had gotten hurt too, and Elijah and Elliot had needed out for their own reasons. Losing our baby sister's husband had just pushed us forward.

Finding out that Eliza's husband had been a cheating asshole had just cemented the fact that we needed to spend more time together as a family so we could be there for one another.

In retrospect, it would have been nice if Eliza would have been able to come down to Texas with us, to our suburb outside of San Antonio. Only, she had fallen in love again, with a man with a big family and a good heart up in Fort Collins, Colorado. She was still up there and traveled down enough that we actually got to get to know our sister again.

It was weird to think that, after so many years of always seeing each other in passing or through video calls, most of us were here, opening up a business. And all because I had been losing my mind.

Wilder Retreat and Winery was a villa and wedding venue outside of San Antonio. We were in hill country, at least what passed for hill country in South Texas, and the place had been owned by a former Air Force General who had wanted to retire and sell the place, since his kid didn't want it.

It was a large spread that used to be a ranch back in the day, nearly one hundred acres that the original owners had taken from a working ranch, and instead of making it a dude ranch or something similar, like others did around here, they'd added a winery using local help. We were close enough to Fredericksburg that it made sense in terms of the soil and weather. They had been able to add on additions, so it wasn't just the winery. Someone could come for the day for a winery tour or even a retreat tour, but most people came for the weekend or for a whole week. There were cabins and a farmhouse where we held weddings, dances, or other events. We had some chickens and ducks that gave us eggs, and goats that seemed to have a mind of their own and provided milk for cheese. Then there was the main annex, which housed all the equipment for the retreat villa.

The winery had its own section of buildings, and it was far bigger than anything I would have ever thought that we could handle. But, between the six of us, we did.

And the only reason we could even afford it, because one didn't afford something like this on a military salary, even with a decent retirement plan, was because of our uncles.

Our uncles, Edward and Edmond Wilder, had owned Wilder Wines down in Napa, California, for years. They had done well for themselves, and when we had been kids, we had gone out to visit. Evan had been the one that had clung to it and had been interested in wine making before he had changed his mind and gone into the military like the rest of us.

That was why Evan was in charge of the winery itself now. Because he knew what he was doing, even if he'd growled and said he didn't. Either way though, the place was huge, had multiple working parts at all times, and we had a staff that needed us. But when the uncles had died, they had left the money from the sale of the winery to us in equal parts. Eliza had taken hers to invest for her future children, and the rest of us had pooled our money together to buy this place and make it ours. A lot of the staff from the old owner had stayed, but some had left as well. Because they didn't want new owners who had no idea what they were doing, or they just retired. Either way, we were over a year in and doing okay.

Except for two positions that made me want to groan.

I had an interview with who would be our third wedding planner since we started this. The main component of the retreat was to have an actual wedding venue. To be able to host parties, and not just wine tours. Elliot was our major event planner that helped with our yearly and seasonal minute details, but he didn't want anything to do with the actual weddings. That was a whole other skill set, and so we wanted a wedding planner. We had gone through two wedding planners now, and we needed to hire a third. The first one had lied on her résumé, had given references that were her friends who had lied and had even created websites that were all fabrication, all so she could get into the business. Which, I understood, getting into the business is one thing. However, lying was another. Plus, we needed someone with actual experience because we didn't have any ourselves. We were going out on a limb here with this whole retreat business, and it was all because I had the harebrained idea of getting our family to work together, get along, and get to know one another. I wanted us to have a future, to be our own bosses.

And it was so far over my head that I knew that if I didn't get reliable help, we were going to fail.

Later, I had a meeting with that potential wedding planner. But first, I had to see what the fuck that smell was coming from the main kitchen in the villa.

The second wedding planner we hired was a guy with great and *true* references, one who was good at his job but hated everything to do with my brothers and me. He had hated the idea of the retreat and how rustic it was, even though we were in fucking South Texas. Yes, the buildings look slightly European because that was the theme that the original owners had gone for. Still, the guy had hated us, hadn't listened to us, and had called us white trash before he had walked away, jumped into his convertible, and sped off down the road, leaving us without help. He had been rude to our guests, and now Elliot was the one having to plan weddings for the past three weeks. My brother was going to strangle me soon if we didn't hire someone. And this person was going to be our last hope. As soon as she showed up, that was.

I looked down on my watch and tried to plan the rest of my day. I had thirty minutes to figure out what the hell was going on in the kitchen, and then I had to go to the meeting.

I nodded at a few guests who were sipping wine and

eating a cheese plate and then at our innkeeper, Naomi. Naomi's honey-brown hair was cut in an angled bob that lit her face, and she grinned at me.

"Hello there, Boss Man," she whispered. "You might need to go to the kitchen."

"Do I want to know?" I asked with a grumble.

"I'm not sure. But I am going to go check in our next guest, and then Elliott needs to meet with the Henderson couple."

"He'll be there." I didn't say that Elliot would rather chew off his own arm rather than deal with this, considering we had a family event coming in, one that Elliot was on target with planning. The wedding for next year was an important one, so we needed to work on it.

Naomi was a fantastic innkeeper, far more organized than any of us—and that was saying something since my brothers and I knew our way around schedules, to-do lists, and spreadsheets. Naomi was personable, smiled, and kept us on our toes.

Without her, I knew we wouldn't be able to do this. Hell, without Amos, our vineyard manager, I knew that Evan and Elijah wouldn't be able to handle the winery as they did. Naomi and Amos had come with the place when we had bought it, and I would be forever grateful that they had decided to stay on.

I gave Naomi another nod, then headed back to the kitchen and nearly walked right back out.

Tony stood there, a scowl on his face and his hands on

his hips. "I don't understand what the fuck is wrong with this oven."

"What's going on?" I asked as Everett stood by Tony. Everett was my quiet brother with usually a small smile on his face, only right then it looked like he was ready to scream.

I didn't know why Everett was even there since he was part responsible for the financials side of the company and usually worked with Elliot these days. Maybe he had come to the kitchen after the smell of burning as I had after Naomi's prodding.

Tony threw his hands in the air. "What's going on? This stove is a piece of shit. All of it is a piece of shit. I'm tired of this rustic place. I thought I would be coming to a Michelin star restaurant. To be my own chef. Instead, I have to make English breakfasts and pancakes with bananas. I might as well be at a bed and breakfast."

I pinched the bridge of my nose. "We're an inn, not a bed and breakfast."

"But I serve breakfast. That's all I do these days. That and cheese platters. Nobody comes for dinner. Nobody comes for lunch."

That was a lie. Tony worked for the winery and the retreat itself and served all the meals. But Tony wanted to go crazy with the menu, to try new and fantastical items that just weren't going to work here.

And I had a feeling I was going to throw up if I wasn't careful.

"I quit," Tony snapped, and I knew right then, it was done for. I was done.

"You can't quit," I growled while Everett held back a sigh.

"Yes, I can. I'm done. I'm done with you and this ranch. You're not cowboys. You're not even Texans. You're just people moving in on our territory." And with that, Tony stomped away, throwing his chef's apron on the ground.

I was thankful that the kitchen was on the other side of the library and front area, where most of the guests were if they weren't out on one of the tours of the area and city that Elliott had arranged for them. That was the whole point of this retreat. They could come visit, and could relax, or we could set them up on a tour of downtown San Antonio, or Canyon Lake, or any of the other places that were nearby.

And yet, Tony had just thrown a wrench into all of that. I didn't know what was worse, the smell of burning, Tony leaving, the water in the basement that wasn't truly a basement, or the fact that I was going to smell like charred food and wet jeans when I went to go meet this wedding planner.

"You're going to need to hire a new cook," Everett whispered.

I looked at my brother, at the man who did his best to make sure we didn't go bankrupt, and I wanted to just grumble. "I figured."

"I can help for now, but you know I'm only part-time. I can't stay away from my twins for too long," Sandy said as she came forward to take the pan off the stove. "I wish I could do full time, but this is all I can do for now."

Sandy had come back from maternity leave after we had already opened the retreat. She had been on with the former owners and was brilliant. But she had a right to be a mom and not want to work full time. I understood that, and I knew that Sandy didn't want to handle a whole kitchen by herself. She liked her position as a sous chef.

I was going to have to figure out what to do. Again.

"I'll get it done," I said while rubbing my temples.

"You know what we need to do," Everett whispered, and I shook my head.

"He'll kill us."

"Maybe, but it'll be worth it in the end. And speaking of, don't you have that interview soon? Or do you want me to take it?" His gaze tracked to my jeans.

I shook my head. "No, help Sandy."

Everett winced. "Just because I know how to slice an onion, it doesn't mean I'm good at cooking."

"I'm sorry, did you just say you could slice an onion? Get to it," Sandy put in with a smile, pointing at the sink. "Wash those hands."

"I cannot believe I just said that out loud. I just stepped right into it," Everett said with a sigh. "Go to the interview. You know what to ask."

"I do. And I hope we don't get screwed this time."

"You know, if we're lucky, we'll get someone as good as Roy's wedding planner, or at least that woman that we met. You know who she is." Everett grinned like a cat with the canary.

I narrowed my eyes. "Don't bring her up."

"Oh, I can't help it. A single dance, and you were drawn to her."

"What dance? You know what? No, I don't have time. We have to work on lunch and dinner. Tell me while you work," Sandy added with a wink.

Everett leaned toward her as he washed his hands. "Well, you see, there was this dance, and he met the perfect woman, and then she got engaged."

Sandy's eyes widened. "Engaged? How did that happen? She was dating someone else?" she asked as she looked at me.

I pinched the bridge of my nose. "It was at Roy's place when we were looking at the venue to see if we wanted to buy the retreat here." I sighed, I knew if I just let it all out, she would move on from this conversation, and I would never have to deal with it again. "Somehow, I ended up at a wedding there, caught the garter. This woman caught the bouquet, and she happened to be the wedding planner. We danced, we laughed, and as she walked away, her boyfriend got down on one knee and proposed."

"No way!" She leaned forward with a fierce look on her face, her eyes bright. "What did she say?"

"I have no clue. I left." I ignored whatever feeling

might want to show up at that thought. Everett gave me a glance, and I shook my head. "Enough of that. Yes, the wedding that she did was great, but I honestly have no idea who she is, and she has a job. She doesn't need to work here." And I didn't know what I would do if I saw her again or had to work with her. There had been such an intense connection that I knew it would be awkward as hell. But thankfully, she had her own business and wasn't going to come to the Wilder Retreat for a job.

I left Sandy and Everett on their own, knowing that they were capable, at least for now. And I knew who we would have to hire if she said yes, and if my other brother didn't kill me first.

I washed my hands in the sink on the way out, grateful that at least I looked somewhat decent, if not a little disheveled, and made my way out front, hoping that the wedding planner who came in through the doors would be the one that would stick. Because we needed some good luck. After the day we've had, we needed some good luck.

I turned the corner and nearly tripped over my feet.

Because, of course, fate was this way.

It was her.

Of all the wedding planners from all the wedding venues, it was her.

In the mood to read another family saga? Meet the Wilder Brothers in One Way Back to Me!

From Bittersweet Promises
LEIF

"Not only did you convince me to somehow go on a blind date, it became a double date. How on earth did you work this magic on me, cousin?" I asked Lake as she leaned against the pillar just inside the restaurant.

Lake grinned at me, her dark hair pulled away from her face. She had on this swingy black dress and looked as if she were excited, anxious, nervous, and happy all at the same time. Considering she was bouncing on her toes when usually Lake was calm, cool, and collected, was saying something. "I asked, and you said yes. Because you love me."

"I might love you because we're family, but I still think we're making a mistake." I shook my head and pulled at my shirt sleeves. Lake had somehow convinced me to wear a button-up shirt tucked into gray pants, I even had on shiny shoes. I looked like a damn banker. But if that's what Lake wanted, that's what I would do.

Lake might technically be my cousin, even though we weren't blood-related, but we were more like brother and sister than any of my other cousins.

I had siblings, as did Lake, but with the generational gap, we were at least a decade older than all of our other cousins. That meant, despite the fact that we had lived over an hour apart for most of our lives, we'd grown up more like siblings.

I loved my three younger siblings and talked to them daily. Unlike some blended families, they *were* my brothers and sister and not like strangers or distant family members. I didn't feel a disconnect from the three of them, but Lake was still closer to me.

Probably because we were either heading into our thirties or already there, where most of our other cousins were either just now in their early twenties or still teenagers in high school. With how big we Montgomerys were as a family, it made sense that there would be such a widespread age group. That meant that Lake and I were best friends, cousins, practically siblings, and sometimes the banes of each other's existences.

We were also business owners and partners and saw each other too often these days. That was probably why she convinced me to go on a blind double date. But she had been out with Zach before. I, however, had never met May. Lake had some connection with her that I wasn't sure about, and for some reason Lake's date had said yes to this double date.

And, in the complicated way of family, I had agreed to it. I must have been tired. Or perhaps I'd had too many beers. Because I didn't do blind dates, and recently, I didn't do dates at all.

Lake scanned her phone, then looked up at me, all innocence in her smart gaze. "You shouldn't have told me you wanted to settle down in your old age."

I narrowed my eyes. "I'm still in my early thirties, jerk. Stop calling me old."

"I shouldn't call you old since you're only a few years older than me." She fluttered her eyelashes and I flipped her off, ignoring the stare from the older woman next to me. Though I was a tattoo artist, I didn't have many visible tattoos. Most of mine were on my back and legs, hidden from the world unless I wanted to show them. I hadn't figured out what I wanted on my arms beyond a few small pieces on my wrists and upper shoulders. And since tattoos were permanent, I was taking my time. If a client needed to see my skin with ink to feel comfortable, I'd show them my back. My body was a canvas, so I did what I could to set people at ease.

But I still had the eyebrow piercing and had recently taken out my nose ring. I didn't look too scary for most people. But apparently, flipping off a woman, growling, and cursing a time or two in front of strangers probably made me appear too close to the dark side.

"Yes, I want to settle down, but this will be awkward, won't it? Where the two of us are strangers, and the two of you aren't?" I wanted a life, a future, and yeah, one day to settle down with someone. I just didn't know why I'd mentioned it to Lake in the first place.

"If it helps, May doesn't know Zach, either. So it's a group of strangers, except I know everybody." She clapped her hands together and did her version of an evil laugh, and I just shook my head.

"Considering what you do for a living and how you like to manipulate things in your way, this makes sense. Are you going to be adding a matchmaking company to your conglomerate?"

Lake just fluttered her eyelashes again and laughed. Lake owned a small tech company that made a shit ton of money over the past couple of years. And because she was brilliant at what she did, innovative, and liked pushing money towards women-owned businesses, she owned more than one company at this point and was an investor in mine. I wouldn't be surprised if she found a way to open up a women-owned matchmaking company right here in town.

"It might be fun. I can call it Montgomery Links." Her eyes went wide. "Oh, my God. I have to write that down." She pulled out her phone, began to take notes, and I pinched the bridge of my nose.

"You know I trust you with my actual life, but I don't know if I trust you with my dating life."

Lake tossed her hair behind her shoulder as she continued to type. "Shut up. You love me. And once I finish setting you up, the rest of the family's next."

"Oh, really? You're going to get Daisy and Noah next?" I asked, speaking of two more of our cousins.

"Maybe. Of course, Sebastian's the only one of the younger group that seems to have a serious girlfriend."

I nodded, speaking of our other familial business partner. Sebastian was still a teenager, though in college. He had wanted to open up Montgomery Ink Legacy with me, the full title of our company. There was a legacy to it, and Sebastian had wanted in. So, though he didn't work there full-time, he was putting his future towards us. And in the ways of young love, he and his girlfriend had been together since middle school. The fact that my younger cousin was better at relationships than I was didn't make me feel great. But I was going to ignore that.

"You're not going to start up a matchmaking service, are you? Or maybe an app?"

"Dating apps are ridiculous these days, they practically want you to invest in coins to bid on dates, and that's not something I'm in the mood for. But maybe there's something I can try. I'll add it to my list."

Lake's list of inventions and tech was notorious, and knowing the brilliance of my cousin, she would one day rule the world and might eventually cross everything off that list.

"Oh, here's Zach." Lake's face brightened immediately, and she smiled up at a man with dark hair, piercing gray eyes, and an actual dimple on his cheek.

Tonight was not only about my blind date, but me getting the lay of the land when it came to Zach. I was the first step into meeting the family. Oh, if Zach passed my gauntlet, he would meet the rest of the Montgomerys, and we were mighty. All one hundred of us.

"Zach, you're here." Lake's voice went soft, and she went on her tiptoes even in her high heels as Zach pressed a soft kiss to her lips.

"Of course, I'm here. And you're early, as usual."

Lake blushed and ducked her head. "Well, you know me. I like to be early because being on time is late," she said at the same time I did, mumbling under my breath. It was a familiar refrain when it came to us.

"Zach, good to meet you," I said, holding out my hand.

The other man gripped it firmly and shook. "Nice to meet you too, Leif. I know you might be the one on a blind date soon, but I'm nervous."

I chuckled, shaking my head. "Yeah, I'm pretty nervous too. Though I'm grateful that Lake's trying to look out for me."

My cousin laughed softly. "You totally were not saying that a few minutes ago, but be suave and sophisticated now. Or just be yourself, May's on her way."

I met Zach's gaze and we both rolled our eyes. When I turned toward the door, I saw a woman of average height, with black straight hair, green eyes, and a sweet smile. I didn't know much about May, other than Lake knew her and liked her. If I was going to start dating again after taking time off to get the rest of my life together, I might as well start with someone that one of my best friends liked.

"May, I'm so glad that you're here," Lake said as she hugged the other woman tightly.

As Lake began to bounce on her heels, I realized that my cousin's cool, calm, and collected exterior was only for work. She was bouncing and happy when it came to her friends or when she was nervous. I knew that, of course, but I had forgotten how she had turned into the mogul that she was. It was good to see her relaxed and happy.

Now I just needed to figure out how to do that for myself.

May stood in front of me, and I felt like I was starting middle school all over again. A new school, a new life, and a past that didn't make much sense to anyone else.

I swallowed hard and nodded, not putting out my hand to shake, thinking that would be weird, but I also didn't want to hug her. I didn't even know this woman. Why was everything so awkward? Instead, I lifted my chin. "Hello, May. It's nice to meet you. Lake says only good things."

There, smooth. Not really. Zach began to move out of frame, with Lake at his side as the two went to speak to the hostess, leaving May and me alone.

This wasn't going to be awkward at all.

The woman just smiled at me, her eyes wide. "It's nice to meet you, too. And Lake does speak highly of you. Also, this is very awkward, so I'm so sorry if I say something stupid. I know that your cousin said that I should be set up with you which is great but I'm not great at blind dates and apparently this is a double date and now I'm going to stop talking." She said the words so quickly they all ran into one breath.

I shook my head and laughed. "We're on the same page there."

"Okay, good. It's nice to meet you, Leif Montgomery."

"And it's nice to meet you too, May."

We made our way to Lake and Zach, who had gotten our table, and we all sat down, talking about work and other things. May was in child life development, taught online classes, and was also a nanny.

"I'm actually about to start with a new family soon. I'm excited. I know that being a nanny isn't something that most people strive for, or at least that's what they tell you, but I love being able to work with children and be the person that is there when a single parent or even both parents are out in the workforce, trying to do everything."

I nodded, taking a sip of my beer. "I get you completely. With how my parents worked, I was lucky that they were able to get childcare within the buildings. Since they each owned their own businesses, they made it work. But my family worked long hours, and that's why I ended up being the babysitter a lot of the times when childcare wasn't an option." I cleared my throat. "I'm a lot older than a lot of my cousins," I added.

"Both of us are, but I'm glad that you only said yourself," Lake said, grinning. She leaned into Zach as she spoke, the four of us in a horseshoe-shaped booth. That gave May and me space since this was a first date and still awkward as hell, and so Lake and Zach could cuddle. Not that that was something I needed to be a part of.

"Oh, I'm glad that you didn't judge. The last few dates that I've been on they always gave me weird looks because I think they expected a nanny to be this old crone or someone that's looking for a different job." She shrugged and continued. "When I eventually get married and maybe even start a family, I want to continue my job. I like being there to help another family achieve their goals. And I can't believe I just said start a family on my first date. And that I mentioned that I've been on a few other dates." She let out a breath. "I'm notoriously bad at dating. Like, the worst. Just warning you."

I laughed, shaking my head. "I'm rusty at it, so don't worry." And even though I said that, I had a feeling that May felt no spark towards me, and I didn't feel anything towards her. She was nice and pleasant, and I could probably consider her a friend one day. But there wasn't any spark. May's eyes weren't dancing. She wasn't leaning forward, trying to touch my hand across the table. We were just sitting there casually, enjoying a really good steak, as Lake and Zach enjoyed their date.

By the end of dinner, I didn't want dessert, and neither did May, so we said goodbye to the other couple, who decided to stay. I walked May to her car, ignoring Lake's warning look, but I didn't know what exactly she was warning me about.

"Thanks for dinner," May said. "I could have paid. I know this is a blind date and all that, but you didn't have to pay."

I shook my head. "I paid for the four of us because I wanted to be nice. I'll make Lake pay next time."

May beamed. "Yes, I like that. You guys are a good family."

"Anyway," I said, clearing my throat as I stuck my hands in my pockets. "I guess I'll see you around."

May just looked at me, threw her head back, and laughed. "You're right. You are rusty at this."

"Sorry." Heat flushed my skin, and I resisted the urge to tug on my eyebrow ring.

"It's okay. No spark. I'm used to it. I don't spark well."

"May, I'm sorry." I cringed. "It's not you."

"Oh, God, please don't say that. 'It's not you. It's me. You're working on yourself. You're just so busy with work.' I've heard it all."

"Seriously?" I asked. May was hot. Nice, but there just wasn't a spark.

She shrugged. "It's okay. I'll probably see you around

sometime because I am friends with Lake. However, I am perfectly fine having this be our one and only. You'll find your person. It's okay that it's not me." And with that, she got in the car and left, leaving me standing there.

Well then. Tonight wasn't horrible, but it wasn't great. I got in my car, and instead of heading home where I'd be alone, watching something on some streaming service while I drank a beer and pretended that I knew what I was doing with my life, I headed into Montgomery Ink Legacy.

We were the third branch of the company and the first owned by our generation. Montgomery Ink was the tattoo shop in downtown Denver. While there were open spots for some walk-ins and special circumstances, my father, aunt, and their team had years' worth of waiting lists. They worked their asses off and made sure to get in everybody that they could, but people wanted Austin Montgomery's art. Same with my aunt, Maya.

There was another tattoo shop down in Colorado Springs, owned by my parents' cousins, who I just called aunt and uncle because we were close enough that using real titles for everybody got confusing. Montgomery Ink Too was thriving down there, and they had waiting lists as well. My family could have opened more shops and gone nationwide, even global if they wanted to, but they liked keeping it how it was, in the family and those connected.

We were a branch, but our own in the making. I had gone into business with Lake, of course, and Sebastian, when he was ready, as well as Nick. Nick was my best friend. I had known him for ages, and he had wanted to be part of something as well. He might not be a Montgomery by name, but he had eaten over at my family's house enough times throughout the years that he was practically a Montgomery. And he had invested in the company as well, and so now we were nearly a year into owning the shop and trying not to fail.

I pulled into the parking lot, grateful it was still open since we didn't close until nine most nights, and greeted Nick, who was still working.

Sebastian was in the back, going over sketches with a client, and I nodded at him. He might be eighteen, but he was still in training, an apprentice, and was working his ass off to learn.

"Date sucked then?" Sebastian asked, and Nick just rolled his eyes and went back to work on a client's wrist.

"I don't want to talk about it," I groaned.

The rest of the staff was off since Nick would close up on his own. Sebastian was just there since he didn't have homework or a date with Marley.

"Was she hot at least?" Sebastian asked, and the client, a woman in her sixties, bopped him on the head with her bag gently.

"Sebastian Montgomery. Be nice."

Sebastian blushed. "Sorry, Mrs. Anderson."

I looked over at the woman and grinned. "Hi, Mrs. Anderson. It's nice to see you out of the classroom."

She narrowed her eyes at me, even though they filled with laughter. "I needed my next Jane Austen tattoo, thank you very much," the older woman said as she went back to working with Sebastian. She had been my and then Sebastian's English teacher. The fact that she was on her fifth tattoo with some literary quote told me that I had been damn lucky in most of my teachers growing up.

She was kick-ass, and I had a feeling that she would let Sebastian do the tattoo for her rather than just have him work on the design with me as we did for most of the people who came in. He had learned under my father and was working under me now. It was strange to think that he wasn't a little kid anymore. But he was in a long-term relationship, kicking ass in college, and knew what he wanted to do with his life.

I might know what I want to do with my work life, but everything else seemed a little off.

"So it didn't work out?" Nick asked as he walked up to the front desk with the clients after going over aftercare.

"Not really," I said, looking down at my phone.

The client, a woman in her mid-twenties with bright pink hair, a lip ring, and kind eyes, leaned over the desk to look at me.

"You'll find someone, Leif. Don't worry."

I looked at our regular and shook my head. "Thanks, Kim. Too bad that you don't swing this way."

I winked as I said it, a familiar refrain from both of us.

Kim was married to a woman named Sonya, and the

two of them were happy and working on in vitro with donated sperm for their first kid.

"Hey, I'm sorry too that I'm a lesbian. I'll never know what it means to have Leif Montgomery. Or any Montgomery, since I found my love far too quickly. I mean, what am I ever going to do not knowing the love of a Montgomery?"

Mrs. Anderson chuckled from her chair, Sebastian held back a snort, and I just looked at Nick, who rolled his eyes and helped Kim out of the place.

I was tired, but it was okay. The date wasn't all bad. May was nice. But it felt like I didn't have much right then.

And then Nick sat in front of me, scowled, and I realized that I did have something. I had my friends and my family. I didn't need much more.

"So, you and May didn't work out?"

I raised a brow. "You knew her name? Did I tell you that?"

Nick shook his head. "Lake did."

That made sense, considering the two of them spoke as much as we did. "So, was it your idea to set me up on a blind date?"

"Fuck no. That was all Lake. I just do what she says. Like we all do."

I sighed and went through my appointments for the next day. "We're busy for the next month. That's good, right?" I asked.

"You're the business genius here. I just play with ink. But yes, that's good. Now, don't let your cousin set you up any more dates. Find them for yourself. You know what you're doing."

"So says the man who dates less than me."

"That's what you think. I'm more private about it. As it should be." I flipped him off as he stood up, then he gestured towards a stack of bills in the corner. "You have a few personal things that made their way here. Don't want you to miss out on them before you head home."

"Thanks, bro."

"No problem. I'm going to help Sebastian with his consult, and then I'll clean up. You should head home. Though you're doing it alone, so I feel sorry for you."

"Fuck you," I called out.

"Fuck you, too."

"Boys," Mrs. Anderson said, in that familiar English teacher refrain, and both Nick and I cringed before saying, "Sorry," simultaneously.

Sebastian snickered, then went back to work, and I headed towards the edge of the counter, picking up the stack of papers. Most were bills, some were random papers that needed to be filed or looked over. Some were just junk mail. But there was one letter, written in block print that didn't look familiar. Chills went up my spine and I opened it, wondering what the fuck this was. Maybe it was someone asking to buy my house. I got a lot of handwritten letters for that, but I didn't think this was going to be that. I swallowed hard, slid open the paper, and froze.

"I'll find you, boy. Oops. Looks like I already did. Be waiting. I know you miss me."

I let the paper hit the top of the counter and swallowed hard, trying to remain cool so I didn't worry anyone else.

I didn't know exactly who that was from, but I had a horrible feeling that they wouldn't wait long to tell me.

Read the rest in Bittersweet Promises! OUT NOW!

Also from Carrie Ann Ryan

The Montgomery Ink Legacy Series:
 Book 1: Bittersweet Promises (Leif & Brooke)
 Book 2: At First Meet (Nick & Lake)
 Book 2.5: Happily Ever Never (May & Leo)
 Book 3: Longtime Crush (Sebastian & Raven)
 Book 4: Best Friend Temptation (Noah, Ford, and Greer)
 Book 4.5: Happily Ever Maybe (Jennifer & Gus)
 Book 5: Last First Kiss (Daisy & Hugh)
 Book 6: His Second Chance (Kane & Phoebe)
 Book 7: One Night with You (Kingston & Claire)
 Book 8: Accidentally Forever (Crew & Aria)
 Book 9: Last Chance Seduction (Lexington & Mercy)
 Book 10: Kiss Me Forever (???? & ????)

The Cage Family

Book 1: The Forever Rule (Aston & Blakely)
Book 2: An Unexpected Everything (Isabella & Weston)
Book 3: If You Were Mine (Dorian & Harper)
Book 4: One Quick Obsession (???? & ???)

Ashford Creek
Book 1: Legacy (Callum & Felicity)
Book 2: Crossroads (??? & ???)

Clover Lake
Book 1: Always a Fake Bridesmaid (Livvy & Ewan)
Book 2: Accidental Runaway Groom (??? & ???)

The Wilder Brothers Series:
Book 1: One Way Back to Me (Eli & Alexis)
Book 2: Always the One for Me (Evan & Kendall)
Book 3: The Path to You (Everett & Bethany)
Book 4: Coming Home for Us (Elijah & Maddie)
Book 5: Stay Here With Me (East & Lark)
Book 6: Finding the Road to Us (Elliot, Trace, and Sidney)
Book 7: Moments for You (Ridge & Aurora)
Book 7.5: A Wilder Wedding (Amos & Naomi)
Book 8: Forever For Us (Wyatt & Ava)
Book 9: Pieces of Me (Gabriel & Briar)
Book 10: Endlessly Yours (Brooks & Rory)

ALSO FROM CARRIE ANN RYAN

The First Time Series:
Book 1: Good Time Boyfriend (Heath & Devney)
Book 2: Last Minute Fiancé (Luca & Addison)
Book 3: Second Chance Husband (August & Paisley)

Montgomery Ink Denver:
Book 0.5: Ink Inspired (Shep & Shea)
Book 0.6: Ink Reunited (Sassy, Rare, and Ian)
Book 1: Delicate Ink (Austin & Sierra)
Book 1.5: Forever Ink (Callie & Morgan)
Book 2: Tempting Boundaries (Decker and Miranda)
Book 3: Harder than Words (Meghan & Luc)
Book 3.5: Finally Found You (Mason & Presley)
Book 4: Written in Ink (Griffin & Autumn)
Book 4.5: Hidden Ink (Hailey & Sloane)
Book 5: Ink Enduring (Maya, Jake, and Border)
Book 6: Ink Exposed (Alex & Tabby)
Book 6.5: Adoring Ink (Holly & Brody)
Book 6.6: Love, Honor, & Ink (Arianna & Harper)
Book 7: Inked Expressions (Storm & Everly)
Book 7.3: Dropout (Grayson & Kate)
Book 7.5: Executive Ink (Jax & Ashlynn)
Book 8: Inked Memories (Wes & Jillian)
Book 8.5: Inked Nights (Derek & Olivia)
Book 8.7: Second Chance Ink (Brandon & Lauren)
Book 8.5: Montgomery Midnight Kisses (Alex & Tabby Bonus(
Bonus: Inked Kingdom (Stone & Sarina)

Montgomery Ink: Colorado Springs
Book 1: Fallen Ink (Adrienne & Mace)
Book 2: Restless Ink (Thea & Dimitri)
Book 2.5: Ashes to Ink (Abby & Ryan)
Book 3: Jagged Ink (Roxie & Carter)
Book 3.5: Ink by Numbers (Landon & Kaylee)

The Montgomery Ink: Boulder Series:
Book 1: Wrapped in Ink (Liam & Arden)
Book 2: Sated in Ink (Ethan, Lincoln, and Holland)
Book 3: Embraced in Ink (Bristol & Marcus)
Book 3: Moments in Ink (Zia & Meredith)
Book 4: Seduced in Ink (Aaron & Madison)
Book 4.5: Captured in Ink (Julia, Ronin, & Kincaid)
Book 4.7: Inked Fantasy (Secret ??)
Book 4.8: A Very Montgomery Christmas (The Entire Boulder Family)

The Montgomery Ink: Fort Collins Series:
Book 1: Inked Persuasion (Jacob & Annabelle)
Book 2: Inked Obsession (Beckett & Eliza)
Book 3: Inked Devotion (Benjamin & Brenna)
Book 3.5: Nothing But Ink (Clay & Riggs)
Book 4: Inked Craving (Lee & Paige)
Book 5: Inked Temptation (Archer & Killian)

The Promise Me Series:
Book 1: Forever Only Once (Cross & Hazel)

Book 2: From That Moment (Prior & Paris)
Book 3: Far From Destined (Macon & Dakota)
Book 4: From Our First (Nate & Myra)

The Whiskey and Lies Series:
Book 1: Whiskey Secrets (Dare & Kenzie)
Book 2: Whiskey Reveals (Fox & Melody)
Book 3: Whiskey Undone (Loch & Ainsley)

The Gallagher Brothers Series:
Book 1: Love Restored (Graham & Blake)
Book 2: Passion Restored (Owen & Liz)
Book 3: Hope Restored (Murphy & Tessa)

The Less Than Series:
Book 1: Breathless With Her (Devin & Erin)
Book 2: Reckless With You (Tucker & Amelia)
Book 3: Shameless With Him (Caleb & Zoey)

The Fractured Connections Series:
Book 1: Breaking Without You (Cameron & Violet)
Book 2: Shouldn't Have You (Brendon & Harmony)
Book 3: Falling With You (Aiden & Sienna)
Book 4: Taken With You (Beckham & Meadow)

The On My Own Series:
Book 0.5: My First Glance
Book 1: My One Night (Dillon & Elise)

Book 2: My Rebound (Pacey & Mackenzie)
Book 3: My Next Play (Miles & Nessa)
Book 4: My Bad Decisions (Tanner & Natalie)

The Ravenwood Coven Series:
Book 1: Dawn Unearthed
Book 2: Dusk Unveiled
Book 3: Evernight Unleashed

The Aspen Pack Series:
Book 1: Etched in Honor
Book 2: Hunted in Darkness
Book 3: Mated in Chaos
Book 4: Harbored in Silence
Book 5: Marked in Flames

The Talon Pack:
Book 1: [Tattered Loyalties](#)
Book 2: [An Alpha's Choice](#)
Book 3: [Mated in Mist](#)
Book 4: [Wolf Betrayed](#)
Book 5: [Fractured Silence](#)
Book 6: [Destiny Disgraced](#)
Book 7: [Eternal Mourning](#)
Book 8: [Strength Enduring](#)
Book 9: [Forever Broken](#)
Book 10: Mated in Darkness
Book 11: Fated in Winter

Also from Carrie Ann Ryan

Redwood Pack Series:
- Book 0.5: An Alpha's Path
- Book 1: A Taste for a Mate
- Book 2: Trinity Bound
- Book 2.5: A Night Away
- Book 3: Enforcer's Redemption
- Book 3.5: Blurred Expectations
- Book 3.7: Forgiveness
- Book 4: Shattered Emotions
- Book 5: Hidden Destiny
- Book 5.5: A Beta's Haven
- Book 6: Fighting Fate
- Book 6.5: Loving the Omega
- Book 6.7: The Hunted Heart
- Book 7: Wicked Wolf

The Elements of Five Series:
- Book 1: From Breath and Ruin
- Book 2: From Flame and Ash
- Book 3: From Spirit and Binding
- Book 4: From Shadow and Silence

Dante's Circle Series:
- Book 1: Dust of My Wings
- Book 2: Her Warriors' Three Wishes
- Book 3: An Unlucky Moon
- Book 3.5: His Choice
- Book 4: Tangled Innocence

ALSO FROM CARRIE ANN RYAN

Book 5: Fierce Enchantment
Book 6: An Immortal's Song
Book 7: Prowled Darkness
Book 8: Dante's Circle Reborn

Holiday, Montana Series:
Book 1: Charmed Spirits
Book 2: Santa's Executive
Book 3: Finding Abigail
Book 4: Her Lucky Love
Book 5: Dreams of Ivory

The Branded Pack Series:
(Written with Alexandra Ivy)
Book 1: Stolen and Forgiven
Book 2: Abandoned and Unseen
Book 3: Buried and Shadowed

About the Author

Carrie Ann Ryan is the New York Times and USA Today bestselling author of contemporary, paranormal, and young adult romance. Her works include the Montgomery Ink, Redwood Pack, Fractured Connections, and Elements of Five series, which have sold over 3.0 million books worldwide. She started writing while in graduate school for her advanced degree in chemistry and hasn't stopped since. Carrie Ann has written over seventy-five novels and novellas with more in the works. When she's not losing herself in her emotional and action-packed worlds, she's reading as much as she can while wrangling her clowder of cats who have more followers than she does.

www.CarrieAnnRyan.com

www.ingramcontent.com/pod-product-compliance
Lightning Source LLC
LaVergne TN
LVHW040150250825
819466LV00005B/66